THE MAGISTER

Other Books by Sally Miller Gearhart

Wanderground: Stories of the Hill Women

Other Books in the Earthkeep Series
The Kanshou: Book One of Earthkeep
The Steward: Book Three of Earthkeep

Published Elsewhere
Loving Women/Loving Men: Gay Liberation and The Church
A Feminist Tarot

THE MAGISTER

Sally Miller Gearhart

Spinsters Ink Books
Denver, Colorado
USA

The Magister © 2003 by Sally Miller Gearhart

First edition published March 2003
10-9-8-7-6-5-4-3-2-1

Spinsters Ink Books
P. O. Box 22005
Denver, CO 80222
USA

Cover Design:
Lightsource Images

Interior Design:
Attention Media Group

Library of Congress Cataloging-in-Publication Data

Gearhart, Sally Miller, 1931–
The Magister / Sally Miller Gearhart. -- 1st ed.
p. cm. -- (Earthkeep; bk. 2)
ISBN 1-883523-49-4
I. Women--Fiction. I Title.

Printed in Canada

The Earthkeep Series is dedicated to
Dorothy A. Haecker and Jane Gurko,
its *sine qua non*.

Contents

ACKNOWLEDGEMENTS

In the years since 1987, the EARTHKEEP books, *The Kanshou* and *The Magister,* have been given both substance and form within the network of my friends, enemies, lovers, colleagues, comrades, teachers, students, chance acquaintances and animal companions. In addition to Jane Gurko and Dorothy A. Haecker, who shepherded the EARTHKEEP material through its most major transformations, a number of people have generously blessed the books with their special abilities and their time.

I've had the good fortune to work with two fine editors. The first was my Intrepid Vicki P. McConnell, marvelously astute and skilled, who endowed the bulky manuscript with one of its first professional affirmations, and then streamlined it — and my writing habits — with a devotion far beyond any duty set upon her by Spinsters Ink.

More recently I have been grateful for the guidance of Paulette Whitcomb, whose insight and keen sensitivities have enhanced the clarity, the exactness and the spirit of *The Magister*. Elizabeth Saria, Karla McDermid and Carla Blumberg educated me in crucial aspects of chemistry, zoology, medicine, virology, technology and marine biology. I called upon Vivian Power for aid in Spanish, enhancement of my understanding of science, and audacious challenges to my utopian vision. Adrian Tinsley, ardent aficionada of fantasy and science fiction, refreshed both my memory and my imagination in her analysis of the manuscript. Moreover, I have been companioned throughout this literary journey by a task force of metaphysical gadflies, led at different times by Tamara Diaghilev, Mara, Ari Lacelle, Cynthia Secor and Helen Stewart.

Frequently I have needed rescue from computer panic, and I've often lacked expertise in specific areas such as astrology, firearms, the geography of Los Angeles, how to play the violin, how to survive in the publishing world, Judaism, the Koran, Mandarin, medical terminology, police practices and the scope of human sexuality. I thank the following people for coming to my aid in one or more of these matters: Bryce Travis, Carlin Diamond, Nancy Ellis, Esther Faber, Susan Feldman, Emmy Good, Dick Graham, Maggie Graham, Matthew Holtz, Tony King, Joann Lee, Lyndall MacCowan, Marilyn McNair, Jack Power, Teri Rogers, Sam Sapoznick and Susan Smith.

As well, I offer a special thanks to all the anarchists, animal rights activists, capitalists, developers, environmentalists, hunters, loggers, militarists, pacifists, political radicals, ranchers, religious fundamentalists and vegetarians who, in my ongoing dialogues with them, have toughened up my thought processes and deepened my appreciation of diversity.

I have lived surrounded by a community of women — Peggy Cleveland, Morgaine Colston, Jean Crosby, Esther Faber, Bonnie Gordon, Jane Gurko, Susan Leo, Ana Mahoney, Carol Orton,

Penny Sablove, Mary Anderson and Diane Syrcle — that has provided the atmosphere of support and patient understanding these books have required in order, at last, to be born.

The metaphysics ultimately embraced by the protagonists of the EARTHKEEP books has its best articulation in the teachings of Abraham, available at Abraham-Hicks Publications, P.O. Box 690070, San Antonio, Texas, 78269 (830-755-2299). Abraham teaches joy, and it is the gift of joy that I wish for all those whom I here finally acknowledge with gratitude: the readers of EARTHKEEP, in Aristotle's terms the "final cause of" or "that for the sake of which" these books have been written.

"… such hands might carry out an unavoidable violence
with such restraint, with such a grasp
of the range and limits of violence
that violence ever after would be obsolete."

—Adrienne Rich
Twenty-One Love Poems, VI

PROLOGUE

In *The Kanshou*, Book One of EARTHKEEP, the citizens of Little Blue find themselves faced with 1) the disappearance from the planet of all non-human animals, 2) the effects of widespread natural disasters and climatic cataclysms, 3) the reduction of their population to one-sixth of its 1999 size, 4) a ratio in the human population of twelve women to every man, and 5) the global effects of decades of social and political unrest.

As Little Blue's social, economic, military and governmental power has shifted from men to women, new values, structures and processes have emerged. By 2087, when the action in *The Kanshou* takes place, nuclear families are rare, and the most common living pattern is still that of the extended family, honoring traditional kinship bonds. Women in such families usually embrace men as full partners in the human experience.

Almost as common are the tribes, nations or communities of women-only citizens, who use ovular merging to produce girl-children among themselves or, alternatively, use men or semen banks for reproduction. Sexually, such women partner with other women, seek solitary sexual gratification, or live asexually. Some of them hold to the belief that womanhood or manhood is self-identified, while others claim biology as an immutable physical condition.

ii

By 2087 the ascendancy of women is the norm in all three of Little Blue's tri-satrapies or geo-political territories. The land, sea and air divisions of the global peacekeeping force, the Kanshoubu, are almost entirely female. Each Kanshou peacekeeper — whether she is an Amah, a Femmedarme or a Vigilante — follows a code of conduct delineated in the Kanshoubu's *Labrys Manual,* and a large part of a Kanshou's responsibility is the confining of violent offenders (the habitantes) to the planet's 780 prisons (the bailiwicks).

By the end of *The Kanshou,* a global movement has gained strength in support of a proposal that would require the testing of habitantes in a neurological search for the organic cause of human violence. If such a cause is found, protocols can then be initiated for the surgical removal of that cause. Zude, one of the Kanshoubu's three Magisters, fervently opposes both the Testing and the Protocols. Her old lover, charismatic witch Jezebel Stronglaces, leads the grassroots global forces in fighting for the approval of the Testing and the Protocols. Their struggle as adversaries has escalated with the eruption into violence of bailiwick habitantes who are protesting both proposals.

The Magister, Book Two of EARTHKEEP, opens a year later, in 2088. Though the controversy over the Testing and the Protocols still rages, an unforeseen event now warns of the whole race's possible extinction.

1

> There is a land beyond kindred and stranger,
> a place beyond here and there,
> a time beyond past and future,
> a mind beyond yes and no.
> Welcome.
> *Weaves from the Matrix*

In the director's office of the Dolly Ruark Athletic Center, Jez's and Dicken's immersion in a flatfilm was interrupted by the Urgent signal of Beabenet's comunit. Bea paused the film and opened her channel.

"A message for Jezebel Stronglaces," said the curly-haired woman on the screen.

Jez moved into the viewfield. "I'm Jezebel."

The woman smiled. "A tribesman by the name of Donal Jain from out beyond the Badlands needs to talk with you. He heard you were going to be in St. Paul, and he contracted with a spoon to fly him to the Ruark Center. He'll be here…" she glanced at her chronometer, "within the hour, at eleven."

"Do you know what he wants?"

"The woman who called said the spooners said he said it had something to do with children—he called them youngs. The message just got here and there wasn't a chance for response. They've been airborne for hours."

"Thank you…Tracey," Jez said, sensing her name.

"Thank you," beamed the woman. She nodded to Beabenet and disappeared.

"Well, that's appropriate enough," Dicken observed.

"I'll say," Bea agreed. She looked at Jezebel, who still stared at the screen.

"Let's finish watching," Jez said. "Do we have time?"

"Plenty," Bea replied. "We're near the end." She de-paused the flatfilm.

A dark-skinned child picked up a fuzzy tiger and rubbed her face against it. She kissed the toy and started to set it back on its stool. She stopped, held it at arm's length and cocked her head, as if listening. Then she clasped the tiger to her. She walked toward the mikcam and into the arms of the bewildered woman who sat on the bed.

"Jula," she told her mother, "we're just going to play with our friends." The round little face was earnest. "They're waiting for us." She looked at the tiger and gave it a squeeze. She then curled up in the woman's lap and laid her hand on the woman's bosom. "You can come too, Jula," she said. Then, flashing a brilliant smile, Mary Frances Safful closed her eyes and slipped into an apparently blissful sleep.

Beabenet cleared the flatfield. "And…"

"And she never woke up," finished Dicken.

"That's right."

Dicken fingered the heaviness of her dankee silver necklace. Jez sat utterly still in one of the office's big chairs. Bea closed down the flatfilm casing and activated a tab on her chairarm panel. Skylights and windows came alive again with light.

"That's the only film we've got," she said. "And we wouldn't have had that if Fanny's big sister, Lyn, hadn't had the instincts of a historian. As you saw, she made it almost a daily game with Fanny, getting her to talk on camera about sleeping so much. Lyn let me borrow the flatfilm chip. She said Jula couldn't stand to look at it, anyway."

She picked up a strip of audio chipnests and a flatcopy report. "Here." She set them on the desk. "You can hear or read about the other three. Pretty much the same story. All in good health except that, according to two of the families, their hair changed color. Only one of them had been sleeping more than usual. The others died completely unexpectedly, yet apparently very peacefully. Just didn't wake up one morning. Only one of them had any history of disease or injury—an anti-grav tumble years before."

Bea sighed. She pressed two fingers against one temple. "One of the mothers went wild. Swore her daughter was just comatose, still alive. She kept her lying in state for over a week, refusing to embalm, bury or cremate her." Bea looked from Dicken to Jez, then continued.

"We have this information only because staff members here knew and loved those children. We have no authority to carry out any kind of investigation. And Demesne Services apparently see nothing out of the ordinary in the deaths. 'Nothing to be concerned about,' they say." She snorted, then blurted, "Jez, am I crazy? Is this all just coincidence?" She looked questioningly at Dicken, then went on.

"The death of one child in one of our programs, okay. Not unusual. Might happen even once a year. Two? Well, maybe even two. But four? Four children in the last six months? All between the ages of three and eleven? Like I told you on the flatfone, that's more than coincidence."

Dicken stood by the sculptured fountain in the corner, staring at the trickling water dropping into the small rock-bottomed pool. "You're not crazy," she said finally. "Just waking up." She pulled herself away from the soothing water sounds. "And if you want to get wide awake, then start watching Size Central's population trends. Not much public attention to what's happening yet, but give it another month—maybe just a week—and the gathering energy of this mysterious phenomenon will push the Testing and the Protocols right off the front page."

Bea's eyes narrowed. "You're telling me other children are dying?"

"Yes. Little girls and boys just tipping their hats and leaving." Dicken reached out to let the water course over her long fingers.

"Why?" Beabenet sat, frowning.

Dicken shrugged. "No reason. No consistency. All arbitrary."

Jez's voice startled them both. "That's not totally true. One common factor stands out over everything." They looked at her, waiting. "All of these children go willingly, even happily. Nowhere is there any hint that they resist. Or that they're victims of any illness or injury. They simply decide to die."

Bea stared at her. Slowly her eyes widened and her lips parted. Her head jerked up, then sank. "Like the animals," she whispered.

Jez watched realization sink into Beabenet's cells. "Like the animals," she whispered back.

The director suddenly sprang to her feet. "Look," she said heartily, "we're probably over-reacting. This whole thing might be a fluke. Or just the normal population fluctuation that happens all the time while we don't notice." She searched Dicken's face. Then Jez's. "Listen, if it really were a global phenomenon, wouldn't the world be on its ear? The statistics have been available on a daily basis. Anyone can see them. And some people's only job is to interpret figures like this."

"That's true," Dicken agreed.

"And there would have been stories, individual stories that would have made the news." Bea's arms were outspread, pleading.

"They have made the news," said Jez. "Even as far back as nine months ago, isolated instances of children's dying unexpectedly were reported in quarter-traps and half-traps, though not in full satrapies. The incidence of such reports is increasing. All over Little Blue."

"So then the whole world is in a state of denial?"

Jez looked out the window. Spring was about to come to the Land of Lakes.

"Well, denial's an appropriate reaction, isn't it?" She turned to Bea. "If a whole species sees on the holocast that it is losing its children, it might very well close down the switch and look the other way."

Her arms slowly falling to her sides, Bea stared at Jez.

A musical question, the announcement of an arrival, interrupted the silence. Beabenet let the arpeggio sound a second time before she straightened her shoulders and went to the door.

"Director Beabenet?" The man's near-black eyes looked slightly downward in order to meet hers. "I am Donal Jain."

Bea shook the stranger's hand. "Come in. You made good time. Donal Jain, here are Bess Dicken and Jezebel Stronglaces."

Dicken liked the man immediately. She smiled her greeting and dropped into one of the low comfortable chairs.

As she took his hand, Jezebel read her senses' first-line assessment. He was young, agitated, controlled, anxious, intent, hopeful, moderately open and of good will. "Hello, Donal Jain."

Beabenet gestured to the chairs and made a move to leave. The man stopped her. "This is not private, director."

With a glance at Jez, Bea started to take a seat in the small circle. She paused, "Can I get you tea or…"

Jain held up his hand. "Diane and Elizabeth, the spooners who brought me, kept me warm with tea as we flew." He almost smiled. Beabenet sank into a chair between Jez and Dicken.

A short silence as Jain sat. "They had to be on their way but asked me to give you greeting. Elizabeth Gael met you some years ago."

"Ah, yes," said the director.

"It's cold spooning this time of year." Dicken was lubricating the conversational wheels.

Jain simply nodded. Silently he laid a backpack on the floor at his side, ran big hands through his shock of black hair, then shifted himself to the edge of his seat. His movements were smooth, almost dance-like. He sat motionless for several seconds, his eyes closed, hands on knees. Finally he looked at Jez. "Thank you for seeing me."

By then Jezebel Stronglaces had conducted as much as she wished of a non-invasive energy evaluation. Clearly the man had regained his self-possession. She decided to speak warmly.

"Thank you for coming. Ah, what's appropriate? Donal?"

"Donal is fine. And..."

"Jezebel, of course," she assured him. "Please don't let my infamous reputation put you off."

Donal's craggy face ignited into a relieved smile. "Oh. Oh right, right...Jezebel. But I'm more worried than intimidated." All three women relaxed. "I want to ask a great favor of you," he said, finally. Jez waited. Donal looked from Jez to Dicken and back to Jez. "I want to take you to a small village in the Black Hills. "Rather," he added, both hands opening, "I want you to take me there."

The women shifted in surprise, Beabenet and Dicken starting to talk at once. Jezebel raised her voice above them.

"You mean you want us to spoon you back?"

Again Donal ran his hands through his hair. "I mean..."

"Start at the beginning, Donal," Jez said mildly. "We've jumped into the middle of a longer story, I think."

"Yes," agreed Donal. He gathered his thoughts. "I'm a teacher," he began. "In a settlement called Chimney Corner some miles north of the Jeweled Caves. It is deep in the mountains, deliberately rural and consciously tribal. Inaccessible except by spooning or cushcar. The people operate a hydroponic project powered by mica shims."

Donal drew and released a big breath. "A group of my students, the most articulate of them a young named Taína Renananda Ko, have agreed, at my suggestion, to talk with you. They are planning to die in less than two weeks, just after our Festival of the Returning Sun."

The room went absolutely still except for the smooth trickling of water over rocks. Beabenet found her voice first.

"Say that again, Donal."

"They are planning to die."

The flight bubble was warm and comfortable, a tight fast-moving powerpod encasing three prone bodies: Jezebel and Dicken, with Donal Jain suspended between them. As they sailed into midafternoon, the altitude kept them breathing lightly and talking little—a blessing for Jez, who was indulging in a luxurious reverie that her mind entitled Forests.

No doubt about it: The forests were back. The hills and valleys that flew below her bore woodlands in every stage of returning growth.

Some difference of opinion existed as to why the great greening was taking place so spectacularly. The loss of the animals, insisted some, allowed an over-burgeoning of leaves and blossoms that under natural circumstances would have been devoured by woods-dwellers. Others minimized that cause, arguing that the loss of so much carbon dioxide would have had, in fact, a countereffect on growth; further, they contended, the disappearance of earthworms, beetles, millipedes and maggots would have retarded the functions of decay, thus contributing to the stultification of the wilderness.

Nonsense, would come the rejoinder, it was the fungi and bacteria that took care of the decay and, thankfully, the Exodus had spared the mushrooms and microbes.

Jez smiled. Not only were there nearly five billion fewer people to use the land and the lumber and to pollute the air, but the billion who were left held a near-worshipful attitude toward trees. Sylvan Renewal, with its centers in Belém and in the rejuvenating Black Forest, oversaw cutting, processing, planting and preservation through its growing network of woods stewards. With its rituals conducted around every tree about to be cut, its tithings, its crusades and its hymnody, Sylvan Renewal constituted the closest thing to a global religion that Little Blue had seen since the decline of consumerism.

A voice broke into her reverie. "Are you comfortable?" Dicken was asking their passenger.

Donal Jain loosened the collar of his thermal jumpsuit.

"Very. How do you keep it so warm?"

"It's part of the spoon energy," Dicken answered, "a function of the lonth and not of the focus." Donal nodded.

They were still chasing the sun, about two hours from their destination, when Jez suggested a rest.

"Can we wait until we reach the Black Hills?" Donal asked. "We'll be seeing them near sunset, their most magical time."

"Fine," agreed Jez.

Donal flashed her his boyish smile.

"My people have always called the hills shapeshifters," he said, "because, according to some, in a certain light they take the forms of animals. And of humans."

"One of those mountains has an amazing carving in the granite," Dicken interjected. "Two mothers and a babe."

Donal turned appreciative eyes on her.

"Mount Moraga. It's on the route of our monthly cushcar to Farmingdale, though it's best seen from below."

"Then we'll hold off resting until we get there," Jez decided. "Can we still reach Chimney Corner by dark?"

"Or shortly after," Donal nodded.

"Those children…" Dicken said. "Shouldn't we hurry?"

Donal shook his head. "We probably won't see them until tomorrow in any case." His face became a mask as he stared rigidly into the distance.

The sun was still bright over the western peaks when Dicken pointed to an approaching hilltop. "Look!" Below them the face of a butte broke the pattern of brown hills. A tall figure carved from the stone seemed to hail them.

"That's Morning Star Woman," Donal explained. "And wait. There, there on the north side, too, do you see?" Another figure, smaller and kneeling, pressed against a large animal. "Bear Woman. Our healers now say that the Stone Spirits grow angry if they are brought from the rock by force. They say that the figures are there without the carving if one has eyes to see."

"Of course," whispered Jez, because at that moment her astonished eyes were beholding a veritable menagerie below her. One ridge was clearly a snake. A high plateau became a turtle. As she watched, the timberline dropped from one mountain's back to reveal a beaver. No, it wasn't a beaver. A rabbit. Not a rabbit, for now it undulated with their flight above it and became a slow-moving porcupine. She sought the lower peaks and valleys to her right. Coyote, deer, buffalo, mountain lion, hawk. Her head was swimming with the movement, the changes.

"Jez!" Dicken's voice called her back. "Your lonth! We're losing altitude!"

Jez blinked, and then with effort captured her straying softself and dragged it away from the spectacle below her. She refitted it to Dicken's softself, then called up the spooning incantation for a swift recitation.

Dicken's eyes were closed and she had her hand on her belly. "Fine, now," she said. "Back to lonth." She put one arm around Donal's shoulders and gave him a quick hug. "Relax. She wigs out like that now and then. It's one of the prerogatives of witchhood."

Donal gave her a grateful smile. Then he looked at Jez.

"You saw them, didn't you?"

Jez nodded. Donal nodded, too. They flew on in silence.

"That baby's eyes. They follow you," insisted Dicken, craning her neck and leaning dangerously toward the escarpment. "Like a hologram."

"Now who's wigging out?" Jez called back. She tied the drawstring of her trews and studied the stone portrait above her. "That baby's eyes are hardly open, sisterlove," she teased. "You can barely see them."

"Mothers' Martyrs, Jezebel! I can see them here," Dicken retorted. "And over there, too." Dicken, her fists on her hips, peered at the carving while standing on tiptoe and then from other angles.

Jez stood wide and leaned toward the ground, stretching her legs. She saw the upside-down figure of Donal Jain moving toward her through the horseweed.

"Donal!" Dicken called. "Come help me set her straight. Keep looking at the baby and move this way."

Donal obliged, zipping his jumpsuit against the late afternoon chill.

"Beware, Donal Jain," Jez warned him as he passed her. She swung her chest right and left in spine-loosening torques. "She's not above bribery."

"I heard that!" Dicken shouted. "I ought to—whoa, hey, ooh!"

Jez saw the ground giving way beneath Dicken's feet, and Dicken herself tottering against the sky. "Dicken!" she shrieked, watching her lover's outspread arms pump the air.

Donal hurled himself toward the precipice, grabbing for some part of Dicken's flailing body. He clutched one pant leg, but it twisted from his grasp as Dicken, with an ever-distancing yell, disappeared completely over the edge of the cliff. Jez heard loud thrashing sounds underriding Dicken's cries. But as she reached Donal's side she heard only silence.

"Dicken!" Flat on the cliff's edge, she searched that first steep drop of at least ten meters. It ended in the layers of firebroom and berry fronds that hugged the side of the precipitous chasm below them. "Dicken!" Nowhere could she see any evidence of her lover's fall. Unwitting stalks of scrub brush and chaparral stared back at her, unmoving in the shadows.

"Dicken!" she shrieked.

Behind her, Donal was stepping out of his jumpsuit. "She fell outward. Maybe over there." He was nodding to a section of the thicket beyond the berry creepers.

Jez knelt to look at the broken rock that had given way under Dicken, then to the spot Donal had indicated. She nodded. "But that brush drops off, too. I can't see…"

"Here, hold on to this." Donal was reshouldering his backpack and pushing a leg of the jumpsuit toward her. "I can swing down to the brush." He sat at the edge of the scarp with the opposite arm of the jumpsuit in his hand.

"Good. I'll join you."

Donal almost let go. "You can't…"

"I can," she assured him, urging him past his astonishment. She sat bracing a foot against a small pine tree until she felt the lurch that meant Donal was hanging at the far end of the jumpsuit. "Are you okay?" she shouted.

Her answer was the release of the tension on their makeshift rope, a quick silence, then a loud thrash. "Donal?" She scrambled to the edge of the precipice.

"I'm fine." His voice was far away.

Through growing shadows she saw him, sprawled on briars and firebroom boughs. She threw the jumpsuit after him and retrieved her backpack.

"I'm coming, Big Dicken," she murmured, slipping into the straps.

She closed her eyes, sank into her inside vastness, and swam there a second to recover all her balances. Then she exhaled and waited a very long moment, breathing slowly, shallowly. There it came, the image she sought, wafting toward her on pillows of air. In an instant she was the butterfly, not yet soaring, but hovering above the ground. She felt her feet leave the earth, and an intoxicating lightness infuse her body. She opened her eyes and with slow intent moved over the edge of the precipice. Lightly, like the creature she imitated, she floated downward.

Donal Jain barely believed his eyes. He ceased his attempts to escape the nest of thorns and underbrush that supported him and watched with careful attention as Jezebel bent her legs and landed beside him, balancing half on the brambles and half on the near vertical slope out of which they grew.

"Do you often do that?" he asked.

"Only when I have to," she answered, silently thanking her butterfly guide. "No, I know what you're thinking. I can't lift her out of here."

She began searching the sea of brush that tumbled downward beyond them. There were no trees for hundreds of feet.

"Di-i-cken!" she called. An echo answered.

Donal clambered up beside her. "We are in trouble, Jezebel," he said, looking around. "This brush is supple. It would snap back and cover any place she fell. And it will be dark in less than fifteen minutes."

Jez's heart sank. "Then we have to find her before then. I can float and scud enough to take a look around," she mused, "but I'm afraid you'll have to do it the hard way. You don't happen to carry a machete?"

Donal began struggling back into the protection of the jumpsuit. "No. And I wouldn't want to use it even if I had it. The bushes will let me through. And they will hold me up."

"Here," Jez said suddenly, reaching to take his chin in her hands. Donal started. "Relax, I'm putting a vapor greave over your face so those briars don't get to you. You'll have to crawl." As her fingers made light passes over his head and neck, droplets formed. "Now your hands."

He hesitated. "Wait. We'll need light." Before Jez could respond, Donal had closed his eyes and cupped his hands in front of his mouth.

With growing astonishment, Jezebel watched the man do what she had seen only women do before: He conjured a glolobe, spinning plenum from vacuum, twining the errant spectra spline by spline with such dexterity that she could hardly see them take shape. He worked quickly, finally moving his hands apart to reveal a network of tiny velocities that fluoresced at last into a bright healthy light.

With a smile of satisfaction, Donal held the light out to Jez. "You'll need it sooner than I."

Jez took the glolobe. "You are a man of many parts, Donal Jain," she said.

"I have sat at the feet of many wise women," he responded.

She cast the vapor protection over his hands and then stood, closed her eyes and lifted again, this time scudding slowly over the expanse of underbrush that clung to the steepening decline. The air was chill now, and in the gathering night she could barely see Donal as he crawled about the area at the base of the cliff.

Methodically she hovered in a steady suspension above the brambles and chaparral, moving her light in regular sweeps below her. As she searched the blanket of darkening sameness beneath her, she reached out toward Dicken, toward the source of deep laughter and blessed comfort, toward memories of work, of…

Jez brought herself up short in midair, dipping almost uncontrolled into the underbrush. Something shiny. Now it was gone. No, there, to her left! She drew herself back and duplicated her last series of moves, waving the light slowly. Yes! Something dangled there in the ranks of bigger firebroom brush. She dove toward it.

"Donal, here! There's…" The object was at her fingertips: Dicken's dankee necklace, its tiny silver plates hanging in a broken strand from the branch. Jez pocketed the necklace and swung the glolobe frantically about her. She forced it deep into the tops of the tree-like brush beneath her, trying to discover where Dicken had disappeared. Her eyes fell on a broken branch.

"I'm going down!" she called to Donal.

Activating a vapor greave about her own body, she collected all that she could of strength and drove herself feet first down into the growth beneath her. She plunged twice her height through a shaft of tangled limbs, one that she prayed had been hollowed out by Dicken's body. Suddenly her feet swung in a huge nothingness and then crashed onto solid earth.

She opened her eyes to a different world. And to the body of Dicken.

Jez sat stunned in the silence. Bare ground made a plateau of the slopes around her, almost level for several yards in all directions. Dicken lay just beyond her, sprawled wide on the earth in a pocket of space between the trunks of the immature trees.

Surrounding the small haven, soundless and dark even in the harsh light of the glolobe, was the microcosm of a forest whose floor in another time could have been the wanderground for all manner of small animals up and down the entire slope. For an instant, Jez saw in her mind the warrens and burrows that once had been a part of this firebroom grove. Then the foxes, the marmots, the woodchucks and the rabbits invaded her mind, and as she crawled toward her lover, her mind caught the creatures' ebullient bustle in the flourishing miniature forest.

Dicken was unconscious, breathing shallowly, unresponsive to her touch. Looking up, Jez could see the opening in the firebroom that she, and Dicken before her, had dropped through. With deliberate caution she again protected her body and thrust her arms and the glolobe above her head. Lightly, she lifted herself upward through the passageway, swiveling back and forth where she needed to, until she felt the leafy top branches. Her head emerged into an almost completely black night. A light shone some distance away, toward the cliff. Donal had called up another glolobe.

"I'm coming," he shouted.

The darkness was heavy on them now, and his light was moving very slowly, revealing his wiry body as he crept like a high-wire walker from the top of one resilient little tree to another, calmly making his way toward her.

"I'll station my light right here where I've gone down!" she shouted to him.

"Good!"

"When you drop, shield your eyes!"

She stabilized her own glolobe in the topmost branches beside her suspended body and, without waiting for his response, plunged again beneath the canopy.

In the blackness she scrambled toward the heat of Dicken's body. Setting her own pack aside, she stretched out parallel to her lover, her arm around her, her temple next to Dicken's temple, her free hand on Dicken's abdomen. She began breathing in a measured tempo, diminishing her softself by slow decrements until she was a tiny presence hovering in the spinal cord at the base of Dicken's skull.

Merely a breeze of gentle inquiry now, she flowed with fluids and leapt with synapses up through Dicken's brain, down her back, out every spinal nerve, into every sensory track, from central source to every organ and every extremity. When at last she swam back into the consciousness of her own body, Jezebel encountered the waiting presence of Donal Jain. Both glolobes were re-energized and hung over Dicken's body.

"She has several cracked ribs, one of them splintered," she announced.

Donal was removing his jumpsuit again, spreading it over Dicken as Jez continued to talk.

"Sprains and bruises almost everywhere, and a dislocated shoulder. She's hit her head, but not hard enough to put her out. Two cervical vertebrae are out of line, though I can't find any pressure there on the nerves. Right lobe of her liver is bleeding badly—probably punctured by the rib. I've relieved its distress and stabilized her systems." She looked with wide eyes at Donal. "But I don't know why she's unconscious."

The full recognition of their circumstances assailed her: Her lover might be close to death, in immediate need of healing that was beyond her ken, and they hung on a cold mountainside in a black night, huge distances from any help, with no transportation and no means of communication.

"How far are we," she made herself ask, "from Chimney Corner?"

Donal offered her his canteen. When she refused, he drank a cautious sip. "Another hour in the air. Two days overland. And if we carry her…There is a village south of us, but almost as far."

Jez dabbed with a handkerchief at the scrapes and scratches on Dicken's face. "The cushcar?"

"It's not due for two weeks. And no other aircraft regularly come."

Jez stared at him, then began exploring the contents of Dicken's pack.

Donal pulled a glolobe to him and studied Dicken's dark brown face, almost ashen now. "Jezebel," he said, his voice breaking the silence of their tiny shelter.

"What?" Jez hauled a sweater out of Dicken's pack.

"The flying spoon, how is that working done?"

Jez froze. She looked up to meet Donal's guileless eyes.

"No," she snapped, restuffing Dicken's pack with its assortment of food and woodsgear.

"No?"

"No!" Jez fairly shouted. She looked apologetically at Dicken and then, still clutching the pack, she swung around to face Donal. Her voice was dangerously steady.

"Listen to me, Citizen Jain! You know a great many things that are important to know. I respect your knowledge and the way you use it. But do not be fooled. All your knowledge ten thousandfold would not entitle you to a hint of women's mysteries! Women's mysteries cannot be told, not because we hoard the knowledge but because no language can capture it. The flying spoon is one such mystery, whose power lies in the sacred double vesseling of woman-love, a vesseling that men cannot imagine, much less imitate. You are a man. You cannot experience the flying spoon. Do not even think of trying!"

Donal Jain did not take his gaze from Jezebel. In the silence of the shelter, Dicken's breathing became a rattling wind.

"I asked…"

"Forget it!"

They stared at each other in the cramped little den. Jezebel broke the intensity by moving protectively to Dicken. She placed her fingertips lightly under Dicken's nose.

Donal Jain closed his eyes.

Jez began laying out a well-worn groundcloth, calculating the odds against getting it under Dicken without disturbing her body too much. Donal moved to help her, gently placing one hand beneath Dicken's neck. With his other arm he slowly lifted Dicken's upper torso, raising the head and neck as a unit. Jez did not protest. Together they pushed and slid and maneuvered until the cloth lay fully under the unconscious woman. Jez covered her again with the jumpsuit and her sweater. Then she laid a light torpor over the inert body for further warmth. She looked up at Donal.

"Thank you."

Donal nodded and crawled back to his spot beyond Jez. He sat, his arms locked around his knees.

Jezebel found the sandwiches of sprouts and ginger squash that Beabenet had ordered up for their trip. She tore off pieces of the bag that protected her food and ate them, occasionally taking a small bite of the sandwich itself.

"Mine is wrapped in seaweed paper," Donal said. "What is yours in?"

"Rice paper," Jez said, munching. She resisted the urge to wolf down the whole sandwich and instead returned it to the remains of its ricebag. She allowed herself a sip of water from the canteen.

"Donal…"

Donal held up his hand. "You told the truth," he said.

She nodded.

He extinguished one of the glolobes and rested his head on his knees.

Jez put out the other light and lay on the hard earth beside Dicken, her mind squirreling with anxiety, longing, despair. Briskly she formulated a plan for the morrow. First, she and Donal would fashion a stretcher and, with some help from her levitating powers, get Dicken over the steep underbrush to the mountain path. Then, by following the winding trails, they would come eventually to Chimney Corner and use whatever technology was available there to reach healing help.

She tried to embrace hope, but in her chest her heart hung like a stone. Stroking Dicken's face and body, she chanted softly every blessing that could bring ease. It was perhaps an hour later that she finally dropped into an exhausted sleep.

Her eyes flew open. The darkness that encircled her was alive with molten energy. Jez gasped. Wild fluctuations of a tightly condensed tension alternately rocked themselves outward and withdrew, only to cast themselves forward again, beating without focus or effect upon some invisible barrier. Jez gingerly reached out her own senses, seeking the source. First to her lover's near-lifeless body. Then…Donal! The man was transmitting! But trying to mindreach with wild splays of frustrated intent. She drew herself into focus and slipped into link with his flailing energy.

"Relax," she mentally sent, trying desperately to find the center of the storm that surrounded her. "Donal! Breathe! Breathe deep!" The chaos abated somewhat, replaced by confusion, embarrassment. "Donal! Can you understand me?"

"Yes!" The thought attacked her.

"You are trying too hard! Invite it, invite the ether to carry your intent! It's not a barrier. Do you understand?"

Immediately the turbulence subsided. In her hardself, Jez could hear Donal rein in his breath. An uneasy calm replaced the frenzy.

"Jezebel," Donal sent. "Jezebel, is that you?"

Hardly believing she was doing so, Jez sent back an affirmation. Then, "How long have you known you can mindstretch?"

"Only recently. I was trying to find Ola, my pledgemate," he answered. "She sometimes can receive me. When we hold each other." The energy stirred again into potential disarray.

"Relax!" Jez mentally shouted, relieved to hear her command obeyed. A glimmer of hope teased her consciousness.

"If I could reach her," he went on, still sending, "she could get spooners to us right away. Jezebel, I…"

"You might, Donal," Jez sent. "Or we might."

She held Dicken's hand, still lying supine several feet from Donal, unwilling to disrupt this magic with physical movement. She spoke again to his mind.

"Can you picture Ola, Donal? Good. Draw her in detail. Place her in a setting—the bed, her workroom, wherever you believe she is right now." She sensed his growing focus. "Now center upon something close to her, something she's touching. A sheet, some clothing." Into her own mind sprang the image of a large polished seed, held by a woven string. It rested on a lovely bosom.

"Donal, you have to visit with that necklace, do you hear? And repeat her name. Then, when you feel she is strong in your mind, you begin easing out the energy. Easing it, Donal. Not throwing it. Ask the air to carry it." She felt his assent. "I will add whatever I can to this link. And together," she smiled ruefully in disbelief, "together we might cover the miles to Ola."

And so they worked. Donal would hold the image of Ola's polished seed, silently chant her name, quietly press his energy toward her. Jez would circle his sendings with her own, setting up rhythmic undulations of relaxed surges. But when Donal increased his force, their link would shatter and again his untamed energy would belt forth, bouncing wildly about them, sending them both into abrupt withdrawal. At maximum exertion, they could reach what they felt must be the top of the cliff, but there their efforts would dissipate. Donal would raise more force, and immediately the wild explosions would rock them again.

He's a toggle switch, Jez thought, either on or off. No control in between.

Jez did not tell Donal Jain that she had mindreached with only a few people in her life, and never with a man. Nor did she tell him that his psychic gifts outstripped in their potential many of the witches she had known. He had to learn to discipline that power. He would have to study with Dorothea. She caught herself. What was she thinking? Helping a man to learn the Craft? Get a grip, Jezebel.

They tried again. And again. Far into the dark night. Jez worked every combination of sendings and addressed every node, every windbreak, every mother tree, every strain of mica shimmering within the mountains, every potential source of help that her tiring mind could discover. But never could their message sail beyond the cliff.

She was readying herself for yet another attempt when her focus was disrupted by intense physical sounds. She dropped from her trance back into their dark mountainside den and felt, like sharp knives, the heartbreaking sobs of Donal Jain. Just beyond her feet, the waves of his everlasting despair slammed at her shieldless body. She reworked her shields and crawled to his side.

"Donal," she whispered. "Donal!"

His cries intensified. He flung his arms wide, striking her chest, flailing at the bushes around him.

Ola probably hears this, Jez thought. She physically forced his arms downward and pulled him to her, holding him against her as they struggled like street fighters in the darkness. At last she muscled his flailing body beneath her. Drawing from her doth strength for every ounce of power, she willed Donal into a supine position under her own weight. She lay upon him, pinning his arms to his sides. He raged against her, shrieking his protest, his despair.

She moved her head beside his and held him rigid for an instant, while his body convulsed. He screamed, then collapsed beneath her, giving himself over completely into her custody.

Jez smoothed his hair and allowed him to weep. Moving slowly, she shifted them both to their sides and slipped her arm beneath his neck. Holding him firmly, she rocked a little and hummed snatches of a sleep-chant. She assured him that they would try the mindreaching again after some sleep. Donal shuddered into silence.

Jezebel Stronglaces, disbeliever of any man's sensitivity, and warrior against the male of her species, held a man in one arm while searching the darkness for her lover with the other.

Fortunately, in their struggle they had ended up close beside Dicken.

By the Sacred Yarn, Jez whispered to herself as she eased her free arm under her lover. This is more than I believe.

How long they remained in that blessed peace, Jez did not know. She was simply grateful that Donal was at last quiet.

They slept, the three of them.

It wasn't Carnaval. But there was a piñata. And scores of youngs besides herself. Jez was deafened by their shrieks, their laughter. A small girl nudged her. "Come on, Donal! It's your turn!" Jez shook her head. Someone tried to put a blindfold over her eyes. She snatched it off, amid yells of Shame! and He won't play! The girl pushed her, knocking her off balance to the floor. Then her tormentor put on the blindfold herself and began trying to hit the elusive papier-mâché star with her swinging bat. The others screamed their delight.

Jez, still sprawled on the floor, felt sick. Her head was spinning. Tears were running down her cheeks. She saw the large woman looming over her, urging a bat into her hand. "Donal, don't you want to break the star?" Jez pulled herself away from the woman and scrambled toward the wall. She watched with an awful howling inside her as, one after the other, the party of youngs tried to hit the piñata.

At last one child caught it with an oblique blow that broke one point off the star. With a whoop, fifteen or so small bodies assaulted the piñata with their bats. Jez rocked with each blow. She covered her head with her arms, pushing her body into the corner. She sobbed.

When the piñata broke, sending the candies and favors splashing all over the room, Jez first felt the howl of pain rise from her throat, then become drowned by laughter and shrieks. Suddenly they were all gone, adults and youngs with their candies, all shouting and pushing their way outside. Only the shattered papier-mâché star remained, lying in silence on the floor.

Slowly, with a sadness that hindered her every move, she crawled toward the wreckage of the piñata and began tenderly piecing it back together.

Other fragments. Flashes. Refusing to cut cucumbers...punishment for swallowing her food whole...smoothing out a crumpled sheet of paper, her tears splashing down on it...Donal is a cryyy-babyyy...

Jez hit the baseball far out into the trees but could not run, so horrified was she at the pain she had given the ball. "Donal, run! Donal!" A friend was beside her, frantically pulling her along the baseline, making her touch first base. Then she did run, straight past first base and toward the trees, running to find the ball she had hit before the fielders got to it, running to find the ball and apologize... running...

Tears, pain, a lifetime of jeers, ridicule. And pity. Then the love of an old woman, her worn hands and gravelly voice soothing, healing. Some understanding, balance.

Something balanced in Jez's own softself at that moment. And she dreamed on, in the companionship of Donal Jain, walking, running, swimming, through the years-long night. She learned more than she had strength to carry. She faltered, recovered, then shouldered the load with increasing ease.

Jezebel awoke to the same sheltered den on the same dangerous mountainside with the same stranded companions breathing with her the same hard, cold air. Yet her world had changed so vastly that she could not measure or name it. She lay immobile in the dim dawn light that seeped into their haven, unable to deny the night's journey and yet unwilling to act upon its knowledge. Then a gracious clarity stunned her.

Jez closed her eyes, trying to subdue the clarity. It persisted. She succumbed. She knew what she had to do.

Beside her, Dicken still breathed shallowly. She had not moved. In the course of their sleeping, Jez and Donal had shifted for warmth. Their three bodies were huddled now in the semblance of a spoon and a half, her arm around Dicken's nearly supine body, Donal curled behind her, his arm around her waist. Before she could turn to Donal, she heard his voice just behind her head.

"Jezebel."

"I'm awake."

"Jezebel, we have dreamwalked."

"Yes."

A silence.

"Is Dicken all right?"

Jez hugged Dicken's immobile body as tightly as she dared and then began slowly to sit up. Donal's eyes were barely visible in the dimness.

"She's going to be fine. But she will need more help before noon of this day. There's a healer at Chimney Corner?"

"One of the finest. But Jezebel!"

Jez stopped him with her words.

"Donal Jain." She took a deep breath.

"Donal Jain, you and I are going to make a flying spoon, just as you dared to suggest we might."

She could just see Donal's eyes grow large.

"We are going to carry Dicken in front of us and then between us, up from and over this firebroom brush and north again over the hills on our original path."

Donal started to speak.

Jez placed her fingers over his lips.

"I know that we can do this, you and I. How it will be accomplished I don't yet fully understand, but I don't doubt we can do it." She was on her knees, sitting back on her feet.

"You will hold Dicken before you and open your mind to mine, just as you did in trying to reach Ola. I will teach you the incantation." She almost smiled. "A new incantation," she added. She put her hand on his shoulder.

"Then, Donal, we shall fly."

The sun was fully risen when the clinging firebroom bushes reluctantly let go of the three figures they had so recently captured. High above them, the spooners slipped the inert form between them into a carrying position. The flight bubble faltered only a moment before it stabilized and sailed to the north.

2

> Turn this way, we are many.
> Turn another, we are one.
> Fish swim, a school of beauties.
> Fish turn, a burst of sun.
> *Song of the Lumari*

Chimney Corner did not nestle in the Black Hills. Rather, it clung to two mountain faces that met around a fertile narrow valley. As if to apologize to the inhabitants for arriving so late each day, the winter sun lingered each evening.

In the still hardy rays of that sunlight, filtered through wide windows, Bess Dicken sat upright against a brace of pillows, her head back, her eyes closed. Jezebel and three other women circled her bed with songs and clapping, weaving impromptu harmonies and rhythms around ancient chants, popular tunes, rounds, lullabies, ballads—whatever the patient requested. Dicken smiled weakly as a bright melody showered its final notes over her weary body.

Jez led the low laughter that followed the effort. "Is that enough, you song-greedy soul?" She sat on the low stool and took Dicken's hand.

Dicken's voice was a whisper. "I have wore you to a frazzle." She smiled, trying to raise her head. Gently, Jez pushed her back into the pillows. "The music makes it better," she said, closing her eyes again and waving one hand at the women. "Thank you," said her lips. Jez lowered her into a flat position and tucked the bedclothes around her.

As the women were tiptoeing out, Ola, Donal's pledgemate, stayed behind. "Dicken," she said softly, touching Jez's shoulder as she spoke, "several of the youngs you came to see would like to meet you. Do you feel up to that?"

Dicken interrupted what was about to be Jez's objection. "Yes. I'd like to meet them." She turned to Jez. "As my momah would say, 'If it do not kill me outright, it will serve to make me stronger.'" She smiled wanly. "Then I will sleep."

Jez rose in astonishment as three girls entered the room, one of them about four years old, the other two between ten and twelve. Polite but curious, the youngs approached Dicken's bedside. They were ordinary children, Jez noted, except for one startling aspect of their appearance: Their hair was as white as new-fallen snow.

"Jezebel and Dicken," said Ola, "these are Luisa Maniboz, Taína Renananda Ko and Jida Wood Dancer. Luisa, Taína and Jid, these are Calica Jezebel Stronglaces and Calica Bess Dicken."

Jez knelt by the bed and reached across to touch the hands that stretched out to hers. All three of those bright faces were excited and smiling; their touch was a shade past courtesy, full of what Jez could only term fervor. When they turned to Dicken, their energies were even livelier. Jid and Taína knelt by the narrow bed and held Dicken's arm. Luisa, the smallest of the three, consulted Ola with a non-oral question and then sat on the bed by Dicken, laying her head on the patient's chest.

"Calica Bess," Jid said, "I'm so sorry."

"You got hurt coming to see us," Taína added.

Dicken did her best to rise to the occasion. "Naw, it was my own foolishness," she whispered, "not your fault." She patted them, hushing their apologies.

With kindly touches, Ola began suggesting that the children leave. "Calica Bess has to rest. But Jezebel, will you talk with them now?"

"Yes. If it's a good time for Taína? Jid and Luisa?"

Taína nodded. "Oh, yes." The three girls stroked Dicken in farewell, Luisa in particular kissing and squeezing her hand.

"Whoa," Dicken croaked. "Your hair, how come your…"

Jid shook her long locks. "Isn't it nice, Calica? It just changed to gray. Then to white."

"And the others," Jez asked, faltering, "the others in your, ah, who are…"

Taína beamed. "Most have this color, but one still has brown."

"I see," said Jez.

As Ola began herding the three out of the room, a large round woman, Dulma, came to sit by Dicken.

"Dulma will be with you for a while," Jez whispered to her lover. "She's the one who brought you back to us." She kissed Dicken's closed eyes.

"Wait!" Dicken's eyes flew open. She said something Jez could not hear.

She bent closer. "Again, love?"

Dicken's voice was raspy. "The Koran."

"The Koran?"

Dicken nodded and closed her eyes.

Jez looked at the healer. Dulma shrugged lightly. Then with another kiss to Dicken's cheek and a handclasp with Dulma, Jez stole softly from the room.

In the front area of the house, a company of women and children stood and sat in various poses of unease, talking with each other or holding and caressing Taína, Jida and Luisa. Bredan, another child with white hair, was sitting on the lap of a young woman whom Jez took to be her older sister.

As she met the eyes of those gathered there, Jez's heart sank, and for a fleeting moment she feared that they expected her to repair this awful damage, to turn back the clock somehow to weeks in days past when Chimney Corner had been normal, when the youngs still had their lives in front of them, when an awful announcement had not yet been made.

Ola, bearing a steaming kettle and mugs, came to her rescue. "If you will, Jezebel, sit with all of us for a bit before you speak with the youngs." She set her burden on a low teapoy while an older man slid behind her to deposit bread and cakes on another table, returning immediately to an out-of-sight kitchen for more food.

Jez looked at Jid, who nodded vigorously, and then caught smiles from Taína and Luisa. "Of course," she sighed, releasing breath she had not been aware of holding back.

There was a stir as the group settled around the tables, on the floor and on stools, falling to the feast of soups and spreads and fresh fruit. The tea, Jez discovered, was almost a broth of sweetness cut with a perfect burst of bitterness that left her palate fresh and eager for more. The woman who sat beside her chewed on an unlit briar pipe, sucking and blowing upon it as if it were burning a delicious aromatic tobacco. She explained between sterile puffs that the tea was made from the bark of a highland fir—and that in the privacy of her own nest, her pipe would fill the room with a smoke that could bring visions.

In the midst of the sharing of food and without any ceremony, one of the women addressed her. "Jezebel, we are desperate people here, puzzled and angry, too. We know you're a witch of great power, and we respect that."

The room had become very still. The woman looked around almost nervously and then, realizing she had begun a little speech, she turned back to Jez. "My name is Nancy Fairwitness. We are glad you have come, but distressed that Dicken had to risk her life for us."

There were nods from others.

"And we're grateful to Donal, too, for bringing you here." Nancy abruptly threw up her hands. "Oh, by all that's holy, I'm just trying to say that you shouldn't feel like you have to save us. I don't think anyone can save us."

"Calica Nancy, you mustn't say that! Save?" Taína was speaking. She was not shrill, but earnest. "We are not bad, we aren't!"

Her mother's hand touched her shoulder. "Shhh, Ta."

"Mada, we love you!" Taína flung her arms around the woman, saying again and again, "Love you, love you!"

Just then, Donal Jain emerged from the kitchen. He moved into the group and knelt by Taína and her mother, his hand on Taína's arm, his eyes in conversation with the woman's.

Then he addressed Jez. "We have found it easier sometimes to talk together when the girls and Elan are not here. But only if they don't feel left out."

He leaned back in order to search Taína's face. "Your mada and the other calicas need to explain to Jezebel how they feel. It's important for them to do that, even if they are sad. Then later you can talk with her, too." He shifted as if to rise. "I'm going to the long meadow to transplant aspen sprouts. Who wants to join me?" He turned to the other three white-haired children. "Luisa? Bredan? Jida?"

They were with him in an instant, offering quick kisses or hugs to the adults near them and heading boisterously for the door. All but Taína. She pulled away from her mother reluctantly. As she stood, she looked at the people in the room.

"Why do you cry, all of you?" she asked, her lower lip trembling. "You always told us we would be with each other after we die. And we will." She was a small brave figure, carrying burdens that youngs rarely bear. Then she clamped her lips together and ran out.

Ola ended the short silence that followed. "Taína feels it most, the saying goodbye. The rest…" She turned to the others, then back to Jez. "The rest seem more willing."

"Not just willing," said the young woman who had held Bredan on her lap. "Eager." She shook her head.

"Well, some of them, Kaluntala," another woman added. "I'm Ester Heartseeker, Jezebel. One of the youngs who intends to die is my daughter, Chassel." She straightened on her stool. "I can't speak for the other mothers. Or fathers," she added, nodding to the older man who had helped to serve the food and who had now taken a seat among them. "And I can't speak for the youngs. But Chassel and I have had long conversations. She knows what she is doing. And she rejoices. Who am I to hold her back, even if I could? She might have been drowned, or brought down by some fatal virus, or struck by a boulder. We might have lost her to a thousand accidents. What better way for her to go than by her own heart's bidding? Yes, I was shocked and stricken at first, and yes, yes, yes, I will miss her. But I have another daughter. In fact, all of us who will lose a young have another child or children. And we will love them all the better for the loss of the one."

Heartseeker turned to address the whole group. "What Taína said calls us all to practice what we preach. Do we really think that this life is all we have? That we won't be reunited in spirit after all? What does it matter when we die since we all will do so? We should be rejoicing with the youngs that they see so clearly, understand so much, that they leave us now only for something more important to their own souls!"

Across the room, a loud cry drowned out these last words. A small woman in heavy skirts was on her feet, flailing her arms at Ester. Jez remembered her name: Bita Yorn. Her voice filled the room with its anguish.

"Spare me, Heartseeker! You can kiss your daughter goodbye on Monday and joydance on Tuesday if you like. But others of us will mourn our loss! Elan, my son, will be dying with Taína and her minions. He's bought the whole bill of goods, and he's just a little boy who does not know what he's doing!" She fumed as she looked around the room.

"And did you hear me?" she continued. "He's a little boy. We don't have many little boys! He is that much more special because he's rare. But his hair is turning white with the rest of them, and nobody, nobody in this whole covenant is doing anything! We just wail and talk about how we'll all meet again in the Great Somewhere!"

Kaluntala spoke softly. "Bita, the covenant has been over all this time and again. But we are only a community, not a superhuman power. What would you have us do?"

"Keep them apart," Bita almost shrieked. "Don't let them congregate and go off into the woods together like they do. They're probably planning how to help each other die!"

Ola's voice topped the other woman's. "Bita, have you tried to keep Elan away from the others?"

"Yes, yes I have!"

"And what happens?"

Bita blinked. "He runs away. To them. Or…"

"Or," bit off the older man. "Or he goes into a trance that is so like death that we awaken him and let him go where he pleases." Heads were nodding in understanding. The man stood up.

"Jezebel," he said, "with this talk you are glimpsing the texture of our days. I am Kirk, Elan's father." He moved a few feet across the room to stand by Bita. "We can do nothing. You know it," he said firmly, placing his arm around her shoulders.

Bita glared at him but did not shake off his touch. Then a well of tears sprang from her eyes. "We have to keep them!" she urged, her voice rising in pitch. "We have to separate them from each other so they don't get contaminated—so all our other children, in fact, don't get contaminated by this crazy idea! And that's all it is, you know! An idea, a notion. Probably Taína's notion, and she has infected all the rest. If we don't stop them they will die, just from believing it!"

She collapsed into her partner's arms, shaking uncontrollably.

There was a silence in the room that Jez felt as a vast pain. She lingered in it, testing its depths and seeking its boundaries. These people, the already bereaved, conducted their daily activities in a state of astonished grief. Yet thankfully, there was an element missing: In all the agony and incredulity, even within the aura of the sobbing Bita Yorn, Jez could not discover a single ounce of despair. They were a strong people, dedicated to life and living even in the face of their great impending loss.

A woman was speaking, the one whom Jez had taken to be Taína's mother. She held up her hands in the ageless manner of one telling a tale, and she looked toward Bita as she spoke.

"Two years ago Taína came to me with a story," she recalled. "She and her sister Metl and Elan had been playing near the great rock chimneys. They had made a giant wheel in the dust. Elan was still clearing away the circle and the two girls were searching the surrounding area for rocks that could be used for cairns to mark each of the spokes. When they got back, loaded with stones,

Elan was on his back in the middle of the wheel—asleep, they thought.

"It was a cool day, so they were surprised to see that he was covered with sweat. As they watched him, he began to sing in a strange language. He sang very loudly, enthusiastically. Ta and Metl thought he was teasing them, and after a bit they decided to sing back to him. Before they could do so, his eyes popped open and he smiled. He began wiping off his perspiration, saying, 'That is a song of the Lumari. Someday soon I will go to live with them.' I mentioned this to no one and thought no more of it until Taína told me a few days ago that she now hears in her head that same song that Elan sang, and that the friends who will welcome her on the other side of death will be those same people, the Lumari."

She lowered her hands.

"I tell you this, Bita," she ended, "to suggest that no one of the youngs is a leader. Not my Taína, not your Elan. The voices that call to each of them may be the same voices, but the path that each follows is her or his own path, chosen by each without influence from the others."

Bita listened to the story but gave no acknowledgement of its meaning to her. Kirk held her as she stared at the floor.

"Jezebel Stronglaces," he said, "we are grateful that you will speak with the youngs. And perhaps you do hold some magical power that could convince them not to leave us." He looked at his pledgemate. "But also important to me is why this is happening. If, in talking with them, you can help us to that greater understanding, that would be gift enough for me."

Nancy Fairwitness added her voice again. "I agree," she said. "And furthermore we could use some information from the world beyond these mountains." She looked at Jez. "We live in deliberate isolation here, concentrating on our tomato beds, our

seedlings, our mica nexuses. We have little contact with the outside world. We don't even watch flatcasts. Are we the only ones?
Are our youngs unique among the societies on Little Blue? Or are
there others like them?"

Jez had known that the question must come. As pairs of eyes
turned to her, she touched once more the uneasiness that she and
Dicken had shared the last few weeks, and the memory of the
flatfilm that Beabenet had shown them—was it only yesterday?
She tried to make her long deep breath a calm one. Then very
carefully she spoke.

"Chimney Corner is not alone in this matter."

In the silence, brows furrowed in puzzlement. Then, as the
eyes all around her slowly became aware, several voices began to
speak at the same moment: "You mean…Other children…No!…
How do you…?"

"Wait! All of us, wait!" Nancy Fairwitness held up her hands
until silence came. She stared at Jez. "Please, tell us more."

Jez set her teacup on the low table. As she spoke she searched
the faces surrounding her. "Some people who have watched the
daily figures on Size Central's calculations have discovered a barely
significant rise in the death rate, particularly among youngs. Even
taking into account the ups and downs of such statistics and
the traditional reluctance of Size Bureau analysts to talk about
statistical tendencies, growing numbers of ordinary citizens are
convinced that very soon the trend will be undeniable."

The expected questions came thick and fast. Jez answered
them all, even the one she had hoped they would not ask.

"The birth rate. With so many dying, isn't it increasing?"

"No," she answered, wishing with all her heart that Dicken
were beside her to hold her in her big arms. "In fact, some of
us—again, ordinary citizens, not statisticians—have been following a trend that in a few weeks, perhaps even a few days, will be

obvious to the world. In every tri-satrapy, the birth rate is actually declining."

The eyes before her widened and deepened into full realization. From a corner of the group, the voice of the pipe-smoking woman rose up loud and clear. "It is the Endtimes," she announced.

When all heads turned to her, the woman pulled a long toke on her empty pipe. Then she recited: "In the Endtimes the hair of the children will turn gray."

Ola's voice rang above the tension, "Who says that, Germaine? Where does that come from?"

The woman blew invisible smoke toward the ceiling. "Comes from the Koran, that's where."

It was late afternoon when Jez found Taína and four other youngs at the edge of the long meadow. They were covered with dirt, proof of their enthusiasm for the transplanting of small trees. As he greeted her, Donal Jain shouldered a mattock, a shovel, and a small clump of fatigue that turned out to be Luisa Maniboz.

"Jezebel, this is Chassel Heartseeker. And I don't think you met Bredan Santir." Jez knelt to speak to the two girls, at the same time smiling up at Luisa. Taína had come immediately to Jez's side and taken her hand. "Jid and Luisa both want to go back with me, correct?"

Both children nodded at Donal's words, and Jid added, "Can we come see Calica Bess tomorrow?"

"Indeed you can," Jez answered.

"The sun will be with you another hour if you're on this side of the hill," Donal told her. He stooped so Luisa could give Taína a wet kiss. "Come home when you're hungry. There are always cold snacks if you miss dinner." Donal set out down the path with

Luisa on his shoulder and Jid clinging to his shirt, trailing two empty gunnysacks behind her.

Long after nightfall, Jez still huddled together with the three girls against a warm boulder by a cave mouth. She had discovered both a great joy and an accompanying sadness, for though she had indeed touched spirits that lived in dimensions she had only dreamed of, those spirits were unable, even with their mind-reaching, to help her with the questions that haunted her. Taína, Bredan and Chassel lent her their images, their stories and their sensations, but they could not tell her why they had to leave, where they would be when they left, or what solace Jez could give to their families.

They spoke of animals as if they touched them daily, they conversed among themselves in a language with no pattern or meaning that Jez could grasp, they bubbled with a boundless joy, and they unquestionably called the whole universe their home. But they were in a place that Jez could not reach. When, much later, after delivering them to their families, she sank gently onto the trundle bed beside the sleeping Dicken, she lay restless and puzzled.

Most inexplicable of all was a vision played out for her by a joint mindlink that Bredan and Chassel had engineered with Taína's guidance. Through the children's eyes, Jez saw Zella Terremoto Adverb.

Zude was on a vertical rockface of majestic Kachenjung. She was securely belayed 30 feet above, but she had slid one boot into a crevice. The leg was awkwardly crossed in front of the other, wedged at an off-side angle. Zude manipulated her rope and the mesh of harnesses that traversed her body, sweating in the heat of the freshly risen sun. She tried to shift her body back over the trapped leg as she called up to her belayer, "I'm fine, Flossie! Just give me a minute!"

Then Zude was gone, and the children beguiled Jez with another vision.

A gas-lit city street and the Cathedral of Basil the Beatified, its unmistakable dome and surrounding cupolas covered by much snow. The scene filled the large window of an unkempt studio where a tousled-haired violinist attempted for the sixty-fifth time an unflawed rendition of the sixteen-bar climax of Ruboff's Tyrolean Concerto. Jez knew these particulars because the man's frenzy was evident, and because the words could be read from the sheet music on the stand.

"That's Mick," Taína had ventured in voice-over captioning, "Vasily Mikhailovich Terenski. He's practicing to perform for the emperor. Emperor Nicholas II," she added, "the last emperor."

Then Zude was there again, able to shift her torso at last so as to move it back across her imprisoned foot. But as she did so, she twisted the ankle in the opposite bias. She screwed her eyes shut and howled with pain.

Mikhailovich stopped abruptly in midpassage and flung his arms upward with a loud cry. Bow and violin shook with frustration.

Zude made herself relax and lean on her rope.

Mick held his bow and violin in one hand and withdrew a large handkerchief from his pocket. He wiped his face.

Zude closed her eyes, then drew in and released a deep breath.

Mick closed his eyes and stood for several moments breathing softly.

Purposefully, with tiny movements, the climber began working her boot out of the grip of the crevice.

Deliberately, the violinist shouldered his instrument again. Eyes still closed, he calmly addressed the passage once more.

As Zude felt her boot begin to move about in the crevice, she smiled with relief.

As Mick played, his body eased and lifted, sustained now by a new composure, a sudden confidence.

As her boot worked free, Zude laughed and yelled, "On belay!"
She then began a one-footed progress up the rockface, using the rope,
her recuperating leg dangling limp and at rest. "I'm coming, Floss!"
she shouted as she gathered speed, hastening exuberantly up the face.

Vasily Mikhailovich Terenski's notes flowed brightly into the
accelerating tempo, rising in perfect precision to the finish of the pas-
sage and ending with the triumph of his signature flourish. He kissed
the tingling soundbox of his precious instrument and whooped aloud
to the snow-blanketed cupolas of Basil the Beatified.

Jez had found herself exhilarated by the scene and enveloped
by the laughter of the girls at its close. Now in her trundle bed by
Dicken, she shook her head in wonder at the power that the little
drama had held for her. She pointed the itinerary of her mind
toward the Tall Towers of Gratitude. At last she reached out to lay
her hand on Dicken's and dropped into sleep.

In the days that followed, Jez visited with and worked beside
the bereaved people of Chimney Corner. Over and over she told
them what little she had learned from the children: They loved
their families very deeply, nothing could prevent their dying, for
them their dying would be joyful and absolutely safe. She listened
to the people of the covenant as they bore unbearable loss and,
with their eyes and ears and fingers, made memories of their children.

When Dicken was able, she wove her own modest strand
of presence and love into the texture of the covenant's life. Both
visitors knew that they must leave Chimney Corner a day or two
before the time of the children's dying. By then they would have
done all they could of hearing and holding, all they could of
understanding and learning. The covenant would say goodbye to
its children without the attendance of outsiders.

With white-haired little ones, and often with other children as well, the visitors flew in low spoon over the greening hills. Or they walked to the edges of the mountain stream where the melting of cold snows was swelling the waters into loud babblings. Taína, Bredan and Chassel sometimes tantalized them with cryptic glimpses of new realities that they clearly took for granted.

Once when Dicken asked Bredan where she would be after she had left them, the child swung Dicken's hand and announced simply, "We go with our friends." And once when they were speaking aloud, Taína told Jez about the beings who guard Little Blue.

"Their home is the Great Ear," she said, "which hears us all into Being. And they call us Her Cherished Vividity."

"Us?" Jez frowned.

"Well, I mean, that's what they call Little Blue. The Planet Being. Her Cherished Vividity."

"So she really is alive...a being. Little Blue? Gaia?"

Taína was aghast at the doubt. "Oh, Calica, of course! And she's very busy, trying to get well."

"I see," said Jez.

One evening Donal Jain awaited them, standing like a solitary oak on the side of a steep hill.

"With respect, Jezebel," he said, looking to the sky, "I dare to hope that I may fly again." He turned to her. "When I learn more of what our flight together meant. And when there is a wise woman who will help me to the task."

There was an uneasy moment, for Jez had stalwartly set aside the memory of that desperate night and the magic that had followed, choosing not to think about it or its ramifications.

It was Dicken who banished the tension.

"Donal Jain," she said, "you can borrow fire from my hearth anytime." She shot Jez a glance. "I don't know what it means that you and my Jezebel did what you did. But I'm the one standing here because of it. That makes you family to me, mister."

She held out her arms. Donal Jain welcomed that embrace. He and Dicken drew Jezebel to them, and the three of them swayed together.

When at last Jez and Dicken flew out of Chimney Corner, Dicken had her life and her health. Jez carried with her a deep gratitude for Dicken's recovery and a swatch of white hair that Taína had given her in a small ceramic box. Both of them bore the memories of extraordinary days and sturdy new friendships. Both of them basked in the love of a score of children, eight of whom they would never see again.

3

[2088 C.E.]

> When the mind is melted and used like water,
> it can be sent wherever one wants to send it.
> *Wisdom of the Ancients*

Sky Captain Lila Monteflores, one of the Vigilancia's low solar rocket engineers, turned her eyes from the bright wide Pacific flying beneath her to the pantomime of fierce competition that raged beyond her transparent sound block. Below and behind her an old-fashioned game of spoons was escalating to its inescapable conclusion: Magister Adverb, Commander-in-Chief of the Vigilancia, was just about to realize that she had been outwitted by a very round little boy named Enrique, Regina his raven-haired sister, and Ria their mother.

"Whoa!" shouted Zude, when she discovered that all the spoons had disappeared. Enrique and Regina cast away their cards and shrieked their jubilation. With taunts and whoops they threw themselves upon the defeated one, pummeling her unmercifully with the very trophies of their victory.

Monteflores spun half-circle in her pilot's cup, scanned the ocean again, and noted that their destination was less than ten minutes away. The sound block puffed open and closed again to admit a much-scathed Zude, hauling with her the accoutrements of her full-dress uniform. "Captain," she said, "may I put myself together in here?"

"Indeed, Magister."

"Better question: If we behave, may I bring Reggie and Enrique up here to watch the landing?"

43

"Of course, Magister. No problem."

"Good."

Zude sank into the secondary cup just below Monteflores and began snapping on the belts and scarf loops of a visiting Tri-Satrapy Magister.

Minutes later the pilot spoke over her shoulder. "We're beginning landing preparations, Magister. Shall I open a line to the children?"

"Please," answered Zude. She was about to speak her summons into the comchannel when Monteflores held up her hand. Zude listened. From the bowels of the fore-suite below them came a sound incomparably sweet. Piping childish voices sang in soft tones, with Ria, mother of the voices, sometimes helping:

> *"¿Dónde estás pelícano?*
> *¿Dónde estás cordero?*
> *¿Dónde estás elefante?*
> *¿Dónde estás salmón?"* sang Enrique.
> *"Sólo, sólo, sólo,*
> *Sólo en mi corazón,"* answered Regina and Ria.

Then Regina sang:

> *"Te ruego, salmón lindo,*
> *Y a ti elefante grande,*
> *Y a ti cordero inocente,*
> *Y a ti blanco pelícano."*

And all three sang:

> *"Te ruego, te ruego, te ruego:*
> *Que algún día estés a la mano."*

The song ended with a flourish. At Monteflores's invitation, two animated children tumbled loudly onto the bridge of the rocket. They plastered themselves immediately against the transparent walls, the better to exclaim at the ocean passing beneath them.

In the back of the craft, other Kanshou and civilians were listening to an interactive audio-commentary: "We're slowing to ground speed as we approach the topmost and largest of the Bathsheba Islands. We'll land on Punto, the smaller island just beyond Bougainville, to allow Magister Adverb and her party to disembark. Then we'll depart immediately for Manila and your destinations.

"Just below you and to your upper left are seaweed operations up and down the archipelago. With no animals to curb it, all the phytoplankton—all the plant life, in fact—blocks out its own sunlight with its heavy bloom. If it's not constantly monitored, it literally dies of its own self-shading. You can still note the differences in the color of the seas surrounding the islands. No coral anymore, of course, but you can see the shallow shelf extending some 32 kilometers from the beach before it drops off far to the west into the New Druid Trench. That trench is 242 kilometers in length, northwest to southeast."

"How deep?" asked one of the passengers.

"About 9,200 meters to the bottom," answered the computer. "Less than 500 meters down into it, the wreck of a World War II destroyer has settled onto a wide shelf. The Amahrery's Sea-Shrieves maintain a small fleet of phaetons or underwater jitneys for island undersea watch. They are similar to the old submersibles and available at a hefty credit outlay for tourists who want to see the wreck or explore the upper regions of the trench.

"On the southwestern tip of Punto are three facilities. The first one you see, there, is the Ocean Thermal Energy Conversion tower. The second is Labine Village, the experimental underwater community."

"Is that where they do ovular merging?"

"No, that's the work of the third facility, the McClintock-Saria complex, whose buildings you can see almost below us now on the eastern shore. McClintock-Saria was one of the centers established in the hope that animals might be cloned back into existence. The equatorial conditions seemed the best chance for sustaining the lives of clones if viable subjects were ever produced. As long as frozen embryonic animal cells were available, the work continued. When those efforts met with no success, centers like this one were converted into human ovular merging facilities."

The lecture continued even as the rocket floated to its cushioned pad on the island.

To Zude's immense relief, Punto's welcome of the Magister was relaxed and only minimally official. While Ria and the children were swept off to breakfast at the underwater village, Zude spent the morning in the company of Dr. Jasper Egarber, widely known as Jass, the stocky rosy-cheeked director of the McClintock-Saria Center, and Dr. Hadra Row, his dark-haired partner and the woman who headed up Little Blue's controversial Antaeus Project. With the easy hospitality for which islanders were renowned, the two scientists guided their guest through the egg-merging facilities and the Ocean Thermal Energy Conversion tower, beaming with delight as Zude admired the resources and charmed the technicians with her curiosity.

It was early afternoon by the time they strolled over the pathways crisscrossing the island, bound for the museum. Regina, Enrique and Ria would be emerging there from a holojaunt, the simulation of a deepsea ride.

"You know, Magister," Hadra noted, laughing, "the holojaunt is designed to lure tourists into the real thing."

"I figured as much. Your submersible trip down into the trench?"

"That's it! It was the holojaunt that finally cured me of my claustrophobia and convinced me that the submersibles are absolutely safe. I at last got to make the excursion to the sunken destroyer. And that I wouldn't have missed for the world!"

"You should do it, Magister," Jass urged, "you and your family. Only this week the Sea-Shrieves have completed a total upgrade of the meridian resonances in all the phaetons. Brand new computer codes and all tests passed with flying colors. They'd be delighted to take you on the excursion!"

"Actually, Reggie and Enrique are set on doing it and Ria is tempted. I don't think I can avoid it." Zude grinned. "Nor do I want to."

"Wonderful," Jass exclaimed. "And if you will allow me, I'd like to pilot your phaeton myself."

"He's an excellent pilot, Magister," Hadra assured her. "One of the best. And the phaetons are his passion."

They moved as they talked through dozens of mini-environments—cool groves, multicolored gardens, copses and glens—up hills, by fields, over paths that crunched under their feet in testimony to the island's volcanic history.

"Tell me about Antaeus, doctor," Zude said to Hadra Row, "before we get to the museum. You must be excited that the cloning moratorium is lifted at last."

Hadra linked her arm with Jass's.

"We're not out of the woods yet, Magister, but yes, yes, it is exciting. The leading edge of our work will be the attempt to clone from human prenatal tissue, perhaps catching an embryo at the two-cell stage where functions are undifferentiated and the potential for success is exponentially increased.

"Of course," she continued, her bright eyes sparkling, "our morpho-electronic patterning and our micro-instrumentation still need extensive development. But we'll never develop them until we're pushed by the need."

They were passing a thicket of what looked like ivory nut plants when Hadra interrupted herself.

"There! Do you hear that?"

Both Jass and Hadra were poised like frozen statues. "It's the high lilies," Jass said, "playing in F sharp today."

"A little lower, I think," Hadra observed. She touched Jass's arm. "There they go!" The scientists stood rapt, in a listening attitude, their faces glowing in the sunlight, their bodies tapping together to some rhythm totally inaudible to Zude. Hadra turned to her.

"Do you hear them, Magister? It's those clusters of white flowers there, singing."

Zude had her eyes closed, opening herself to hear whatever would present itself. She shook her head. "Afraid not." Then she hastened to add, "But I believe you when you say they are singing." In a burst of candor she explained, "It's just the sort of thing I've been practicing for some months now. Central sensing, my teacher calls it." She closed her eyes again, made a silent obeisance to the gentle Bosca, and tried again. Finally she sighed, "No. I fear that magic is not my strength. I hear only the sea."

"It takes practice," Jass offered, kindly.

Without guile or apology, Hadra flung her arm around Magister Zella Terremoto Adverb. "Believing is seeing," she urged, giving the Magister a small hug. "And if you truly want it, it will come."

They walked for a moment in comfortable silence.

"I've been in touch with Magister Lin-ci Win," Jass said after a while. "She told us you'd be coming and directed us to give you full access to any and all information."

Hadra's voice had a hard edge now. "She is withholding approval of the pre-natal research, Magister."

When Zude showed surprise, the doctor continued. "The Central Web may have approved a window in the moratorium on human cloning, but even so, Antaeus can't begin its work without an executive order. Magister Win says she's delaying the order because she needs first to reassure some of her conservative constituencies that human life is not about to be sacrificed on the altar of immoral science, as they term it."

Jass gave a short laugh. "The irony is that human life may be sacrificed if we don't conduct such research."

Zude looked at him sharply. "Why do you say that, doctor?"

"I think you know, Magister." Jass let a pause grow. "Babies are just not being conceived."

"That's far too strong a statement, Jass," Hadra objected.

Jass nodded to his lover and corrected himself. "Babies are not being conceived in numbers large enough to offset the death rate."

Zude slowed her step. "A decline, yes. But experts are not calling it 'significant' yet."

But they're arguing," Jass said. "And more and more publicly."

"Indeed," Zude admitted.

"At any rate," Jass continued, "Magister Win has assured us that she will let us know whether or not she will issue the executive order allowing work to begin. We've been expecting news from her daily."

"Hourly." This from Hadra.

"Any minute," said Jass. "I've directed everyone on the island that I'm to be found and notified the moment any word comes from her."

As they resumed their pace, the talk turned to the occasional failures being reported in ovular merging centers.

"We're pretty sure it's in the denucleating process," Hadra explained. "Something in the donor's egg nucleus is being rejected by the receptor egg. Concern is limited to individual centers so far, but in the India Satrapy correlative data are being studied. And the decline in egg unions is significant."

"Heterosexual unions? Inseminations?"

"Same story," Jass said. "A decline in egg and sperm alliance. At least that's the news from hospitals and merging centers. Very unofficial."

Abruptly he came to a stop.

"Magister." Zude and Hadra halted with him. "Magister," he began again, "from your vantage point, would you say that an inordinate number of children is actually dying?"

Zude resisted lighting up a cigarillo. She looked carefully at the doctor. "The answer is yes." Jass and Hadra exchanged glances. "And from your vantage point?"

Hadra took up the gauntlet. "Well, Magister, there are no deaths here, except for one child in the village, frail from birth, who died in her sleep a few weeks ago."

As they walked on, Hadra added, "There is a phenomenon my sister in Ho Chi Minh tells me of, however." She paused. "There's apparently a rash of child deaths there, Magister."

"The incidence? Do you know?"

"No, but my sister is convinced that the end of the world is at hand."

Hadra stopped them all again. She sought Zude's eyes. "She quotes the tradition of Nechung, an ancient lama who said that in the last days children will be wrinkled in countenance and walk with canes as symbols of the fact that they are grown old before their time."

Zude's dress uniform was hot and uncomfortable.

"Well?" she barked.

"Well?" Hadra was taken aback.

"Are children there wrinkled and do they walk with canes?"

"No, not that, my sister says. But often, before children die, their hair turns white."

Zude's dress uniform was cold suddenly, and clammy. She spun away from her companions and began walking toward the museum. Then, regretting her rudeness, she stopped and waited for her hosts. The three of them entered the museum in silence.

The holojaunt had worked its magic and the children's curiosity about the real trip was whetted to a fever pitch. Moreover, Ria had lost any fear for their safety. Now, from the deck of a large floating barge surrounded by an enormity of sky and ocean, they had descended over 30 meters to the Seadrome, the underwater launch station. They were about to embark upon an undersea excursion into the trench.

"Show me again!" cried Reggie to Commander Raola Ark, chief engineer and presently the omnipotent manipulator of the Seadrome's tractor beam. Obediently Commander Ark fixed the beam onto yet another of the huge cargo hoppers in the far distance and hauled it rapidly toward them, to within a handspan of the wide viewport. Laughing, Reggie tried to touch the car as it hung there, just beyond her grasp.

"You're magic, Ark! Could you tow the big pod back, the, the, you know!"

"The phaeton? Indeed," nodded Ark, straightening her red tabard, "if it is in a line with us." She turned to Jass. "Will you be piloting, doctor?"

"Yes, if you'll authorize that."

"Always," she replied.

At the other side of the control room, Zude watched a monitor's display of the Seadrome's fleet of three phaetons, each waiting in its launching bay for activation by teams of sea-searchers or inquisitive tourists. "That, Rique, is what we'll be in," she said, pointing to one of the pods.

"She's the *Sojourner*," said Ria.

"*Sojourner*," Enrique repeated. "Just like in the holojaunt."

"Exactly," said Ria. "And here's a diagram of our trip, see? Here's the drop-off of the ocean floor. We'll go down into the trench…"

"How will we see?"

"Lights. We'll have lights." Ria pointed to the destroyer. "Look how she hangs out over the shelf here. We'll go all the way down beneath her and come up here on her other side." Enrique was galvanized.

"Commander," Ria asked Raola Ark, "couldn't the control room monitor us by vidcorder, that is, see us the whole time we're away?" Ria smoothed Enrique's hair over his ears.

"An enlightened question, señora. But actually, no. That technology is available, but the Kanshoubu has never authorized its use in vessels of any kind. We can do both audio and onscreen communication at the will of both parties, but more than that is looked upon as, well, as a kind of spying."

"Five more minutes," Jass called to them from Mariner First Class Tiny Nauru's station, where Regina now charmed that exceedingly tall woman.

"Doctor!" Ark called back. "I have the new computer codes for you. They just got proofed."

Zude lazily watched the screen while the commander brought up a list of six codes and pushed a tab labeled Manifest. Jass joined the group in time to receive the comcube that catapulted from the slot below the screen.

"They need to be plugged into the master display on *Sojourner*," Ark told him.

"Done," said Jass, pocketing the comcube. "Magister, I am proud to announce that we've got a mission. A task for our expedition. If we want it, that is."

"We haul the destroyer back with us," Ria said, trying to guess.

"Almost as good," said the doctor. "We're to get holofilms of the destroyer. Preparatory to adding the close-up experience of the ship to the holojaunt."

"Good," said Ria. "That was the only thing missing."

"Magister." Commander Ark stood by Zude. "I am due at the shelf's drillsite to get our microresonators online. I regret that I'll not be able to see you off." She pointed to another Sea-Shrieve who stood examining a mission capsule by Tiny Nauru's station. "That is Commander Kiang Tung-Po, who will be in charge of the Seadrome. Mariner Nauru will be your communications contact. She'll get you launched and will stand by to check in with you at short intervals during the excursion." Ark saluted smartly.

"Bon voyage, Magister. I shall see you tomorrow."

Zude returned the salute. "Thank you, Commander. You've been very kind."

With a wave to the children, Ark disappeared into the back corridor. In her off-ear, Zude heard Jass still speaking to Ria, who was nodding with his every sentence.

"It's very preliminary work. Won't take long. We can almost do it as we explore the wreck ourselves. Any hesitations on your part, Magister?" Jass was donning a subvention belt and stuffing its compartments with holocartridges.

"None of course, doctor."

Zude had been ready for this excursion for hours. She had shed her cape, folded it carefully and laid it at-rest in her subvention belt. She hadn't had a cigarillo all day and didn't even want one.

At last the word came. A strong voice overrode all other activity. It pronounced the launch bay and Sojourner ready for departure. The mood of the control room altered: Voices heightened, movements accelerated. Zude's excitement rose with that tide. She picked up Enrique and looked about for Regina.

Regina, as it happened, appeared on the arm of still another Sea-Shrieve. "Zude, this is Maizie," Reggie burbled. "She's a pilot, too, like Jass."

Zude's dark eyes met the pale eyes of the whitest woman she had ever seen.

"Lieutenant Commander Nicola Maiz, Magister," saluted the newcomer. "I was told that Dr. Egarber might need an auxiliary pilot as he's handling a small holoproject." Her skin shone, almost like alabaster, and her full shock of hair must have clearly defied Amahrery regulations. Zude had seen pictures of horses whose manes were this white and this regal but never had she seen such hair on a human.

She returned the Amah's salute and was about to respond orally when a new voice intervened.

"Commander Maiz trains pilots for undersea vessels, Magister," said Commander Kiang Tung-Po. "I summoned her because I thought Dr. Egarber might use help. And because there is plenty of room in the phaeton."

"Of course," Zude responded.

"Enjoy your trip," Tung-Po smiled brightly. With a nod to Maiz and the children, and an extended nod to Zude, she returned to Nauru's station.

Jass beamed when he saw Nicola Maiz.

"Maizie! Good, you're with us. Here." He handed her three microcorders, which she dutifully hung from her shoulders. "And here." He added a light meter and stabilizers. "I've got the holo-cartridges."

"We'll be in voice contact with you all the way," Tiny Nauru assured them. She helped Jass through the control room door.

"Except for the sweep under the destroyer," Tung-Po corrected from Nauru's duty station. "We lose you for a while there."

"But only minutes," added Nauru, giving Regina a salute and a farewell pat.

Jass shed all his hologear by *Sojourner*'s central shaft. "At last," he breathed. "This is a dream come true. I've been nagging the museum for years to upgrade the holojaunt." He began activating the comchannels, running yet again the check sequences and safety procedures.

The phaeton's design was of the simplest and most time-honored of the shapes friendly to water: a marvelously round, double-convex saucer, compact and efficient but without a crowded look. The upper half was transparent for observation, and its central control shaft cleverly housed not only the crystals that drove it but the vessel's toilet and storage areas. The control cylinder's outer surfaces were covered with power and disposition panels, monitoring sequence displays, communication and manifest catchments, and biodirectional sensors. The pod's five seating cups were situated around the phaeton's perimeter, rising and falling in response to their occupants' subtle weight shifts.

Zude sat in the formfit cup, facing outward in what she mentally labeled the aft position of the circular craft. She spun inward and gave a wink to Regina, who screwed up her face in a mirror of the gesture.

"All systems at ready, doctor, and we are standing by." Mariner Tiny Nauru's voice filled the phaeton from the control room. "We'll begin bay fill on your mark."

"Fine," Jass replied. "Maizie, have we rerouted the duranium conduits in this vessel?"

"Negative, doctor. Refer to your standard array board. There." Jass sighed in relief and smiled broadly.

"An improvement, hmmm?"

"Definitely," Jass nodded.

Tiny Nauru's voice summoned them and then faded. There was some background conversation in the control room. Zude's heart began to sink even before Tiny's voice resumed.

"Doctor, Magister Lin-ci Win has asked that you call her."

"What!"

Commander Kiang Tung-Po's voice replaced Tiny's. "Doctor, Magister Lin-ci Win wishes to speak with you."

"Patch her through to the comscreen here. No. Belay that."

"Magister Win is not waiting now, doctor. She asks that you call her back at 1400 hours." A pause. "That will be in forty minutes."

Jass muttered an obscenity. "Hang on one minute, Tung-Po." He looked around the phaeton, his eyes halting at Zude's. "Magister, I'd flat out forgotten. I'm sorry."

"Nonsense, doctor. You must speak with Magister Win." Zude scanned the devastated faces of the children. Ria looked even more disappointed than the little ones. "And your conversation could be a long one."

"See here," Jass said, "I'll go make the call and the four of you can continue the expedition with Maizie. She's top of the line as a pilot. And a great tour guide, too."

Zude read the look on Ria's face and the renewed hope in the eyes of the children.

"Good! We can do that. We'll miss you, doctor," she said to Jass, "but I have no doubt that Lieutenant Commander Maiz can carry on. Right, Commander?"

Maiz was quick to respond. "No problem, Magister. I'd be honored to be your pilot." Regina and Enrique whooped with joy.

"That settles it." Jass opened the comchannel. "Delay launch fill and get me out of here, Tiny." Within seconds Jasper Egarber had thrown them all a kiss and disappeared, the phaeton's hatch had been resealed, and the launch bay had begun its transformation from air into ocean.

Nicola Maiz, her high white hair occasionally bouncing, spoke smartly into the comchannel with Tiny Nauru. Zude followed most of the technical language, growing inwardly more and more content with their new pilot's obvious efficiency and comfort in the command chair.

"The Commander is reviewing the mission orders," she told the others, "just to be absolutely sure she understands all we've planned. And now she's officially laying in our course."

"I could handle the holocorders," said Ria speculatively. She was examining the equipment Jass had left behind. "If I knew the kind of shots he wanted of the destroyer."

"Do it," Zude said. "Use your own judgment and fulfill your old dreams of being a holojournalist."

Ria grinned. "Then help me, Zude," she said, fumbling with clips on a microcorder. "He had his cartridges, ah, there, in the subvention belt."

Minutes later Ria was rigged like a media correspondent, with small cameras, flat and laser, each with a different lens, stuck to her jacket, light sensors banded to her head, and audio inputs secured to her jaws. "I'm ready!" she declared.

"We're all ready," said Nicola Maiz. "Launch bay is filled. We are cleared for departure. On my say, Mariner Tiny." She scanned the phaeton's controls.

"Good wind at your back, sailors!" "Bon voyage!" Shouts from the control room.

"Now!" said Lieutenant Commander Nicola Maiz.

It seemed hours before the bay ports were adequately spread apart, days before the saucer crested at its opening, and an eternity before the full diameter of the vessel was able to clear the ejection canal and ease into the great South Pacific. They were on their way.

Vastness immediately drew them all into a deep silence, punctuated only by the soft beeps of Maiz's dampened sensors and her lowering of the phaeton's cabin illumination. Now her passengers could see the Seadrome behind them, its diminishing lights glistening eerily in their wake. *Sojourner* spun into the blackness like a brave ember banished from its hearth.

"Wow," breathed Ria, finally, as they released their stasis fields.

Lieutenant Commander Maiz smoothly shifted the phaeton's direction 90° to the right. Ria, who had been riding sideways, now found herself moving forward. They swept into the open ocean, losing more and more of the dim surface illumination as they gradually dropped.

"Commander!" Zude was sitting upright. "What are those noises! There's no animal…"

"Interesting, Ma'am, isn't it? You expect to have the great silence of the deeps. But it's constantly sounding off." Maiz glanced at the bathometer. "Particularly at this depth. Some of it's our own noise echoing back as we cut the water. Some of it is just the so-called big groan, the Ocean's residual expression of Her own presence. Some of it is shore noises—boats, top slaps, currents, tides. Clicks and whistles and gongs. Over hundreds of miles. Maybe even drags and creaks from the destroyer. All of it amplified for your delight."

Tiny's voice intruded. "Looking good, Commander Maiz. Still on course, bearings on the money. Do you read 260.3 meters?"

"Affirmative, Mariner. We're full ahead."

They were settling into the motion of the phaeton now. For a short time Maiz let Zude control the craft from a remote helm, guiding her carefully as the Magister made minute course or attitude changes and then corrected them, each time with more confidence. Handling a circular vessel, with pitch that became yaw and yaw that became pitch again, proved far more demanding than Zude had anticipated. She sat in a dark world, delicately poised between flipping over and tumbling over, every cell in her body ablaze with each small triumph of skill. Finally she shifted the helm back toward Maiz.

"That made my day, Commander. Thank you."

"You'd be a good undersea pilot, Magister," Maiz said as she transferred the helm back to her own station.

As they sailed deeper and deeper into a new world, the darkness outside the vessel seemed complete. Tiny Nauru spoke at greater intervals. "On course, *Sojourner.* At 7.3 and 155." Or, "At 343 meters, Commander Maiz." Maiz would confirm briefly.

They paused to examine a pocket of bioluminescence that sparkled like a host of fireflies just beyond the vessel.

"An angel!" Regina said in hushed tones.

"Patches of bacteria," said Maiz. "They show up now and again."

They sat in silence as the pocket of light floated to the side and upward, soon to be lost in their own wake. Enrique waved goodbye.

"Are you all right, *Sojourner?*" Nauru's voice came through. "We read your drive at one-third."

"A little sightseeing, Mariner," Maiz assured the control room. "We're on our way again."

Regina and Enrique, still side by side, let Maiz guide them as they manipulated far-reaching search lights that pierced the blackness around them.

Nicola Maiz spoke into the comfield. "44.8 atmospheres and approaching the trench."

Ria sat upright. "The trench? How far?" She began adjusting her holocorder equipment.

"Less than a minute. We'll circle above the edge so you can see what we'll be going down into."

Zude was alert now, peering into the tunnel that Regina and Enrique were making with the lights. Maiz leveled the phaeton and added more beams from the ship's full perimeter until the whole ocean on all sides of them was illuminated.

"We'll keep those lights pointing downward, Reggie," she said, urging Enrique's joystick forward with her finger. She kicked back the pod's advancing motion to half impulse. "What looks like the bottom of the ocean should be coming up any moment now." She divided her attention between the bathometer and the height soundings of the vessel's belly sensors.

Ria saw it first. "There!" she pointed.

Dimly emerging below and in front of them was a change in the ocean's texture. It looked to Zude like the ocean floor below them was bisected by a straight line. Just beyond them lay the edge of a cliff.

Both children bent and craned. Maiz swung the phaeton out and over the precipice. Ria and the children shifted to keep the cliff in view.

"It's huge," said Ria. "Can you take us back and over the edge again? So I can get the approach?" She altered the holocorder's settings.

"Done," said Maiz, upping impulse power and spinning easily into a wide arc over the chasm below and back toward the cliff top. She ducked the phaeton until it was closer to the floor, easing it back into a slow approach to the drop-off.

"Good," Ria muttered, stretching the holocorder to the edge of the pod's transparent upper half.

"We are at the trench and rigged for diving," Maiz reported, "in explore pattern alpha two, preparatory to our vertical descent."

Thirty seconds later, after confirmations from the Seadrome, she said, "Beginning vertical descent."

No one in the pod spoke as Maiz eased the phaeton across the cliff's edge, letting her sink gradually into the deeps.

Reggie held Enrique's hand, her eyes only half as big as his. Ria lay supine in her passenger cup, holocorder poised at the disappearing cliff's edge above them. Then she sat up to focus upon the smooth rock wall that was rising past them even as it plummeted for miles beneath them.

"Great Gifts of the Goddess!" she muttered, closing off the microcorder. "If only I could be outside, showing how we look as we go down!"

Precisely, thought Zude, and in an instant, as if from 50 meters away, she saw exactly how they looked: a silver saucer, outlined against a gray-blue wall and surrounded by a hazy aura, drifting aimlessly down into a measureless abyss. The image disappeared as quickly as it had come. Zude blinked. She was back in the pod again.

Ria panned over the nondescript ocean around them in an ambience shot. "It's already clear to me," she observed, "that our most dramatic display of the destroyer will be from beneath it. Shooting up toward the surface."

"The feeling is totally different from that angle," Maiz agreed.

"Mami, you're glad we came?" Regina was grinning.

Ria reached out and touched her daughter's cheek. "I am, precious. Just like you are."

The phaeton sank straight down in the silence, occasionally moving out to avoid protuberances or shelves that jutted from the cliff, only to smooth herself back into the sheer vertical drop.

Tiny Nauru's voice from the control room shook their reverie. "Report, *Sojourner.* Are you at 389.2?"

"Affirmative, Mariner. The destroyer is inferior by 100 meters. We have just passed the Holiness Fissure and expect to sight the ship in another two minutes." Maiz continued to control the helm, moving her hand over the steering orbs with practiced subtleness.

Regina was on Zude's lap now. "Why is Tiny's voice so funny?"

"Because it's bouncing off a ricochet trough," Zude answered. "Jass explained that, preshi. Remember? How the trench wall blocks the sound?"

"What's that!" Enrique pointed at the wall beyond them.

Maiz paused the phaeton, letting her hover gently at the level of Enrique's interest. "Magister, bring a light to this, if you would."

Zude obliged. The beam struck a fluttering strand that seemed to explode and disappear, taking with it Zude's light. Now the shaft of light that Zude controlled was cut off clean a couple of meters from the ship. Zude moved the beam away from the wall, and the shadowy strand reappeared. So did the full shaft of light. "Amazing," she breathed, experimenting again and again with her beam, always with the same effect.

"It swallows the light," Reggie said.

"It's a Swallower," said Enrique.

Zude blinked. Something stirred at the edge of her memory. That name…But Maiz interrupted her thoughts.

"A tiny black hole perhaps?" their pilot speculated. "I regret that we have no probes on this pod so we could reach out to it." She released the hover and eased the phaeton away from the cliff. They started slowly downward again.

"Maybe the holofilm will show something," Ria mused, pausing the holocorder and staring back at the disappearing Swallower.

Maiz was addressing the comunit. "420 and still on descent."

"Are you dawdling again, *Sojourner?*" chided Tiny's voice.

"Affirmative." Maiz smiled. "I suggest you expect an unusually long silence from us when we go under the destroyer some minutes from now. We have inquisitive passengers, and our holo-artist wants to experiment with both figure and color." She glanced up to catch the Magister's smile. Ria grunted and replaced a holocartridge.

Tiny's acknowledgement was the last they heard from her for a long stretch. The phaeton continued her drop.

"Destroyer ho!" Zude whispered suddenly.

And there she was, still many meters below them, the huge old war vessel lying almost upright, listing only slightly against the cliff wall. Her hull was broken by several craters, one of which might have been a torpedo's point of exit. Over half of her bulk was supported by a wide ledge, but a huge portion of her stern cleared the shelf and hung free, cantilevered over the deeps.

Zude studied the abandoned form below them. She thought she could make out anti-aircraft stations on the bow, and certainly those unsubstantial protrusions further aft were hangers for depth charges.

"My usual rap," Maiz told them, "would inform you now that this was a U.S. Navy war vessel with a displacement of 1,700 tons. Her propeller was driven by diesel power or perhaps by steam turbines. She cruised at 36 knots, about 64 kilometers an hour."

The Lieutenant Commander shifted her attention to the comunit. "*Sojourner* reporting. We are at the destroyer site holding steady." Her eyes roamed the screens and manifold reads. "All systems in peak condition. We will notify you when we dip under the vessel. Give us 10 minutes there for our holocordering. We will hail you upon emergence."

"Acknowledged, *Sojourner*."

To Ria she said, "I'll take us in as close to the cliff as I can. We'll drop to her starboard side, there where she juts out off the shelf. Then you can get a continuous shot of the descent and the hull bottom as we go below her."

Ria nodded and balanced herself in a flexible squatting posture. Zude, across the pod from Ria, gathered the two children to her, placing them at good vantage for the approach to the ship below. The destroyer was bathed now in the full range of lights from the phaeton. As they drew nearer, the ship's features, though still a monochromatic blue-gray, seemed to emerge from the darkness. From a bent hook swung a heavy chain, describing a short slow arc. Glassless ports stared empty-eyed into the ocean. A collapsed railing scraped the deck at eccentric intervals. Zude could not shake the feeling that the vessel was alive, if only with memories of the men who had sunk with her to their deaths.

"We are moving down the gunwale now," Maiz told the Seadrome, noting the time. "You will hear from us in 10 minutes, Tiny. *Sojourner* out."

"Acknowledged, *Sojourner*. Hurry ba…" Tiny Nauru's voice snapped off abruptly, seconds before the pod reached the bottom of the destroyer's hull and slid beneath her. Zude was struck by the utter stillness that followed the loss of contact with the Seadrome. The soft subliminal hum of the comline had accompanied them since their launching. Without it now, the phaeton was a silent circle moving soundlessly in the deeps.

Here behind the ship with the cliff so close, the mood was vastly changed. Space was more cramped, the lights bounced off the destroyer with a subdued resilience, and Zude felt somehow the servant of this ancient wreck rather than its explorer.

"Yes! Ah, what a sweep!" Ria bent to keep the destroyer's hull in her viewer. "Great, Maizie."

Maiz drew the phaeton to a hover stance, an arm's length, it seemed, from an ungainly apparatus protruding from the very end of the ship.

"What is it?" Regina cried, pointing.

"That's the propeller, Redge," said Zude.

It was at that moment, out of her years of lazy rest against the cliffside, that the destroyer executed one of her tiny shifts in position. Perhaps she scratched a microscopic itch, or accommodated with a minute shrug to some texture in the corner of a dream. In fact the old ship had frequently shifted her various slopes and planes over the decades, nestling herself ever more inexorably into the rock that lent her its couch.

This particular shift differed from countless others only in the fact that it gave at last a long-awaited margin of movement to one of the vessel's depth charges, one that had been wedged between its packing and a crushed portal placement. Deprived of its purpose of destroying enemy submarines, it had languished disappointed in its watery prison, tapping incessantly against its strictures and awaiting the moment of release. Now it suddenly floated free and drifted out over the port side of the stern. It dropped into the triangle between the cliff and the suspended hull, descending slowly into the lights of the Sea Shrievalty's phaeton just below.

"Look out!" Ria cried, sighting the drum only a split second before Maiz saw it. The Commander's quick response was in time to prevent full impact of the ancient little bomb, but the drum brushed against the pod on its way to the depths beneath them. That brush and the force of Maiz's evasive action thrust the phaeton hard into the cliff behind it.

A crash. Lights died and alarms sounded. *Sojourner's* passengers were thrown against the walls of the phaeton and its center shaft. The children shrieked.

"Reggie!" Ria reached for her daughter even as she cushioned the assault of Enrique's body against her chest.

"Mami!" called Regina. She hung on to the arm of a seat cup as it wheeled out of control. Zude caught her before she struck the console.

"Ria! Are you all right?" Zude realized that the searchlights were out, the pod in almost total darkness. Only control panels glowed or blinked urgently. She hugged Regina and felt for the solidity of Ria and Enrique.

"Fine. Fine, Zude," Ria said. Enrique shrieked. "He's hit his head. But he's okay. Reggie?"

"I'm here, mami. Here." She reached out to find Ria's lap, her eyes showing her fear. Ria held both her offspring. "Great Goddess, what happened?"

"Don't know." Zude moved toward Lieutenant Commander Maiz, whose fingers were shadows flying over orbs and through force fields.

"Damages?" Maiz asked the computer. "Damage account!" Her voice was louder, her fingers flew faster. "Computer, assess and recount!"

The compuvox was steady. "Hull intact. Core crystal coherence 100% dispersed and lateral matrices splayed in polaric stasis. Pressure at 80%. Life support at 83% and falling. Emergency measures require manual initiation."

"I'm cold!" cried Enrique.

"Yes, preshi," cooed Ria. "We'll be okay."

"Commander, what was that drum?"

"A depth charge, Magister. Shaken loose. It only brushed us. Not hard enough to explode." Maiz's hands were flying again. Her white head bounced back and forth from one monitor to another. The compuvox spoke.

"Oxygen at 79.1%."

"If it could still explode," Zude added, a question in her voice.

Maiz did not meet Zude's eyes. "It could, Magister."

Suddenly Zude was cold too. Like ice. "It will drop to the bottom?"

Maiz nodded. She pressed in a calculation. "It will take almost an hour for the charge to reach the bottom of the trench. I'm not sure how much danger we are in from its impact. More urgent is the fact that *Sojourner* is becalmed, and I can't raise the emergency systems. Excuse me, Magister." She circled the center shaft, issuing occasional vocal commands, her hands weaving over tabs and activating the array of screens.

Zude spoke to Ria and the children. "We're in trouble." She stroked Enrique's head. "Relax and breathe shallow. Slow." She demonstrated for Reggie and Enrique.

"Oxygen?"

"Don't know, Ria. Maizie will tell us in a moment. Important thing to do now is to keep warm and relax."

"Relax!" Ria began again. Then she caught herself. "We can do that, huh, Reggie? Rique?"

"Sure you can." Zude grinned at the children, both obediently intent upon being calm. "Close your eyes and pretend you're in your hidey-hole, sleeping away until Boisterous Bear finds you and brings you breakfast."

"Of honey," Reggie said bravely.

"Of real honey," Ria echoed, nodding to Zude. "Real honey and corn cakes." She adjusted the seat cup and jostled them to more comfort on her lap, kissing the small bump rising on Enrique's forehead.

Zude turned back to their pilot. Her chest felt tight. The compuvox sounded.

"Oxygen at 61.8."

Maiz was muttering in the dim lights, her face a map of growing consternation. "Magister," she said, finally letting her hands drop, "our emergency procedures fail to respond. We can sustain pressure in the pod, but I cannot activate the reserve air and heat necessary for us to survive until rescue."

The two Kanshou looked at each other wordlessly. Zude broke the connection by leaning over Maiz's shoulder. The list that filled the screen in front of them seemed vaguely familiar.

"Those are codes? For accessing emergency measures?"

"Affirmative. Checked and double-checked before launch and now inoperable."

Maiz's jawline tightened. Zude studied the screen.

"Commander, when you check the codes before launch, do you put the measures into full operation?"

"Negative, Magister. That would activate them unnecessarily. All that's required is assurance that the codes are in place."

Without warning, the voice of Commander Raola Ark prodded Zude's memory: "Doctor, I have the new computer codes…" Zude dropped to one knee beside the pilot and pointed urgently to the monitor before them. "Commander, that's what happened. Jass took the new codes!"

Lieutenant Commander Maiz looked askance at the Magister kneeling beside her. Zude tapped the screen. "The codes were revamped, right, after the regular upgrade of the phaetons?"

"Of course. And locked into the system."

"Wrong on that count, Commander. Before you got to the Seadrome, Commander Ark gave Dr. Egarber the comcube for the *Sojourner*. When he left he took it with him."

Realization crept over Maiz's face. "Then these are the old codes." She shook her head. "Magister…"

Zude leaned toward Ria. "Jass's subvention belt," she said abruptly. "The comcube may be in one of the pockets."

Ria pointed with her chin to the belt on the floor, now couching the microcorder. "There."

Zude snatched at the belt, exploring its compartments. She shook her head. "Nothing." Again to Maiz. "Are there patterns to the codes, Commander? Could you predict what the new ones might have been? Run a search?"

"Right." Maiz was already at work inputting variables and calling up probabilities. The air was distinctly chilly. The compuvox reported.

"Oxygen at 50.1."

"Ri," Zude said, now back in her seat cup.

Ria stroked Regina's black curls. "We're in big trouble, right?"

"Maybe. The oxygen has crashed, and we can't access the reserve. They'll get a rescue phaeton to us. We just need to last until then." She checked her tacto-time. "They won't even start worrying about us for another eight minutes. Then it's a twenty-minute trip to the trench."

"We'll freeze first." Ria rubbed the bundles on her lap.

As if on cue, Enrique bawled, "I'm cold!"

"You are, you are," Zude told him. She unfolded her Magister cape from its pouch. "This will keep you warm as toast." She draped the tekla over the children and secured it behind Ria's back, making a cocoon of its special textures. "Can you breathe in there?" She ducked her head under the cape.

"It's a tent, Zude," Reggie said.

"Right. It allows you your air. Can you go to sleep?"

"We'll try," Ria answered for them. "But Zude…"

Zude stopped her. "Relax. We're not licked yet. Look, I saw those codes on the screen. If it's true as Bosca says that everything we see is still in our cells somewhere…" She reclined the seat cup and stretched out. "I'm about to attempt total recall."

"Magister, we need only the first two codes to activate our life support." Maiz spoke without interrupting her task.

"Good. Now just let me relax. I might be able to do this."

"I can't reach your hand, Zudie," said Ria. "Imagine that I'm holding it."

"Your foot will do," Zude whispered, laying her hand on the toe of Ria's boot. She closed her eyes. As she breathed herself down into a lighter state, Zude heard the compuvox register oxygen at 38.2. She took one precious deep breath of air and let some ease soak through her muscles.

Deliberately she replayed the scene in the Seadrome. There was the comcube, leaping out of the Manifest port; there was Jass pocketing the cube. The screen, what was on the screen? Zude breathed herself deeper still. There, the list of numbers! But what were they? She peered at the memory of the screen. Each line had consisted of some twenty numbers, interspersed with a series of letters. Just the first two lines, that's all she needed. Just the first two lines.

Bosca, where are you! she muttered under her breath. I may have seen them, but not a one of those numbers is coming back to me! She tried for another deep breath and panicked at the realization that she couldn't execute it. The phaeton was becoming stuffy.

"Relax," Bosca's voice suddenly echoed. "Get to a feeling-good place. Think of sunsets. Making love. Find joy!" Zude sloughed off her panic and envisioned their rescue. Her heart lifted. She upped the feeling.

Maiz's console beeped and whistled. Ria's fear pulsed in little ripples beside her. The children stirred now and again, struggling to be brave.

Zude kept herself feeling easy, even light. She watched herself breathe, belly moving slowly up and down, rhyndon bodysuit glowing softly in dimmed light, glowing like a…

Holy Hound of Hera! She was watching herself breathe! And she was up, up here! Above her body, watching herself breathe! There, there was Ria with a huge tekla-covered belly that housed humps of small children, and Maiz doggedly calling up options for codes. She saw all of it clearly, as if brightly lit, from her position on the ceiling of the phaeton.

Zude swallowed. And the scene pulled further away. She was outside the phaeton now, viewing the whole vessel, watching everyone inside, even Zella Terremoto Adverb. There was the Magister, holding onto the toe of her compañera's boot.

Slowly Zude tried moving her arms and legs. The body of the Magister below her lay completely still. Then her perspective changed, and she floated across and under the phaeton, up by the propeller of the old destroyer. Experimentally, she slowed down. Speeded up. She turned her observer-body in different directions.

By Persephone's Pajamas, she said very calmly to herself, I'm having an out-of-body experience. She was watching the interesting manner in which she breathed ocean water in and out of her lungs when she was visited by a tiny flash of brightness. It swept past her, then back over her again, beckoning to her.

Zude followed it, moving her arms and legs effortlessly. Her direction seemed to be determined just as in swimming, by the placement of the top of her head. Yet it was not, she found, any swimming motion that propelled her, but rather her intent to chase the little light. Up and away she soared, away from the phaeton and her friends, up and above the destroyer, up the vertical path they had followed into the trench.

With a start Zude recognized her guide. It was the tiny light-gobbler, the Swallower, that had hung so compellingly on the cliff wall. She was just below the top of the cliff when the little being swooped back toward her, passing quickly over and around her again and again, wrapping her in golden cords of light.

And then it happened: an explosion of cacophonous echoing sounds, a blast of vigorous colorful life! A surging of a thousand tails turning and ten thousand fins finning—schools of dolphins, pods of whales, diving sharks, sailing turtles, dancing squid, bass, mackerel, salmon, seals, shrimp, sardines, seahorses, rays, molluscs, and all of their friends and families. Delegations from all the creatures that ever roamed the deeps or the shallows of the Great Pacific flowed around her, singing to her soul and magnifying her joy.

She heard the Swallower calling to her. "Come on! There's no time to lose!" She tore herself apart from the vision, but not before she heard a sweet promise falling on her ears. She paused deliberately, as if to acknowledge the promise. Then she arched upward after the Swallower, following rapidly, smoothly, exuberantly, up to the top of the cliff and over the ocean floor toward the Seadrome.

In the control room, a purling stream of Sea-Shrieves went about their tasks. Commander Kiang Tung-Po sat in her desk, surrounded by exhibit panels. She spoke to Mariner First Class

Tahang Nauru, across the room at her station. "Let me know the second they are back in contact, Tiny."

"Acknowledged. Commander, I'm willing to bet that they will be out of range longer than ten minutes. Apparently they have an accomplished holocorder operator aboard who will want a variety of angles."

Tiny kept her eyes on the three show-screens, any one of which could herald the return of *Sojourner* to communication with the Seadrome.

Zude floated through the wall of the control room precisely at the moment of Kiang Tung-Po's emergence from her desk. Magnopad in hand, Tung-Po made for the array of screens by the far viewport, there to examine ambience panels for Seadrome maintenance. One utility station displayed a screenful of long numbers, useless now.

That's it! thought Zude, propelling her weightless self toward the viewport station for a better look. Yes! It was still there! That was exactly the list she'd seen before the comcube was delivered to Jass.

Tung-Po was reaching for the Clear tab.

"Stop!" shouted Zude at the top of her lungs. "Don't change that screen!"

Commander Tung-Po was deaf to the cries of the Magister of the Nueva Tierra Tri-Satrapy. Her hand did not falter but continued its irrevocable progress toward the numbers' annihilation.

"No!" barked Zude in her best command voice. "Commander, attention!"

Tung-Po halted, not because she heard the command but because a young Amah suddenly stood beside her handing her a magnopad for approval. The Commander tucked her own magnopad under her arm and stepped toward the Sea-Shrieve to scan the proffered magnopad.

Zude's hungry eyes turned to the first two lines of figures on the screen.

"LS 2416 7463082 AN 480. TUX 3840\303," said line one to her, glowing calmly, as if its very existence were not being threatened. Out of the corner of her eye, Zude saw Tung-Po, now nodding as she signed the magnopad. Zude set her mind into memorize mode, quickly zapping each of line one's number groups into a place of secure recall in her mind. She was just focusing on line two when Tung-Po dismissed the Sea-Shrieve and turned back to the utility screen, her hand vaguely reaching again for the Clear button.

"Not yet!" shouted Zude. She pushed her whole buoyant body toward the numbers, trying to see around the bulk of Tung-Po's shoulders. The Commander's hand continued to advance. Zude shouted louder, frantically insinuating herself into a standing position between Tung-Po and the screen. To her horror, Tung-Po's arm moved through Zude's own substance, still on its path to the clearing tab.

Zude gathered all the intensity her diaphanous body would allow her. As the Commander's arm moved forward through her, Zude ducked her head and raised it again carefully, thus placing her eyes firmly on a level with those of the Chinese woman.

Remarkably, Tung-Po stopped. Both hands dropped and she frowned. Slowly she widened her eyes, as if taking in the hues of a stupendous sunset.

"Kiang Tung-Po," Zude whispered, looking deeply into the soft brown eyes, "I want you to rest a moment before you continue your work." Her hands framed the Commander's head, caressing her black hair. "Just rest," she cooed. "You've been working far too hard, and you're righteously tired." Zude began blowing sensuously around the woman's hairline, her ears. "Take a deep breath and relax now. Just for a moment."

Mariner First Class Tiny Nauru heard a small clatter as something dropped to the floor of the Seadrome. Casually she looked up from the monitoring of her three show-screens. Over at the north viewport Commander Tung-Po stood like a statue, a magnopad at her feet and both arms outstretched as if embracing someone. Tiny craned her neck to see if the Commander's companion would retrieve the dropped magnopad. And to determine, if she could, the other's identity.

To her consternation, Tiny then saw that the Commander was alone and was in fact staggering and turning backwards to brace herself against a convenient console. She was leaning there as if in some shock, her right hand on her chest and her left still cupped as if holding another's chin. Her lips curved in a warm smile.

"Commander!" called Tiny. Torn between her duty and what seemed to her to be Tung-Po's distress, she then addressed an Amah retreating through the control room door, the same officer who had obtained the Commander's signature.

"Sea-Shrieve, front and center!" she shouted. "Look to the Commander!" She pointed to Tung-Po, who acknowledged the eruption of noise with a slow turning of her head. The Amah sprinted across the room to Tung-Po, taking her by the arm.

Tung-Po patted the young woman's hand. "I'm fine, thank you. Just fine."

None of the preoccupied officers noted the bundle of energy that hovered over the utility station, carefully absorbing the sequence of numbers that constituted line two of the screen.

Grinning with satisfaction, Zude floated again toward the ocean outside the control room where the bright Swallower awaited her. As she passed over the cluster of Sea-Shrieves surrounding Tung-Po, she dropped to a delicate head-first hover and brushed the Commander's cheek with her lips. Then she was gone.

Hand to cheek, Commander Kiang Tung-Po turned her head quickly toward the wall of the Seadrome. When at last she gathered herself again into the proper conduct of her duty, she dismissed with thanks those so concerned for her health.

Only Mariner First Class Tiny Nauru puzzled about the deep flush that adorned her Commander's cheeks.

The Swallower sped out and downward through the ocean. Zude sped with it, focusing as she went upon holding the number sequences in her mind. She knew without consulting her tacto-time that less than two minutes had passed since she had left the Sojourner. *Still she must hurry.*

Her guide led her under the destroyer and back to her precise spot of exit from the phaeton. Zude barely thanked the strange little Swallower before dropping into the vessel. She saw Ria motionless, her eyes closed, holding what Zude hoped were sleeping children; Lieutenant Commander Maiz sat like a statue of white ice, her eyes open but not seeing, her hands resting on the console bank. "Oxygen at 6.6%," *the compuvox intoned.*

Zude's own body anxiously awaited her, drawing her like a magnet back into its confines. This body was very cold. And obviously it was not breathing. Well, maybe twice a minute. Slowly, Zude initiated short shallow breaths. Then longer ones. She could barely move her hands and feet. What had been freedom was now a tomb. And she was having trouble orienting herself. Things recently bright and clear were now murky. Urgently she made herself repeat the sequence of numbers. Twice, to be sure this body had them in its cells. Then, heavy and uncoordinated, she finally pulled herself to a standing position.

"Maiz!" she called. Her voice was a rasp.

Maiz seemed not to be breathing, much less moving.

Zude saw Ria's chest rise and fall.

"Ria!"

Ria nodded, trying to smile. Zude reached out toward the children. Ria stopped her with a grunt. "They're okay," she mouthed.

Zude nodded. She tried for a shout. "Lieutenant Commander Maiz!"

Maiz jerked. Her eyes flew open. "Magister." It was a whisper.

Zude found a small swallow of air. Her lungs hurt. "Quick, enter these numbers." She began reciting the first line.

Maiz's fingers started to move.

Zude put her mouth to Maizie's ear. "Seven four six three zero eight…"

She could barely whisper. Maiz's fingers fumbled at the keys. Zude pushed out the remaining figures of the codes between small intakes of breath. Both lines. Maiz's fingers struggled.

At last the Commander drew in a large precious batch of oxygen. She expended it in one mighty whoop. "That's it! Systems responding!"

Sojourner came alive again as emergency systems moved online. Air hissed. Lights seeped into brightness. The promise of warmth and comfort surged from reactivated ducts and boosters. Zude and Maiz pushed themselves to the limp forms of Ria and the children, beginning the task of reviving them fully.

They were drinking hot coffee and tea when the comunit burst into full presence with the arrival of two phaetons bearing a tractor beam. They were dizzy with delight and relief as they were towed out of the abyss and back to the Seadrome. And they rejoiced with a huge party of Sea-Shrieves as they clambered out of the launch bay and into the safety and comfort of the control room.

Magister Adverb's first act upon debarking was to speak with both Commanders Ark and Tung-Po, convincing them that no Kanshou could be held responsible for the consequences of the missing comcube. In fact, the Kanshoubu's *Labrys Manual* immediately featured the incident as a dramatic testimony to the eternal imminence of disaster even in the face of procedures perfectly followed.

Lieutenant Commander Nicola Maiz could hardly wait to tell her Sister-Shrieves the remarkable tale of how Magister Adverb had gone into alpha state and emerged with one hundred percent accurate recall of figures she had only casually noted when she had first seen them.

As they emerged from the Seadrome, Zude understood that her world had changed beyond telling. Her sleep that night was deep.

The next morning, when she and her family boarded the low rocket to Australia, Zude saw another whole dimension of change that was to come. Buckling Regina into her seat cup, she froze at the sight, in the child's black hair, of a single white curl.

4

> When madness beckons, go there.
> When reason beckons, beware.
> The paths of the Journey are not straight.
> *Vade Mecum for the Journey*

eep in the Brazilian jungle, a setting sun touched the headwaters of Río Itanhaua and the glassy surface of Lago Tefé. The sounds of the village wafted through the damp afternoon, soft voices chattering together through tinkling chimes and rustling branches.

Jezebel lay alone, on her back, in a treehouse. She was seeking rest—and sleep, if it would only deign to come. She was resisting an old familiar chill, her most reliable symptom of an impending loss of consciousness. Her head ached. She licked several bubbles of foam from her lips and swallowed a metallic saliva. "You can hold this off," a voice told her. "You used to do it all the time." Oh yes, she thought, I used to. Forty years ago.

Deliberately she concentrated on the wooden windchimes, bringing herself into their resonances. "Good," said her voice. "Now stay there. Hold with the chimes." Then, unbidden and in spite of her focus, the old sweet taste came, cloying and insistent. "Listen!" Heavily she shifted her attention back to the chimes, sucking in their sounds, willing them to fill her universe.

But in the next instant she knew there was no escape. Not when the head-to-toe blasts of sweat had begun, not when her body started its old familiar arching upward, navel to the sky, not when she moved like a dutiful slave into her curving backbone as it completed its inexorable rounding and stiffening. Its arch fitted her like an old pair of shoes. This daemon had slept for decades, dreaming of the time when it could again be the companion of her nights and days. She was completely in the arch now, surrendered to its stasis, braced on her shoulders and heels, in full-body paralysis. And there they went, her eyes, backward into her skull, back, back...

In her last moment before total darkness and the convulsions that were sure to come, she remembered to tuck her tongue behind her lower teeth.

"She's eased," Dicken said. "She'll be okay after some rest."

Oaliu, Trustholder of the Acuai tribespeople, took the damp cloth from Dicken. "Last night, before we began the culture and language transfers, her sleep was very disturbed. Why was that?" Dicken sat at the end of the pallet, holding Jez's head. "She calls it 'my childhood affliction.' It's been on her for three nights now—just some symptoms. But even our spooning got to be affected. Nothing dangerous, but a little shaky."

"You have not seen such seizures before?"

"No. She's described them, but this one here is the first I ever saw. Wait, she's stirring."

Oaliu laid her lips close to Jez's ear. "You do not have to move. We have healers who will help. I have sent for them."

The eyelids fluttered mightily with the effort to open. Then Jez whispered the Acuai word of agreement.

"Good." Oaliu nodded. "We have gotten you cleaned up and in fresh beddings. You will be able to understand all that the healers tell us." She looked at Dicken.

"I am right here," Dicken told Jez. She wiped the wet brow again with the cloth.

Jez's eyes flew open. She sat bolt upright and tried to get to her feet.

"Lavona," she croaked, "we've got to get to Lavona!" She pushed Oaliu's arms away.

Dicken brought her partner gently down to the pallet again. Oaliu helped her to soothe the wild-eyed Jez. "Jezebel, sweet love," she whispered.

Jez still struggled. "Now, Dicken! We have to go now!"

Dicken held her down, effortlessly. "Jezebel, we cannot be going right away. We could not even raise the spoon, you in this shape. So hush now."

Jez sank back, fighting nausea. "An hour. I'll rest an hour." She was lost again in slumber.

"Lavona?" Oaliu asked.

"An old friend. She's a weekday childkeeper, I think. She lives up in the Alleghenies."

"Nueva Tierra Norte?"

Dicken grinned ruefully. "Yes. West Virginia." She pulled a light blanket over Jez and spoke to the room at large. "I got no notion why we got to go to West Virginia."

Two days later, after long legs of hard flying over jungles and high plains, and a rocket hop across the Caribbean, Jez and Dicken spooned due north again. The air whipped by their powerbubble at 100-plus miles per hour, disturbing not at all the two navigation and monitoring systems that were linked in perfect coordination. But things were not peaceful inside the flightpod.

When Dicken suggested a layover in Atlanta, Jez took her hand out of a warm pocket and reached toward her lover. "I'm not tired, Dicken."

"Well I am!" Dicken exploded, flinging Jez's hand away from her. She pushed more sustaining ki toward the edges of their bubble and rubbed her eyes with both hands.

"God's Green Eyeballs, Bella," she said wearily.

"And I am not Bella!" Jez's voice was tense.

In a swift shift, Dicken rolled onto her back, readjusting her monitors so that she flew supine just a scant space below her lover. "Look at me," she challenged, shaking Jez's shoulders. The eyes that stared back at Dicken were surrounded by gray circles. "It's just that you will not lay down your head to rest," Dicken whispered.

"I can't rest! Quit protecting me, Dicken!"

"I'm trying to keep you from killing yourself."

"Don't do me any favors! Let me kill myself!"

"Fine! Get to it!"

Dicken flung herself back into the side-by-side prone position and steadied the staggering lonth maintenance.

Dregs of anger settled within the quiet flightpod. Dicken was breathing hard. For the first time since discovering the power of womanlove and stepping up into the high reaches of paired flight, she considered calling for spoonbreak.

Jez was speaking softly. "We can't do that anymore, Dicken. That's poison."

"Spare me."

"Hear me. It's fueling all the violence, everywhere."

Dicken raged. "All the…our fighting? Oh, come to mama, Jezebel!"

"I'm tired of doing it." Jez stretched out her arms for a sky-high embrace. Dicken hesitated, then let her tension dissolve. With a grateful sigh she moved into the waiting arms.

They did rest in Atlanta, and from there they informed Lavona of their impending arrival. They took off again with a refurbished intimacy and somewhat restored health.

Like their ancestors, those who still lived in the mountains of West Virginia died with the conviction that there was no such thing as flat. Nowhere in these overlapping ranges were any two adjacent feet of terrain at the same natural altitude, and it was the forever up-and-down demands of those green-clad majesties that assured natives they were home.

It was no wonder, then, that in the heart of those mountains the abandoned Welchtown rocketport stood out to Jez and Dicken like a skeptic at a Goddess gathering. Its hundreds of rows after rows of solar panels shone like a vast cold flat lake, reflecting a pale sun that was setting abruptly behind the higher mountains to the west. April in West Virginia still felt like winter.

Almost hidden in the trees that climbed close to the port's edges were hillside homes, and a winding road that bound the houses into a visible unit probably called a town. The rocket's landing was hailed by the cheers and laughter of a welcoming group. One woman stood out from the others.

"Witchwoman!" she shouted.

"Hillbilly!" Jez flung out her arms. Their hug encompassed Dicken and set the tone for the lively evening of food and music.

Long after the cornbread and greens had disappeared, long after the women had sung and drummed themselves to satisfaction, and shortly after the goodnight voices had faded into the sky or down the hillside, Dicken and Jez stood together listening to the loud flow of the branchwater behind the house. When they returned to the warmth of the kitchen, Lavona was emptying a coal scuttle into the cookstove's firebox. She scraped the round cover back into place with the eye-grip and wiped her hands on her apron.

"Well. Set." She motioned toward the hefty straight-backed chairs in front of the stove and dumped cold tea from cups she identified as theirs. She felt the belly of the teapot and, satisfied it was warm enough, filled the cups.

Dicken and Jez tilted their chairs, bracing their feet on the stove fender. Lavona put the cups in their hands and drew up her own chair. She chewed on a toothpick. "So. Jezebel, it's time fer you t'do some tall talkin'."

Jez looked briefly at Dicken before she spoke.

"Hillbilly, you tell me why in five hours' time, in the presence of thirteen women and children who are a part of a small town that is clearly in contact with the rest of the world, over a blessed meal and good conversation, why two outlanders like us haven't heard a word about a world disaster that's bigger than anything that has happened to any of us in our short lives."

Her words hung in the air. Lavona scratched under her light brown hair. "Y'mean…"

"I mean, hillbilly, why is nobody talking about the dying children? Why did the little ones we put to bed two hours ago sing a strange song together before they went to sleep? Why do they all three have gray hair?"

Lavona sucked on her toothpick and studied her guests. Then she dropped her chair to all four legs and leaned on her knees, addressing the stove.

"We done lost six. An' it looks like no more's a-comin'." She looked back at them. "Jezebel, we been a long time parted so maybe you forgot." She shifted the toothpick to the other corner of her mouth. "It's a fam'ly thing. Fer us t' take keer of, here in our slopes an' hollers. We got no need t' tell the world 'bout it."

She wiped her forefinger across her upper lip.

"T' boot, we don't hold with weepin' an' wailin' more than's common. We figure it'll either git better or 'twon't. Th' Goddess gives an' She takes away. We come t'gether regular-like, fer as long's we need to, t' shake out our cryin' cloths fer th' day. An' we pray with each other till there's no prayers left in us."

Lavona was blinking hard. Her voice got louder.

"Then we go home an' fold up little dresses an' jeans an' sneakers an' ribbons an' we put 'em all away in a trunk. An' then we git back t' work. Or we have a party. An' we don't invite th' wailin' an' th' prayin' to th' party. Y'see? They just ain't on th' invite list."

Neither of her guests moved. Lavona stood up, wiped her palms on her apron. Then she took the toothpick from her mouth and tossed it into the coal scuttle. When she turned again to the visitors, her head was up, her eyes were bright, and her long face was creased in expectation.

Jez still looked at Lavona. Then, deliberately, she lifted her cup and took a big sip of her tea. Dicken followed suit.

"Okay," Jez said, setting down her cup.

Dicken stepped in. "First, you tell about this conjure woman."

"Mad Becky." Lavona filled her own cup, settled into her chair again. "She's one of th' legends 'round here. Only one, two

85

people maybe, ever seen her. Lives down in one of th' mines. Some say as her mouth is black from eatin' coal." She took another sip of tea.

"Dennis, th' fella what come on her jist last fortnight, says she weren't never borned but got biled up outen a sulfer spring over near t' Blue Stone Gap. Got reared by church folks, then run off up north t' be a actress. Forty yar later she come back crazy an' they throwed her in a half-way house over in Princeton. She excaped, an' taken to th' hills. Nobody never found her, Dennis said."

Lavona paused. "Dennis is one of th' old liners 'round here. He up an' told his story all over Matoaka an' at th' Apple Harvesters Grange meetin' last week."

She sighed, then spoke more briskly. "Seems he had t' go up t' Powhatan Pass t' scavenge some old iron pipe. He was a-settin' by th' creek early one mornin' jist tryin' t' figure how he'd git downstream with his pipe, when th' godawfullest screamin' he ever heerd come bustin' outen th' draw. Dennis, he hunkered down in th' bushes so's he could hide an' see.

"Well, th' yellin' come closer, givin' our Dennis a purdy good scare. It were Mad Beck, tumblin' outen th' woods an' pert near fallin' in th' creek. Dennis said she done stood there with'n her arms spread wide an' hollerin' out a name. She jist kept a-callin' that name an' screamin'. When she looked like she was all wore out, she taken off back up th' hill, still a-screamin' now an' agin, jist to be sure Old Dennis was still shakin' in his boots."

Lavona looked from Dicken to Jez. "He said near as he could make out, th' name she kept a-callin' was Jezzybell."

"My oh my!" said Dicken. "We are talking a first-order crone!"

"Yep." Lavona reared back and pointed at Jez. "Now, seein' as how you are th' only Jezebel I know, I tried t' find you. But with all yer gallivantin' I kept missin' you. Then what? You call me on th' company flatchannel an' tell me you been hearin' a voice callin' out to you an' that you got t' come see me. Well now, reckon what I been a-thinkin'!"

Jez smiled a little, her tiredness dissipated by the strong tea. "Let me tell you my part," she said. She grounded her own chair, closed her eyes in the time-honored preparation for a dreamtelling, and mustered her narrative mode.

"I had one of my seizures. And a dream. In the dream, I am holding an old flatview screen, trying to get a picture to match the sound. On every channel is a woman's voice shrieking my name. Jezzzeee-belll!"

"Cerridwen's Sweetcakes!" Lavona breathed, sinking back in her chair. Jez went on.

"I know she's trying to reach me, but all the rest of her message is garbled. I can't get sound or picture except for her calling my name. So I pray for a spirit guide. And what appears as my spirit guide?"

"Don't say!" said Lavona. "A animal, right?"

"Right," answered Dicken. "Humans are hardly worthy."

"A bear," said Lavona. Jez denied it. Lavona tried again: "King snake!" Jez shook her head.

"Think smaller," Dicken advised.

"It were a spider!"

"Closer," nodded Dicken.

"This spirit guide," Jez said, "turns out to be a slug."

"A what?"

"A slug. A banana slug. In fact, a whole bunch of them."

"Slimy things. Ugly." Lavona shook her head in disgust.

"Slugs were amazing," Dicken pointed out. "They could crawl over the upright blade of a sharp razor and get only a good tickle out of it."

Jez resumed. "Well, slugs it is. The flatview screen is real quick streaked with luminous lacy lines in fancy patterns. I keep trying to figure out what the patterns are telling me since this is the answer to my prayer, right? When the screen is totally covered with this slug slime, about twenty-five of them stand up on their tails and sing to me in eight-part harmony, telling me I got to take the aerial to higher ground. It sounds like a Bach cantata, you know?" She sang, "'You must take, you must take, you must take the aerial, you must, you must, you must take the aerial, the aerial, to higher ground, to higher ground, you must take the aerial to higher ground…'"

Lavona and Dicken joined in Jez's laughter.

"So they all crawl on my arms and neck and shoulders for a free ride while I haul this bulky antenna unit up the hill with this vast-voiced woman yelling in my ear the whole time. Somehow I make it to the top, I set up the antenna, and I'm in immediate communication with the woman. I still can't see her, but she tells me, 'Find Lavona. Now!'"

"Goddess's Goose Eggs," breathed Lavona. She sat hunched, chin on fist.

"You know the rest," said Jez.

"I know what-all's t' know." Lavona shook her head. "Lordy, girl!" She sat for a long quiet moment with her arms braced on her knees. "Well. I reckon we got t' get you to her. Quincy and Brit'll take you, about sun-up tomorrow."

Jez nodded. "Quincy and Brit weren't here tonight."

"Nope. They're tree stewards, both of 'em here on three-yar assignment. Brit lived over in Prospect Dale most'n her life afore she give that up t' study woodcare up in Ontario. She's tickled t' be back home agin."

"Quincy?" Jez asked.

"A strange one. She trained with Brit in Canada. Yonder's where they got t'gether. But she hails from Newfound Land. Had a ear fer languages an' taught a good while afore she pledged Sylvan Renewal. She's might nigh gone native here. Even talks right." Lavona grinned. "They both love this country. They'll be downhome guides for you."

Over an hour later Lavona banked the fire and led the outlanders through the cold house up to a many-quilted bed.

Two spoons broke the low cloud cover just above an aging superhighway, half of which had been allowed to return, as they said, and the other half of which sometimes accommodated cushcars and bicycles. The road wound southeast below the four women.

Brit was an expert guide, once she understood that they didn't need to know the history of every ridge or every cluster of trees. Gray curls seeped out from under her tight red watchcap, and her voice easily bridged the flight bubbles.

"Charlene's Town is northwest." She blew a puff of cold air in the direction of the old capital city. "Between here and there we got traces of more than one hundred company towns, all of them surrounded by mines. These hills are pure honeycomb underneath, what with natural caves and then the mining. When the Twin Quakes hit, folks got scared and moved out."

Quincy, carrying a large pack like each of the other women, was handling the double-spoon logistics while Brit talked. She spoke for all the hills to hear. "It weren't fear what took 'em away. This here was heartland to too many of 'em. They'd lived with coalmines all their natural lives. Their blood even ran black. A little quake or two wouldn't scare 'em." She sank her fists into her overall pockets.

Brit took up the explanation. "Well, nobody knows for sure what took them away. Some say folks just didn't give a care about hanging around after Empty Monday. It was home to them right enough, but home included hogs and crows and skeeters. One of the venables down in Matoaka will tell you how his daddy just set him down one day and told him he figured 'it warn't worth livin' a-tall if'n he couldn't have his hound dog.' Then he just took up his shotgun and walked off into the woods and never come back."

Jezebel squeezed Dicken's arm. "Fog coming up."

Immediately their guides pushed ahead to lead the group through the mountain mists. When they broke the clouds a second time, it was to drop onto a frosty hill by a creek.

"We got to go on foot from here," Brit informed them, the unspoken message being that somehow it would be a breach of reverence to come the easy way. True pilgrims had to walk.

It proved to be hard going. They made their way single file up and down a cold, densely covered path where no sun could have reached—even if there had ever been a sun, which Dicken was beginning to doubt. The morning passed into afternoon before the guides pulled them up for a rest.

Brit and Quincy talked about a mine known as Upper Thirteen, and of its railroad spur. They pored over contour maps and took compass readings. Dicken refrained from telling them that Jezebel could give them a deadly accurate perception of their location, their destination, the altitude, the temperature, the barometric pressure, the time of day to the second, and the constellation at that moment ascendant on the eastern horizon. But Jez was strangely withdrawn.

They had just negotiated a narrow log that bridged a small ravine when Quincy stopped the company with a "Shhh!" that held them all motionless in the fog-filled woods. "Did you hear it?"

"Hear what?" Dicken murmured.

"Quincy hears voices a lot," Brit whispered. "She says there's something in these parts that speaks to shyers."

"Shyers?" asked Dicken.

"Folks that can go shy," Brit answered. "Disappear." Then she added, "Quincy's learning to go shy."

Dicken began to perceive Quincy as fading, no longer with them. She blinked. Quincy was definitely there, still standing motionless, her head upturned. A trick of the fog, Dicken decided. She turned back toward Jezebel, whose hand at that moment took her own.

It was late afternoon and a psychological hundred miles deeper into the hills when the party thrashed through some brush and broke into another world. Confronting them was a huge open slip-slot freight car still bearing the block letters, Red Flame Coal Company.

The dull clouds that had so far blanketed the treetops now fell in quiet drifts over a large, sparsely vegetated clearing. Wisps and puffy billows brushed soundlessly past long-collapsed buildings, over piles of thin metal and silent rusting towers of belts and bins, cables and coils.

Jezebel broke from the group and began moving purposefully into the mists, crossing the broad clearing to its far side. She stopped at a boarded-up mine portal and turned back to her companions as if to say, "Here."

The others joined her, and Quincy began examining the layers of two-by-twelves. "Behind this is bound to be the slope shaft," she announced. "Slants so we can walk down it. Iffen we can get into it," she added, pushing half-heartedly on the heavy boards.

Jez stepped in front of her and faced the barrier. She ran her fingers over the wood and the corroding metal staves. Carefully, she grasped the critical cross-timber and closed her eyes. With slow inevitability the beam moved, nails screamed, bands snapped, and the entranceway virtually opened before them.

"Pretty impressive," Brit observed. Quincy nodded.

Dicken looked askance at her lover. "You think she's down there, don't you?"

"She's down there," Jezebel said.

The Welchtown women activated two glolobes from their packs, and the group began a descent into the wide passageway. Jez led them, outdistancing the light and looking neither left nor right. Dicken captured her and slowed her pace.

Some fifty meters later, black walls surrounded them as the shaft cut its way into the coalfield itself. Over their heads, decaying timbers and rusty bolts still held the black ceiling in place.

Looking up, Dicken asked, "You figure we're safe?"

Jezebel spoke in a voice Dicken barely recognized. "We're safe," she said, plunging forward again.

They followed Jezebel deeper into the mountain. At the intersection of another tunnel, Quincy secured a heavy string to the wall at waist level. She talked as she played the string out behind her, occasionally twisting it around a protruding piece of coal to keep it visible and graspable. "There was small tunnels for pick minin' but these here big passages was for the heavy machines. They could dig half a ton in less than ten seconds. An' load it onto the belt, all in one operation."

"We're actually in a network of rooms supported by big pillars of coal," Brit added. "Could get lost easy."

The footing was good, even though the air seemed staler and the dankness more pronounced. Dicken didn't like it. She didn't trust the walls not to collapse behind her, cutting off any escape.

They came upon an underground workroom where wooden shelves bore dusty tools, machine parts, hardhats, pieces of clothing. Dicken hauled Jezebel to a stop on an overturned cart. Brit and Quincy squatted, inspecting the walls.

"She's very close," Jez said. Then she looked squarely at Dicken. "I have to meet her alone."

"No," said Dicken promptly, sitting beside her.

"Yes." Jez's eyes brooked no contradiction. "Brit, Quincy, can the three of you stay the night near the entrance?"

"We could…" began Brit.

"Jezebel!" Dicken was in full protest.

Quincy stopped her. "I got no hankerin' to sleep down here, Bess Dicken. Maybe we ought to go back up, set up camp and get some rest. Try again tomorrow."

"Good," said Dicken. "You two go ahead. Jez and I…"

Jez took Dicken's head in her hands.

"I haven't often said this," she said, as Quincy and Brit moved discreetly back the way they had come. "You can't go with me, Dicken. There's an elevator shaft further on. Mad Becky is at the bottom of it. I can drop down to her slow. But I can't take you with me."

Dicken's face was full of consternation. She took Jez's hands in her own and held them against her cheek. Slowly she nodded. "Okay. But how long?"

Jez shook her head. "I don't know. Maybe I can meet you or leave you some message. Somewhere near here. She's not going to hurt me, Dicken. I'm sure of it. But she knows something important that I'm supposed to learn. I'll stay with her until she's ready to tell me." She reached to take Dicken in her arms. "You could go back to Welchtown?"

"Girl, you have lost your pluperfect mind!" Dicken pulled Jez to her feet and held her close.

Group consultation resulted in a modification of Quincy's plan. The three women would camp at the mine entrance, sending Dicken back to their present location at regular intervals for word from Jezebel.

Jez held Dicken and kissed her soundly before striding off into the darkness.

5

> I must be you to know you
> and only through your eyes will I ever see.
> *Vade Mecum for the Journey*

Ever since they had landed in this forest, Jezebel had been aware of three dangers. Most tangible now, as she stood at the brink of the deep shaft, was the peril of black walls and damp, tight air. The immediate danger was the summoning of the frantic unhinged mind, now so close after beginning from so far away. Most terrifying was the threat of her own madness, the wisps of disorientation and lightheadedness that had been intensifying throughout the day. The icy wind had begun again, sweeping from the soles of her feet upward through her body, until it swirled in the rigidity of her skull; the sweat and the sweet saliva were not far away. She had to hurry.

Jezebel fashioned a short-life glolobe and dropped it into the shaft, watching it die out some forty meters below. Then, propelled toward the sisterstress of that other mind, she stepped into the void and drifted downward in the pathway of the glolobe. She landed just as the sweat burst out and blackness overcame her.

Jezebel lay on a hard stone floor. A light whose source she could not discern showed her she was no longer in the mine, but in a cave; clammy breeches told her she had peed. She could find no blood under her nose or on her shirt; she identified the dampness there as saliva and phlegm. Without moving, she took an internal inventory: breath near normal; metabolism galloping; head clear; body very strained, parts of it bruised. Certainly she had been in convulsions.

She closed her eyes, beginning the slow, barely perceptible stretches that relaxed traumatized muscles and calmed the body's systems. With warm torpors she dried her trews and extended her smell and kinesthetic senses beyond herself. As she called up more sophisticated scanners, she dared a deliberate movement that twisted her onto her back in the manner, she hoped, of an agitated dreamer.

Through barely slitted eyes, she determined that where she lay was not where she had fallen. This ceiling was low and smooth, and stone walls crowded her from behind and from either side. She made out a pattern of wire rectangles stretched across what would have been the fourth wall of her confines. Fencing wire, she mused.

She was in a small makeshift cage, she decided. The wire looked to be embedded in heavy rock on one side; on the other, it terminated far out of her reach in an elaborate system of bolts, stones and wooden staves.

Immediately and deliberately alert now on her survival level, Jez cautiously extended her inner sight toward the noiseless passageway from which the pale light emerged. There! Mad Becky, the old woman of her dream! Jez judged her to be no more than ten meters away.

Surrounding the conjure woman was a field of vibrating bodies. Crystals. Jezebel was sure of it. That would be the source of light. She risked again, extending a quick scan toward the being beyond the corridor: perfect physical health and vibrancy, flexible joints, many missing teeth, sharp sensory awareness, and—there it was again!—the chaos and ecstasy of a mind unbound. Jez sent an enfoldment of greeting. No response. The old woman was preoccupied.

A heavy penetrating pulse resounded in Jez's head. She raised her eyes to the cave wall beyond her. On that wall was a moving shadow, almost sticklike in its thinness, and broken in its perpendicularity only by the lift of knees, the high swing of skinny arms, the bounce of plumes of hair. It hopped in stark justice to the beat, spinning and kicking, in repeated patterns, arms in synchrony.

She's dancing, Jez thought, dancing split naked to the music in her head!

The pulse suddenly stopped. The shadow of the long figure stood motionless, arms raised. Jezebel extended an enfoldment. It bounced back. Slowly the silhouette drew a thin rod from out of nowhere and raised it noiselessly to a striking position above its head. Then it crept along the wall toward her. Jez waited, watching the sharp lines of the shadow dissolve into a growing amorphous blob.

The rod emerged first, a long walking stick that poked its crafty way into her line of vision. It was followed by Mad Becky, not naked at all, but immaculately clad in a red leotard of skin-tight spandex. The red contrasted with iridescent silver tights that hugged the thin legs and disappeared into the tops of red aerobics shoes.

Jez barely breathed.

The old woman stared at her out of cavernous black eyes and from under a shock of silver hair that grew in billows around her dark leathery face. Suddenly, she leapt toward Jez with a shriek. Jez cringed back from the fencing, and Mad Becky slipped the stick through the wire to poke at her belly, her breasts. Jez doubled over.

"Stop it!" She yelled. "Stop it, Becky!"

The prodding continued, accompanied by grunts of satisfaction and, Jez sensed, edges of fear. She reached up suddenly and caught the end of the stick.

"Rebecca!" she shouted. "Reeba! Beckla! Becka, Becky, Beck!"

Instantly the old woman howled and pulled back. Jez lost her balance and fell forward. With a mighty twist, Mad Becky jerked her weapon from Jez's hands and, with her own arms inside the fencing, began beating the stick all over Jez's body.

"Stop, you crazy woman! Stop! I'm Jezebel! Jezebel!"

Mad Becky halted. She frowned. Before she could move again, Jez had seized her hands and pinned them to the wire. "I'm the one you called," she whispered tensely. "I'm Jezebel. Jezzybell!"

The old woman jerked free, letting her stick fall into the cage. Jez seized it. "You can have this if you'll let me out." She waited. "Open the cage, Becky."

She pointed to the place where the wire was secured, surrounding Mad Becky with images of her hands on the rocks and wires, rolling back the fencing.

The brightly clad figure did precisely that. As her cage bulged open, Jez thrust out the stick. "Here." She waited on her knees until Becky slowly took it. The black eyes were canny now, warily scanning the crouching figure before her.

Jez spoke quietly. "I'm here. I came because you called me." She extended her hands.

The old woman's eyes widened, then blinked twice. When they met Jez's eyes again, their blackness had softened, and for a moment an impish merriment flickered in their depths. With infinite slowness, Mad Becky reached out and took the proffered hands, folding them within gentle fingers. She raised Jez to her feet; releasing an audible sigh, she laid her hand delicately on Jez's cheek. Then gesturing to the passage from which she had come, she began to urge Jez toward it.

When Jez started to speak, the old woman motioned her into silence and drew her insistently into the passageway. Jez followed with difficulty, stretching her cramped muscles into obedience and struggling to match Mad Becky's pace. They moved through tunnels and open areas where mounted crystal stalks revealed smaller corridors branching left and right. The walls were rough and gray at times, smooth and almost glassy at other times. Some mixed-texture surfaces seemed composed of figures that reminded Jez of shells and tiny sea animals.

As they twisted down new passageways, Jez had the strong sense that they were drawing deeper into the mountain, toward some center of activity. She fought off the return of her lightheadedness, at last stopping the old woman so she could rest. She sank to the floor, dizzy and trying to balance in the midst of nowhere. Then she heard Mad Becky's voice for the first time.

"Jezzybell."

Jez raised her head.

"Girl, I can't get to you." The conjure woman leaned on her walking stick, shaking her head. "You got a job to do," she went on softly. "You got a job to do, you ain't near ready for it, an' I can't get to you!"

Jez summoned every mechanism of focus. "Becky, I...there's something here...I can't..."

Then cool hands pressed her cheeks. The old woman knelt beside her, holding her head, washing away tightnesses, easing pressures. Jez drew a long breath and unleashed it in a sigh.

"You got all it takes," she heard the old woman whisper, "all it takes to do what you come here to do. But girl, you got to trust me."

Jez met the dark eyes, searched the craggy face. Tears rose in her eyes and moved her head into a nod. The old woman nodded with her, her eyes dancing.

"I aim to take you to that room yonder." She pointed with her chin. "You close your eyes and lay your hand in mine. You ain't about to come to no harm."

Jez pressed her lips together and let the conjure woman help her to her feet. As she gave herself over to her guidance, she heard a low musical note pulsing through the mountain, suggestive of a tremendous subdued power. It matched their footsteps, growing stronger by the moment and calling her to its center until at last she felt Mad Becky halting their progress at the opening to the room.

Even through her shielded eyes Jez felt heat, and the intense brightness. As Mad Becky took her by the shoulders and turned her toward the source, every cell in her body trembled, her eyes flew open, and she suddenly stood bathed in a blinding unearthly light. At the same moment a pure vocal tone rose from the mountain crone's throat. It grew to full volume and steadied as she flung out her arms to the stark incandescence before them.

"Becky, don't!" Jez cried, lunging forward to stop her singing. Then something brought her up short: Hundreds of crystals were being called into exquisite attunement by the ringing of the old woman's fundamental note. Jez put her hands to her ears as the proliferating overtones washed through her, echoing in her head.

She felt herself stiffen and cry out even before she fell to the floor. Her dutiful monitor told her that the cold wind had already yielded to sweat, that her supine body was rounding to a high arch, and that tumultuous paroxysms were on their way. With a locking of her breath, she opened to the inevitable.

And landed, swaddled by chords of crystal song, right in the middle of Mad Becky's fertile brain.

At the same moment, she felt the conjure woman inside her own head, dwelling with her in a presence that distinctly differed from softself exchange – this was too high and too exhilarating, too unreal to be mistaken for that more earthbound phenomenon. She was aware of the thin leotard-clad body still transfixed by the crystals, and of the other body garbed in woodswarmth, bent grotesquely upward and pulsing with brutal spasms. But she and the old woman inhabited some third terrain.

"I am filled with your whole life," Jez said, choosing a language unspoken for centuries.

"And I with yours," her companion replied in still another ancient tongue.

In the person of Hadashida Perkins, stage-named Rebecca Tsunami, Jez bowed to the applause of yet another enchanted audience, fed flocks of ducks and geese on a parkland lake, screamed at Becky's level-headed doctors, heaved Becky's bed through the window of a dingy little room, and lived again with Mad Becky the terrifying separation-from-self that had sent her wandering in the darkness of West Virginia's defunct coal mines.

She saw with Mad Becky's eyes the beams of sunlight that broke through the clouds over endless green hills of oaks and sugar maples drenched with rain.

For her part, Mad Becky found her hands braiding the long black hair of Jezebel's mother, her knees brown and wet from working carrot rows at the collective farm, her eyes dropping Jezebel's tears into the ashes that had been Jezebel's baby girl, her lips forming Jezebel's lectures on transmog operation, and her heart locking with Dicken's in a storm-soaked soaring over the Caribbean.

At the end of the hundredth story, with laughter and sadness linking their two suspended minds, the two women approached the matter of their present meeting. The descent from their high exchange of minds began when Becky's voice hummed through the crystals, "You have a rock in your chest, Jezebel, blocking your flow." Her attention was focused on the distorted and arched body, still in light spasms, that Jez identified as her own.

"A rock is causing me to do that?" Jez asked.

"That and lots more." The old woman's mind textures were grumpy. "And I can't teach you what you must learn while you block your flow."

Jez examined the rock that Becky was perceiving. "Men. You see my distrust of men."

A rising unease threatened their link.

"That is your rock," Becky's mind acknowledged.

Before Jez could control it, defensive rejoinders rushed from her memory toward Becky. They flooded their mutual mindspace with images of Jez's encounter with Shaheed, her learnings from being in the body of Wundu, Dicken's rapist, and her dreamwalking and spooning with Donal Jain.

"And they are men, Beck!" her mind contended.

Mad Becky agreed with her.

"You've done some good work. You've begun to understand that violence could live within your own skin. And you've softened toward some men, become more understanding. But these men are exceptions for you. You still put the rest of their sex into a cage that you won't open."

The old woman growled audibly, her mental textures tinged with resignation, then with decision. Her meanings began to come less from their shared mindplace than from the sticklike figure in the doorway to the crystal room.

"We got more to learn than I figured on." Becky's mouth and head moved again with her words.

The crystals were dimming now, the sound dying. Becky jerked her finger at Jez's body, limp at last and sprawled on the floor of the cave.

"You got to climb back into yours, too."

"Why?"

Becky squinted.

"Because you are the beggar, girl, and I am the conjure woman. Because I got the answers and you don't. That's why."

She pointed again. Reluctantly, Jez slid back into her body, cringing at its confinement and its distress.

Her clothes were dry, but stiff and uncomfortable. She rubbed blood from her chin and rolled her tongue around in a sore mouth. She was nauseated and exhausted. The old woman took her to a rockface whose dampness drew itself into a slow trickle. It terminated in a hollowed-out stone basin. Jez knelt before its clear coolness and immersed her lips in the water, drawing it into her parched throat.

Later, when she stood to dry off from her long hot soak in Becky's big washtub, Jez breathed in with delight the freshness of the flannel nightgown handed to her.

The old woman, long since deprived of her upper incisors, grinned back at her through the cuspid gap.

"Crystal-cleaned," she said, then tucked Jez into a warm bed under layers of quilts. She squatted by her guest. "Jezzybell, you got to go easy for a while so's to be up for this work."

Jez squeezed the old woman's arm. "I'll rest. But I need..."

"You ain't wantin' half as much to get crackin' as me, girl. We got to git you educated fast. You git to sleep now. We got all the time we'll need."

Before she dropped off, Jezebel scanned the environs of the mine in search of Dicken. She found her standing by the elevator shaft, her face a puzzle of calculation in the light of her glolobe. Jez formed another glolobe in her mind and sent it roaring upward from the bottom of the shaft. It flew around her stunned lover, brushing against her cheeks and lips. Then it fluttered in farewell just at Dicken's eye level and disappeared whence it came.

There, thought Jez. That ought to let her know I'm okay. She was asleep before her next full breath.

Jez awoke with a refreshed body to a breakfast of mushroom and sourgrass salad with a cooked root that tasted deliciously like a potato. They ate in companionable silence, the crone and the witch, sisters in madness now, embarked upon a quest for meaning that Jezebel could not foresee.

She followed the sharp white light of Becky's crystal candle through honeycombed tunnels to a room containing trunks of theatrical costumes. Their designs spanned cultures and centuries, and Jez could not imagine by what manner of transport they had come to that cavern. At Becky's direction, she draped herself in a spaghetti-strapped chemise while her companion wiggled into shrunken long johns that looked and smelled squeaky clean. Then the mountain crone rummaged in a foot-locker labeled Mothertongue International Tour 2004. She withdrew a crumpled pair of orange culottes for Jez and, apparently satisfied that they would at last be properly attired, padded off down the corridor with her quartz light. Jezebel zipped up the culottes' side placket and strode after her.

She then gave herself over to the discoveries of that day, absorbing all she could of the subterranean dwelling place of this legend of the West Virginia hills. More than once in the morning's activities the old woman's eyes would turn cavernous again as she stared at a crack in the rocks or fondled some bizarre artifact.

"Becky," Jez would whisper, "are you…"

"I'm okay," Becky would assure her, focusing once more. "I'm okay."

As their explorations became easier and more playful, Jez saw less and less of Mad Becky's empty black eyes, and more and more of their dancing joy. During those hours, and with Becky as her guide, she knelt to meals of boiled tugroots and anise-spiced kale, topped with the nutberry shreddings of tasty chinquapin; sipped a sinus-blasting tea that immediately sent her to a three-gallon galvanized bucket for relief of her bladder; probed without success the secrets of quartz filings that not only instantly heated both food and atmosphere, but also transformed her shit into an ash so fine and pink she could powder her nose with it; harmonized minor Hungarian folk songs and American show tunes; mastered, but never won at, a three-dimensional game of stones in wooden cups; learned, to the sound of a near-toothless cackle, that there were scores of non-invasive ways to observe, identify, catalogue and remember the multifarious rocks and minerals, plants and fungi that lived in the surrounding hills and hollows.

In her fatigue at the end of the day, Jez declined any dinner and in fact found satisfaction in emptying her insides of every trace of food or water. She sank onto the cushion-covered stones in the old woman's living area, resting her head against the wall. She reached out toward Dicken again, sending forth another glolobe of reassurance.

Lazily, she watched as the conjure woman went about her preparations for bed. Old Becky moved in silence, and apparently with some new sense of purpose, adjusting the glow of crystal candles, cleaning food bowls, heating bathwater, arranging quilts and pillows over flat stones. Jez became uneasily aware that their comfortable visiting together had come to an end, that it had been only a preparation for a more important enterprise upon which they would embark the following day.

"Becky," she began.

The old woman silenced her with a gesture. "Time for sleep, girl," she said, motioning her to the washtub. She bathed Jezebel, then enfolded her in a heavy quilt and eased her to her bed. Jez was asleep before her head touched the pallet.

Hours later she burst into wakefulness. She threw off the quilt, careful not to disturb the figure that sprawled face down just beyond her. Her flesh was sore and her bones ached, but sleep had rejuvenated her spirits. In the low light of warmth-making quartz filings, old Becky's bare body lay under a sheen of sweat. The skinny brown back rose and fell with soft snores.

Jez watched the movements, lulled by the sounds. In the crystal glow, the crone's scrawny arms and legs had a lean vibrancy, and her skin stretched wrinkleless over rounded ribs and joints. Barely perceptibly, the flat buttocks were rising and falling with the rhythm of her long breathings.

She surveyed the movement of those twin mounds of flesh, increasingly aware of how her own hips could exactly cover them. In a lazy slow motion, she began to shed her nightgown, breathing in time to Becky's gentle noises. She sat for a moment, free of her clothes and absorbing the motions of Becky's lanky body.

Jez edged closer to the sleeping figure and with quiet movements suspended herself above it, leaning upon her carefully placed hands and feet. She braced herself there in a rising anticipation, her breath moving now in its own cadences, her blood vibrant against her skin. Smiling, she closed her eyes and began her slow descent toward old Becky's body.

Barely short of contact, the snores ceased and the body beneath her came alive. It grew rigid, softened suddenly into an invitation, and then into desire. Jez stopped her progress and held herself in prolonged expectancy. Below her, Becky strained upward toward the canopy of Jez's body. A low cry was being born in the old woman's throat.

Jez took in one last breath and lowered her torso onto the woman beneath her. As she fitted her hips to Becky's backside, she felt her pubic bone lock into the cleft beneath the crone's buttocks. Becky gave birth to her cry and pressed herself hard against Jez's weight. They rolled, Old Becky hooting with pleasure.

She laughed her own pleasure as she plunged her hand into the prodigal silver curls that tossed beside her. Becky turned upward into the embrace so that Jez could stroke and knead the dark, finely wrinkled skin of her breasts. Becky crooned. Both women grazed over their face-to-face bodies, Jez's hands and her lips purposefully seeking every fold and crevice of the mountain woman's skin. They plunged and tumbled amid exclamations of desire and delight.

Jez hovered over Becky's mouth, and her eyes began to dance with the prospect of delicious discovery. She found a wild tenderness in those extraordinary lips. As her own tongue fell through the toothless hollow, she yielded to the welcome of that mouth and its ardent greeting of her every attention. Jez lingered there in long luxurious exploration.

She tamed her teeth into a gentleness they had rarely known, the better to entrap Becky's eager nipples, the better to conspire with her own lips and tongue below the hairless mound where Becky's thighs converged, there delicately to tease a tiny button to a long and breath-halted burst of joy. To her astonishment, the old woman rose to a second climax. And with very little encouragement from Jez, to another, and still another and another, dancing and driving to the touch of Jez's hands, her fingers, her tongue.

At last Jezebel put her arms around the conjure woman, kissing and stroking her head and hair, while Becky moved her own wise fingers in an act of self-love that was the artful acme of all previous climaxes. Awed and incredulous, Jezebel Stronglaces held Rebecca Tsunami while the old woman came, and came, and came.

It was later, in the crystals' dim light, after Becky's intimate loving of Jez's body, that Jezebel noticed a difference in the cave room's ambience, as if solid objects were becoming unstable, subtly straining to hold their form in place. At first she assumed it was simply an effect of their afterglow, but as she changed her position, the stone floor beneath her felt soft and unsteady.

"Becky," she whispered.

"Pay no mind, it's just surface tensions relaxin' a little. You've seen it before."

"It feels like…"

"That's what it is. A shapeshift tide, just passin' through." She draped her arm around Jez's shoulders. "Come here to me, Jezzybell."

Instantly the words reawakened Jez's blood. She stretched toward Mad Becky, and felt herself pulled into the embrace of a younger woman, a stronger woman, a woman whose hands lay both heavy and gentle on her back and thighs, a woman who pressed upon her the warm weight of smooth muscles. This woman's lips covered a full complement of teeth, and her short-cropped hair was dark, almost black.

Jez opened to the probings of the woman's powerful fingers, spreading her legs to them in a rush of longing. She gasped at the first touch of the silver tongue on her nipple and encouraged the rhythmic rasp of the rough cheek on her breast. She raised her legs and bent them into an embrace of his buttocks. With her hands she maneuvered his torso to its proper place, drawing his head near her own, and urging him toward her open thighs.

He made deep easy love to Jezebel, moving in and out of her with gradually increasing intent. At the top of the highest wave, he held the moment so that both of them crested, plunged and rode down together. Jez was crying, holding him close, when suddenly she wanted him again, wanted him more ferociously, more profoundly. They rose another time, her cries driving them high with a keen desperation utterly strange to Jezebel Stronglaces. They blazed together in a passion all the wilder for the precision and balance of their mutual husbanding of its power.

Her cry filled the West Virginia mountain and sang its way back to the pallet where her partner lay, withdrawing from her body but pushing his hand gently against her crotch, sealing a sacred doorway.

Jez narrowed her eyes and peered at him. Another figure roved the terrain under his muscles and smooth skin, the shadow of a crone, almost emerging, then subsiding once more into his solid physique.

He kissed her lightly, then slipped down her body to spread her legs apart and set his mouth into her dense thatch of brown hair. His tongue and lips caressed the dark rosy flesh there, as if to open again that avenue of delight. He focused his attention upon the tiny rod, massaging it with his tongue, lightly then insistently. Jez felt a deep change overtake her blood and tissues, animating his efforts. His hands slid under her, lifting her hips. His tongue and lips stroked on.

She embedded her fingers in his short-cropped hair, pushing and kneading, savoring her phallus's tantalizing engorgement as it filled his mouth. The knowings of her every cell centered in that newborn agency and the vessel that it probed. She was cast into an unparalleled world of bright intensity.

She matched her rocking hips to the sliding suction of his tongue and palate as they drew her into him, expelled her and encompassed her again and again. He took her to the edge of release, denied her the fulfillment, took her there once more and again retreated. When at last he brought her exploding into freedom, her long scream shook the caverns of her consciousness.

She hardly felt him turning her body to its prone position, his hands separating the cheeks of her buttocks. Unthinkable hunger flooded her haunches. She arched her back, her hips rising to an entreaty.

His fingers made ready the passage, easing the flesh and sinking deep to awaken in her an unaccustomed core of craving. Jez caught her breath as his phallus played at the entrance, pushing gently against her sudden tautness. He reached under her and clasped her testicles. Jez's own penis stiffened and her buttocks relaxed. She opened herself and engulfed his phallus, drawing it smoothly in again and again, until it reached into the center of her strange, her huge new appetite. There his steady thrusts brought her to a deep fulfillment, totally new, totally unlooked for.

And when he held her in the long embrace of their afterlove, Jez placed her rough-shaven face alongside his as they marveled at their maleness and their muscled beauty.

The circles of their loving spun on through the night. Buoyed by a tireless energy, Jezebel Stronglaces and Rebecca Tsunami moved in and out of the shapeshifting tides, generating countless combinations of bodily love.

In one of her female bodies, Jez lay long and languorously with a man of delicate touch, weaving together rainbow webs which bound, unbound and bound them again into a single tapestry. At the center of this Oneness, a phallus lifted and a softness rose to meet it, and Jez understood at last the male and female yearning for each other, their organs fine-tuned by nature for simultaneous excitation.

And there was no trace of violence in either—not in him, not in herself.

It was in that same body that her mind beheld a wondrous parade. Its participants were all the bodies and personalities that she had ever inhabited over the millennia: the female ones, the male ones, the ambiguously sexed ones, each unique in its attraction to another individual body or personality. Those who suffered or themselves brought hurt—all, all were herself.

And it was in that particular man-loving body that Jezebel Stronglaces at last set aside the rock.

In this finale, her lover was a short man, a little over five feet in height, corpulent in body yet with long elegant fingers and a smooth hairless head. He rode her high, driving her short breaths into tiny taut vocalizations. Together they filled a seed pod that every second promised to explode into lush flowers. On the thin edge of its breaking open, Jez sensed the familiar and unmistakable rush of the icy wind sweeping through her chest, bound toward freezing any life to come. Instantly, she intercepted its progress, consigned it to the conflagration in her groin and swam into full-body throes of rapture and release. Bright blossoms covered them both.

They slept.

The Earth had moved more than a quarter turn on Her axis when Jezebel awoke. She lay still and spoke to each of her bones and organs, each of her body's intricate systems: blood, nerves, air, lymph, electromagnetics, digestion, elimination. The ardors and ardures of the long night had entirely subsided, and she felt washed by a joyous yet unfamiliar peace. With a deep certainty, she knew that she would never endure seizures again, that her cells had realigned into health. She felt brand new.

Becky was already up and brewing something over a glowing mound of quartz filings.

"Pokeweed tea," she said, squatting beside Jez with a battered tin cup. "Starch you right up."

Becky wore fresh white long johns. Her black eyes were shining. Jez took the cup, set it aside, and held out her arms. Becky grinned.

"Jezzybell, I don't aim to jump back in bed with you. Else we get nothin' done all day." She took one of Jez's hands in her own.

Jez searched the old woman's face and for a dizzying moment watched the sensuous passage of all the faces she had worn so recently in their loving. Reluctantly curbing the wanting that rose within her, she settled her eyes again upon the woman before her. She saw warmth there, and happiness. And a firm resolve. She nodded, then spoke with her own determination.

"So. What do we do today?"

"Lots. You ready?"

Jez braced herself with a sip of tea. "Yes. I am."

Becky nodded as well. She dropped Jez's hand and settled cross-legged by the pallet. "Watch close," she admonished, as Jez obediently blinked her eyes into full alertness.

The conjure woman sat before her, framed against the gray stone of the wall behind her, her eyes closed, her hands folded over her belly, her face a picture of snaggletoothed joy. She began breathing, full and deep. As Jez watched, the old woman's energy rupa expanded and then brightened; her hands shook with tiny vibrations. Suddenly, Jez saw through her to the gray wall behind her.

The mountain crone had disappeared, long johns and all.

Jez cried out, reaching to touch the emptiness. At that moment Becky bounced back again into full visibility, her body a very present entity.

"That," she said through another tooth-gapped display of satisfaction, "is how you go shy."

"Go shy? You just…your clothes…"

"Everythin' that's vibratin' goes right with you." She picked up the battered cup and disappeared again, with the cup. Seconds later she was back.

Jez was agog. "Beck, where do you go?" She hung onto the old woman's leg lest she escape again.

"I don't go nowhere," Becky grinned, "cept'n maybe into a faster place where your eyes can't fasten on me." She sobered. "You can do it too, girl."

Jez swallowed. "But I…"

The conjure woman was on her feet.

"Nothin' to it. You get quiet, you focus, you get happy, you're gone. Refocus and you're back." She set her fists to her hips. "That's it," she beamed. Gently, she eased Jez's torso back against the cave wall. "Now close your eyes."

Jez obeyed, flattening her diaphragm to take in long breaths, wrapping herself in composure.

"Get shut of all your thoughts. Head for that sweet restin' place where you float. There, where you touch your soul, your peace."

Home! Jez thought, and caught her breath as she stepped into deep space. Home, she smiled, floating on empty eternity.

Becky crouched beside her like a bench-press coach. "Now you're truckin'," she rasped, "you're settin' right there where it all is. Everything. Stay there, Jezzybell. Hold it like a cloud."

She waited a full minute before she spoke again. "You're goin' to start changin' the energy now," she said softly. "You're goin' to move that sweet peace up into hallelujah joy. Easiest way to do that is just to pick somethin' and focus on its best parts. Just start lovin' it. Pick that rock wall, Jezzybell."

Deliberately, Jez shifted away from the vast stillness where no thing existed into a tiny movement toward the wall behind her. It was a thing now, an object of her attention. She felt its hardness, its rough texture. She imagined its dimensions, its heaviness.

Becky's cracked voice reached her.

"Bring in appreciation, Jezzybell. Get grateful! Tell that granite wall how amazin' it is. Thank it for gettin' belched up from the boilin' bottom of these mountains, movin' in a red-hot flow, coolin' down, bein' mica and feldspar! Praise that rock for makin' up this mountain, Jezzybell! For holdin' up the soil and the trees, the blacks and the browns and the greens that live together on top of it. You got to love that rock, girl!"

And Jez did love the rock, loved it with a wild admiration and respect, loved it with the tears that fell in thankfulness for its being. She was exhilarated, riding a high energy that did not somehow carry her with it but rather flowed through her with a tremendous passion and joy. Her ki rotations were soaring. Her whole body trembled.

"Good!" cried the old woman. "You're close, right on the edge." Her voice modulated into a higher key, its tempo doubled. "Now stay focused on that rock! Keep up that pure energy! That's it!"

Jez concentrated on the great granite wall, praising its every quality. Her passion escalated and a surge of light covered her.

"You're gone!" laughed Becky.

"Am I?" Jez laughed back, her eyes still closed.

"Gone!" repeated the crone. "Your bones and muscles ain't nothin' but pure ecstatic vibrations, Jezzybell! You are gone from this world!"

Becky was right, Jez realized. She had no body.

"Stay high, and don't focus on anything, else you'll come back!"

The warning was too late. Already Jez had rematerialized. She sat on the pallet rubbing her arms, her chest.

"Becky, I did it!"

"You done good," said Becky, leaning against the wall.

Then Jez did it again—disappeared and moved around the cave room while Becky's eyes passed right over her. As they prepared and ate a hot mush sprinkled with tangy seeds, Jez experimented with her new skill until she felt adept at it. On her last return to material form, she fell on the old woman with hugs and gratitude.

"What gifts you have given me, Rebecca Tsunami!" she announced.

Becky held her a moment, then moved away from her to scrape her bowl, busily. "There's one more of them gifts," she said. "It's the one you come for." She downed the last of her mush. "We got to go outside for it. You up to that?"

Jez pushed Becky's bowl aside and took her hands in her own. "Of course I'm up to it." She lifted Becky's hair back from her eyes. "We've stepped into tall sistership, you know."

"Yep," Becky grinned. "Wrote up the affidavy last night." She sat stroking Jez's hand. "Girl, you've done give me a gift too, you know."

Jez searched the craggy face before her.

"You've done parted me from my madness," Becky said quietly. "I feel all of a piece now."

They sat without stirring, there in the deepest pool of their kinship.

Finally, Becky said, "Jezzybell, you got to be on your way soon. We're both knowin' that."

"I'll be back."

"Maybe."

"I'll come back. And," Jez smiled, "I'll teach you…to fly."

Becky's eyes were bright. "Mebbe." She laid a soft kiss on Jezebel's cheek. "So we got to get dressed now."

She leapt up and boosted the crystal-lume to a hot brightness. Then she rummaged in yet another trunk, this time for a down vest that she donned over her long johns. She pushed her bushy hair into a snood; on top of it and at an angle precisely parallel to the floor, she planted a ladies' flat, straw sailor hat bedecked with artificial flowers.

It was midafternoon when they entered the woods, Becky clad like a scarecrow come to tea and Jezebel in her trews and softshirt. They stepped from the cave through a narrow vertical crack that spilled them out near the bottom of a deep ravine. Just beyond them, waters wound their way down the narrow but deep draw. Jez stood with her companion, captured by the quiet, the remaining chill of winter, and the chuckle of the stream. They were much lower, she calculated, than the mine entrance, which she estimated to be almost directly behind and above them on the other side of the mountain. Her sensors told her that Dicken and the Welchtown women sat there awaiting her.

Becky led her down a rough path through the underbrush, holding back whipping arms of vegetation for her passage. The old woman walked with purpose but without speed and some-times, Jez thought, with a touch of reverence to her gait. Once or twice she stopped to smell the bark of a tree or to scrape at it softly. Once she dropped to her knees to examine the earth.

They came to a small clearing, where the land sloped gently down to marshy ground that bordered a rill, flowing silently. Jez was marveling at the hold that winter still had on the forest when her companion halted them with a Listen! gesture.

Jez did hear something. Rather, she heard absolutely nothing, but felt as if she were hearing something. Or she heard an impending something. She sent out enfoldments. They vibrated as if about to surround someone, and then dissipated into emptiness. She looked to Becky, who was on her way again, straight into the underbrush, still careful but determined, her hat still balanced precariously on her head.

At long last they stopped at a spot where the terrain called back some of the water into a modest inlet, almost a pond, two to three meters wide. The old woman directed Jezebel to get comfortable atop some dry stones, as she herself was doing with the folding of her long bones into a compact bundle. They braced their backs against a bank and settled in for what was clearly to be a vigil.

The spring sun shone from a winter sky, allowing the forest only a dulled uniform illumination, yet the light of the lengthening day seemed fairly strong for late afternoon. Jezebel identified a willow tree above them. Then a hickory beside it. The rest were, she thought, maples of some sort, though one on the far side of the inlet resembled a fruit-bearing tree. She concentrated on stillness, curbing even slight movements, lest her companion frown at the disturbance.

There was no wind. Now and again Jez sensed a strange impending presence, as if someone were lurking behind them. Or around them? She scanned the area several times in vain. Nor was Becky open to mindreach. Forget any attempts at words. Jezebel suppressed a snort.

The old woman had closed her eyes.

They sat in the stillness.

The late winter afternoon stretched on.

A falling leaf intruded on Jez's peripheral vision, just a flicker of movement to her left, there, at the edge of the inlet. She turned her eyes without moving her head but failed to catch the leaf's landing.

She was about to close her eyes when the same leaf movement stopped her. She leaned forward carefully and shifted to change her sightline on the bundles of wet brush, the plant stems and bracken that lined the far side of the still water. It wasn't a leaf at all. It must have been that smaller piece of stick, the one that had just disturbed the surface of the water. It had fallen. She sighed her relief and eased back against the bank.

Then the piece of stick fell upward.

Jez stared. Yes, that was unquestionably what it had done. It hung there, a handspan over the water. Or did it? She could not see it at all now. She leaned far forward as quietly as she could.

She must have been mistaken. No, there it was again. A thin brown, no, blue, ah, a blue stick? She shifted her bottom slowly and noiselessly toward a neighboring rock. Sure enough, the stick was blue, and sure enough, it was dropping to the edge of a leaf, ducking one end of itself into the water.

Jezebel blinked. Then she leaned toward the slender stick, enfolding it, extending to it, determined to hold it in the center of her perception. It did not move. Her eyes had fooled her, then. All was right with the world, after all.

But a blue stick? She had no sooner formed the thought than the object in question floated upward once more and disappeared, only to appear again instantly, this time perched on her extended elbow. It balanced on legs cornered at precise right angles, and for her fascination it twitched a double pair of delicately veined diaphanous wings. Jez stared into enormous eyes and felt her heart quicken when the insect drew the distal end of its blue-stemmed self into a rounded arch and began poking at its blue-tinged wings as if to separate them or perhaps clean them of some drifting debris.

Tears sprang to her eyes. As if in response to those tears, the frail figure pounded its wings into a lift, sailed to within a wing's breadth of her nose and hovered there at the edge of her astonishment, daring her to see what she could not be seeing.

"Shut your mouth or it will fly in."

The words snapped her head toward Becky. The movement banished the dragonfly. But Becky was nowhere to be seen.

"Get shy, girl. You gotta see this," the voice came again. A mindreach at last from the old woman!

Jez wasted not a moment, but breathed deep and found her inner place of stillness. She shifted to focus upon the image of her double-winged little visitor, praising its lightness, its iridescence, its mobility. She felt her vibrations rise. Still she focused and appreciated. As she began shaking from head to toe, she acknowledged that she was about to enter another world.

It was the sounds that struck her first, sounds her ears had never heard but had only heard about. The forest, this quiescent winter forest, was ablast with them: the crackles and the croaks, the slaps, the pecks, the rasps and the buzzes, the swishes and the cheeps; the susurrus of an established tonic of life; sounds made by things that lope and jump and dart and swing and hop and crawl, by things that climb and slither and fly and pad and swirl, that sniff and suck, chew and ooze, that snap and hiss and claw and sting; sounds that had once told of interwoven strands of life, folding over and around each other, leaning upon and into each other; sounds testifying that here in this dimension such embedded concourse thrived again.

Jezebel sat immobile in a sound-drenched forest, bathed in tears. Beyond her, Becky stood by a spruce tree immersed in a world gone shy. She had taken off her flowered hat and was now holding it over her heart. Jez followed her gaze, expecting to see the Goddess Herself. She saw instead the grubby white suspended body of a young 'possum, probably snoring, its bare rattail coiled around the substantial horizontal branch of a persimmon tree.

For a long time in the chill afternoon, Jez moved her eyes around slowly, letting them rest on sights that no one of her generation had ever seen. Birdflight. Fishglide. Chipmunkscamper. Tadpoletwirl. Snailcreep. Moleburrow. Tickbloat. Spiderweave.

The forest's canopy faded, and a flock of geese covered the sky. A herd of buffalo thunder-trod a canyon. A school of minnows flipped on a lake's surface. Walruses basked, oysters rocked, crayfish crawled, penguins plunged. Visitors came to Jezebel: A nail-tailed wallaby laid its head in her lap, received her affection, sprang away; a Barbary ape investigated her ear; a black-bellied pangolin swept its long tongue down her ankle; and a giant tortoise let her touch two huge eggs buried deep in white sand.

Dusk came and went. They stayed there, the two celebrants, into a foggy night, both of them oblivious to the chill. They listened to the dark sounds of a living forest and watched the prowl of beings that Jez had loved only through the words of Afortunadas or the charity of flatfilms and pictures.

Becky was hugging a pine tree some distance from her, silently searching for the moon, when Jez first heard the singing. Heart pounding, Jez turned uphill, toward the music that was all too familiar to her by now. She had last heard that haunting tune from the little ones in Lavona's house just after she had tucked them into bed.

A band of children was winding down the mountainside, following a deer path and calling out parts of their song to specific animals, to a squirrel here, a rabbit there, their voices light with laughter, their hair almost indistinguishable from the mists rolling about them. Jez could make out at least eight small figures, one of them with her arm raised in greeting.

"Taína!" Jez shouted.

"Calica Jezebel!"

Becky witnessed the conference from her vantage point by the pine tree: Jezebel Stronglaces and a girl-woman, standing transfixed and smiling at each other for a very long time in the heart of an oak and maple forest, while mists and moonlight wove wonder around their motionless bodies. At last the small figure moved out of sight behind the band of singing children, and Jezebel stood waving at shades and spirits in the trees.

In the dawn, with the awakening of the sunlight world, the old woman and her companion moved one nanosecond away from those who were shying, and from the magic of the night. In that second they returned to silence and emptiness.

Jez and Becky sat for the last time around glowing quartz filings in the old woman's cave room. They toasted each other with crystal-cooled root wine, drinking their farewell with appreciation and thanksgiving.

A long embrace.

Then Jezebel turned swiftly and ran down a labyrinth of tunnels to the bottom of the old elevator shaft. When she lifted and floated to its top, she held herself suspended there for fully a minute while she watched the shallow breathing of Dicken's sleeping form, sprawled on the cold black floor. She stretched out beside that body and received the flood of joy that threatened to consume her.

It was hours before Jezebel could make words work for her, and days before she could articulate the urgency that she carried from the bowels of the West Virginia mountain.

"I have to talk with Zude," finally she said to Dicken. "Very soon."

6

[2088 C.E.]

> Listening is the highest expression of wisdom.
> *Vade Mecum for the Journey*

H*e-e-e-e-e-ya!*
  The sands and shadows by the rivers!
  Seh nuh w-a-a-a-n-yu! The ayllu and all its people!
  E-e-e-e-yan-wu! Stones, hold me!
  Stormclouds, shake the oleander blossoms!
  I cover the fog with my hand!
  My strong foot drags. My follow foot awakens.
  I breathe the air of change.
  I drink the water of silence.
Hey ya anah ah ah!

Thus sang Eti, Acuai tribeswoman, with her wide mouth and
big throat. Similarly sang all of the tribespeakers of Nueva Tierra
Sur's steaming green jungles. They sang in response to the tidings
brought by footpaths and windstreams, by runnels and brooklets,
by drumsong and dreamshare. From as far south as the waters of
Rogagua, from as far north as the Guiana Highlands, across the
broad continent from its mountainous western backbone to its
eastern sea, came the news: The tribes, the People, die.

Whole villages in the selva realized simultaneously that few
women were pregnant or that many who were, miscarried. Babies
not stillborn often lived healthily for months only to refuse
to awaken one morning from their apparently peaceful sleep.

123

Increasingly, children below the age of puberty—some with white or gray hair, some balding, a few with unaltered brown or black or yellow locks—calmly announced their intention to die, then did so. Children who had achieved full puberty lived as adults, without incident or apparent threat.

Throughout the selva the outcries of grief throbbed long into the nights, long into the days. In every corner of the forest, learning centers closed, small fresh graves filled up the burying fields, and streets and pathways grew quiet. Parents and would-be parents encountered each other silently with hollow eyes, drawn cheeks. And always, always among the women and men of the People, one heart would speak to another to say, "Your loss is my own."

As on other continents, sexual activity was at an all-time high as efforts at conception intensified. Both the hearths of mid-wives—who supervised ovular mergings—and the daily schedules of the men who could give seed were very busy. Amid ceremonies of grief and loss, tribes danced in ceaseless rituals for fertility and virility. Cults of child-worship emerged in some ayllus; sometimes a village's remaining children were lionized by the affection of stricken adults; sometimes adults would stay close to the children, insisting upon watching them even while they slept, until the children themselves had to hide in order to escape the obsessions of their elders. Madness and suicide among adults increased in direct ratio to the amount of a tribe's industrialization.

But among the People, in every household and communal orb, there emerged as well another and more widespread response, for a radical understanding was settling upon their hearts. After a hundred tales of barren women, after a hundred anguishings of impotent men, after a hundred goodbyes to those who had lived among them for such sweet short seasons, they knew with unshakable certainty that the time had come for their forest home to say goodbye to the only animals left within its depths.

Many believed that the demise of the People was the natural extension of the exodus of non-human animals. They reminded each other that the People had become extinct many times before in the history of the forest, and that always they had respeciated and returned. Many more believed that the vanishing of the People would mean a return to the selva of the boar and the monkey, of the black warbler and the slow anaconda. All knew that, like the death of one woman or one man, the death of all women and men was but a sleep and a passing.

And so they attended to their daily tasks, reflecting upon the dust stirred by the broom or the sway of water in the gourd. Now and again they anticipated the changes to come and praised their gods and loved one another, especially their children. They cleansed themselves in the waterfalls in order to be worthy of the unfolding that was upon them. And they rested, as they always had, under giant ferns or babassu palms when they tired of their tasks.

On that same continent, in Nueva Tierra Sur, in South Brazil, was Belo Horizonte. The city was near the Atlantic; almost the whole width of the continent lay between it and the mighty Cordillera de los Andes along the Pacific Coast. Partly because it had been a planned city from its birth in the late 19th century, and partly because the crash of the meat industry and epidemics had inflicted huge population losses, Belo Horizonte had yielded gracefully to its transformation into a bailiwick.

The city was surrounded by iron mines, returning forests, and plains once devoted to intensive livestock production. The containment fields that marked its outlying sectors accommodated 2,200 bailiwick habitantes and the free citizens who chose to live near them or, in the case of habitantes who were trusties, with them. Within the city, large buildings now housed modest bureaucracies.

Most of the city's pavements had long since been allowed to revert to dirt, historically a matter of hot contention in South Brazil's quarter-trapy web and in its demesne bar. On this day, the streets that had been mud the evening before were now puffing dust with each footfall. The air was sharp. Paraná pines swayed with quick alertness to every change in the breeze.

In the southeast sector of the bailiwick, a large dust dervish erupted and began collecting a crowd. At its center, two men rolled on the ground in a loud curse-filled contest. Each attempted to strangle the other while spectators shouted encouragements and criticisms.

In the adjacent square, from their cement bench and portable stools, four women left off their finger-weaving to watch.

"It's Diogo. Inés's husband," Camila Lins Gonzaga informed the others.

"Where's Inés?" asked Alfreda Gala do Rego.

"Who knows?" shrugged Tui Machado.

"The gringo is on the bottom," observed Camila.

"That's no surprise," commented Tui.

The fourth woman had divested her fingers of the brightly colored cloth threads. She brushed back a wisp of graying hair and looked for just a moment as if she'd join in the disruption. Then she stilled herself and leaned back on the bench, her legs wide under her faded green print skirt.

"What do they fight about, Ti Tui?" she asked.

"Who knows?" answered Tui. Then she turned to a young man who stood nearby. "Diniz," she beckoned, holding up bottled water.

Diniz moved closer and with a bow of thanks drank from the bottle. "Craziness," he muttered. "Pombal, there on the bottom, was delivering feijão to the food stalls." He addressed the oldest woman. "He said Diogo tripped him, Ti Camila."

"And that's all it took," nodded Camila. She moved her threads with tight jerks.

In the street the crowd was larger, the voices louder. The fight was escalating to brawl proportions.

The woman in the green skirt fingered her long braid. Then she took off her hemp sandal and deliberately dislodged a pebble from its thong. Her eyes casually searched the streets, the square, even the sky.

The young man wiped his cheek on his sleeve. "Pombal is dangerous," he said. "His daughter just died. Foot-Shrieves found him yesterday in the mercado with a knife. He was asking others to stab him. To kill him."

A shriek came from the crowd. One of the bystanders threw himself into the brawl, pulling Diogo off the other man. Diniz left the women and moved into the street. The green-skirted woman stood up.

Camila pulled her down again. "Leave them be," she growled.

"The Vigilantes. Where are they?" whispered Gala.

"Who knows shere…"

Tui was interrupted by the arrival of Vigilantes, a gert of Flying Daggers who landed to flank the fight. With strong hands the two Kanshou separated and subdued the men, got them to their feet, and began breaking up the crowd. "Get along, now!" they urged. "Show's over!" As the crowd dispersed, the Vigilantes drew the three men aside, talking with them, listening and nodding.

The woman in the green skirt watched the interchange until it seemed that all was well. The two original assailants were grudgingly apologizing to each other. The taller Kanshou, still in conversation with one of the men, eventually walked off with him. Her partner, also still talking, went in the opposite direction with the other man and his friend.

A sigh or two, and the women resumed their mid-morning finger-weaving. "That is how it is these days," said Camila, pulling her strands tight.

"How is that?" asked the fourth woman.

"It is the pain," answered Gala. "The pain."

"Even here in the bailiwick," mused the inquirer, biting through a thin string.

"What do you think?" Camila exclaimed. "You think just because these men are habitantes that they have no pain? You think they do not mourn the loss of their children! You think…"

Gala overspoke the older woman. "Roma visits us, Ti Camila, here in the bailiwick. She visits Braga and Carolina. In the trusties' sector."

"She has no understanding. Or she would not ask such a question." Camila yanked a strand of red into place.

"A thousand pardons, senhora," said Roma. "I spoke not so much a question as a reminder to myself that the whole world shares a great grief."

Mollified skepticism passed over Camila's face. She grunted.

"I shall bind my tongue," Roma said.

"Never," Tui interceded, then addressed the older woman. "No one can be hushed in these days, Camila."

"Speak then," Camila grumbled, waving her hand.

Tui took up the turn. "I do not live with Basilio, my habitante," she explained to Roma, "for he is not a trusty. But I have lived here, near his barracks, for five years. This bailiwick has always been very orderly, maybe because so many free citizens choose to be here near their habitantes." She paused. "Dying children have brought many responses. Particularly from the men."

She held up her hand with its web of covered fingers so that Gala could splice its threads into the strings on her own hand. Then she eased her hand out of the creation she had woven upon it and handed the fabric to Gala. "Like this fighting," she finished.

"Some have tried to escape," said Gala, leaning forward on her knees as she integrated Tui's contribution into her own weaving. "Some try to kill others."

"Do many try to kill?" asked Roma.

"No. Only some. Three days ago a man set a fire in the hospital saying, 'What does it matter now, since we will all die?'"

"Baboseira!" snorted Camila. "Always we have known we will die."

Gala was patient. "Ti Camila, he meant the way it happens, the way we outlive the children. We die without the children."

Camila grumbled as she fished about in her string sack. A stout woman with a small child approached the group.

"Chia," Gala said. "And Fidela." She took the child's hand and kissed it. Fidela rewarded her with a smile. "This is Senhora Roma. And you know Ti Tui." The child ducked her head in acknowledgement.

Camila grunted and pointed with her chin to the stool at her side. She watched while the newcomer sat on it and withdrew a soft hairbrush from her bag.

Chia held the brush in front of Fidela's face and asked a question with her eyebrows.

Fidela smiled and nodded vigorously. She drew Chia's tote bag under her and settled herself between the woman's knees.

Chia began brushing the child's long black hair. For a moment all the women ceased their activity and watched as the child closed her eyes to permit the gentle stroking.

Tui broke the silence, tightening a new row of orange strings around her fingers. "The world is changing," she said. "Every person has been touched by losing the children."

"First the animals," said Camila, "then the men." She pulled on a single thread. It responded by unraveling itself.

"Now the little ones," Gala nodded.

Tui added bright blue thread to her pattern. "But it is not all fighting or frustration."

"No," agreed Gala. "There is also magic." She tied off the juncture of her two fabrics and set them aside.

"Faugh!" Camila barely refrained from spitting.

Gala pushed a finger-splayed hand toward Camila. "It is true! Watch the flatcasts, Camila! Every day a thousand more people will do an impossible thing. They move rocks with their minds, they levitate, they talk with the dead, they dance with joy at funerals!"

Camila stared at Gala from heavy-lidded eyes. "I watch the flatcasts. And I do not see your magic. I see the riots in big cities. I see people who do not know what to do with their anger. They attack public buildings. Sometimes they attack Vigilantes. I watch the flatcasts. And that is what I see."

Roma, the visitor, listened and wound her threads.

"In Diamantina," Chia said to Camila, "two men flew together from noon until dusk. They flew. Like spooning women. Two men."

"You saw them, my Chia." Camila pulled outward on each of her unraveling strings, ungloving her fingers. "You of course saw them."

"No, but others did."

"Ti Camila," Gala urged, "a time like this has never been before! Not just earthquakes and volcanoes. The people of the selvas, they speak of forest noises. And right here in this bailiwick there are huge religious services, all kinds, every day! You have seen them. You know it! The people of the world stand on tiptoe, breathing great waterfalls of air. They wait, Camila. They wait."

"They wait for God? Tola!" Camila spat.

Tui shook her head. "Not for God." She worked with new threads of many colors, setting them swiftly between her fingers.

Camila pursed her lips and rested her eyes on the child near her feet. "We die," she announced.

"'Baboseira!'" Gala imitated Camila. "'Always we have known we will die!'" The others laughed as Gala put her arm around the grim figure beside her.

Camila looked at the hand on her shoulder. She looked at Gala, then at the others. "Death is one thing," she snorted. "An end to birth is another."

The faces around her sobered. In the silence Camila began a smaller cantlet with her unraveled threads.

Chia paused in her brushing, her hand on Fidela's shoulder. "There is the heart of it," she said. "No babies coming." She brushed. "They are cloning humans now, the scientists."

"They have not been successful, Chia," Gala interposed. "They only hope."

"They are crazed," Tui added, her colored threads flying. "Madwomen, trying to save the race."

Roma, the visitor, listened and wove her threads.

The sun blazed. The many swift fingers made no sound.

Gala wiped one sleeve over her sweating face. "In the cities they freeze people," she observed. "Cryosleep, they call it. They will wake up in a hundred years."

"They will wake up alone," Camila scoffed.

"I heard," said Tui, "that in Beijing they have frozen a girl child and a boy child." She made a sound that registered her disgust. "They think they can make Adam and Eve." She wove all the faster.

Chia brushed on. "We never imagined this before. The earth without people."

"The Earth will be happy without us." Tui wove without looking at her work.

"Will She?" asked Gala.

Tui waved a hand. "Of course. Then She can bring forth something different. Already She is gestating. The Earth is our only expectant mother."

Gala watched a pair of women set up a flimsy stall on the far corner of the square. Long Life Guaranteed! shouted the sign, 20 Credits Per! Gala spliced two strings.

"We may not all die," said Chia. She spoke through the two barrettes she held between her teeth, one hand still parting Fidela's hair, one still brushing.

"Ha!" growled Camila. She wound a curly thread into a broadening ball.

"It may not happen, avoa," Chia insisted, keeping the barrettes dry with small sucking sounds. In the silence she inserted one of the clamps over Fidela's left ear, snapping it closed. She looked around the circle of women. "Hope is a choice," she said, a shade too heartily. She drew the brush again and again through the hair over the child's right ear. The women wove their strings.

"You don't fear that death, Ti Gala?" Roma spoke in the silence.

"Of the whole race?"

"Yes." Roma bit a string.

"The Imandade, the Sisters, ask the same question," answered Gala. "No. We do not fear it."

Chia set the last clasp through the child's hair.

"Only the men fear it," said Tui, standing and bending forward. She handed a multicolored clump of strings to Fidela, who grinned her thanks and sank to the dust in a focus of unscrambling. Before she reseated herself, Tui let her hand rest a moment on the child's shining hair.

Chia still brandished the brush. "Tui, you're a sourpuss. Men? Why do they fear it more than women?"

"Because they are not women," Tui said, impelled by Chia's shrug and upward-rolling eyes to complete an intricate knot over her thumb with a wide flourish. "Death, like birth, is female," she went on. "We all know that."

"I know that," said Gala.

"Certainly." Tui resumed her work. "Men think of themselves as unique and separate. They fear losing that separateness in death." She cut her eyes from Camila to Chia, then to Roma. "Do you fear it?" she challenged.

Roma met her eyes. "Not for myself. Not even for the race." She looked away. "I only fear it for those I love."

Camila grunted. The other women nodded. Chia hugged her legs closer around Fidela.

Roma corrected herself. "No, that's not it." She drew her knees together and leaned on them, her weaving dangling. "I fear my own loneliness."

In the long silence Camila did not grunt.

"Some say the habitantes will now go free," said Chia brightly.

"Lies," said Camila. She picked up a snarl of Fidela's hair cast aside by Chia and examined it carefully. "They want to make them docile."

"You mean the Testing? Wake up, Ti!" Gala punched Camila with a playful elbow. "Nobody's about to get experimented on.

Central Web canceled consideration of the Testing and the Protocols. Indefinitely."

"Maybe," said Camila. She tucked the ball of hair into the deep cleavage between her breasts. "Maybe."

Chia began the small stirrings of impending departure. "And the rules are getting looser," she assured the others, motioning Fidela to gather her strings. "Antero will stay again tonight with Fidela and me. He was with us twice last week, too."

"Before you go, Ti Chia," said Roma, "tell me something." Chia halted her movements. "Tell me what you think things would be like if it were true, if the rumor were true."

"What rumor?"

"That the habitantes will now be freed," answered Roma, fanning her green skirt against the increasing heat of the sun.

"Ah, what a blessing! And why not, I ask, why not…"

Chia's response was cut off by the group's shift of attention. Two uniformed figures approached them from across the square. The taller of the Flying Daggers said, "Senhoras, excuse us. We are Vigilantes Truza and Satores. We need to ask if you know one of the men fighting. Pombal Tranco."

No one spoke for a moment. Roma was rummaging in her string bag.

Then Gala said, "Diniz, a young habitante from Sabara. He told us he knew him."

"Is Diniz family?" asked Satores. "We need someone to accompany Pombal to Rio. He must have extensive care."

"I know Diniz," Chia said, rising and taking Fidela's hand. "And he knows the man's friends. Diniz will be in the hemp shop." She pointed.

"Good," said Satores, making a sign to her partner and setting off alone for the shop.

"May I ask you questions about Diogo?" Vigilante Truza scanned the faces of the group.

Chia called suddenly to Satores. "Kanshou! Over there! It's around the corner!" Then she looked at the tall officer. "We're going that way. I'll show her." Anticipating Truza's nod of approval, she said short farewells to the women.

"I must leave, too," said Roma, standing and holding Chia back for a moment. "I am a visitor, Vigilante Truza, and know none of the parties involved."

The Vigilante studied Roma's face. "Of course," she said, her brow furrowed. "Of course. Your name, though, senhora?"

"Roma Alves Nabuco. I registered at Northgate Two last night and I visit Brag Callo, trusty of third district." Roma's voice was soft but she looked directly at the Kanshou.

"I see," said the officer slowly. Then she nodded and smiled a dismissal. As she turned back to the other members of the group, she cast a puzzled look over her shoulder toward the two departing women. Chia and Roma each held one of the little girl's hands.

Senhora Roma Nabuco said affectionate farewells to Chia and Fidela before they caught up with Vigilante Satores. She waved an abrupt goodbye to the young Kanshou and then made her way slowly down a long street lined with trees. No one saw her turn into an alley and quicken her step. She assured herself that no eyes watched the alley, then raised her green skirt and vaulted over a chest-high fence with the agility of a teenager.

In the privacy of a banho cubicle, Roma Nabuco sat upright on the waste stool, her eyes closed. She breathed slowly, evenly. She invoked an inner companion.

"Swallower," she whispered, "I'm frayed and frazzled."

"Breathe," came the response.

Roma breathed. Questions, duties and fears swirled inside her brain.

"Empty," said the voice.

Minutes later, the chaos in Roma's spinning head was gathered and ordered into discrete enclosures, and her mindspace glowed with a welcome serenity. She forsook the worries of that inner territory and hung above it in a bubble of nothingness. She held the balance there, breathing delicately. She was content.

"Now remember joy."

Joy, she thought, like at the acme of a stick dance, her body swooping and bending to the escalating beat, the delight of her duet with the flashing stick, the bright high leap and the twirl into ecstasy. She laughed aloud.

"And now to work!"

Roma Nabuco emerged from the restroom on the back of a new-found energy. A tiny light flickered around her, dipping and dancing as it led her back to the responsibilities of her day in the Belo Horizonte Bailiwick. Before sesta, Roma Nabuco had visited two electronic assembly lines, talking to three habitantes who worked there; dallied at dice on a short break with habitante employees at the solar conversion plant; and washed dishes with free citizens at a bailiwick common kitchen. By dusk she had changed clothes and hairfalls twice—and had made the acquaintance of trade liaisons, free citizen roustabouts, crematorium grips, habitante rights advocates, and extra-bailiwick communication clerks.

Clad in the dark blue coveralls of a trusty, she delivered supper to habitantes confined to barracks rooms, assessing the words and looks, the sounds and textures of those who would chat with her. In the evening, she unobtrusively attended meetings of habitantes where she would not be challenged, sitting with them in common rooms, listening to their interactions until the call to quarters was signaled.

She spent the night with old friends and rose early the following day to talk with more habitantes: credit balancers, public cushcar operators, hospice counselors, food processors, musicians, dental technicians, fabric designers, bereaved lower-school teachers. By late afternoon, when she said goodbye to road maintenance crews and water purification monitors, she felt satisfied that she had heard opinions from habitantes strictly confined as well as from those who participated in every working part of the infrastructure that supported the Belo Horizonte Bailiwick operations.

The only elements of bailiwick society she had assiduously avoided were the Vigilantes. More than once she had skulked around a corner or waited impassively before proceeding when Kanshou passed close by.

But in the early evening she presented herself without disguise to a quiet room in the Bailiwick Vigilancia. There she made three requests: The immediate use of a comstation for two brief calls, the good company of the Vigilancia's commanding officer over a light meal, and the gerting services of Vigilantes Truza and Satores, who, if they were willing and available, could fly her to Rio de Janeiro.

"Ria." The comchannel was occasionally distorted but the audio was clear. "How are they?"

"Oh, Zudie!" Ria exclaimed. "I'm so glad to hear from you. She's fine. Both of them are fine. You can hear Enrique now, can't you? He's banging around, making a fort out of the garden shed."

"A fort?"

"A fort. I wonder how he got so inspired by the military?" Ria's face was all innocence.

"But he's okay?"

"Fine. And so is she." There was a pause. "Her hair is a little more white." Ria's eyes filled up. She smiled brightly. "It's very pretty." Then she pushed her palms into her eyes. "Shit!"

"Ria."

Ria shook her head. Her eyes had almost recovered. "She insisted on going to classes today. And their group, I mean, you know, the little group that…"

"I know."

"Well, the group went to a midcity hospice this afternoon and sat with several old people. All of them, all of the hospice residents they visited, well, all of them were so delighted to see the children. And then all of them, all of the residents, I mean, they all…Zude, they all died. Zudie, it was very strange. The workers said that it was wonderful, that the whole room was filled with light. One of them, they said, one of them died holding Regina in her arms, and laughing and singing a jazzy song. Can you handle that?"

"Yes. Yes, I can."

"You sound tired."

"A little. But I'll be home in another day. I'll take a rocket tonight to Bogotá. That's my last stop. Then home."

"Good."

"Eva? Kayita?"

"All fine. Kayita gives Regina a very funny look sometimes, like she…"

"Tell her I'm on my way, Ria. Don't let her get any ideas."

"Oh, she wouldn't do that. She may be old, but she still loves all this too much. Besides, she wants to hear about Brazil. Says you promised her a travelogue."

"Right."

A pause.

"Bosca has been here every day," Ria said.

"She is good."

"Yes. Yes, she is." Ria was nodding, her eyes shut tight.

"I'll try to call tomorrow night. But no matter what, I will see you day after tomorrow."

"Right." Ria smiled a little.

"Abrazos."

"Y besos. Travel safe."

"I will."

"Edge, are we on a secure channel?"

"Double damper, Magister. But audio only."

"That's okay. I want you to send a protected comcube to Yotoma and Lin-ci Win, if you can find her, saying the following: 'Phasing out bailiwicks must be an option, maybe a certainty. Will call.' Add anything you feel important, and tell them I'll be back day after tomorrow."

"Done."

"You okay?"

"Fine, Magister."

"Everything else okay?"

"Lots of things to interest you when you get back. Nothing urgent."

"Thanks, Edge. I'll check in tomorrow night."

"Indeed, Magister."

"Indeed, Captain."

It was well after dark when two Flying Daggers lifted a precious cargo over Belo Horizonte, circled the city, then headed for Rio. Before Vigilantes Truza and Satores landed, they were each privileged to own a square of marajó finger-weaving, a personal creation of their Magister.

7

[2O88 C.E.]

> Threads move back and forth
> through universes
> over moons and under suns.
> Your breath on my cheek
> stirs wind on a pond
> ten thousand light-years away.
> *Weaves from the Matrix*

"Adverb, tsa-a-ah, if you had any horse sense, tsa-a-ah, you would know I got a few matters of my own to deal with, tsa-a-a-ah."

Yotoma panted as she hugged the vertical rope with her arms, then forced her knees to bend deep once more so her feet could grasp the rough hemp for the next push upward. "You think maybe, tsa-ah, you're the only one digging short graves? Tsa-a-a-ah!" Her panting got louder but so did her voice. "Think you're the only one, tsa-a-ah, got processions of self-flagellates in the streets, or crazy women trying to nurse dolls? Tsa-a-ah! Or broad-daylight kidnappings, tsa-a-ah, or homemade bombs in the suburbs? Tsa-a-a-ah!"

Yotoma pushed out her last puff of air as she triumphantly reached the top of her climb and swung there at rest, talking toward Zude's holofigure. "Look at me, child!" Her free hand was on her hip.

In her office nearly half a world away, a lethargic Zude obediently pressed out her cigarillo of treated seaweed and smoothed the arms of her softshirt. Then she folded her hands and leaned on her console table, staring at a holo-image from the faraway Aegean: Flossie Yotoma Lutu, Magister of the Africa-Europe-Mideast Tri-Satrapy, swaying like a chorus girl seven meters above the holocameras.

For a moment Yotoma studied the subdued visage of her colleague and friend. Then she unwound herself and dropped like a stone onto the trampoline below her. She did not bounce.

Zude's attention was arrested in spite of herself.

"You're working in augmented gravity?"

"Yup. It's up by thirty percent." Yotoma heaved her body off the tramp and stood, rubbing her close-cropped gray hair with a towel of bright Femmedarme Green. Then she sat on the edge of the trampoline and leered at Zude. "But oh, Might of the Mbeles, do I climb like a bug when I switch back to normal! Ha!" She gave a special dig into her ears and then swung the towel down to her lap. "I've been rough on you," she confessed. "So say me. About Regina."

"Not much to tell, Floss." Zude sank back into her chair. "I've been around the world and back. Nobody can help her. That magus you sent me did manage to tune into her songs. Did you know that all of them who are dying are singing the same melodies and doing the same rituals? All in that same strange language. All over Little Blue."

Zude's eyes sought Yotoma's with a deep weariness. "We've run every test known to health and healing, and she's fine. They've magnified her tissues up to the thousandth power and read her circuits in every possible combination of tracks. Traced her whole life electromagnetically. I sat for hours and watched that little soul of hers producing cell after cell, beautiful cells, healthy cells, in every part of her body. All the healers declare her compound energy anatomy to be in top-notch condition." Bleakly, Zude watched her thumb as it rubbed against the edge of the console table. "She's just quiet." She looked again at Yotoma. "And she says she thinks she will leave us in six days."

Abruptly, Magister Adverb's face contorted. She struck the console top with both hands and shot out of her chair with an exclamation that Yotoma could only call a howl.

Magister Lutu watched her friend lunge toward the wall of glass that revealed, below and beyond, the sparkling blanket of the Los Angeles city lights. When Zude seemed about to fling herself against that wall, Yotoma stood and called out, "Zudie!"

Zude rested her head on the window surface. "I am okay, Floss," she responded. She turned to face Yotoma's holo-image. "But it's not like there are other niñas just around the corner, you know!" She threw up her hands and paced the wall's length. "Flossie, I never thought I'd pray for babies to be born." She leaned on the back of one of the sofas. "I've always worried about us having too many of them. Now I'd like it to rain babies! Let them be born by the litters! By the hundreds! I just want to see a baby again, one that's not going to squeeze my finger and grin at me and then die tomorrow!" Zude flung herself onto one of the deep sofas, head in her hands.

Yotoma eyed Zude in silence. Then she said, "Have you got a body to hold you, child? I'll be there on non-stop rocket."

Zude smiled a little. "Thanks, Flossie. Not necessary. Ria and I have been doing lots of holding." She checked her tacto-time. "And Bosca's coming." The floor captured her stare. When she spoke again, her voice was a whisper. "We can't reach Reggie. She seems loving, lets us put our arms around her and all that. But she's, ah, polite, almost. It's like she's in another place, a place we can't go."

Yotoma said nothing.

Zude still stared. "I will handle it, Floss. We'll lose her. And Enrique, too." She glanced at Yotoma. "He's okay, so far." She leaned on her knees. "I'll survive. We'll all of us over twenty going to survive. But what then? Or does it even matter?"

Yotoma wiped her face. "Pretty natural, wouldn't you say, to resist death? That's all we're doing, Zude. No business as usual anymore." She paused, then spoke vigorously. "You ought to see the pink lather that Medicine is in over here. Downright frantic. Every research institute staff's working and worrying around the clock, most of them on double shifts. All the blessed night they prefigure and test and titrate and fluoresce and precipitate! And they come up with the same big nothing as before. And all that time they got crowds screaming at them, sitting in their foyers or in cushcar lots shouting, 'Save us, save us! The race is dying!' And the researchers themselves drag home 72 hours later and cry with their own barren partners and use up a mile or two of holofilm on their own white-haired children." Yotoma wiped her face, rubbing her eyes especially hard. "It will make a weeper out of an angel."

Zude was quiet.

Yotoma tried again to raise some collegial interest. "In Medina," she said, cataloguing as she paced, "the 'Darmes confiscated a so-called fertility drug that's already killed 300 women. In Johannesburg and Helsinki, pharmaceutical houses have given up trying to do business and closed down completely. For that matter, whole bunches of demesne webs have quit, too, for lack of a quorum. Everybody's either shrieking in fear or drowning in a pot of depression. The whole Mediterranean coast is jammed with religious ceremonies, and when they're not praying they're fornicating. Orgies block the streets of Leipzig, all night, all day. Everybody in rut, everybody hoping to reproduce."

Zude was nodding. "Here, too." She reached for her seaweed cigarillos, threw the package down, and clasped her hands. Calmly she said, "Flossie, could I be incompetent?"

"What?"

"I know, I know. Everybody's feeling that way, I guess. But my mind's been doing spooky things. I can't think straight sometimes, couldn't remember Edge's pager sequence the other day. And I get these impulses, like today I started humming salsa tunes in staff meeting. Had to keep myself from dancing. Wild dreams, silly notions…" She ran her hands through her hair.

Flossie Yotoma Lutu narrowed her eyes, taking full measure of Zude's state of mind. She reconfigured the holo-angles and brought her image into close-up capacity on Zude's receptor field. She sat on the floor in front of her trampoline.

"Magister Adverb," she said, "trust me. You are not incompetent and you are not even a little crazy." She paused. "Now. You don't sound at all interested in the affairs of this planet of ours, but we got some business. You feel up to it?"

Zude raised her head.

Flossie gave her neck a broad swipe with the towel. "I finally ran down our dragon. Magister Lin-ci Win."

Zude gathered her attention. Then she activated her own close-up link and put her colleague's life-size image right across from her. "Where was she?"

"Doesn't matter. Off in some Fujian convent. Retreating." Yotoma took a long breath. "Zudie, you and I, we been talking this thing into the ground. About freeing the habitantes." She held up her hand to stop Zude's interruption. "And I have not given you an ounce of support about it." She leaned against the trampoline. "Fact is, when you first said it to me, I did figure you'd gone one brick shy of a load. I said to Self, 'Self, am I hearing right? She wants to put a million people back on the streets?

All of them violent, some of them killers, and bingo! right now! Why, Self, we'd have to double the number of Kanshou overnight to handle that change!' And Self says to me, 'Yes, that seems to be what the girl is suggesting.' But then Self reminds me, saying, 'But Flossie, nobody knows more about bailiwicks than Zudie does. Bailiwicks are her thing, remember? So you just take a balance-breath and think about it,' Self says to me."

Yotoma watched Zude carefully. "Now I figure maybe our Zudie hasn't lost her cookies after all." She hung the towel around her neck and leaned forward. "By the time I'd laid out all your arguments to Lin-ci Win for closing down the bailiwicks—and added a few of my own—your crackpot idea was not just logical. It seemed like our only option. Let the habitantes live out their lives in freedom, like the rest of us. Send them back to their families, to their children if they've got any. Given the state of the world, it's only right."

Zude relaxed a little, into the cushioned sofa. "No joke?" She smiled wanly.

"No joke." Yotoma smiled back. "Look, Adverb. What's the worst that could happen? Let's say we let them go, and then all the children don't die after all. Let's say the human enterprise has not ended, that it's only paused a little to shake us up some. So then the worst we got to do is say to these released habitantes, 'Sorry folks, we thought we were finished as a species but we're not. So now we have to remand you into custody, put you back into your bailiwick again.' Or maybe we wait and see if they need to be sent back. Maybe they will have learned all the lessons they need to learn. Maybe we all will."

Yotoma paused.

"I figure it's worth it, Zudie."

She paused again.

"So I'll line up my boots beside yours when you lay out the proposal for the Heart and the Central Web."

Zude swallowed against a big welling up of tears. "Floss!" she cried, and in the next instant found herself laughing ruefully. "Flossie, Flossie!" she exclaimed, hugging herself. "Here's a little irony: You're finally ready to let the habitantes go free, and I just spent this afternoon convincing myself that we shouldn't try to do it after all!"

She leaned toward Flossie, excited now. "Admit it, Floss, the bailiwicks work like nothing else ever has! They contain violence, keep it out of the way of ordinary citizens, and they do it without taking away the dignity of the habitantes! Looked at historically…"

A roar from the Aegean stopped her.

"Zude! You're shuffling back and forth like a drunk crossing heavy traffic!" Yotoma was bending into the holofield toward her Co-Magister, thrusting each word across the distances with her pointed finger. "How in All the Fields of Glory are you and me and our Nirvana-bound Lin-ci Win going to hold this lunatic show together if you keep switching ground? How am I going to convince Lin-ci…"

"Floss, maybe nobody can hold it together. Maybe we shouldn't try!"

Silence filled the holowaves. Yotoma stared at her friend. "I take it all back," she said calmly. "You are crazy." She rested her back against the trampoline. "Maybe I am, too."

Zude stared at her.

Yotoma chuckled. "Zudie, you give me such soul-smarting grief."

Zude relaxed. "We're tired," she offered. "And we don't live in very ordinary times."

Yotoma finally spoke into the silence. "Today's Monday. I am due in Vancouver Thursday. I'll come to Los Angeles that night. I want to see Regina. And you, child."

Zude nodded. "Thanks, Flossie."

"And now I got to perish on this rope. Two more climbs before I go to work." Yotoma's eyes imprisoned Zude. "It is all just like it is supposed to be," she said slowly. "And when a soul passes, Zudie, any soul, always it is carried on the backs of a thousand cranes. Always."

Then she was gone.

"Yeah," Zude whispered, staring at the empty spot that a moment before had held Yotoma's image. She pushed herself up, and deactivated the holo-unit. Aimlessly she moved around the familiar furnishings. She picked up magnopads and laid them down, she brushed off consoles and arranged sofa cushions.

With a sigh she activated her wall panels. Statistics and graphics flowed in and out of the room. She noted that bailiwicks still reported small salvos of vandalism and anti-social behavior. No big revolts. Just yelps of pain, sporadic bursts of impotence and grief. Public forums and chat-chambers, gathertalks and vent meetings—all were busy, all were doing their job. She wiped the screens and closed her eyes. "Swallower," she whispered.

A tiny light flickered in her mind. "Joy," it whispered back. "Joy?" Zude yelled. "Ha!" She reached for the silver case that held her real cigarillos, then rethought the desire and explosively flung the case across the room. It hit the taxidermed calico cat, knocking it from its perch to the floor. She was instantly at the animal's side, swooping it up with apologetic murmurings.

When Captain Edge escorted Bosca to the office's dissolving entranceway, they found a casually clad Magister, sitting cross-legged on the carpet, stroking an armful of very stiff cat.

"Dealing with my nurturing instincts," Zude explained, trying to smile in welcome.

"I see," the tall woman smiled back.

In contrast to the dampened energy field that accompanied the departing Captain Edge, Bosca blazed like the noonday sun. Zude allowed herself a bit of congratulation that she was able now to observe this phenomenon.

Bosca slipped off her cotton shoes and drew her feet onto the sofa beneath her long skirt. Zude came and sat beside her.

"Well," Zude began, carefully setting the cat aside. Her grin was genuine but truncated. She covered Bosca's hand with her own, holding it tight for a moment.

Bosca searched Zude's face. "How are you?"

"Good," Zude boomed, for emphasis shaking the hand that she held. "I'm good, Bosca." Her heartiness faded. "Wipe that," she almost whispered. "I'm no good at all." She looked at Bosca. "Barely holding it all together, in fact."

Bosca waited.

Zude let her head droop and rested her elbows on her knees. "It just seems like so much pain right now." She imprisoned her hair in her fists and tugged, first one hand and then the other, as if her distress lived in her scalp and she could uproot it by hand. "A season of pain."

Bosca touched Zude only with her voice. "A season of pain," she echoed.

Zude nodded. Then her chest expanded with a huge intake of air. Her downward sigh became a sob. She fell against Bosca, lodging her head in the long neck and inviting the long arms to surround her. The arms obliged her, cuddling her like a child and catching her drenching tears. Zude cried hard, filling the office with her wails. And Bosca held her, a firm, gentle bower for the sorrow.

Some minutes later they sat more easily in the sofa's deep cushions, Zude breathing smoothly again and Bosca enclosing one of Zude's hands with both of her own.

"I had a visit with Regina," Bosca said.

Zude matched her voice to the texture of the moment. "You saw her today?"

"Well, yes, but only briefly. My real visit with her was last night."

"Oh?"

"We dreamwalked," Bosca said.

Small hairs rose on the back of Zude's neck. "You what?"

"We met. In our sleep."

"You mean like spooners?"

"No, no, no." Bosca shook Zude's hand. "You keep thinking that magic only happens between lovers." She spoke slowly, as if to ensure Zude's understanding. "Last night Regina called to me. From her sleep." Zude stared at her. "So I went dancing with her on the High Road," Bosca finished.

Zude felt dizzy. Carefully she took a large open breath and nodded very slowly.

"Like you did in Punto," Bosca resumed briskly, nodding with Zude, "when you left your body to get the computer codes." She squeezed her friend's hand. "Zude, I want us to walk with Regina together, you and me." When Zude's mouth flew open, Bosca hurried on. "I understood so much from her! Things she can't tell us in her body. I felt like I had dropped a huge burden. You might feel better, too, if you met her there."

Zude shot off the sofa. "Bosca! I can't!"

"You can, Zude!" Bosca's voice filled Zude's body, down to her toes. "You're getting to be a regular card-carrying psychic, Magister Adverb."

Zude combed her hair with her fingers. There was a long pause. "All right. I'll try, but…"

"Good! We can do it whenever you're ready. Tonight."

"You mean right now?"

"Why not?"

"Ah, well…no reason, I guess." Zude looked toward the door. "We could. We certainly wouldn't be disturbed."

"Regina's been in bed," Bosca said, closing her eyes, "hmm… she's been in bed for over three hours now. It's eighteen after eleven."

As she sat again, Zude checked her tacto-time. It was 11:18. "How do you do that?"

Bosca sank back into the deep sofa. She stretched her arms above her head. "Anything you really want to know is available to you, Zude."

"Ah." Zude drew a breath and sat up. "Well. How do we do this?"

"You're sure you want to?"

"Bosca, I'm not sure of anything anymore. I know that I want to understand Regina. I know that I trust you."

"Trust yourself." Bosca let her hands massage Zude's neck and shoulders. As Zude relaxed, Bosca's words took on a formal tone. "Tonight's working will be different from our usual patterning. Your Swallower will guide you as usual, but through me. I will configure the passage and escort you to our appointed station. You will leave the earth, much as if in flight, and discover yourself on a thoroughfare, empty of visible travelers. Stay in touch with the energy spline that connects you to your body. There is no danger. I shall step aside when Regina arrives but will return when you call. Regina may or may not appear in her echo-body, but you will have no difficulty recognizing her."

Bosca's hands withdrew from their massaging. Her voice was smooth again. "Here, stretch out." She placed Zude supine on the sofa and dimmed the lights. She stood for a moment at the windowed wall, watching the city glowing below.

"The paque-trap is to your right," Zude told her, "there." The window disappeared. Zude waited and watched. Bosca's long body was encased in a bubble of subdued brightness. Her back was to Zude. Both her hands were moving upward in front of her face, enclosing an object that Zude could not see. She spoke words that Zude could not distinguish. Abruptly, her arms fell, and without a glance at Zude she strode to the precise opposite side of the room, faced the wall, and repeated her actions.

Now to the south, Zude thought. And Bosca moved to the point on the south wall at right angles to the line she had just walked, repeated her actions, and walked to the opposite wall for her last repetition. With her final low incantation, the room jerked. The walls and the ceiling of the office were suddenly misted over, as if she had struck a protective dome within their confines.

Bosca surveyed the dimly lit area and returned to the sofa. "I'll sit here in the recliner by your side." Her voice seemed muted, without full overtones. She settled into the big chair and closed her eyes. Moments later she leaned forward and showed Zude a many-faceted crystal. "It's a trisoctahedron," she explained. "Twenty-four sides, eight for each aspect of the Glad Self. It's our talisman. I'll hold it and you'll hold my other hand. Like this." She took Zude's hand and leaned back in the reclining chair. "Are you about to drop off?" she asked easily.

"No," Zude answered. "But I could."

"Stay alert. We won't be on a dream vector."

Zude closed her eyes, feeling Bosca's steady hand, listening to her warm voice. "Just call yourself home now, like you always do. At your own pace." Zude felt herself floating, moving toward spaciousness. Minutes later the voice said, "Reach for your highest vibration." Zude began her shorter breaths, letting the voice carry her upward. She rested, at ease but courting a more animated bliss, until her fullness began tugging against its belaying lines and the ballast of her body. She focused on Bosca's voice, aware that it was drifting away from her. "You are absolutely safe," it whispered.

Those were the last words Zude heard, for suddenly she was swept upward by a cold rising wind. It lifted her off the sofa and thrust her through the protective dome and the walls of the Shrievalty, catapulting her outward over the wide city lying resplendent below her. It spun itself into light-year swiftness and set its course for the stars. Zude clasped Bosca's hand, now a braided cable of light unfurling behind her as she hurtled through space, the wind roaring in her ears.

The wind died suddenly, and with it the sound. Zude stood in boundless silence on a moonlit country road that traveled the crest of a high treeless ridge. Below her and to each side, tall grasses, wooded hills and ancient stones lay motionless, vigilant.

She started walking toward the white moon, her footsteps on the dirt and pebbles the only sound. She was clothed as she had been in her office, though her body was not solid and exuded an iridescent sheen. The air, cold and fresh, held a trace of the sea, and behind her a thin strand of light rounded into a cloud and settled on a rock. "I'll wait here," it said in Zude's mind.

She walked on, her feet moving now to a rhythm not her own, but one she knew well. The familiar song of the children floated on the thin air. She hummed along until the tune faded.

"You came!" Regina—a shadow of Regina?—landed on Zude's back with a tactile thump, her legs straddling Zude's torso, both hands holding Zude's head.

Zude disengaged a small finger from the socket of her eye and peeled the frail burden from her back. "Reggie!" She hugged and stroked, trying to give substance to a form that declined to be substantial. At last she simply held the child on her arm, letting the white hair rest against her shoulder. "Reggie, you are so…weightless!"

"You, too, my Zudie!" said the child, giggling and poking at Zude's softshirt. "Carry me?" she added.

"Of course," said her friend, moving toward the moon once more. "Where shall we go?"

"Everywhere!" Regina exclaimed. Zude dutifully strode forward, bouncing her laughing bundle with each step.

"Stop, Zudie." When Zude obediently halted, Regina told her, "We have to play now."

"A game, preshi?"

"Eye-swap," the bundle said, wiggling to be put down. "Come on."

Regina slid from her perch and squatted in the middle of the road, her feet flat and her buttocks swinging just off the ground, her armpits on her overalled knees.

Zude imitated her position. "So what's this eye thing?"

Regina's smiling head bobbed from side to side. "Zudie, I can see me. Can you see you?" Zude frowned. Regina bubbled on. "Put your feet here, Zudie, inside mine."

"Mine are so much bigger, Reggie." She started forward.

"In your head, Zudie, do it in your head!" Zude closed her eyes. "There!" Regina crooned. "Now look!"

Zude opened her eyes to a squatting, slightly gray-haired woman in plastiped boots and a softshirt, earnestly squeezing her eyes shut. Zude gasped and giggled, her head bobbing left and right. "That's me!" Her voice was a child's treble.

"Yes!" said Regina from inside Zude's child-body, "yes, and I can…" The voice slipped away.

And continued flowing from the mouth of the figure across from her.

"…jump into you!" said the warm mellow voice from the shiny-eyed Magister. Before Zude could respond, the voice was back with her, her companion again inside her tiny body. "Oh, Zudie, I've missed you so!"

Zude was plunged gloriously into the heart of Regina's love. She basked there only a moment before a cavalcade of characters paraded by her: Ria, Enrique, Eva, bisabuela, Bosca, cousins, friends, Zude herself, all perceived from the vantage point of a small being. She saw with Regina's eyes both the accented memories and the daily commonplaces of a cheerful young life.

To her astonishment she realized she could halt the progression and examine as deeply as she wished any one of Regina's experiences, vividly remembered or long-buried under armor deliberately or fortuitously forged. Zude investigated a scene or two, feeling the feelings that pervaded them: big joys, stark disappointments, bald angers, lavish generosities. There, in the still and frosty countryside, on a road with neither origin nor destination, and inhabiting the echo-body of her cherished child companion, the Magister explored them all with appropriate awe and attention, all the while aware that Regina was happily allowing her scrutiny.

She even survived with dignity and full appreciation her introduction to Regina's Source Self, that vital spirit from whose center the child's life energy and well-being surged. I-Bear, Regina called her Source Self, and Zude in fact felt it as a great ursine presence.

"She has something to tell you, Zudie."

"Your I-Bear?"

155

"Yes. It's important, she says. Listen!"

Zude was surrounded by a delicate tuneful humming and a fuzzy breeze that swaddled her and held her close to an enormous heart. She swung there, embraced by a big innocent joy and a vast affectionate curiosity. If this was what an I-Bear felt like, she thought, she wanted one too. Such comfort!

Then it came to her like an ocean seeping into her bones.

"What you are proudest of," the I-Bear told her, "you must destroy."

Then it ebbed quickly away, back into the light-year stars, leaving her in her echo-body again, cold upon a moon-drenched road with a white-haired child beside her.

Zude reached toward Regina to gather her into her arms again. She held the child close, while the words resounded in her mind, over and over.

"I have to go, Zudie."

Startled, Zude squeezed the little hand. "Will I see you again, preshi?"

"Oh yes, Zudie. In my real body."

"But then you will go away?"

A dazzling smile covered the child's face. "Yes. Soon." She kissed Zude's cheek. The overalls and the shirt became translucent, then transparent.

The Magister watched the precious shape fade entirely. She did not reach out. She did not weep. She only nodded. A deep ease settled around her, one in which she wished to abide forever.

Some time later a spline of light circled her head, took her hand, drew her back to earth.

Zude was cold and shaking, even under the warm tekla of the Magister cloak that was spread over her. Tears rolled down her cheeks. She was on her side, and beneath her were not hard dirt and pebbles, but the cushions of a sofa. Her arms held her knees close under her chin in fetal position.

The voice from beside her was no longer muted. "I found your cloak in the wall abditory," it said. "I hope that's all right." Zude managed to nod, then slowly unfolded her legs and rolled onto her back. The office was as usual, no longer under a misted dome.

The lights were still low, and Bosca sat on the recliner holding a cup out to her. "You should have flightbane to soothe you after an episode like this, but it's not on the transmog's menu. This is a double-steeped herbal."

Zude pushed to a sitting position, keeping the cloak around her and closing her eyes to steady the room's spin. She could manage only a small sip of the liquid.

"Did we do what I think we did?" she whispered.

"We did indeed."

Zude nodded. She blew on the tea, then took a large swallow and sat back. The hot drink eased her insides. She rubbed her forearms and thighs, assuring herself of their solidity. "Bosca," she whispered, "Bosca, I held her! She was so light!"

"I know."

Without warning Zude's eyes filled and overflowed. She took the handkerchief Bosca offered and wiped her eyes. The tears did not stop. "I'm not sad," Zude insisted, still unable to keep her cheeks dry, "I'm not sad, Bosca." A short laugh escaped her lips. "In fact," she stammered, "I felt, I mean, I think I know what peace is. For maybe the first time ever in my life."

"You're a Peacekeeper."

"I am now."

They sat in a long silence.

"Bosca."

"Here."

"We have to close down the bailiwicks."

Bosca nodded. "You're sure?"

"Very sure." Zude set her tea on the end table by the taxi-dermed cat. "It's so obvious." She took Bosca's hand. "Regina's Source Self told me. It said, 'What you are proudest of you must destroy.' I don't think it could be any plainer."

The chime of the intercom sounded at regular intervals on the far side of the room. It grew gradually louder. Zude started to consult her tacto-time. Instead she closed her eyes and tried to sink into the ambience of all that had just occurred.

"I get 1:40," she said.

"Close," Bosca replied. "It's 1:33."

Zude smiled. She rose unsteadily. "I know I can handle this," she said, and made her way to the desk console.

Edge's voice was subdued but clear. "Magister. Sorry to disturb you."

"No problem, Edge. What is it at this hour?"

"Two spooners from Denver just landed and insist on seeing you. In person. They say they have a message for you. They, along with a package that they bring to you, have cleared all security checks." There was a pause. "I informed them that you are officially not here. They informed me that the matter is of the greatest urgency."

Zude looked at Bosca, who started to rise. Zude stopped her with a shake of her head. "Give me one minute. Then you can bring them in, Captain." She spoke to Bosca. "Stay, if you don't mind, will you? This can only take a moment or two."

"Of course." Bosca began arranging the furniture more formally. She folded the Magister's cloak, then respread her long skirt and settled back into the deep sofa.

Zude brought up the lights and depaqued the broad window, letting the night's cityscape in again. She was smoothing her softshirt into a proper uniform when Edge ushered in the visitors and left.

The spooners introduced themselves as Margarita and Viva, explaining they were to deliver to the Magister a small bag that came from the Alleghenies via three other spoons.

Zude took the pouch that Margarita extended.

"There is a note enclosed in the bag," said Viva, the designated spokeswoman.

"So I'm to open it now?"

"Yes. The sender is anxious for your reply and wants us to wait."

"Oh?" Zude let her puzzlement show.

"Magister, I'm not sure why it has to be this way," Viva said, shifting her weight left and then right again. "We understand that there's a comspot code for you indicated on the enclosed note if you wish to make your response yourself. But we are to remain here until you send that answer. Or you can give us your answer, and we'll get it to the sender at once. If you decline altogether to respond immediately, then we are to inform the sender that your answer is, No."

The speaker relaxed momentarily. "The sender just wants to be sure there's no delay to your response."

"I see," said Zude. She glanced at the cotton bag and then at the messengers. "Please sit," she said. "This is Bosca, a heartsinger and dancer. Spooners Margarita, Viva."

Nods of acknowledgement, glances around the office, and the two women collapsed gratefully into their chairs.

With a look of apology to Bosca, Zude retreated to a lamp near her desk. She studied the pouch and then addressed its intricately braided drawstrings. The braiding was of a texture that quickened her heart. It would fall open in an instant, she recalled, if she tugged the right string... yes.

Bosca, watching Zude in the periphery of her vision, saw the Magister close her eyes. To the visitors she said, "Would you like tea or hempbrew? Or coffee?"

"No, thank you," Margarita smiled back. "We're fine."

"We had a good meal before we left. And we flew fast," Viva added. "We're looking forward to staying the night with friends as soon as we've finished here."

Zude had undone the drawstrings, Bosca noted. "I admire spooners," she said, deliberately shifting her attention from Zude. Then, as the glances of both women invited her to say more, she added, "I've been carried by a spoon but haven't flown myself. Yet. I mean I haven't, that is, I'm not..." She felt suddenly very vulnerable. Against her will, her eyes were drawn back to Zude. The Magister was staring at something she had withdrawn from the pouch. Around her pulsed an intense field of multicolored and agitated luminescence.

"There's nothing like flying," Margarita was saying, seeking to ease Bosca's discomfort and clearly unaware of the electromagnetic turmoil presently surrounding her Magister.

Bosca smiled her thanks at Margarita. "I'm sure I'll, well, that I'll do it someday," she finished. In her periphery, she saw Zude taking charge of renegade emotions, pulling in her turbulent energy rupa. It was a controlled and calm Zude who now read whatever words comprised the urgent message.

"We passed over the de-desertification project," Viva was saying excitedly. "It's very impressive from the air." She was about to elaborate on the beauties of water reclamation when she realized that Magister Adverb was rejoining them. Both she and Margarita stood.

Zude looked at each of them and then addressed Viva. "Tell the sender that the answer is, Yes. An unequivocal and immediate Yes." She held out her hand for the Earthclasp valedictory. Viva and Margarita each in turn covered Zude's hand with both of theirs.

"Will you allow us to treat you to a hot meal and lodgings?" Zude asked.

"No, thank you," Viva replied. "We only need the use of one of your comstations to send our message. May we?"

"Of course," said Zude. She dissolved the entry wall with a motion at the corner of her desk. "Captain Edge will help you."

Margarita turned to Bosca. "Here's to high adventures!" she said. Her thumb subtly gestured to the sky.

"Thank you!" Bosca laughed. She waved her farewell as both women passed into Edge's competent custody.

"High adventures?" Zude said, dropping to the sofa.

"Colloquial reference." Bosca cast it all aside with a vague hand movement. She was sitting forward again on the sofa. Neither woman spoke for a long moment.

Zude fingered the object that had arrived in the pouch. She looked at Bosca. "It's from Jezebel."

Bosca's head fell back in the first half of a long nod. She pressed her tongue between her teeth.

Zude held up a small silver earring delicately shaped into a unicorn that rose majestically on its hind legs. Bosca's head completed its nod. Her eyes went to the unicorn's duplicate, the one dangling from Zude's ear.

"She was to send this to me if ever she needed me," Zude said.

Bosca examined the figure without touching it. "So," she whispered.

Zude handed her the note.

> *Hello, Zude. Will you meet me*
> *Tuesday evening, sundown, on the roof of*
> *the Give Away Casino in New Nagasaki?*

> *I hope you are well. Jezebel.*
> *1.36\earthkeep.4773.biz\lavona*

Bosca searched Zude's face as she handed back the note. "That's tomorrow. No, today. New Nagasaki is down in the old New Mexico desert."

"Yes. Isn't that the town that's grown up near White Sands?"

Bosca nodded. "A healing town. And a gift society."

Zude fingered the earring. "I wonder..."

"You'll know soon enough."

"Indeed I shall," Zude agreed.

8

[2088 C.E.]

> Love is a leap of faith, a leap off a cliff.
> Are you ready for such joy?
> *Voices of the Stream*

Anarut, originally a Naga tribeswoman of the lower Himalayas, was now the manager of the Give Away. She swept around the spacious rooftop garden in her elegant long-flowing gown, showing Jez the sumptuous upper dominion of the casino.

Near a fountain surrounded by hearty desert flora, she leaned over the chest-high protective wall. "There's a colony of Afortunadas there," she said, pointing. "Visitors can hear animal stories for days at a time, if they're willing to camp out." Then she looked to the far-off snow-capped mountains. "See the timberline that cuts north? And that bald escarpment?" Jez nodded. "Just to the right of it, a slightly lower peak? There, that reflected light! That's it. That's our observatory, monitoring for extra-terrestrials."

A barely audible tinkle of chimes interrupted them. Anarut touched her earlobe, silencing the sound. She sighed. "Well," she said, "the dome over there paques and depaques so you can see the action down on the promenade and in the main gaming hall. You can even magnify any quadrant, with no danger of spying on the dealers or..."

"No necessity for that," Jez assured her.

"Sorry I have to leave you." Anarut held out her arms. "It is good to see you, Jezebel."

163

Jez hugged her hard. "You too, Anarut, you too."

"I'll have your friend sent up the minute she arrives." She made for the drop shaft, waving her arms to encompass the roof as she went, calling, "It's all yours, my dear! Enjoy!"

Jez drew a deep breath and looked at the sun, flatbottomed now as it began its disappearance behind a southwestern ridge. Zude would be prompt. Always Zude was prompt.

Carousel music from below drew her to the parapet. She looked down upon a children's playground. Two niñas hung from a bright yellow pipe-bridge, one by her legs, the other in a hand-over-hand progress across the bar. A sudden irony struck Jez: The children were not so much playing as performing. She herself was part of an audience that watched the niñas; her fellow voyeurs were a man and a woman on a bench by the pipe-bridge, three people just beyond them who stood by the empty carousel, and two young adults who had just halted in their cleaning of the shallow pool to observe the small acrobats.

The only children on the playground.

Deliberately, Jez turned away from the scene and began exploring the rooftop. She strolled over pathways and through occasional nooks, where cushioned chairs or lounges sat with tables and transmogs, all inviting human use and occupation. She marveled at the hand-wind-water pollination that must have been required for this variety of vegetation. There were at least twenty kinds of cactus. And all over the garden, yuccas flowered vigorously as if, in spite of decades of disappointment, they still stubbornly expected the visitations of a dainty double-winged moth to propel them into fruition.

The wide dome rose out of the floor, holopaqued to resemble a serene pond, complete with water lilies and reflections of a blue sky. Ripples and tiny expanding circles played across its surface, teasing the viewer into coolness and reminiscences of amphibian and insect life.

Jez touched the patchpad by the low wall that surrounded the dome, and the pond dissolved to reveal the casino below. The teeming madness of gambling transactions was accompanied by a riot of sparkles, shimmers, brightly lit colors. She decided not to activate the audio field, instead focusing her attention on the figure of Dicken at a blackjack table. Jez leaned stiff-armed on the edge of the low wall and watched.

"Pardon, señora." The voice was close behind her. "But have you perchance lost a unicorn?"

Jez made herself turn slowly.

Nothing in all the annals of alchemy or the Craft could have kept down the swift sharp tears that rose at the sight before her: the proud Kanshou bearing, the uniform, the warm brown eyes, the long, slightly aquiline nose, the waves of salt-and-pepper hair. Handsome. Compelling.

"Zudie." She held out her hands.

Zude took them, smoothly, with none of her old characteristic awkwardness, holding them firmly, with all of her old characteristic gentleness.

"Jezebel," she said, matching the brightness of Jez's eyes with a fullness in her own. The presence that faced her pulsed with vigor, from the crown of the shoulder-length hair to the high cheeks and long hands, from the strong easy shoulders down the lean body's flow to the brown sandaled feet.

They were blanketed by keen memories and barely contained longings, pervaded by such an intimacy that neither could speak further. They stood transfixed, there on a rooftop in the last rays of a desert sun, daring neither breath nor movement.

"The unicorn is yours, Vigilante Magister," Jezebel said at last, with a small formal bow. "In pair with its proper mate, it celebrates the rebirth of magic."

Zude took the earring from her ear and held it up. "But the magic is not yet fully born, señora." She pressed the tiny unicorn into Jez's hand and held it with both her own. "And you may have need of it again."

"Then I shall take it, Vigilante Magister." Jez placed her other hand on Zude's.

Long moments later, some handmaiden of impermanence broke the spell, catapulting them into self-consciousness. They relinquished each other's hands and attempted to laugh easily. They made big gestures and spoke a little too loudly.

"So," Jez said. It felt like a bark. She tried again. "So how did you get here?" She pocketed the earring and busily repaqued the dome. They began to walk.

"Low rocket to Albuquerque." Zude cleared her throat. "The Mat Rangers brought me from there."

"Mat Rangers?"

"A kind of flying carpet. They carried me on it." A pause. "And how did you come?" Zude ventured.

"I came with Bess Dicken, my lover. We flew."

"Ah, I see!" Zude's smile did not achieve full-blown status. She drew in a swift breath. "Well, you should see the Mat Rangers, Jezebel. They are sort of the passenger-and-cargo branch of the Flying Daggers, you know. They come up to you and say, 'We are Vigilantes Crane and Mercedes, Magister, admiring your person and honoring your office.'" She shot Jez a stiff grin in the midst of her impersonation. "Well, I mean, they wouldn't come up to you and say that but they…"

"Zude." Jez had stopped some feet behind her companion.

Zude turned, her eyes anxious.

Jez stood with that old light grace, her arms alive by her sides. She sent her words directly to those uneasy eyes.

"Zude. It's been eighteen years since we last saw each other. There has not been a day of any one of those years in which I have not thought of you, pictured you, wanted to come to you. You will always be the one who first called up in me the best I've ever known of love. And passion." Jez paused. "So we've got other allegiances now, both of us. But please know: You will never be replaced or diminished in my heart, no matter what gifts any other woman may bless me with. Never."

Zude stood like a statue. In her search for words, she found only her tight throat and stinging eyes. She opened her mouth, closed it, cleared her throat, swallowed. "Jez."

"I had to say that."

"I know. I just…" Zude tightened her lips. She drew a deep breath. "I don't have to tell you, do I?"

Jez shook her head. "No." She smiled. "No, I knew."

Zude laughed softly. "You always knew." She lingered for just a moment on the sight before her. Then she looked around the roof-garden. "Well. Shall we order the house special on drinks? Are you hungry?"

"I couldn't eat. Or drink."

"Actually, neither could I."

They both nodded, just a splinter short of unison. Jez drew Zude to one of the chair circles by the parapet and they sat, more easy now with each other. In the closing in of the desert night they spoke carefully but comfortably of the events of their lives since the Amah Academy, each acknowledging with ironic smiles the increasing distance between their diverging paths.

The threat of full nightfall prompted Zude to reach out for Jez's hand. "Let me look at you a minute, Bella-Belle. I feel so thirsty just for the sight of you."

"Well, I've had the advantage," Jez replied. "I've seen you on public flat-transmissions many times." She pressed Zude's hand. "My Magister."

"And," Zude paused, "your adversary."

Jez dipped her head in brief acknowledgement. "Once, in Toronto, I was waiting in the back of a live street crowd to challenge you. About the Protocols, of course. I had my strategy all laid out."

"But you didn't. Challenge me."

"No. I just watched you." Jez covered their clasped hands with her free hand. After a moment she disengaged her hands entirely and stood up. "Zudie."

Ah, thought Zude, here it comes.

Jez turned to the protective wall, looking out. "The Anti-Violence Protocols. They're a lost cause now."

Zude followed Jezebel with her eyes. "I'd not say that. I'd call them a non-issue."

"No. The issue is still there."

Zude stiffened. "I don't know how it's been in your part of the world, Jezebel, but from where I sit it's pretty clear that nobody's life is normal anymore."

Jez turned.

"I know. I know, Zude. I've watched it happen all over. In every tri-satrapy." She suddenly understood even before she caught the stricken look on Zude's face. "You've lost someone," she said abruptly.

"Well, not yet. My chosen daughter. And eventually, I guess, her brother."

"I'm sorry."

Zude smiled a little. "It's okay. Now." She put energy into her voice. "We've all lost. Or we all will."

It was Jez's turn to nod. "Zude, about what's happening—you must have lots more hard data than I do, and I've got plenty. I've also got theories by the score, all of them with some sense to them, none of them satisfying me." She sat again. "None. Except for one."

Zude looked at her intently.

Jez searched the deep brown eyes. "I'm not sure how to tell you what I've just learned."

Zude placed her forearms on her knees. "Jez." She leaned forward, smiling. "Jez, it's got to be important. You're here, by the Blessed Yarn, you're here!" She laughed a little. She flexed and extended her toes inside her boots. She rubbed her hands together. "Look. I have something important to tell you, too."

Abruptly Jez sat back. "Do it."

"Do what?"

"Tell me."

"Why me first, Jezebel?"

Jez's voice was playful and insistent. "Because this is the most important scene in our story, Zude! Look at it: A meeting of old lovers and adversaries after many years, when civilization is about to crumble, and in the story you have more political power. It's only decent for you to begin disclosure." She grinned as she recalled a rubric from their past. "And besides, Zudie, I called it first!"

"Okay, okay, I'll tell!" Zude laughed. There was an easy pause. "Jez, I don't know where to begin. And," she held up a forefinger, "I've got to have a guarantee."

"Of what?"

"That you won't say, I told you so."

"You've got it."

Zude picked up a small stone from the graveled rooftop and studied it, rolling it between her fingers. "Jez." She looked up. "I've got an angel."

"You have a what?"

"Well, she's probably just an electronic emission. She follows…no, she leads me. Everywhere. Through everything. I call her the Swallower."

"Is she here now?"

"Yes, but hiding." Zude dropped the stone and turned her chair so she could face Jezebel. "And," she began. She looked away, then back to the night-darkened face before her. "Jez, I've talked with the animals."

Jez simply looked at her.

Zude laid her words carefully on the air between them. "The Swallower led me to them. In the ocean. Every kind of sea life the world has ever known. I swam with them, moved among them. For an eternity, it seemed. And I talked to them. No, scratch that. They talked to me." She took Jez's hand again. "What a tale it is to tell!" She stopped suddenly. "What is it, what did I, what?"

Jezebel's cheeks were wet and her lips were trembling. "Zudie," she began. Her voice was strong even through the fast-flowing tears. She sat very still, erect, her eyes closed. Her tears continued to fall, patterning the softshirt that caught them. Zude peered at her face, that moving landscape of sorrow and wonder. She could barely see it in the accumulating darkness. She waited.

Fortuitously, the coming of night caused a dusky glolobe to ignite within the branches of an overhanging mesquite tree, highlighting Jez's next remark.

"Part of what I have to tell you, Zudie," she said, "is that I've done that, too. Talked with the animals."

Zude simply looked at her.

"I got the air-and-land contingents." She released Zude's hand and pulled a handkerchief from her trews. "No! There were fish. But not many. It was mostly mammals. And insects. And snakes and birds." She wiped her cheeks. "Tell me, did they say words to you?"

"No words. Some of it was pictures, extraordinary vast pictures, eons old, but it was more like...knowings, like what is, and what they are...I can't explain it."

"You don't have to."

"Was it the same for you?"

Jez nodded. "I seemed to know it all: Where they came from, why they left, how they're only a vibration away from us right now. It was like looking into the heart of the universe."

A long silence.

Then Zude whispered, "I haven't been the same. Not since then." She paused. "And there's been more," she said, "more, ah, psychic stuff." She shot a glance at Jez, then hurried on. "It's prepared me for losing so much, for all the changes that are coming."

She was on the High Road again, holding Regina.

Then she added, as easily as she could, "Everything's going to be just fine, no matter how many children die, no matter if no more are born. We've had our moment in the sun and it's time to go. And that's okay. It's all been a gift."

Jez started to speak, then stopped.

"But that's another world," Zude was saying, "another order of knowing. We're still here, here on this physical plane. And there are things we can do. Things we must do."

The subtle desert sounds modulated into another key. Jez lifted herself into the new ambience. "Do you believe that?"

Suddenly, Zude wanted a cigarillo, even a seaweed cigarillo. She took a deep breath and spoke. "That there are things we must do?"

"Yes."

Zude hesitated. Something had changed. A judicious sharpener had brushed lightly over the words Jez was speaking, over the posture of Jez's shadowed figure. Zude felt her own idling defenses leap into alertness. She studied Jez's face. "Yes," she said, finally. "Yes, I do believe that."

"I'm glad," Jez said. She rose and faced the desert.

Zude folded her hands between her knees and waited, watching Jez's back.

Jez looked toward the mountains. "Because, Zude, there's something you must do."

Zude frowned, even as her voice attempted lightness. "Are you trying to persuade me, my righteous, non-combative Jezebel?"

Jez turned. "I am."

Zude stared. "I see."

Jez spoke steadily. "It's maybe the only thing that will guarantee that human beings survive. I know that sounds grandiose. And impossible. But I believe you can do it. In fact, you're the only person who can do it."

"I'm flattered." Zude leaned back in her chair, interlacing her fingers around a lifted knee.

"Zude, don't you go numb on me!"

Zude was immediately forward again. "Jez, I didn't mean to be flippant. You just make me sound so powerful. I promise you, I've never felt less powerful in my life!" She covered her face with both hands, then pushed her knuckles against her eyes.

"You're a Magister, Zude!" Jez insisted. "And, what's more, you're probably the most highly regarded person on the planet! What's more powerful than that?" Suddenly, Jez pulled herself up short and dropped to her knees in front of Zude. "Oh, Zudie," she whispered, "Zudie." With a light touch she drew the reluctant forehead toward her until it touched her own. She closed her eyes. "I'm not listening to you. I wish it undone. Erase?"

Zude took Jez's head in her own hands. "Erase," she said.

They let themselves be held in the sway of the old ritual.

It was Zude who broke the contact, urging Jez into the chair so they could face each other once more.

"So, my worthy misanthrope," she ventured, now dry-eyed, "why are you trying to save the human race? You used to say we're a flawed species, an evolutionary blunder, that we're up way past our bedtime."

Jez pondered. "I've changed."

Zude trod carefully. "Even about men?"

Jez stared beyond Zude, out into the desert. "Particularly about men."

Zude waited for several heartbeats. "What is 'it,' then, Jezebel? What's the 'it' that I must do?"

Jez placed her face in the full light of the glolobe so there would be no mistaking her words. She drew in a long deliberate breath and spoke very slowly.

"Zude, you have to dismantle the Kanshoubu."

Zude stared at her, the remnant of a smile still dwelling at the corners of her mouth. Then the remnant faded.

Jez repeated the words in her mind, pushing them one by one into the guarded eyes before her. At last she spoke aloud again. "All of it, Zude. Not just your Vigilancia, but the Amahrery and the Femmedarmery, too. The Foot-Shrieves, the Sea-Shrieves, the Sky-Shrieves, the Flying Daggers. The whole of the peacekeeping forces on Little Blue. It's all got to go."

Zude closed her eyes and shook her head, fiercely wrinkling her brow. Then she released her eyebrows, letting her eyelids snap open so she could blink several times—at her boots, at the mesquite branches above her. "I'm not hearing this," she told the roof-garden very softly, still moving her eyes over its many varied parts.

Jez waited.

Zude looked sideways at her. "Say it again."

"You have to dismantle the Kanshoubu."

"I have to dis…"

"Dismantle. Disassemble. Dissolve." Jez spoke faster. "Abolish, undo, erase, eradicate." Relentlessly now. "You have to demolish it, Zude." She could not read beyond the unwavering brown eyes before her. "You've got to annihilate it," she concluded.

Zude's head was spinning. She stifled the impulse to shoot out of her chair. Instead she closed her eyes and masked her face with one hand. She spoke calmly. "Now tell me why I must do this."

Jez leaned forward, arms on her knees. "Because the whole human enterprise has been about understanding violence. Not about stopping it. About understanding it. But right now we're at a strange juncture, because we can't hope to understand it until we do stop it. The Kanshoubu is the biggest barrier we have to stopping it. The Kanshoubu perpetuates violence."

"You mean the vicious circle. That violence begets violence."

"More than that. As long as there is the fear or the expectation of violence, there will be violence. The Kanshoubu exists out of fear; it exists in the expectation of violence."

Zude said nothing.

Jez continued quietly. "You have participated in a great epic, Zudie. The Kanshou have literally held things together on Little Blue for sixty years—over half a century! They've done it justly and worthily. We're as good as we are today only because of your work and the work of the Vigilantes, the Amahs, the 'Darmes."

She shifted herself slightly forward, anticipating some dismissive gesture from Zude. When it did not come, she continued. "But their work is no longer appropriate. It is done. Finished. The Kanshoubu has to move out of the way and let the next step take place."

"And what's that?"

"Zudie, we can no longer believe in violence."

Zude threw out her hands. "Just like that!"

"Yes, just like that!" Jez leaned forward again. "Change it, Zude! Change it by thinking differently!" She paused. "Or, change it by an extraordinary act of faith that is born of your deepest desire, the desire for real peace! Find a place somewhere in your heart that knows we can demolish the Kanshoubu and still survive."

Zude pulled away from the force of those words. But Jez's voice still held her.

"We're talking about a watershed in history, Zudie, one that probably outstrips the discovery of fire or the development of language. We're talking about the rebirth of the human race."

Zude was on her feet in an instant, striding past Jez toward the chest-high wall behind her. She leaned into it, shaking her head and pulling into her lungs long drafts of night air. When at last she spoke, to the desert as well as to Jez, her words were equanimity itself. "I know you are serious. You may be the only person who could say these things to me and expect to be taken seriously." She turned once again toward Jez. "But even if I were capable of doing what you ask, I wouldn't do it."

Jez's shoulders sank a barely perceptible millimeter. She spoke without looking up. "Well. That's plainly said."

Zude made herself wait.

Jez rose. "Zude, I have to say more. Will you hear me?"

"You know I will."

Jez thought a moment before she spoke. "The Kanshoubu itself knows that force invites force. Why don't Kanshou train in the use of heavy arms? On some duty tours they don't even carry standard police batons. Just bare hands and moral courage. All three of the academies meticulously train Kanshou in how to use the least necessary force in every circumstance. Why? Because, Zude, they know that simple and profound presence is the only true antidote to potential violence."

She stepped toward the shadowed figure by the wall.

"And your Kanshou Oath, Zude. All I'm asking you and the Kanshoubu to do is to enact your own statement of faith." She turned away to recite: "'Thus my primary and unalterable purpose in becoming Kanshou will ever be to render obsolete my own profession and the Kanshoubu itself.'"

She faced Zude. "It's that time, Zude."

Zude slapped the parapet's ledge. "It is not that time! Jez, you don't know what you're talking about! Have you seen the stats on the rising incidence of violence? Have you heard the stories about armed bands of women castrating men? Are you aware that the Femmedarmery is so short-handed that it's had to solicit volunteers? And in Rangoon some crazy piece of work planted a bomb, a bomb if you please, in the middle of the city's administration plaza!" Zude raised a hand in entreaty. "Jez, people fear lawlessness now as never before in recent times. And you want to dismantle the Kanshoubu? Now?" She ran her hand through her hair and shook her head.

Jez stood silently. Then she sighed. "I had to come today," she said. "I had to try, even though I doubted that I could reach you. Then, we met. Here on this rooftop. And I saw how you've changed. Your children, your Swallower, the sea animals. And for the first time I felt hope."

She leaned on the heavy chairback toward Zude. "What I don't understand is how you could experience such changes and still close yourself off from what you are so clearly being called to do."

"Jez, hear me." Zude's voice pleaded. "Understand me, if you can: I don't believe it. I just don't believe this is what I'm being called to do!"

And suddenly, as she uttered the last words, the I-Bear's words rolled into her head, turning themselves toward a different sun, taking on a new color, a firmer design.

"What you are proudest of you must destroy."

With a bitter bark of a laugh, Zude whirled toward the parapet. The more fool you, Adverb! she told herself in bewilderment. You thought you were proudest of the bailiwicks!

"Zude!" Jez's voice was anxious. "What is it?"

Zude pressed her palms hard against the ledge. "A little irony, Jezebel," she answered, "just a little irony."

She stood stock-still, a silhouette against a starry sky.

Jez approached the silhouette. She spoke gently, matter-of-factly. "Zude, in the past week you've visited four bailiwicks in four different regions."

Zude snapped her head toward the words, her eyes searching Jez's face.

"You've been trying to decide," Jez went on, "if the dying out of the whole human race warrants some change in peacekeeping practices. You've been thinking of closing down the bailiwicks, of setting free every habitante."

Zude's lips barely moved. "How do you know that?"

"Just tell me. It's true, isn't it?"

Starlight covered them both. Zude nodded slowly.

"Then," Jez whispered, "it's just one more step to…"

"I know, I know!" Zude spun away from the wall. "Jez, I don't know how you know what you know, but yes! Yes, I'm ready to free the habitantes, for lots of reasons, all of them good. But you're asking for far more than that!" She faced Jez, speaking faster. "Look. The whole species is about to ride out into oblivion. That's the only thing that most people understand. And when they realize that, they panic. They cling to familiar possessions, to the things that have always given them stability and security. They cling to their Kanshou!"

"No!"

Zude stared at her.

"You're selling us all short, Zude. You might have been right a century ago, even two decades ago! But we are a better race of beings now. Look what's happened to us! Look what we've had to learn! First the animals, then the men, and now our children! Look how it's all unfolded, like a magnificent illuminated manuscript! Like a proclamation, Zude, from the Universe Itself, telling us in no uncertain terms what we must now do!"

Jez held up both hands. "The Protocols! Zude, do you remember the Protocols?" She leaned on the chairback, reaching for Zude's eyes. "The Protocols distilled and intensified the issue of violence. They brought to a head the very thing we came here ultimately to understand! And what happened with the Protocols, Zude? There was no way out of that dilemma. It was clear that, in order to quell violence, we'd have to abrogate a basic human right. How could such a decision be made?"

She raised one hand. "The answer? Don't make it! Instead, turn your attention to something far more devastating that just coincidentally happens to be happening. Instead, turn your attention to the most important lesson we'll ever have the opportunity to learn. Instead, deal with the big possibility that there may be no more humans, violent or not, to be a part of whatever decision is made!"

She stood again in front of Zude at the parapet, her face flushed and animated.

"Zudie, people aren't looking for security anymore. We've learned too much about love and hate, about right and wrong, and about how fear has always fueled those dualities. We know that, whatever comes, it will have to be big and different, something equal to the big and different things facing us. I've seen it in people all over the world, Zude, that excitement about what could come. I've heard it in their voices, seen it in their eyes. In every satrapy, in every kitchen, by every dock, around every village fire, under every veil."

"Jez, Jez!" Zude shook her head helplessly. "You're not talking to the people I'm talking to."

"Of course not!" Jez exclaimed. "Of course not, Zude. You're the Magister, and I'm the Witch! We have different constituencies." She found Zude's eyes. "But I promise you, people are ready. Hundreds of millions of them."

Zude turned away from her.

Jez followed and stood behind her. Her voice was low, intense. "They're scared, yes. But ready. They know we're all about to step into a brand new episode in our evolution, and they need some guidance."

She leaned over the shoulder of the Kanshou uniform, looking outward with its wearer, her words brushing a unicorn earring.

"You can show us the way, Zude, you can give us a model for dealing with our fear." She felt Zude's head moving left and right. "You've got the power. Take the leadership now in this crucial moment of history, and we'll rally behind you in the blink of an eye, rejoicing as we go!"

"Jez…"

"We need a metaphor, Zudie, a symbolic action that states our desire to let go of fear."

Gently, she stepped in front of Zude's rigid figure. She captured the brown eyes, holding them with her own. "Zude, dissolving the Kanshoubu is that metaphor!"

Zude stood very still. She closed her eyes.

Heartbeats ticked by.

Zude spoke quietly. "I'll think about all this, but I'd be lying if I told you there's much hope." She closed her eyes again and shook her head.

No sounds came from the desert now. The silence was the stillness of the stars, in which all had been spoken.

Both women sighed—Zude because she saw them floating rapidly apart on a widening sea of disparate perceptions, and Jez because she saw the two of them standing together facing a stone wall. If, at that moment, Zude had not been scrutinizing her big hands in an agony of distress, she might have sensed that her companion was trimming the sails of discourse to catch a different wind.

"I want us to relax a little," Jez was saying. She moved as if to slide her hand through Zude's arm and then caught herself abruptly and drew back.

"Here," Zude said quickly, holding out her hand.

Jez took it with a rueful smile. They fell into a leisurely walk, rhyming their steps as of old.

"You're not finished, are you?" Zude observed.

"Almost."

"I figured."

They strolled on, swinging their hands between them.

"You won't persuade me, Jezebel."

"I know that. The only person who can persuade you is you."

There was a long quiet in their strolling. Jez urged them toward the dome at the center of the roof. "Let me add one last thing, and then I'll say no more."

She stopped their progress and held Zude's eyes. "If you decide not to take this risk, then we'll all be the losers. I don't know if we'll ever have another chance to understand violence. Or who we are. Or what our proper function is as a part of this particular biosphere. We'll pack our tents and pass out of existence with our little whimper, like other species that were invited to do the job and ultimately also failed."

"You make it sound so cosmic."

"It is cosmic."

"But then Little Blue will be Paradise again," Zude mused. "Maybe better than before. The animals will return and take up where they left off, without the awful hazard of Homo sapiens breathing down their necks. And clouds and trees and oceans, Jez, they'll all rejoice with relief and gratitude. Hallelujah! they'll sing. Hallelujah, they're gone!"

Jez sank on the low wall that surrounded the dome, inviting Zude to sit beside her. "Maybe," she said. "Then a few million more years of evolution, and another species will emerge to be charged with the task of understanding negativity and violence."

"Whoever they are," Zude said quietly, "I wish them well. They may not make it, either."

Jez nodded. "And so it will go, until the sun grows cold, and other galaxies are invited to host such experiments."

They sat without speaking for a long minute, Jez staring into the quiet desert, Zude worrying the gravel with the toe of one boot. Behind them, dim versions of casino noises bounced against the depaqued dome.

"Jez."

The name floated on the cooling air.

Jez looked up.

"You were right."

Jez cocked her head in query.

Zude searched for words. "What you used to say, that we are all just forms of energy, eternal and infinite." She paused. "Do you remember?"

"I remember, Zudie."

"Well, I know it now. And I know it's changed my understanding of death. I no longer fear it."

"Zude, that's it!"

"That's what?"

"That's what we both have to think about. Don't you see? The critical factor in having real presence is lack of fear. If all of us lost our fear of death, then violence would have no hold on us. And…"

"And we'd have no reason to keep the Kanshoubu," Zude finished, her eyes laughing. Then she sobered. "Jezebel, best beloved." She sought true words. "I don't know what my decision will be. We're left—the Magisters, the Webs, the Kitchen Tables, the Cabinets—we're all left trying to hold it together…"

Jez stopped her with the touch of her hand. "Hush, Zudie. We've said enough." She rose, drew Zude to her feet. They faced each other in the starlight. "We'll meet again. Either to observe the new human animal, or to watch us all fade away."

"I would like that, Jezebel."

"So would I."

Jez took the unicorn earring from her pocket and deliberately set it back in her own ear. Zude watched her.

Then Jez spoke in a limber voice, almost light and chatty. "Will you come and meet Dicken?"

"Of course."

"She's only a little bit in awe of you."

"As I am of her."

They nodded, and walked hand in hand to the drop shaft.

Much deeper into the Aztlán night, it was Magister Adverb who stood alone by the dome above the casino. She waved to the departing spoon with a dignity becoming her station. Then, walking slowly and carefully over the roof-garden, she retraced each movement of the evening's encounter and reheard each of the evening's words. When the Mat Rangers arrived near dawn, they thought they saw a tiny spot of light accompanying their Magister, alternately sitting on her shoulder and sweeping before her in what appeared to be an animated conversation.

9

BURIAL BARQUE ———————————————————————
[2088 C.E.]

> By the mind the world is led.
> *Wisdom of the Ancients*

It was midafternoon of a calm sunny day on the brightly decorated deck of a large barque. The barque rocked gently on the swells of the ocean just off the Los Angeles coast, beyond the channel where the semi-deeps begin.

The barque was a recreational and ceremonial vessel of the Vigilancia's Sea-Shrieves, the *N.T.S. Steinem*. Over 35 meters long, she resembled an ancient trireme. She had been propelled by her fusion cells from Huerta Beach to the Channel Islands and from there by three tiers of long oars on each side of her hull. One hundred Vigilantes and more had labored at the oars on the final leg of the barque's journey to her appointed destination: the burial site of yet another burden of small bodies.

The satrapy's children preferred burial at sea above any other disposal of their bodies, for they said that in the depths of the Pacific where no one can see, the fish had returned, lovingly to consume their human shells. The Sea-Shrieves had rowed many such ceremonial voyages over the past six months and knew they would row many more.

On that day, seventeen small bodies would be consigned to the deeps. Regina's was one of them. The huge, high-railed forward deck was crowded with families and friends.

Magister Zella Terremoto Adverb was clad shoulder to ankle in the cobalt blue and silver cloak of the Vigilancia. To her right, Magister Flossie Yotoma Lutu was similarly cloaked, but in Femmedarme green and black. To Adverb's left, Bosca stood draped in her woodswarmth cape. Clustered in front of them were Kayita, Eva, Ria and Enrique. Surrounding them were aunts, uncles, cousins. Behind them, covering the after deck, a group of Vigilancia Oarswomen stood at parade rest.

Friends, parents, family members, learn-togethers, playmates, priestesses, shamans, ministers—all had just offered stories, images and expressions of love and loss. The barque drifted in a silence of memories, recent and short. Softly, an adult chorus hummed the minor intervals of the most haunting of the children's melodies, now famous the world over: the *Song of the Lumari.*

With other parents and family members, Ria and Enrique stepped forward to balance the flower-laden wooden pallet that held Regina's body over the edge of the barque's railing. As the wordless song gathered power, the braces that secured the fulcrums of the seventeen rectangular frames were released, allowing those who guarded them to lift or lower their ends of the litters. The melody was crowned by a flood of sustained harmonies, and each survivor, in her or his own time, raised high the pallet's end and felt its precious burden slip into the sea.

Ria waited until the music rode its way downward toward completion before she nodded to Enrique. She steadied the wooden frame while he stood on tiptoe and pushed up with his arms, giving over Regina's body to the waters below. When the last litter had been tipped, silence fell again upon the crowd, broken once by a cry, once by a loud enduring wail.

The tune rose once more, the whole assemblage chanting the strange Lumari syllables and calling out goodbyes. The melody repeated, again and again, as if the crowd could not let it go, as if it still held within it the voices of those who had first brought it to their ears. A zither player stood forward to solo and then to lead the singing. She was followed by other musicians of all levels of accomplishment on flutes, guitars, a horn, a harp, an accordion. A group of drummers kept the rhythms until they became aware that another musician waited her turn to play.

Zella Terremoto Adverb had thrown off her cloak and stood among the crowd, anticipating the song's next point of entry. When it approached, she shouldered a violin and began translating the melody into yet another language. The Magister played imperfectly but with scrupulous care, gaining a measure of aptitude and sureness as she moved into a repetition of the song.

Faintly, then more assertively, the ambience altered. The tune awakened and the tempo quickened. For a split second the musician faltered, her eyes wide with consternation and resistance. Then she rallied, raising the instrument high, playing to the heavens and to the sparkling ocean. Crowd voices united with their violinist; the notes became fuller; other instruments joined in.

As if buoyed by the wishes of the group, Magister Adverb modulated into a companion key and raised the tension and the complexity of her rendition. Her eyes were closed. Her body swayed with mingled rhythms. Voices and instruments followed her lead, blending with and supporting her escalating recital.

In the crowd, Magister Lutu was suddenly charged with an uneasy sense of the irregular. She stared at the performer. Without moving her eyes, she whispered to the woman beside her. "Bosca! In the name of All That's Given and Blessed, what is she doing?"

Bosca's eyes were alternately fixed on Zude's tour de force and upon a bank of thunderheads far beyond the barque. "I'm not sure, Magister," she breathed, "I'm not sure!"

Magister Adverb's hand hastened as never before over the fingerboard of her violin. She played with perfection and exhilaration, texturing the melody with mixed cadences and crafty embellishments. Another modulation. Another acceleration. The music drove inexorably to a fulfillment and its final measures, a paean to freedom and hope.

The barque exploded with jubilation and release, every voice enlivened, every heart aloft. The last full note of the Lumari tune lingered, dying only when clouds, sky and sea carried it to realms beyond the ears of those who had launched its elegant flight.

The chaos of cheers and embraces hid the fact that the violinist staggered slightly before she was supported by two friends and guided to a resting place. "Bosca," she kept muttering to one of them as they wended their way through a grateful and astonished crowd, "Bosca, I didn't…something else, somebody else…"

"I know, I know," Bosca whispered back, still nodding to well-wishers. "I saw him. He was playing."

"Captain Maggie? Good." Flossie Yotoma Lutu spoke to her aide in Tripoli. A very British voice spoke back to her through the flatfield. "Yes," responded Yotoma, "yes, it was…it was fine. Maggie, I'm going to be delayed. Maybe by as much as six hours." She looked at her tacto-time. "Magister Adverb and I are arranging a three-way conference with Amah Magister Win. By secure channel holo hook-up from here at the Shrievalty Building. As soon as we can reach her. You shouldn't look for me before ten tomorrow morning, your time."

On the other side of her office, Zude could hear Yotoma as she and her aide continued to readjust schedules. She was back in her long cloak, standing motionless by the empty recessed wall panel that customarily housed her violin. Finally she lifted a case from beneath her cloak, opened it and removed the violin and its bow. She put them in their proper place on the display rack under the alcove's tiny spotlight, arranging their positions with slow delicate touches.

She studied the instrument. It seemed to rest happily and proudly from its recent exertion. It was old and even valuable. Certainly it carried precious memories. Nevertheless, it was a normal violin. It did not glow with enchanted light. There was no hint of sorcery or sortilege on its dark brown body. Its bow smelled only of resin, not of sulfur or of angel dust.

"I said, Zudie!" Yotoma's voice was brusque. Zude turned to see her friend waiting, two cups in hand, by the transmog.

"Coffee, please, Flossie. Strong and black." She threw off her cloak and sank to a sofa, smiling as she stared at the ceiling.

Yotoma placed the hot drinks on a low table, settled herself across from Zude, tested the temperature of her tea. "You sure you don't want to tell me about this? Before we talk to Lin-ci?"

"About?"

"About whatever it is you have made a decision about." She took a full swallow of tea, her countenance barely masking her concern.

Zude sighed and stretched. Her eyes brightened, and she shot a quick grin at Yotoma. "I wanted to weigh it all out with you on Thursday when you visited Regina, but it didn't seem appropriate then."

"And then I took off for Denver."

"And it's a good thing it happened that way." Zude picked up her cup. Her face was relaxed. "I thought at first you could help me decide, Floss. But now I know it's better that I tell you and Lin-ci together."

"So whatever it is, you've decided."

"I've decided."

She looks about twenty years old, Yotoma thought. Maybe twenty-one. Her eyes squinted. "I'll lay you eight to three I can tell you the exact moment you decided."

"You're on! When?" Zude sat up, set down her cup.

"You decided standing on that boat, with that violin, about twenty seconds into your first repeat, right after the music got away from you. You decided when your whole body started playing, when you lit up like a dervish gone to glory and began performing like a maestro."

Zude shot up from the sofa, her arms wide. "Yes!" She spun a full circle. "Flossie, was there ever such a moment! I can't tell you even now what happened! It was like I turned it all over to another part of me. I let go and let something else move my fingers! And Bosca, Bosca said she saw him, a violinist…in the clouds…" She stopped herself and frowned at the far wall. "Actually, Floss, that wasn't exactly the moment. I didn't decide until the ending, when everything lifted up into another world, and sorrow turned into, well, into joy! When all the emptiness was filled up with life again!" Zude looked at Yotoma.

"You are touched, Adverb."

Zude pushed her fingers through her hair. "I know. Sounds dippy as a dinghy on a choppy sea…"

Yotoma cut her off. "No." She wasn't smiling. "I mean you're touched. By the Wings of the Dove."

Zude stared at her. Then she sank down onto the arm of the sofa. "I am, Flossie. I guess I am." She shook her head gently. "But we've been calling it wrong. It wasn't a decision. It was more like…a knowing. I just knew what I have to do." She held Yotoma's eyes.

The chromatics of the intercom interrupted them. Zude opened its flow to the voice of Captain Edge. "Word from

Magister Lin-ci Win, Magister. She can confer in five minutes. We're ready and waiting in the Peace Room."

"Good. We're on our way." Zude closed the circuit. She took in a deep breath. "Well. This is it, Flossie."

"Zudie, you make me nervous, talking like that. Like it's the end of the world."

"Al contrario, mi amiga. It's maybe the beginning."

Yotoma grunted. "Don't get cryptic with me." She finished off her tea as she stood.

Zude swept her Vigilante cloak around her body, chuckling as she adjusted its clasp. Yotoma's voice made her turn.

"Zudie," said the formidable figure in front of her, "tell the truth and shame the devil." Zude looked back evenly as Yotoma's eyes hunted down and demolished every possible camouflage. "Are you figuring on quitting?"

"Quitting?"

"Spit it out. No gilding the pill."

Zude's eyes were laughing again. "Flossie, I am no more going to quit than you are." She took the green and black Magister cloak from Yotoma's hand, shook it and held it up so she could step under it. She settled the cloak around Yotoma's lean shoulders. Then she hugged the taller woman from behind, resting her cheek for a long moment against her friend's back. She depaqued the wall of the office, and the two women set off together.

"If you have called this conference to discuss the closing of the bailiwicks, Magisters, I congratulate you on the shrewdness of your timing." Beneath her red cowl and over her red and silver cloak, Lin-ci Win's face was drawn and her eyes were sunk in gray circles.

Circles of fatigue, wondered Yotoma, or of grief? She studied her Co-Magister. Circles of torment? Yotoma set her elbow on her chair and her fist to her cheek. She watched.

Lin-ci's holo-image leaned without animation on the arm of her mobile Greatchair. Zude and Yotoma sat elevated in restricted sub-channel ambience, holo-projected to their colleague in Hong Kong. Below them, the sounds of the Shrievalty's Peace Room hummed with technological activity.

"How so, Magister?" Zude, too, was disturbed by Lin-ci's devitalized countenance.

The Amah Magister allowed herself a rueful smile. "In this moment, I am ready to fling wide every bailiwick gate and never incarcerate another soul, just to be relieved of the responsibility." She held up a warning hand. "I won't be held to that!" She leaned back in her chair, almost relaxed. "It's a moment of weakness only. I shall recuperate."

"Lin-ci," said Yotoma, risking much on the informality, "you look like soaproots after a hard day's washing."

The Amah stared a moment, then reluctantly nodded.

"If you wish, please tell us," Zude urged. "It can serve as a such-and-such."

Lin-ci sighed. "Here is one item, the most recent. Vice-Magister Khtum Veng Sanh has asked to be relieved of her duties and to be transferred to some remote post commandership." She raised one eyebrow before she continued. "That I share this with you is a measure of my distress."

Then she spoke rapidly. "Amahs had just quelled a routine and minor outburst of hostility inside Sambor Bailiwick, on the Mekong in Cambodia. At the same time, hundreds of habitantes were beginning to gather for what Sambor's Post Commander took to be further violence. She immediately began standard response procedures. That is, she ordered a blanketing of the entire bailiwick with slumber vaporose—with Amahs masked against it, of course. From Hanoi, Vice-Magister Veng countermanded that order and informed the Commander that the habitante gathering was not related to the hostility but was instead a part of a peaceful assembly for the purpose of prayer for the children, and why-had-the-Post-Commander-not-remembered-that?

"Unfortunately, by this time some vaporose fumes had already been released. The habitantes responded with outrage, chaos ensued, and a pipe bomb was thrown. Two Amahs were badly wounded, one of them probably fatally. The Commander then overrode Veng's countermand, filled the bailiwick with the complete allotment of vaporose, and thus restored order."

"It was to have been a peaceful gathering?" Yotoma asked.

"Who knows? Facts, motives and responsibilities are hopelessly entangled. It did not end peacefully." Lin-ci's powerful arms braced on those of the mobile Greatchair and lifted the inanimate lower half of her body into a variation of her sitting position. She looked at her colleagues. "Veng challenged me. Without any request to speak freely, she exploded into a tirade in which, among other things, she catalogued the symptoms of my fascist behavior and informed me that citizens in all three satrapies believe me to be completely out of touch with their needs and their reality. She justified her action at Sambor by blaming me for the incident. The violence of habitantes throughout the tri-satrapy, she informed me, is the residue of my own anger. She had the grace to add that other angry or disgruntled people, herself included, might also be contributing to the emotional stockpile that fuels such violence. I countenanced Veng's behavior only because she had clearly taken leave of her senses."

The Amah Magister lowered her eyes. "I assigned her to immediate rest and recuperation. I accepted her resignation and granted her transfer." She spoke despondently. "I have lost an able Vice-Magister. And a friend."

The visage of such pain astonished Zude. In her experience, Lin-ci Win had rarely confided internal crises, and never had she exhibited personal feelings of this kind.

"A loss beyond measure," Yotoma said simply.

Lin-ci looked up. Quietly, she observed, "Nighthawk, Hong Kong's municipal tapestry artist, says that to live well one needs to embrace only two rules: Be nice, and make pretty things." She smiled ruefully. "Perhaps Nighthawk is right."

Zude also spoke quietly. "If everyone believed so, that would be a world worth living in." More pointedly but still gently, she added, "We wouldn't need bailiwicks."

"And we could all retire," added Yotoma. "We wouldn't even need the..." The Femmedarme Magister's words slowed, then ceased. Yotoma dared a look at Zude. Her friend's dark eyes were full of laughter and love. "Adverb!" Yotoma whispered.

Lin-ci Win's voice sundered the moment. "Colleagues! What secret do you share now?"

Yotoma unclasped her cloak. "Get set, Lin-ci," she said, still looking at Zude. "I think we're about to address the subject of this hastily called conference." She began removing her cloak, keeping her eyes on Zude.

"By my oath as a Kanshou," Zude said to Lin-ci, "I have not breathed a word to Magister Lutu about the substance of this meeting." She straightened to an upright position and said with unaccustomed formality, "Magister Win, Magister Lutu, the three of us are the titular heads of government on Little Blue. We are also the Commanders-in-Chief of the planet's peacekeeping forces. I submit to you that at this time in human history the only conscionable action open to us is not only to close down the bailiwicks but, as well, to initiate and carry out the complete and irrevocable abolition of the Amahrery, the Femmedarmery and the Vigilancia—the abolition of the global Kanshoubu."

Amah Magister Lin-ci Win stared at Zude with no visible reaction. Flossie Yotoma Lutu frowned and began barely shaking her head.

"I have not yet put together even a full prima facie case," Zude continued, still formally, "for I came to my present understanding only a few hours ago. Still, I am acutely aware that there is no time to lose. I would like to begin moving toward our consensus on the matter as soon and as rapidly as possible, with the hope that in the next few weeks we can present to Kanshou world-wide a plan for their discharge, their relocation and, if necessary, their re-education. The Heart of All Kanshou must approve the measure, and I suggest that we set our case before the Heart no later than a month from today."

Lin-ci Win moved not a muscle, but her eyes blazed. "You are mad!" she whispered. Suddenly, she ignited like tinder. "You would throw away all we have worked for, all we have gained of peace!" Her flushed face looked ready to explode.

"Magister," Yotoma soothed.

"And you, Flossie! You stand with her!"

"Negative, Lin-ci! I don't know where I stand. I haven't heard Adverb out yet. And neither have you!"

"I've heard her propose the destruction of the Kanshoubu!" The Amah Magister seemed almost to dodder in her fury. "It will never work, Zella Adverb! You forget the women you are talking about. These are Kanshou! They would never allow their own destruction! Their total identity is committed to fighting violence. That is their reason for existence!"

Yotoma's Hausa oath split the air. "Lin-ci," she boomed, "you forget who the Kanshou are! You talk like they'd wither and die if they couldn't be fighting violence!" She drew back deliberately to a more moderate demeanor. "The Kanshou wouldn't want for jobs, Lin-ci. Kanshou are tailor-made to deliver the discipline and the integrity that are needed in a world that has been turned upside down, whether they're in uniform or in mufti. They'd take the lead, they'd be the role models, and they'd empower with knowledge and know-how anybody who wanted to learn. You know that as well as I do!"

Lin-ci Win listened to Yotoma with increasingly narrowed eyes. "You misunderstand me entirely. I do not say that Kanshou would be incapable of living as civilians. I do say that they would not allow the abolition of the Kanshoubu." She looked at Zude and then back to Yotoma. "Astute women, both of you," she mused, shaking her head, "and yet you misjudge so appallingly the true meaning of a Kanshou's commitment."

Zude was visibly taken aback.

"What do you mean, Magister?"

Lin-ci Win had settled again into her Greatchair. She studied her counterparts but did not answer.

"I don't know what you're getting at, Lin-ci," said Yotoma. She drew a green kerchief from a belt pocket and wiped her face. "And Zude, don't count me into this lunatic scheme." She scratched her short-cropped head and gave a kerchief swipe to her upper lip. "Lin-ci may be right. The Congress of Active Kanshou won't knuckle under to a notion like this. What line to heaven have you suddenly got that says our peacekeeping forces will go belly up and agree to wipe out their own Kanshoubu?"

Zude sighed, but her eyes were bright again. "I'd be disappointed if you two didn't fight me on this." She sat up straighter. "But I assure you, my sole purpose in life from now on is to persuade you and 600,000 other Kanshou that the Kanshoubu must cease to be. I intend to stand with both of you before the Heart of All Kanshou as we all three argue for its blessing on this enterprise. If you don't join me, I'll be sad, but I will carry out the task alone."

She paused. "It is what must be done. I have not the shadow of a doubt that it will be done."

Abruptly Lin-ci Win turned her head and looked over her shoulder. Yotoma was certain in that moment that the Amah Magister was summoning those in her Hong Kong Peace Room who would physically and summarily remove her and her Greatchair from this conference. Instead, Lin-ci spoke to an Amah behind and under her, then drew from the nebulous air beneath her a max-monitor magnopad. She activated several control orbs, then held up for Zude and Yotoma's perusal a scrolling screenful of names.

"Are you responsible for this, Magister Adverb?" she asked as the names rolled slowly upward.

"Who are they?" Zude peered at the list. "Amahs?"

"Amahs indeed. Two regiments of the Asia Satrapy's finest Kanshou." The names scrolled on. "From Sri Lanka and Lower India." She sat back in her Greatchair still holding out for her Co-Magisters the seemingly endless list of names.

Zude draped her cloak over the back of her chair and sat forward to watch the movement on the screen. Yotoma studied Lin-ci Win's face.

"They have retired," said the Amah Magister.

"Retired?" Zude began.

"They have left their offices and their careers. They have laid down their capes. Over 800 women."

"And some men," Yotoma added automatically.

"Only in your tri-satrapies," Lin-ci snapped, "not in this one. I remind you that men have never been a part of the Amahrery." She watched the scrolling screen again. "This is a list of women."

"I don't understand," Zude murmured.

Lin-ci recited in an orator's voice, "'We will no longer fuel the violence,' their statement said. 'We will live now thinking of and believing in a world of lovingkindness.'" Lin-ci paused. "Answer my question, Magister Adverb."

"Magister," Zude answered, "I have in no way participated in this action on the part of the Amahs of Sri Lanka and Lower India. That they have pre-empted my proposal, however, at least in regard to their own lives, testifies to the appropriateness of the Kanshoubu's abolition."

"It testifies to no such thing!" If Lin-ci Win could have stood, her presence would have towered over her colleagues. "It testifies to the panic that assails every township on Little Blue, and to the false spirituality and unctuous piety that have beset even the most rational of women in the face of that panic—Vice-Magister Khtum Veng Sanh its prime example. And now, the Magister of Nueva Tierra its secondary one!" The Amah's eyes were ablaze.

Yotoma's cool reason met Lin-ci's fire. "The accusation is unjust, Magister. Adverb speaks from exigency, from…"

"Enough, Flossie!" Lin-ci proclaimed. The air shuddered under the weight of her rage. The red-cowled woman faltered a moment, then said earnestly to Yotoma, "Magister Lutu, you are my respected elder in both reason and political sagacity, but if you even consider endorsing Adverb's madness, you are no better than the perpetrators of violence who will rise up in self-vindication and triumph at the suggestion of this idea! You are courting chaos! Anarchy and pandemonium! Both of you!"

"Magister." Zude matched the energy with a steady composure. "What will come is as yet unimaginable, but I'm certain it will not be chaos. Or, if so, then not for long. Will you open the ear of your ears to me for a moment?"

Zude proceeded as if Lin-ci's motionless countenance were an affirmation. "In a public context this afternoon, I was challenged by an unfamiliar aspect of myself to surrender the most carefully cultivated part of my personality: my control. I was dared to trust that my training, my preparation, my passion and my good intent would be sufficient for the difficult task at hand. I resisted, fearing failure and humiliation. In the same instant, I understood that it was my effort at control that was dooming me to failure."

Zude glanced at Yotoma, then said urgently to Lin-ci, "Magister, it was a moment of supreme daring! I did relinquish control, and I found to my astonishment that I was participating in a small miracle!" She bent forward, toward her Co-Magister's uncompromising facial lines. "We're at just such a juncture now on Little Blue, Lin-ci Win. Our heart is whispering that we must give up our attempt to control violence because that attempt, that expectation, merely guarantee that violence will exist, and in fact thrive. But if we listen to the promptings of our best selves, then in another moment of daring we may forever transform our understanding of violence!"

Zude hesitated. "No human act means the same thing today that it meant a year ago. Everything has been made extraordinary, and we must open ourselves to vast changes." She studied her hands for a moment. "I know now that our beloved Kanshou, our peacekeepers, are part of what creates and sustains the violence that has been our most ancient and agonized birthright." She looked up at the other women. "Uncreate the Kanshoubu, and we at last begin to uncreate this most relentless legacy. When we renounce our fear of becoming victims and our pride at protecting victims, then what we have known as violence will disappear."

"Ah!" Lin-ci Win's interjection was edged with sharp sarcasm. "We will slip into a parallel reality! An alternative universe!

Is that it, Zella Adverb? We shall simply deny the existence of violence—or, as you might say, we shall lift our eyes from the violence in this world and rest them on a nonviolent world instead." She smiled derisively and dusted her hands one against the other. "And, since only what we focus upon is real, the violence we have looked away from merely evaporates!"

Zude took the words seriously. "I don't know. But unless one person raises her eyes and thus emboldens a second and a third to do the same, then the collective lifting of eyes will never happen. A change in our collective beliefs is what is required. You may actually have stated the matter correctly: A hundredth monkey, a critical mass of people lifting their eyes, may make a qualitative difference in material reality." Zude shrugged. "We can't know what will happen when we abolish the Kanshoubu. But we must find out."

Lin-ci's voice was matter-of-fact and uncompromising. "You betray us all, Magister Adverb."

"You are out of line, Magister Win!" Yotoma's equanimity was fraying beyond repair. "Betray is hardly the word," she finished grimly.

"What then is the word?" Lin-ci's voice suddenly approached stridency. "We speak here of over 600,000 women, each of whom has sworn to the Kanshoubu her mind's finest functioning, her heart's best devotion, and her body's last ounce of strength. Now a leader in whom these women have placed their trust, and for whom they would lay down their lives, announces that their gifts of mind, body and heart are no longer needed, that for no reason that this leader can articulate, the Kanshoubu is going out of business, and they will simply have to find some new thing to give their bodies, minds and hearts to." Lin-ci was breathing hard. "Instruct me, please, Magister Lutu. What is the appropriate word for that leader's action?"

Yotoma sat withdrawn in her chair, distaste blanketing her features. She folded her lips inward and clasped them there. She looked at Lin-ci Win's irate countenance, then at Zude's composure.

"Lin-ci," she finally said, "you have got sand in your craw from beaches that Adverb never stepped on. And I have listened to your naysaying just one straw past my patience. I walked into this Peace Room with no notion of what Zude had up her sleeve. And if an hour ago you had told me we'd be considering wiping out the Kanshoubu, I'd have wrapped you in flax stems and sold you for homespun. But I swear, Lin-ci, your contrariness, your mistrust and your blame-fixing are pushing me right into Zude's camp."

The Amah Magister sat immobile, her eyes cast to one side, away from her colleagues. The Vigilante Magister sat, watching and waiting.

Yotoma folded her kerchief, shaking her head in puzzlement. "I said to Self I said, 'Self, how come I feel so good when Zude talks and so rotten when Lin-ci has the floor?' And Self said to me, 'Because Zude's got a vision and a hope, Flossie, but Lin-ci's got nothing but pain and misery and fear.' 'But Self,' I say, 'Zude is talking pure craziness!' Then Self says to me, 'Trust your feelings, Flossie girl. They are the only real guide you've ever had.'" Yotoma glanced at each of her Co-Magisters. "And if feelings were all there is to it, I'd have to say I'd rather go walking with Zude's hope, Lin-ci, no matter how crazy it is, than with your fear, no matter how sane it seems."

Lin-ci Win snapped her head downward, sitting for a moment with her hand shielding her face. She shook her head twice, then released a long sigh. When she looked at her colleagues again, her voice wore the endlessly patient tone of master to student.

"We are talking here of an ancient and fundamental truth, at least in my culture: That humanity must be governed by all-encompassing social mandates so that its essential goodness can be realized, and so that what violence erupts can be controlled. That wisdom has for millennia weathered the insidious teachings of a lesser philosophy which you, Adverb, seem now to be championing. 'Never resist,' that way suggests, 'for resistance only intensifies that which is being resisted.'" Lin-ci's eyes bored into Zude's. "That submissive and servile philosophy is at this moment running rampant on this planet, infecting minds otherwise courageous and stable."

She sat back in her Greatchair and her eyes swept those of both her colleagues. "I know once more why I am Kanshou." She lifted her head higher. "I am Kanshou today for the same reason that I chose to be Kanshou over forty years ago: Because in the rising of the power of women I found my first hope for the appropriate handling of violence. I could see that humanity's goodness was no longer to be endangered by corrupt police and military forces which had only in theory protected and nurtured it. I could see basic human virtue for the first time contained by a formal but organic structure of reason, by a social order that was not imposed from without—as men's social order had always been—but which grew from within, from the Inner Virtue itself."

Lin-ci Win leaned forward. "I could trust the Kanshoubu. The hands of women are accustomed to the nurturing and protection of goodness and of life. And you, Zella Terremoto Adverb, you would have us abolish the only agency that has given meaning to the human need for social order. You would have us forsake that very Order itself for the chaos that will reign without it."

Her last words echoed in the holochamber and faded into silence.

Yotoma studied her Kanshoumates. She took in a long breath.

"I am not this world's oldest living Kanshou," she said quietly. "I am not even its oldest active Kanshou. But I've been around a good while. I had already spent over twenty years on Little Blue before the Kanshoubu even got born. I got to sit at a table with the women who were creating the Femmedarme Cadet Academy. And one of the first gerts from the Vigilancia's new division, called the Flying Daggers, carried me over the Atlantic and back to southern Sudan for my momah's funeral."

She looked hard at the Amah Magister. "Lin-ci, I had your same feelings when I discovered I wanted to be Kanshou. It was a new kind of law and order, the kind that I could trust, the kind that gave a sweet pride to being a woman."

She clasped then unclasped her hands twice, three times.

"I'm trying to figure what's happening here, where you two are parting company, and where I stand. In some ways, Lin-ci, you are more optimistic than many of my own, who say folks are bad from the start and need a lifetime dose of law and order to keep them from getting any worse."

Yotoma wrinkled her spacious forehead, then spoke again.

"By this way of thinking, violence and peacekeeping would be two inseparable and eternal halves of the human coin. The Kanshoubu just put the law and order into the hands of women where it belonged in the first place. But then you bite your thumb at Zude here, accusing her of turning into one of those nonaction-action people who go lingering in rivers and soil and star spirits and let the civilized rest of the world go to perdition in a pitcher. With all due respect, Lin-ci, I think you're mistaken about what our colleague here is proposing."

Magister Adverb was staring at her old friend, alternately amazed and puzzled. Magister Win made an impatient gesture and hardened her mouth. Zude rushed into the widening gap. "Flossie, does it matter..."

"Hush, woman," Magister Lutu admonished. "I am trying to understand you, and the task is not easy." She turned back to the red-caped Amah Magister. "Whether we're talking your people or mine, Lin-ci, we would have to believe that violence is inherent in the human condition, yes? That it will always be with us and the question is how to handle it?"

Lin-ci spoke through a mask of tolerance. "That is my understanding, Magister Lutu."

"I hear Zude saying that violence is not inherent, that it is born from our deepest fears and expectations and nourished by our need to control it. Thus, if we were willing to change ourselves enough, it could be undone."

She paused. No one spoke for a moment. She scratched her close-cropped hair. She waited for some response. Zude supplied it.

"Flossie, what I'm saying isn't new. It's just that..."

"It's just that only mystics, poets and philosophers ever took it seriously, Adverb, because it says loud and clear that we do indeed create our own reality. We've got to take that idea seriously now."

"You neglect the final and most obvious possibility."

Zude and Yotoma swiveled toward their Kanshoumate.

Lin-ci's voice wavered. "This is also the most devastating one, and to my eternal dread, the one that is most likely our destiny." The face that shone from the red Amah cowl looked ready to flood the earth with tears.

Yotoma deliberately softened in the face of Lin-ci's demeanor. Clearly the woman was at the center of some internal storm of which neither she nor Zude could guess the dimensions.

"When I was very small," said the now carefully measured voice of the Magister of Little Blue's largest tri-satrapy, "both my mother and my father were killed in the battle that made Hong Kong a free city under women's rule. They had both been career officers in China's New Army, and they were both a part of the rebel forces who defied that army from within its ranks. I spent my childhood reading tales of warriors, battles, and the emergence and destruction of great kingdoms. I spent my youth poring over military science texts.

"The swearing of my Kanshou Oath was the most meaningful moment I had ever experienced. I believed I was saying the words earnestly: 'I hold in my heart the vision of a world where peacekeeping forces are unnecessary…and my purpose in becoming Kanshou will ever be to render obsolete my own profession and the Kanshoubu itself.'" The Magister's face was pinched. "Veng's betrayal and the desertion of the Asian Amahs set me to a re-examination of that oath. I now know that I had never said those words earnestly. I had said them blithely."

Neither Zude nor Yotoma stirred. Lin-ci spoke harshly.

"I thought that to render the Kanshoubu obsolete meant that we would have won, that we would have made a world where men controlled their own violence, where civilians were so enlightened that only a civilian social order would be necessary to handle any infraction. I thought in my innocence that it would be a shame to lose the Kanshoubu, and of course I would miss it. But, my young heart told me, what a victory that loss would testify to: That we had at last harnessed and controlled human violence!"

The red-clad Amah smiled wryly.

"But here is what I found, my Kanshoumates, in the depths of my despair. Here is the root of my rage at your proposal, Zella Adverb. Here is what both of you have failed to understand from the start, the reason that Kanshou will never sanction your scheme."

Her words came very slowly. "Adverb is wrong. Violence will never disappear. But not because it is built from the start into every synapse of our consciousness, not because it lets us sin so that we can be redeemed, not because it provides karmic ribbons by which we must learn compassion, and not because it is the human form of some universal necessity for imbalance."

Lin-ci Win arched one eyebrow high, and her smile bespoke self-contempt. "Violence is an inherent part of the human condition, and we will never choose to live without it," she over-enunciated each word, "because we like it that way."

"Doubledamn!" The words exploded in a whisper from Yotoma's lips. Immediately her head swung back and forth in denial. Her voice rose. "Lin-ci, not so! You don't anymore believe that drivel than you think you can catch wind in a cabbage net!"

"Why not, Magister Lutu?" The Amah Magister was relentless. "You can submit to me that through the ages human beings have fought for food, for territory, for God, for glory and for love, and I can show you that such motives constitute only part of the story, that they only mask a crude but remarkably dependable rush of adrenaline that quickens in every person at the prospect of blood and conquest. Sing me ballads about the rise and fall of mighty empires and the triumph of just societies over barbarism, and I can disrupt your harmonies by unveiling for you the spark of violence that lies at the birth not only of every army but of every police force or peacekeeping agency since the dawn of human consciousness. Even the Kanshoubu."

Lin-ci's laugh was empty. "Even in times of justice and plenty we will look for an enemy, we will cultivate evil, we will find a reason to defend, a reason to take violent action." She surveyed the grim countenances of her Co-Magisters. "We have institutionalized violence simply because we desire it." She paused. "And if all other proof fails, we as Kanshou have only to look honestly into our own hearts in this very moment and see there that same stark desire. To disband the Kanshoubu is to rob myself of the thing I love most: The violence for which I have lived my life."

The three Magisters sat transfixed in the silence.

Zude spoke at last, quietly. "You have not lived your life for violence, Magister Win."

"I have done precisely that, Magister Adverb."

"I don't believe you."

Lin-ci Win looked directly at the younger woman. "That is my truth as I see it. I will not shun it, ugly as its image may be. Let me confront my own failure, Zella Adverb."

"Your only failure, Magister Win, is one of imagination," Zude countered. "And we've all suffered from it! It is hard to visualize what we would do in a world without violence because we have lived with it for so long. But we know—Kanshou know —-that there are adrenaline rushes aplenty from sources other than quelling violence. We know the thrill of competition and of teamwork. We know the exhilaration of a hard job well done. We know the ecstasy of seeing our creations come into being. Kanshou are not dependent upon violence for the joys of their existence. I ask you to consider that, Lin-ci Win, and to trust it. I suspect you know it as well or better than either Yotoma or I."

In the long silence, Lin-ci dropped her eyes and studied her hands. Then she straightened in her Greatchair.

"So!" she said with a hollow vigor. "I will watch with interest, Magister Adverb, as you approach the Heart of All Kanshou, as you attempt this worldwide conversion of our Vigilantes and Femmedarmes and Amahs. I will listen with care as a highly regarded Magister turns mendicant preacher and slaps the back of every sensible, trustworthy and responsible Foot-Shrieve on Little

Blue, assuring her that all she must do to ring in a new reality is lift her eyes from the pain and violence that constitute the very fabric of her life and look to a sweeter vision in the clouds where the violence that she secretly loves will be no more. I will observe her response carefully, Magister Adverb."

Zude shot a glance at Yotoma, who sat unmoving behind a scowl. Then she focused on her own big hands clasped before her.

"Magister Win, even if you are right, that we have chosen violence in the past—and for the reason you give—still, we are not bound to make that same choice again. To the extent that we can imagine or expect a world without violence, to that extent we can choose to create that world."

No one moved or spoke. It was clear that the final meeting of Little Blue's Magisters was drawing to a close. The holochamber held thousands of words in its embrace, awaiting an as yet undetermined departure ritual.

Flossie Yotoma Lutu cleared her throat. "Lin-ci, I do not believe what you are saying about Kanshou or about your own Self, that you love violence. Every interchange we have had over the decades that we have worked together gives the lie to your words here tonight." Yotoma's figure was ramrod straight. "But your words have pushed me unequivocally to my decision, because from them I realized something. I realized that not to support Adverb in her effort to abolish the Kanshoubu would be at the very least to affirm what you call our desire for violence, and at the very most it would be to affirm the inevitability of violence in human beings. I can't affirm those things, Lin-ci. And I don't think you can either."

Yotoma wiped her face again with the green kerchief and restored it to her belt.

"So," she said, "I will walk side by side with Magister Adverb when she lays out her plan to the Amahs and the Femmedarmes and the Vigilantes of Little Blue. I will also be right there with her when she presents it to the Heart of All Kanshou. And, Spirit Willing, when this old world shifts on its metaphysical axis, me and Magister Adverb, we will be holding hands together, just waiting to step out into splendor!"

Then Yotoma added softly, "Nothing would give me more joy than to be holding your hand as well, Lin-ci Win."

Lin-ci Win raised her head high. Yotoma thought she might be trying to smile. "A vision appropriate to your madness, my colleagues." She adjusted her Amah cloak. "My companion in these times to come will be my own Heart of Darkness, whose presence has been articulated and intensified in this, our last meeting."

Lin-ci's voice became high and brittle, and her face flushed. "Whatever our differences, Magisters, I will always deeply value the association we have shared." She began searching the Peace Room below her for her attending Amahs.

"Magister Win." Zude's voice halted Lin-ci Win in her movements. Zude held the woman's eyes. "I want nothing more on this earth than to have you join us at the meeting of the Heart of All Kanshou. Even if only to be our adversary on that occasion."

"If I came, which is highly unlikely, that would certainly be my role, Magister Adverb."

Zude nodded.

"Go well, Magister Win," said Yotoma.

"I shall, Magister Lutu. Thank you." She signaled her staff.

The figure of the Amah Magister, mobile Greatchair and all, disappeared in an instant, leaving for the eyes of those still sitting there a pulsing afterimage of red and silver.

10

> You cannot harm me, you cannot harm me,
> one who has dreamed a dream like mine.
> *Wisdom of the Ancients*

"She will never agree!" argued a passionate Amah in one of the common rooms of the Places for the Heart. "Nor should she! Magister Win is our only hope!"

"But if the Magisters agreed, we would follow!" objected a Vigilante. "All of us!"

"Not I!"

"Yes you, you too!"

"We'd all follow!" came another shout from the crowd of Kanshou. "We always have!"

A chorus of voices rose in approval; others roared, "No!"

To one side of the clamorous discussion, a Femmedarme—a bit tipsy—drained her nukupunch. "They're right," she drawled to her Amah companion. "We'd follow in a minute if the Magisters agreed, even if it meant no more Kanshou. The Magisters are supposed to find a way to agree with each other. They always have. That's their job!"

"I'm not so sure, Darmie," replied the Amah Jing-Cha, pinching off a bite of breadfruit. "The consensus of the Magisters is important, but it's not law. In fact," she observed, wagging a finger at her Kanshoumate, "a Magister's decision to go against the tide is not only her right but sometimes her duty."

211

The Femmedarme lifted a flagon, then set it back down on the table with a thump of belligerence.

"Well, I say it's a betrayal. And it's not just me. Jing-Cha, if the Magisters' decision were unanimous—whatever it was—then every Kanshou of the name would stand up and cheer. She'd feel like all's right with the world again at last!"

"You make us sound like mindless automatons, Darmie, never questioning the Magisters." Jing-Cha began clearing her breakfast crocks. "Anyway, I'm heading for the flatcast. The Heart's about to begin and I don't want to miss it. They may even decide today." She studied her Kanshoumate. "Come on. Both of us could use some fresh air."

Outside, the well-tended paths and hillocks of Nuku Hiva in the Marquesas Islands teemed with color, some of it from bright native prints of civilian observers, more of it in the greens, reds and blues of visiting Kanshou. In the arcades and media areas, the Daily Voice coverage had already begun. Scrolling upward on the flatcast screens were the results of the one-vote-per-person-per-day straw ballot of both free citizens and habitantes on the radical propositions before the Heart. Each morning, before beginning their deliberations, Heart Members studied these global figures as well as summaries of widespread individual feedback.

The flatcast announcer spoke in voice-over. "Mere minutes from now, the Heart of All Kanshou will reconvene for its eighth day of study and deliberation in the meeting rooms of Global Kanshoubu Headquarters. Heart Members, as you'll recall, are elected by the entire body of global Kanshou. They are retired Shrieves of every rank and every satrapy. They have ultimate authority over the policies of the Kanshoubu, and their decision, whatever it is to be, will in these critical times undoubtedly be ratified immediately by our legislative and judicial branches, the Central Web and the Kitchen Table.

"As you can see, the polls show habitantes continuing to favor the dismantling of the Kanshoubu—understandably, because that proposal entails their freedom. But there is still little consistency of opinion among civilian citizenry; their votes continue to vacillate from yea to nay by as much as forty percentage points over each twenty-four-hour period.

"The 600,000 Kanshou themselves, whose careers are in question, are also sharply divided on the proposal. Many believe that these are exceptional times, calling for profoundly new ways of thinking and acting. Others resist what they view as any affront to their beloved Kanshoubu.

"And now, Magisters Flossie Yotoma Lutu and Zella Terremoto Adverb are about to enter the Rotunda Gather-Room of the Places for the Heart. There they will present their final arguments for the abolition of the Kanshoubu. The Heart Members are taking their seats."

Bosca sat with her eyes closed, holding the tiny short-band communicator tab in her hand. She read the tacto-time in Zude's desk and checked once more the comstation monitor for incoming messages. With a sigh of resolve, she held up the comunit and slid the tiny Call orb to the right.

Zude's flattened voice crackled through the small silver pad in Bosca's hand. "Adverb here." A background of animated voices surged around the words.

"Still no message, Magister," Bosca said. "I'll continue to stand by."

"Okay. Thanks, Bosca." The voice held both an excited tension and a shade of disappointment. "We're about to go in," Zude added, "so you're on your own when the call comes through."

"I know." Bosca paused. "¡Qué la fortuna te mire con buenos ojos!"

Zude chuckled. "Abrazos." The silver tab went silent.

Bosca set aside the comtab and closed her eyes again. Almost thirty minutes passed before a chime broke her reverie. On the comscreen appeared the head of a woman with long brown hair and a silver unicorn dangling from her ear. Bosca's hand rose involuntarily to rest gently upon the screen so that it covered the lower part of the woman's cheek. Technology augmented the moment, intensifying the dynamic contact that flared between the two women—Bosca in the Taiohaé Bay quarters of Zella Terremoto Adverb, and Jezebel Stronglaces on the North Island of New Zealand, 3,200 kilometers southwest of the Marquesas. Both women smiled, their eyes closed.

"A pleasure to meet you at last!" Bosca heard in her head.

"A pleasure for me, too," she replied, basking in the moment.

"How late am I?" Jez finally asked aloud, her eyes meeting Bosca's.

"Too late to talk with Zude, I'm afraid. They are already in today's session."

Jez sighed. "We just now found comunits that are back on line. Storms had taken out long-range transmissions."

"And Magister Win?" Bosca asked gently. "You were chasing her all over China."

"China and the islands," Jez added. "We finally found her here. Bosca, I spent last evening with the Magister of the Amahs in a bed of hot springs on the side of a volcano. Apparently it's one of her favorite retreat places."

"And you talked?"

"Yes, for all the good it did." Jez sighed. "She was not overjoyed to see me. But we've had some special ties, so she did me the honor of letting me be with her alone there in the pools. She's a large woman, you know, and it takes three of her Amahs to lift her in and out of her Greatchair, or to shift her around in the water. She wouldn't let me help her. Always called on them. We Sat Hearkening for three hours together and I left her just after midnight—that's three in the morning your time."

Bosca waited quietly.

"She still won't commit either way," Jez said at last. "I know Zude has hoped that she'd make some decision, yes or no, maybe even rocket at the last minute to Nuku Hiva to announce it to the Heart." She didn't conceal her regret. "There's no chance she could make it to the meeting now. It's three hours by rocket, and anyway she's still too racked by indecision." Jez pushed both hands through her hair, a gesture so reminiscent of Zude that Bosca caught her breath. "So," Jez finished, "the Heart will do whatever it does without the participation of Lin-ci Win."

Bosca shook her head. "Zude is still convinced that she and Magister Lutu can sway the Heart. Neither of them has slept much lately. They've been through every satrapy…sometimes together, usually alone…talking with Kanshou and Kanshou cadets night and day, one on one or in small groups. They've held forums, discussions, parties and weight-free dances, even primp-light performances."

Bosca slowed her speech. "And just by their presence, Jezebel, people are often moved to follow them. It's a little awesome to watch." Bosca paused altogether. "Both of them are transformed. It might not even matter if the Heart says, No, because they are so entranced by their own vision."

Jez laughed quietly. "Maybe if the Heart says, No, the two of them will just discorporate. Fly away together into the Great Stream, leaving us all behind."

"That may be truer than you think." When Jez raised her eyebrows, Bosca explained. "Have you watched the flatcasts of the proceedings?"

"Only the first one in full."

"Well, Magister Lutu has been behaving unconventionally. Her original presentation was wonderful, and then for three days she very respectfully and thoroughly countered all the opposing arguments and evidence. But at the end of the fourth day, she didn't respond to one of the questions. Instead, she sat staring at the far wall. She hasn't participated since."

"Flossie Yotoma Lutu?" Jez exclaimed.

Bosca nodded. "When a member of the Heart addresses her, she snaps to attention, apologizes, but declines to respond. Then Zude steps in and covers for her. For a little while every night she and Zude sit together in silence in the beach-house tower. Then Zude helps Yotoma's aides tuck her into bed." Bosca paused. "Zude isn't worried about her." She smiled. "Zude isn't worried about anything."

"So I gather," said Jez. "Speaking of unusual conduct, I hear that one member of the Heart was also behaving, ah, irregularly."

"Winifred W. Glee, retired Vice-Magister of the Vigilancia, Nueva Tierra Sur?"

"The same."

"It's true. In the middle of one of the investigative committee reports on the third day, Vice-Magister Glee announced that, the night before, her spiritual guides had enlightened her about the proposal from their cosmic perspective. 'I'm now in absolute accord with the recommendation to abolish the Kanshoubu,' she essentially said, 'and since each of you, my colleagues, must also have been visited by your personal spiritual guides and seen the same truth of the matter, the present proceedings are clearly a travesty and a waste of time.' Then she calls for the immediate vote on the question."

"High drama!" breathed Jez.

"Yes," agreed Bosca, "particularly since Vice-Magister Glee is one of the best-loved Members of the Heart. They had quite a time silencing her, but then she lapsed into a happy trance, like Yotoma." Bosca herself smiled. "One rumor has it that Vice-Magister Glee and Magister Lutu exchanged a wink yesterday. Zude says she didn't see it, but that it could have happened."

Jez laughed. "Well. Please tell Zude I wish I could have been more helpful with Lin-ci." When Bosca nodded, Jez added, "And give her my love."

"I will," said Bosca. "I will."

Jez held up her hands, palms forward. "A privilege, Bosca."

"A privilege, Jezebel." Bosca placed her own hands over those of Jezebel on the monitor. She closed her eyes.

After the screen went blank, Bosca lowered her hands and sat quietly. Then she tuned the comchannel to Zella Terremoto Adverb's final speech to the Heart of All Kanshou.

Communication and comfort had been the design priorities for the Rotunda Gather-Room that housed the Heart's present deliberations. The round-domed space spanned a diameter of some one hundred meters, and the technology of shield harmonics allowed the walls to be paqued to represent a wide range of holo-options. On this day, the walls were a simple transparent stasis field that revealed the lush gardens, arcades and foyers that surrounded the Gather-Room. Sunlight, filtered by a dense cover of leaves, drifted through the transparent roofing at the top of the dome and added to the sense that the Heart of All Kanshou conducted its business out of doors.

Each of the 18 Members of the Heart wore the tunic color of her tri-satrapy and sat in a chair covered with a wide-spread tekla cape of royal purple, the emblem of the special Kanshou duty she performed in her retirement. Each light but well-padded chair was capable of tilting to recline, of spinning full circle to face any speaker, or of rising on silent jets to offer its occupant better sightlines or greater visibility. The unit also provided for the Heart member her own personal reader light and writing board, her own augmented fresh-air shaft and visually enhanced magnopad, and her own amplification for voices too soft for her ears.

The chairs on this morning, including those of Zude and Yotoma, were in the northeast quadrant of the room. They had been placed in an approximate double circle formation, those in the back row raised slightly higher than those in the front. There was an intimacy to the grouping that separated it from the unused and empty part of the vast room, and from the distant south-western door that stood beyond the wide expanse of the carpeted floor. Parked on the carpeting near the group was the jill-jogger whose air jets and standing straps had carried the Heart's oldest member, Sub-Aga Mollie Mordecaia of Jericho, from the visitors' quarters to the meeting.

Seated together in the back row were the Communication Escorts, Vigilante N. Louise Mead and Femmedarme Jovana Gorodhov. It was Marshal Mead's turn to hold the gavel.

Inconspicuous mikcam stations in the walls and dome were focused on a space of about five meters in diamenter that separated the circled chairs. In this enclosed area stood the Magister of Nueva Tierra, wearing a formal tunic of cobalt blue and her dress sash of silver. She was in the midst of her address to her colleagues, the Heart of All Kanshou.

"So," Zude said, turning slowly to include the full circle of her audience, "we've tried to show that the proposal is practical, that it could be carried out with ease." As she continued, her eyes sought some rapport with Flossie Yotoma Lutu. But the relaxed and immobile Femmedarme Magister gave no indication that she had heard Zude, remaining calmly attentive to one of the swaying tree limbs beyond the wall of the Gather-Room.

"I declare for all who will hear," Zude continued, "that there could never have been for me a calling more rich in pride and satisfaction, a calling more necessary in its time to the smooth operation of this planet's social processes, than that of the Femmedarme, the Amah or the Vigilante."

A long silence held the speaker and her listeners in its custody.

"But our job is finished. Well done, and finished." She studied the faces that surrounded her. "In the traditions of public discourse," she went on crisply, "my task would be to remind you now of our need to abolish the Kanshoubu. But I shall not speak of that, because focusing on need merely emphasizes a negativity, a sense of lack, and…"

"May I interrupt, Magister?" The voice rose from Femmedarme Aga Malika Katir. There was a general stir at the breach of protocol.

"To be sure," said Zude, graciously.

"Magister Adverb," the Aga's crusty voice continued, "it sounds like you are about to launch into another of your happiness lectures. I can't sit still for much more of that empty and excessively cheerful verbiage." She looked at her colleagues. "I think others may agree."

Vigilante Marshal Mead pounded the gavel.

"Out of line, Aga Katir. And it doesn't matter who agrees with you. Magister Adverb has the floor."

Zude smiled easily at the Communication Escort. "Marshal, the proposal before us is of unprecedented importance. I'm glad to yield to any comments or questions, as long as I have opportunity for final appeal."

Mead's eyes swept the room. "Granted," she announced. "Without objection then, you are open to questions." She gave a sharp rap to the gavel and settled back in her chair.

Zude faced Katir. "Aga?"

"That's all," Katir mumbled. "Just curb your enthusiasm, Magister Adverb. Stick to causes and material issues, to good reason in controversy."

The Escort intervened coolly. "The Magister can stick to whatever she pleases, Aga. Any attitude on the part of a speaker is appropriate, unless it becomes disruptive." She cast her eyes around the gathering. "A little enthusiasm about anything might not hurt the Heart right now."

"Escort Mead," said Amah Jing-Cha Honora Wang, one of the few in the room still sporting dark hair. At Mead's nod she addressed Zude. "Our proceedings here have been thorough, but we haven't looked hard enough at the fact that Magister Lin-ci Win is not with us. I want to hear it from you, and from Magister Lutu if she will speak: How can you hope to convince us to act on this proposition when Magister Win opposes it?"

Zude drew in a breath and intentionally relaxed. Heart Members stirred and focused on Zude with sharpened attention. "Jing-Cha," she said, "Magister Win has not opposed the abolition of the Kanshoubu. Her lack of comment must be interpreted as neutrality." She paused. "Any member of this body, for instance, has the option of silence. She can step aside when the Heart's Desire is taken, so as not to block the will of the group. Magister Win is stepping aside, allowing you," her hand swept the assembly, "to make the decision. She cannot be said to be opposed. She is simply silent."

Amah Matrix Major Joann Nikobishi objected. "I know Lin-ci Win well, Magister. In my experience of her, she has an opinion on every subject. She is fair-minded, yes. And careful in her weighing of the evidence. But indecisive? Never. She has been asked countless times over the last month to support the abolition of the Kanshoubu. And she is silent. Clearly, she has decided not to do so."

"Marshal," growled Sub-Aga Mollie Mordecaia, "she has also been asked countless times over the last month not to support the abolition of the Kanshoubu. Her silence might equally mean she has decided to support it."

Malika Katir exploded. "Negative, Sub-Aga! It's not the same thing!"

"Order!" Marshal Mead's gavel cracked. "We will not drown ourselves in speculation here!"

"With respect, Aga Katir," Femmedarme Mordecaia exclaimed, gesturing forcefully with her functional left arm. "Escort Mead is right. We can't dicker around trying to second-guess Magister Win." She focused on Amah Wang. "I've been in the Heart a long time and, to be honest, Jing-Cha, I'm like you. It galls me to think I have to act on this proposal when it comes from only two of our Commanders-in-Chief."

Slowly, she rotated her deeply reclined chair and scanned every member of the group.

"But, like it or not," she grimaced, "we're going to have to decide this thing without Magister Win's opinion. I think the Heart is capable of doing that."

"Sub-Aga," said Zude quietly, "I think you are right."

"Magister Adverb," Vigilante Mariner Myrtha Bisbruja interposed, looking at Zude over her old-fashioned glasses.

"Mariner Bisbruja," Zude acknowledged, meeting her gaze.

"And Magister Lutu," Bisbruja said pointedly. All eyes turned to Yotoma, whose concentrated stare had shifted from the outside tree to a seam in the wall segment across the circle from her. When Yotoma did not respond, Myrtha Bisbruja audibly released a short breath and turned her attention back to Zude.

"Magister," she said, pushing her glasses further down her nose, the better to see Zude over their rims, "though we have requested it a number of times, you have given us no realistic hint of what the effect would be of abolishing the Kanshoubu."

Zude shook her head.

"Mariner, I can't tell you—and neither can anyone in this room—what would happen if we kept the Kanshoubu. Would the preservation of the Kanshoubu stop the children from dying? Or bring back the animals? Would it produce an answer to the question of why they have chosen to leave us? If we kept the Femmedarmes and the Vigilantes and the Amahs, would children suddenly begin to be born again? If we kept the Kanshoubu, would the existence of the human enterprise be guaranteed?"

Zude put her hand on her chest. "If I could do so without offending Aga Katir, I would sketch for you the glorious visions of the future that to me are the clear consequence of abolishing our peacekeeping corps. But, alas, there is no reasoning behind these visions, no material causation, only my desires and my convictions."

She smiled broadly at Katir. "And so, I will refrain."

There were low chuckles and some modest shifts of position in the big chairs.

Bisbruja moved forward in her seat and leaned on an armrest. "Magister, many of us here in this assembly are amazed that this proposal of yours has even gotten as far as this body." She still peered at Zude over her glasses. "We listen to you only out of respect for your office...and, some of us, still out of respect for you." She removed her glasses and rubbed her eyes. "We also listen to you because we are desperate," she looked up, "desperate for any hope that there may be some future for our species."

The Mariner shook her head, reclaimed her assertiveness. "I agree that, in our present distress, some simplifying of government structures might be called for, that we might best be moving toward some changes that would allow us merely to accept our fate and live out these final days in peace." Her voice rose in volume. "But why the Kanshoubu? Why target for oblivion the one agency that can guarantee us that peace, the one agency that can save us from widespread anarchy and sheer chaos? Why not the Central Web or the Size Bureau? Why do you choose the largest group of public servants on the planet—and not only the largest, but the most efficient and most dedicated. Why single out our Shrieves?"

The Mariner shook her glasses at Zude. "Where is the justice, or the good sense, in focusing upon the Kanshoubu?" The glasses trembled visibly in her outstretched hand.

Her question echoed in the silence of the Gather-Room.

"I am far from believing in the death of our species, Mariner Bisbruja," Zude said. She turned and looked into the tough old eyes of Vigilante Captain Luz Adelia Zurbarán of Nicaragua, whose unfailing support she, as a brand new Matrix Major, had once so heavily depended upon. Zurbarán's countenance revealed nothing, only an alert attentiveness. Zude continued.

"I pick the Kanshou because there are some jobs that only Kanshou are capable of performing. The eradication of the expectation of violence is one of those tasks."

Zude quietly, slowly scanned the circle, inviting each woman there to question further. When no one responded, she looked again at Yotoma. The Femmedarme Magister still gazed into space.

"Vigilante Bisbruja is wise to ask about justice," Zude continued, "because that's what our work has been about. Justice, in the face of malevolence. Justice, in the face of exploitation or ignorance. Justice."

Zude closed her eyes briefly and drew in a long breath.

"I have to tell you all of my truth now," she declared, "for you deserve to know it, whatever the consequences." She tilted her head upward and said, "I can no longer serve the law. I can no longer serve justice. The time of law and justice has passed."

No member of the Heart moved even the smallest muscle.

Abruptly, Zude turned toward Flossie Yotoma Lutu. Sure enough, the Femmedarme Magister's warm brown eyes were smiling now into her own, alert and present, as they had not been for days. Heartened, Zude's voice rose in volume. "Colleagues, in the new world that is on our doorstep, justice and the law are antiquated concepts. I am ready—I believe we all are ready now—to see that laws create crime, that prisons create criminals, and that what we have called justice is actually a hindrance to human freedom."

Zude addressed Vigilante Bisbruja directly. "Far from fearing the anarchy that you mention, Mariner, I now understand that anarchism has been a pathfinder for the next stage of human evolution. Kanshoumates, the old wineskins of law and justice cannot contain the flood of forgiveness that is upon the world."

Out of the corner of her eye, Zude registered the forward movement of Adjutant Major Rabia Nuruk of Istanbul, her face a landscape of suppressed emotion. Zude waited, calm and respectful, for the woman's outburst.

Nuruk expelled a short disgusted breath, waved a dismissive hand, shook her head. She sat back in an attitude of enforced patience, looking grimly at the speaker.

Zude spoke again. "In the vocabulary of peacekeeping officers throughout history, I have just uttered an indecency: forgiveness. Forgive the murderer, Magister Adverb? Forgive the rapist? And I reply, 'Precisely. Forgive them all. Do not arrest them, do not prosecute them, do not imprison them. Any punishment due them resides in their own full knowledge of the act they have committed, and not in the meting out of punishment by any human tribunal. Let them be.'"

Zude surveyed the room. She found the bobbing gray head of Vice-Magister Winifred Glee, and the raised thumb, inconspicuous but explicit, of Flossie Yotoma Lutu. Some of the faces were astonished or puzzled, others incredulous. Still others registered distaste or anger. Some faces Zude could not read. None, she observed, wore the mask of boredom.

Her gaze fell upon Amah Mariner First Class Kit Lunming from Shanghai, an old friend. Zude noted that Lunming had not dropped her head in embarrassment, but sat in concentrated attention, her chin leaning on the hollow molded by her forefinger and thumb. A wave of gratitude passed over Zude. It eased her more massive bodily tensions and refined the edges of the path before her. She pressed her lips together in a half-smile at Lunming for the gift that the Amah had unwittingly bestowed.

She turned to Malika Katir, who had originally interrupted her. "Aga, you ask me to stick to 'good reason in controversy,' as rightly you should. At least in principle, reason has always been our straightedge, the standard by which we measure our ideas and actions. I have been first to say to those who would fight, 'Come, let us reason together.'"

Zude clasped her hands behind her back and turned casually, assessing another broad range of response in her listeners.

"But reason has imprisoned me in its own closed system, in its own rules and fallacies. It has limited my thoughts and thus my reality. Reason is only a one-minute increment on a world-wide spectrum. It is the contour of one snowflake in the swirl of conformations that comprise the storm of my human capabilities. I have focused upon that one tiny increment, upon that single snowflake, to the exclusion of the spectrum and the storm, and I have granted to reason a supremacy that must give way now to my full human legacy."

Rabia Nuruk slumped further back into her chair, a heap of disapproval. Zude deliberately turned to her.

"Adjutant Major, reason can no longer serve as my sole measuring stick for value or policy decisions in human affairs. Alone, it's too confining. I'm using other abilities now, abilities that, in the service of reason, I have belittled and disparaged: My feelings, my hunches and, most of all, my ability to visualize beyond my daily experiences."

Zude had grown breathless in her description. Purposefully, she calmed herself and met the eyes of individual Members of the Heart, addressing some by name. "It's the magic of my life that I'm speaking of, Sea Captain Victoria Painter. I'm talking about the things I've always called coincidence or miracles. Crazy things, Sky Commander del Dragón, which I now realize are among the proper guidelines for human action."

Zude opened her arms. "Perhaps, my colleagues, the rumors are true. Perhaps I have lost my mind." She laughed and dropped her arms. "Whatever I may have lost," she said quietly, "I have gained an extraordinary peace and an exhilarating passion." She extended her hand. "I invite you to join me in those newfound joys."

"I'll join you, Magister Adverb," said a voice from behind her. Every eye turned to Femmedarme Magister Lutu, who sat calmly surveying the Heart. "And, if you'll permit me, I will speak briefly now."

"With great pleasure," said Zude, sinking easily into her own chair.

"Marshal Mead?" Yotoma addressed the Escort.

"Of course, Magister," Mead nodded. Heart Members stirred in their chairs with renewed interest.

Flossie Yotoma Lutu rose. She was tall and smooth in her green dress tunic, her Magister's sash marking the bottom of her long upper torso. "A question first," she said. She turned to the Heart's resting Communication Escort. "Hedwoman Gorodhov, we've done a good bit of hard work together for the Femmedarmery. Would you agree?"

"Lots of it, Magister Lutu," replied Jovana Gorodhov. She smiled. "The Central Ural Garrison and Europe's military tribunals testify to that."

"And would you say, Hedwoman, that I have been a reasonable person?"

"A relentlessly reasonable person," Gorodhov replied with a wry smile, "more hidebound by reason than any Kanshou I've known. A stickler for law and logic."

Yotoma nodded her thanks, then addressed the assembly. "I ask," she said, "because it's got to be clear that no one is exempt from the changes afoot on this planet. In fact," and her eyes fastened briefly on Aga Katir, then on Rabia Nuruk, "it may be those of us most dedicated to reason and justice who are most vulnerable to the changes."

Yotoma's stance took on a formality only partially military in nature.

"I speak now as a Rememorante Afortunada," she intoned. Immediately her audience was compelled to a new mood. Resistances lowered, all heads came up, all ears awoke.

"I speak, calling back my childhood near Juba in Sudan, two days' walk from the White Nile, calling back a jackal named

Koussi, calling back Koussi as he came into our village from the desert almost every night, usually just before dawn, to scavenge our garbage and rubbish heaps."

Her voice took on the storyteller's cadence.

"We had good communions, Koussi and I. I would squat low at a distance from him, watching him tear at bones or shucks. He never got his belly full, but when he had eaten all he could find, he would sit with me for a while, his small gray body hard to see against the sky behind him. I knew he belonged to a pack, but other jackals never came near.

"Now and again Koussi would all of a sudden lift his nose high to the sky, then relax again. Or sometimes he'd point his nose up and then take off, fast as the wind, like danger was just around the corner. I always wondered why he raised his nose like that. He seemed to be listening raptly to something finely tuned. I listened too—at the time, and long after the time when he ever came again. I have been listening on and off all my life. Sometimes, it has seemed, I could actually hear it, far in the distance, a single tune like my momah's voice, or the faint chords of a choir, or instruments. I would hunker down and try harder to hear it, because it sounded comforting, like a true home. But the harder I tried, the sooner it would fade away. I could never hear it clearly."

Magister Lutu's voice became matter-of-fact.

"And then I got educated. I practiced law. I became a police officer. And after the Kanshoubu was born, I held seats of judgement in Femmedarme and civilian tribunals, listening to other voices, hearing no music. Hearing only the summons of law and justice." She sighed. "The only internal work I ever did was to carry on conversations with my Self—rational dialogues, usually, in which I weighed the value and efficacy of one path or another."

Yotoma cut her eyes at Zude, noting there a barely perceptible nod. An old merriment sparked the features of both women.

Yotoma stood in the precise center of the circle and announced, "I know now what Koussi heard." She turned in an irregular pattern so as to spread her attention throughout the assembly.

"He heard the music of the Source Self." She paused.

"Several of you Afortunadas here have heard the howling of jackals and you know how haunting those cries were—even terrifying. But to Koussi those howls were music, the music of the jackal pack—not only the music that warned them of danger but the music that was their home, their center, their joy. No matter how far apart they had wandered."

Yotoma drew a long breath. "Kanshoumates, you deserve to know why I have withdrawn from our proceedings these last few days, why I've left the hard work to Magister Adverb."

She rested one hand on the half-hitch of her sash and turned her eyes for a moment to Femmedarme Rabia Nuruk. "Simply put," she said, "I have at last been listening to the music."

No one moved.

Yotoma continued. "By the grace of that music—that magnificent symphony—I have been recalling every executive decision that I have made over the last twenty-odd years for the Africa-Europe-Mideast Tri-Satrapy. I have been measuring the sympathetic vibration of every one of those decisions by the music in my soul. I found some of them to be in harmony with my symphony. Some others, though they may have seemed wise enough at the time, are now loud and dissonant, a cacophony of inappropriate thoughts and actions. I could never make those same decisions again. Never."

Yotoma contemplated the group.

"There are four of you right here in this room, Members of the Heart of All Kanshou, who have also been hearing the music, who have come into full contact with your Source Selves, who now know where your true guidance lies. I won't point you out. You know who you are."

As she explored the faces before her, she carefully focused on foreheads rather than on eyes.

"When I heard you listening with me, even as we also heard Adverb's words, I knew for the first time what the Heart's decision will be. You have given me faith. And I thank you."

Yotoma waited for many seconds before she bowed to Escort Mead and took her seat beside Zude.

In the silence of the Gather-Room, Amah Sea Admiral Sulan Ka'ahumanu's voice was a piercing whisper: "Thank you, Magister."

Gently, Yotoma nodded to her.

Zude rose. She let the silence lengthen while she gauged the mood of her listeners. At last she spoke.

"My colleagues, if we close our eyes and settle our minds into the comfort of the best that is within us, into our memories of a child's laughter or our first breathtaking discovery of love, if we can touch the Inner Self that reminds us of who we truly are, then we can see there the meaning and the beauty of our lives."

She paused, watching some pairs of eyes as they closed, other pairs as they focused upon her. She kept her own eyes open, her voice matter-of-fact.

"We can also see the linear progress of Time as we have conceived it. It presses toward us out of the vivid and magnificent narrative that we call our history, flowing forward from this moment into the countless unknown possibilities that we call our future. In that flow of Time is a window. It has been opening gradually over the past weeks, and now it is closing again. Once it closes, it will be lost forever."

Zude held the moment carefully.

"This window frames the most splendid of our possible futures. It urges us to shake off fears and old beliefs. It dares us to test our identity as women of uncompromising courage and good will."

Zude now spoke slowly, firmly.

"The present is the only thing we have, and the power of all human wanting, in all past moments of human experience, is visiting us in this present moment. Here. Now. At the sill of this window in time."

She turned within the circle, looking directly at whatever eyes would meet hers.

"We cannot step through the window of yesterday or a few hours ago, for those moments have fled. We cannot step through it tonight or tomorrow, for by then the window will have closed. We can only step through it now."

Zude realized that she was holding her Magister's sash, her thumb stroking it lightly. Unhurriedly, she studied the sash and then gently pressed its ends against her cobalt blue tunic. She raised her head.

"You are the only people in the world," she said, "who can take us through the window. You are, right here and right now, the key players in humanity's most crucial decision. What you are called upon to do will come from the deepest knowledge of your truest Self. With your dissolving of the Kanshoubu, every Amah, every Femmedarme, every Vigilante—and every other person on Little Blue—will be released to the rich achievement of this next step in human evolution."

Zude's eyes were alight. Her audience was motionless. An audible sniff came from someone behind her. Casually, Zude turned to see Flyer First Class Niki Keya of Calcutta pressing a handkerchief to her cheek. The old Amah had been merciless in her hounding of Zude and Yotoma during the past week. As she caught Zude's eye, Keya coughed several times and blew her nose, conspicuously dealing with the symptoms of a bad cold.

When the Magister spoke again, she did close her eyes.

"You are Our Heart," she said. "You are those in whom every Kanshou trusts. We thank you for keeping us these many years in such safety, in such honor, and in such love."

There was no sound. For one fragile moment, the will of every Kanshou in the room rose into a singularity of understanding and acceptance. Zude held her breath. The moment endured. And still endured. It did not begin to fray until Amah Keya's sniffing nudged the group into small tension-relieving movements.

Zude dared to open her eyes. The array of faces around her wore a wide spectrum of feelings, some of them changing—even as she watched them—from a deep wonder to a smiling conviction. Others were frozen in bewilderment or concern. Still others fought to control displeasure or frustration.

Zude released a slow sigh and started toward her seat. She was halted in her tracks by the steady voice of Vice-Magister Winifred Glee, who was on her feet and staring across the rotunda at its southwestern entrance.

"She's coming," Glee announced, her smile dazzling. "Magister Lin-ci Win is coming!"

Chairs swiveled. Eyes began looking with those of Vigilante Glee toward the doorway. The hum of excitement mounted. Communication Escort Mead pounded the gavel to still the rising voices. "Colleagues!" she called out, at the same time pressing her fingers to her earphone. She struck the gavel again. "Colleagues!" Chairs swiveled back toward her. The clamor subsided.

"Colleagues," she announced. "I'm told that Vice-Magister Glee is correct. Magister Lin-ci Win is presently approaching the Rotunda Gather-Room."

No sooner had Mead made the announcement than a commotion arose on the southwestern arcade. Suddenly, the doors were flung open. As both protocol and their excitement decreed, every woman in the room began respectfully to stand, each welcoming the entry of Magister Win's familiar mobile Greatchair, its air jets puffing boldly as they bore her smoothly over the carpet toward them.

No Greatchair appeared. Nothing, in fact, appeared.

Zude put her hand on Magister Lutu's shoulder. "Flossie!" she breathed.

"Watch!" whispered Yotoma.

Just then, an audible gasp rose from the Heart of All Kanshou. The Gather-Room's entrance framed a sight that no one present had ever seen before: Magister Lin-ci Win, an imposing figure in red and silver, stood tall in the doorway, leaning heavily on elbow crutches. Her long Magister cloak hung regally from the back of her shoulders, and no cowl covered the short-cropped black hair. She paused for a moment, a portrait of vigorous womanhood, backed by her three Amah aides. Then she began a slow, majestic journey across the expanse of carpet.

She walked awkwardly but unaided, save by her crutches, her eyes aflame, her lips parted in a proud half-smile. Her modest entourage followed her, their radiant faces lighting their Magister's way toward the astonished Heart of All Kanshou.

At the Amah Magister's approach, three Members of the Heart began in impromptu unison the soft intoning of a high, open-throated Ah-h-h! Others took up the sound, until the full assembly held the note and sustained it. Kanshou and the civilians crowding the doorway poured in uninvited, lending their voices to the sound that filled the vast chamber.

As Lin-ci Win coaxed her unaccustomed legs into their triumphant march toward the meeting circle, the moving sound about her swelled in volume. When the Magister was a short distance from the edge of the northeast quadrant, vigorous applause began from all parts of the now crowded rotunda. It buoyed the chanted sound to a still higher plateau and grew in its force and volume. Shouts and cries replaced the chanting. "Lin-ci Win!" "Brava!" "Our Magister!"

As the Amah Magister approached the Heart, the group before her parted, pushing its chairs into a welcoming horseshoe. As she drew nearer, she halted and dropped her handgrips, letting the crutches hang from her arms. Slowly she extended her hands, lifting one in the direction of Zella Terremoto Adverb, the other toward Flossie Yotomo Lutu.

The applause and the shouting soared.

Zude and Yotoma stepped to Lin-ci Win, each taking a hand to steady her as she covered the few paces remaining. The ovation roared to its climax. The three Magisters of Little Blue's Kanshoubu stood together, holding hands and facing their Heart.

Zude found herself panting with the effort to take it all in. She looked to her left and saw the runnels of sweat that coursed down Lin-ci Win's face, and the tears that coursed down Yotoma's. Both of her Co-Magisters were laughing softly. Zude surveyed the throngs that were still flooding into the Gather-Room—both Kanshou and the civilians who had followed Lin-ci's entrance and now stood only a short distance away from the Heart, at a boundary tacitly and unanimously acknowledged. It was their applause and shouting that still swelled and subsided, swelled and subsided, in a pattern that seemed destined to last forever.

Zude felt the Amah Magister squeezing her hand, and apparently Yotoma's too, at the same time. She squeezed back.

Then Lin-ci dropped their hands and stood by herself, addressing the Communication Escort. "Marshal Mead!" she shouted above the noise of the crowded room. "Marshal Mead!"

Mead's gavel cracked, again and again. Members of the Heart, ready by now to resume their seats, left off their clapping.

"The Heart recognizes Magister Lin-ci Win of the Asia-China-Insula Tri-Satrapy!"

Lin-ci's voice carried to the limits of the rotunda. "Marshal Mead," she boomed, "and Members of the Heart, I have come to ask you…to dissolve the Kanshoubu!"

In the split-second between the word dissolve and the reaction to Lin-ci's words, Zude sensed a grand stirring in the depths of a vibrational sea, a tsunami of exhilaration beginning its skyward lift. The lucent wave rose high, crested and broke into a canopy of brightness against the domed ceiling. It fell in sparkling shards of light over the colors of the Kanshou and the bold prints of the civilians. It leached the scowls and tensions from their bodies, it drained away the aches and stiffnesses, it washed aside all resistance. And it left, emerging from the departing deluge, the drenched and dripping, healthy and vibrant bodies of everyone in the Gather-Room.

"YES!" The word was one voice. It rang in a colossal chorus from the crowd. "YES!" It was shouted again and again in concert with loud sustained applause. "YES!" There was no ambivalence among the visitors to the Heart's proceedings. "YES!"

As Zude scanned the ranks of the Heart of All Kanshou, her incredulity stopped her breath. Fourteen women, clad in green or red or blue, stood in front of or leaned upon their padded chairs and applauded in unison with the crowd. Some of them shouted while they clapped their hands. Zude counted them again, to be sure. Fourteen! She quickly identified the four Members of the Heart who were not joining in the ovation. Femmedarme Adjutant Major Rabia Nuruk and Amah Sky Captain Anapaya Mogok had taken their seats; they observed the clamor through narrowed eyes. Two women in Vigilante blue were standing but pointedly not applauding; they were Lieutenant Carla Elana Díaz and Marshal N. Louise Mead, the Communication Escort.

Zude saw that Magister Lutu had also completed her calculation of the Heart's Desire. Yotoma called to her above the din, "Not to worry, Zudie! It's only four! And they will stand aside!" She continued her clapping. "Only four!"

Above the noise Lin-ci Win was also shouting to Zude. She stood supported by her aides, her face aglow. "Zella Adverb!" she called. When Zude harkened to her, Lin-ci shouted, "All will be well!"

11

> Be free. Fly free.
> The dream of sky is limitless.
> *Voices of the Stream*

I. Shifting Habitantes

"The bailiwicks will open their gates at exactly the same moment all over Little Blue," said Anastasia N'basi, public airwaves correspondent. "Some habitantes will thus be released at night, some at sunset, and others at dawn. Still others will Step To Freedom in broad daylight."

The correspondent's black hair was studded with gold buttons, colorful pins and silver beads. They took turns sparkling around her animated face. Sustained crowd noises in the distance lent urgency to her words.

"As you know," she said as she resumed her flatcast, "there have been worldwide protests of last week's action by the Heart. Tuesday, rioters panicked Yokohama citizens by encircling a bailiwick, pledging to kill any freed habitante. Striking government workers in London still insist that they will refuse food until the Heart revokes its decision. Citizens dedicated to, and I quote, 'preserving public safety,' infiltrated the Teheran bailiwick yesterday and killed or fatally wounded 62 habitantes."

N'basi drew a deep breath. "We will remember always the scattered acts of vengeance visited upon members of the Heart of All Kanshou, and the death of one of those members, Femmedarme

237

Sky Captain Bushona Talabele, at the hands of demonstrators in Bujumbura."

She shook her head gently. "Many of us will puzzle over the movement within the bailiwicks themselves, called We Like It Here, the rebellion of habitantes who do not wish to be released."

With another deep breath, the correspondent went on.

"During these next weeks, while the disbanding of the Kanshoubu begins, we can expect more dissention. Street-corner prophets and diviners in every satrapy daily blame the loss of our children on too lenient a government."

She consulted her notes. "Some urge us, and I quote, 'to cease our folly, to double the number of Kanshou on our streets, to strengthen the walls of the bailiwicks, and to hold our children close lest the future of the race be swept from us by the overwhelming forces of rape and massacre that will be unleashed upon the world if the habitantes are freed and the Kanshoubu dismantled.'"

Anastasia N'basi looked directly into the mikcam. "I note these circumstances and these opinions because, in fact, they are more the exception than the rule in the world at large. Next to the waves of acceptance and hope that seem to billow around Little Blue in the wake of the Heart's decision, the resistances to that decision pale in significance." She moved toward the roaring crowds in the background of her flatcast.

"Today we find few people, in or out of a bailiwick, who harbor serious regret that the bailiwicks will be abolished." N'basi was now strolling into the thickness of an assembled crowd. "Everywhere today habitantes will emerge rejoicing, and everywhere they will be greeted by throngs of friends, family and well-wishers. The celebrations will of course continue for hours, maybe days."

The yellow and brown of her large-print caftan stood out now against the background of Amahrery Red tunics and light-maroon habitante coveralls. "It's 1:51 in the afternoon here at the Hanoi Bailiwick," she continued, "where, less than a year ago, at this very moment in the day, habitantes were in the last minutes of preparation for an uprising that would be coordinated with revolts in Bucharest and Caracas—three separate bailiwicks in three separate tri-satrapies carefully timed to explode simultaneously."

The mikcam dissolved the flatimage of the correspondent, bringing into focus the crowd of approximately 4,000 habitantes who were shouting and waving behind the main gateway to the Hanoi Bailiwick. The long shot revealed the low buildings of the city's outskirts and, to the sides of the gate, it caught the shimmer of the hurtfields that still encompassed the bailiwick proper. At the gateway itself, however, there was no barrier except for the wide red ribbon that stretched across the street between the guard booths. The ribbon bulged outward with the press of eager habitantes, then inward with the passing of Amahs urging them back. Minutes later the ribbon would be pressed outward and inward once more—time and again, in a dance of liberty and restraint.

In several streets perpendicular to the gateway and a distance beyond it, lines of Amahs monitored huge throngs that stretched back into the city: those who waited for the release of their loved ones. The mikcams panned the masses of people, zooming occasionally upon a single item in the wild array of mannequins, drawings, hats, kites, balloons, goggles, toys, and papier-mâché figures. Signs affixed to upraised sticks waved and bounced: Sani, Here We Are!—Tong-se The Lightfingered!—Tuscan Wine for Dinner, Sam Woo!

Other signs, held by small groups of somber citizens, protested the entire scene: Don't Do It!—Stop The Liberation Madness!—

Protect the Few Children We Have Left!—No Criminals on Our Streets!

Now and then the colors of the crowd were punctuated with Amahrery Red as pairs of Foot-Shrieves moved among the people, urging them to patience, re-forming the rough organization of groups, exchanging greetings.

The correspondent's warm voice spoke over the flatfilm of the noisy crowd. "Friends, a scene similar to this one is taking place right now in every bailiwick on the planet, and you will be able to access flatfilms of the occasion from your demesne or quarter-trapy by tomorrow. But today the public airwaves are bringing you the brief Step To Freedom ceremonies in simultaneous live coverage from each of the three bailiwicks that so recently exploded in violence. Let's go now," N'basi urged, "to Alana Gold in Bucharest."

The crowd noises altered in volume and texture, early afternoon light gave way to the fresher brightness of a morning sun, the buildings lining Hanoi's streets dissolved into rolling open country, Amahrery Red turned to Femmedarmery Green. More than 3,000 people, mostly men, stood behind a bright wide ribbon of green at the bailiwick's gates. They waved, shouted and sang, as the Third Femmedarme Division Marching Band lent a sedate, military precision to a medley of rowdy drinking songs. The mass of thousands outside the bailiwick had swelled beyond the shoulders of the Bucharest highway and into the expanse of crimson clover fields that flanked it. Its members waved and shouted in the direction of the habitantes. The smiling face of Public Airwaves Correspondent Alana Gold filled the screen.

"As you can see, the atmosphere here, just south of Bucharest Proper, is almost universally one of celebration," she said. "That may partly be due to the fact that this bailiwick will undergo a minimum of physical change, and many of its habitantes will continue to work here as free citizens in the sewage conversion facility." Gold brushed a wayward curl from her cheek. "There will be no speeches today, only the eagerly awaited appearance of Magister Flossie Yotoma Lutu. In just a few minutes Magister Lutu will cut the ribbon that will symbolically allow the habitantes to take their Step To Freedom."

The correspondent was about to lead her mikcams toward the gate when she stopped herself.

"I'm told that Magister Zella Terremoto Adverb has just arrived at the Caracas Bailiwick, where it's nearly 2 in the morning. Are you there, Long Ron?"

"I'm here," answered a deep voice. It belonged to one of the lankiest Japanese men anywhere on Little Blue. Correspondent Ron Haniku stood by a brightly lit building beside the blue-cloaked Magister of the Nueva Tierra Tri-Satrapy. He struggled to be heard over the music and chaotic street noises that surged around them. "Caracas is exploding with happiness and anticipation tonight," he announced, "and I have the honor of being here with the person who, many believe, is responsible for this joy. Will you speak to us, Magister Adverb?"

"Ron, I'm running short of words these days," Zude said, "but I can tell you that, of all the duties I have ever executed as Vigilante, as Kanshou, or as Magister, the duty I will carry out only minutes from now, when I cut that blue ribbon, will be by far the happiest duty I have ever performed."

Wild cheers erupted from the dancing crowd. Magister Adverb was hoisted to the shoulders of a shouting civilian and an off-duty Vigilante. She was borne by the crowd to the gateway of the Caracas Bailiwick, while around her roared the cries of "Adverb! Libertadora!"

Around the world, viewing screens great and small split into thirds as the three Magisters simultaneously approached their habitantes, the thousands of laughing, clamoring free citizens to be. Lin-ci Win walked easily without the aid of crutches or Amahs; Zude was carried; but Flossie Yotoma Lutu moved most smoothly of the three because, observers insisted, her boots never touched the ground.

Sudden silence fell. In Bucharest. In Caracas. In Hanoi. The Magisters positioned themselves by their ribbons, facing their habitantes, their bodies slightly turned toward the prime mik-cams. Together they opened their ceremonial shears.

"What the animals knew," said Yotoma in Bucharest.

"What the children knew," said Zude in Caracas.

"What we are learning," said Lin-ci in Hanoi.

"Is that the most precious gift of all," said Zude, "is free-dom."

"Freedom," said Yotoma.

"Freedom," said Lin-ci.

With precise uniformity the three Magisters severed their rib-bons.

The ribbons dropped into an incredulous silence of approxi-mately three seconds. Then cheering habitantes swarmed from the bailiwicks, some to reach their friends, some to touch their Magister. Lin-ci, Yotoma and Zude stood unprotected while thousands of men, and some women, surged by them. Or stopped to touch them, to speak, or to look them in the eye.

Ron Haniku's face was an inset in the upper right-hand corner of the aerial view of the Caracas celebration, emblazoned now by the fireworks splitting the sky above the bailiwick. Haniku's inset enlarged to present his full-screen interview with a woman who carried a small boy. The boy's black hair was streaked with gray. "Then you've traveled a long way for this celebration!" exclaimed the correspondent.

Both woman and child were smiling. "We have friends here," she said.

"Zudie!" affirmed the boy.

"I see," laughed Ron Haniku.

Almost straight through the middle of the earth, on the other side of the world, Anastasia N'basi had captured the Magister of the Amahrery in her interview inset. "The world is crazy with curiosity, Magister! Will you tell us how you came to your decision to support the abolition of the Kanshoubu?"

Like the traditional Chinese rulers who had gone before her, Lin-ci Win faced the Equator as she spoke. Folding her arms under her red Magister cloak, she said, "Not for a while, Correspondent N'basi. Perhaps I shall someday record my memoirs."

"Then we must wait?"

"You must," smiled the Magister.

In Bucharest, Alana Gold plunged behind her mikcams into the sea of habitantes flooding through the bailiwick's gates. The full screen showed her in pursuit of a near-teenage girl whose long flowing gray hair was in stark contrast to the black face of the habitante she was hugging. Gold drew the pair to the side of the gate.

"You are family?" she inquired, indicating with her hand the mikcams that carried their images around the world.

The man lifted the girl into his arms. The two looked at each other. Then they both smiled at the correspondent. "Yes," they said in unison.

"And where are you going now?" Gold shouted above the din of human traffic.

"Well," said the broad-shouldered man, "I'm going to go looking for snakes and eagles."

"Snakes and eagles!" exclaimed Gold. "Do you expect to find them?"

"I do."

Correspondent Gold nodded, then spoke to the girl. "And how about you?"

"I'm going to go join the Femmedarmes," she replied, giving the man's neck a squeeze.

"But the Femmedarmes won't be here!"

"No," laughed the girl, "but they'll be somewhere."

Alana Gold held out her arms in resignation. "Then you will certainly find them!" she affirmed.

The big man grinned and nodded goodbye to the reporter. The girl in his arms waved vigorously at the mikcams as the two of them moved back into the stream of liberated habitantes. Again the screen split into thirds to cover the opening of bailiwick gates all over Little Blue, from the Urals to Tasmania, from Mar Caribe to the Philippines, from Greenland to the Kalahari, from the Northwest Territory to the Falklands. A Kanshou concert band played tirelessly in the background. The flow of habitantes went on and on, on and on, out of the bailiwicks and into freedom.

II. Shifting Kanshou

It was a fully appreciated irony that the century's most heinous explosions of violence took place during the next two weeks, just before the official dissolution of the most effective peacekeeping force in history. Prior to those two weeks, the responses to the Heart's decision had been within the expected boundaries of public dissent. In every satrapy, small pockets had exploded with thievery, fraud and physical abuse, as if to herald the lawlessness that would prevail without the Kanshou. And in every satrapy, self-appointed individuals or groups had stood ready to defend themselves and the commonweal against such affronts: Renegade groups of paladin protectors had sprung up along the Yukon, anointing themselves the fearless armed guardians of endangered innocents; Bedouin tribeswomen near Damascus had engaged Femmedarmes in a conflict of heavy weapons, hurling loud condemnations at the "cowardly, irresponsible Kanshou, the puppets of treason"; a brigade of Amahs in Seoul had resigned their posts and established themselves as "the New Amahrery, the true sentinels of public safety."

Zude and her colleagues had observed such discord and nodded with understanding at the protests and rallies, the marches and picket lines and confrontations. They had reminded themselves that they could not expect far-reaching acceptance of their decision overnight, that the world, after all, was fast being robbed of its children, its most precious possession. They had dutifully acknowledged to each other that all of Little Blue's people were not only wrenched and frightened by personal loss but also threatened to their core by the knowledge that their determination to preserve their species might well come to naught.

Again and again, Zude and her colleagues had turned their eyes to the concomitant river of hope that had leapt its banks and seemed now to be flooding Little Blue. That flood included a deep bonding of the members of the Heart of All Kanshou, even in the face of Bushona Talabele's assassination, and their daily reaffirmation of trust in the appropriateness of their decision. It included the increasingly compelling reports of changes that daily were transforming the individual lives of Little Blue's citizens. And most heartwarming of all, it included the overwhelmingly supportive response of some ninety percent of active Kanshou to the leadership of their Magisters and their Heart.

But during the two weeks prior to the first ceremony of the Kanshoubu's dismantlement, negative rejoinders to the Heart's decision, at least in some parts of the world, increased almost exponentially, requiring the presence of Kanshou themselves in exceptional numbers. There were riots in eleven major cities; in Zanzibar, rebels proclaimed the joint states of Tanzania and Kenya to be sovereign entities independent of any satrapy, tri-satrapy or global jurisdiction; in Novosibirsk, a demesne governor challenged Zude to a public duel.

Most devastating to Kanshoubu officialdom were two incidents that occurred over a two-day period just a week before the initial dismantlement ceremony of the Kanshoubu. First, a 24-hour rash of mass suicides in the southeastern sector of North America stunned the world. Atlanta, Birmingham and Jackson were hardest hit, but almost every part of the Old South was affected. The dead totaled over 4,500 persons, all but three of them adults, and one of them, it was later reported, a Vigilante Lieutenant. Second, in Prague, two distraught parents murdered their three children in their sleep.

With the news of these incidents, Little Blue's three Magisters stopped in their tracks and spent sixty-odd hours in holo-conferences with Heart Members and other Kanshou all over the planet. All Kanshou, both mighty and modest, painfully re-examined the Heart's decision and their own participation, their own motives. They argued with and despaired of each other, they ate little, and they slept not at all.

It was the Congress of Active Kanshou who officially stepped into the morass of agonized self-examination and helped the Magisters and their colleagues to come again to a clear and common decision. The message read:

> To our Magisters, Vice-Magisters, and our Heart.
> We speak as 180 Kanshou and we speak for, at our
> best estimate, 556,000 of the 600,000 Kanshou
> whom we represent. We urge you to stand by your
> decision to abolish the Kanshoubu, and to leave the
> victims of recent unfortunate events with only your

deepfelt compassion. By your leadership and your trust you have empowered us to assess extreme situations and intentions. Our assessment of the present dissent on Little Blue is that it is only the dying gasp of violence itself. We look forward to joining you in a world where being a Kanshou is simply an internal state, expressed by every appropriate action that we take each day in the living of our lives. You have decided wisely.

The leaders of the Kanshoubu heaved a grateful sigh and turned with new resolve to the carrying out of their decision. By the time the first disbanding rites were held, there were globally only occasional protests of the decision; by the time the third and last ceremony took place, the planet's dedicated and diligent Full Spectrum Opinion Services experienced difficulty in finding citizens willing to criticize the Kanshoubu's abolition.

The Vigilancia, last of the Shrievalties to be founded, was the first to be disbanded. In their final duty as Shrieves, the Vigilantes sailed, low-rocketed, gerted, cush-carred or marched from the furthermost reaches of Nueva Tierra to Los Angeles in Aztlán, where they were to spend two days in rituals that would close the doors forever on their careers as peacekeeping officers.

They began arriving days before the exercises, claiming a need for parade-ground practice, or for flight tests for air shows, or for briefing on sea-vessel and flex-car maneuvers. They joined immediately in the complex organization of work assignments that would assure the smooth execution of the closing rites. They sang and danced and drank long into the nights in the bars and gather-rooms and aboard the Sea-Shrieve vessels anchored in or beyond the harbor. They established communication networks that would keep them forever bonded to one another. They sat on hillsides and watched the lights of a civilian metropolis, speculating about what their lives would be like when they returned to whatever satrapy they called home. They relived the old times and made plans for the times to come. They shared personal agonies about giving up their careers, and they described with wonder the magic that seemed to have touched their lives since the moment of their letting go of being Kanshou.

When the first day of the formalities arrived, so did Lin-ci Win and Flossie Yotoma Lutu, each with her three Vice-Magisters. They joined Zude and the Vigilancia's top-ranked officers on hot review stands, officiating at full-dress parade exercises, Sea-Shrieve maneuvers and Sky-Shrieve routines.

To the delight of every Vigilante and the hundreds of thousands of civilians who crowded the basin's spectator fields, Nueva Tierra's Magister herself, in gert with an old lover, Sky Captain Claudia Anzaldúa by name, led the Vigilancia's Flying Daggers in a dramatic air show that climaxed with an entire wing's quarter-mile perpendicular dive toward the choppy waves of Santa Monica Bay. Zude-Gert-Claudia (and the wing) finally pulled out of the dive just short of the water's surface. Breathtaking, concluded the proud civilians and Kanshou of Nueva Tierra.

Zude stopped trying to count the Vigilante marching bands, the visiting Amah and Femmedarme drum-and-bugle units, the honor brigades, the regiments of Vigilante cadets, the drill teams and the light-weapon demonstrations that filled the afternoon. She stood, she saluted, she smiled, she nodded, she applauded and cheered with the appreciative crowds. And she felt no weariness whatsoever, only a light-headed pride and a priceless gratitude.

When at sunset the spectator fields were transformed into a highly organized small city complete with street markets and art fairs, the Magisters, Vice-Magisters and top Vigilante officers visited the open-air banquets and fiestas of representative Vigilante corps or divisions. They put in an appearance at major carnival areas, cheered the splendid pyrotechnics display, and took in whatever street performances they encountered on their sojourn into the regiments of Vigilante officers and cadets.

It was past midnight when Magisters Lutu and Win sought their quarters for rest before the next day's final proceedings. Zella Terremoto Adverb, still fresh as a daisy, returned to her Vigilantes, talking and laughing with them far into the morning hours when, often quite literally, she tucked them into their camp beds. Like generals from time immemorial who spent the night before a great battle walking softly among the silent tents of their troops, Magister Adverb covered miles under that cool starry sky, stepping carefully past battalions of dreaming figures in regulation bags or bedrolls.

On the deck of the flagship *Nora Astorga* of the Nueva Tierra Central Vigilante Coastal Fleet, Zude smoked a rare cigarillo with Sea Commander Nancy Chevarría of Matagalpa and watched in the dawn for the gulls that the Commander insisted would swoop over the bow to greet early risers. Zude heard their squawks and felt the breath of their wings, but only Chevarría actually beheld the gulls, her eyes bright with appreciation and wonder. What Zude did see in the gray waters of the bay was the triple leap of a shipfish. On each high arc of its thick body it imparted a word to her: Yes! Praise! Soon!

By 9 the next morning, the spectator fields were cleared of any remnant of the previous day's celebration. They hosted instead the spit and polish of 180,000 Vigilantes at parade rest and the masses of citizens who encircled them on temporary but sturdy scaffoldings of feathersteel. Media dirigibles dotted the sky, transmitting to aerially mounted audio-view-screens the close-up activity of carefully specified companies or battalions; most friends and families seated themselves according to the mikcam location of their favorite Kanshou. It would be a day to remember.

The complex exercises were conducted with appropriate pomp. Each Vigilante or Vigilante cadet was recognized, called by name and congratulated for her service by her Magister, Vice-Magister, Brigadier, Admiral, Captain or Commander. Each individual Kanshou or Kanshou cadet received from a superior her collar pips, a merit scarf or token of any special honor she had earned, and her warrant of service. Each Vigilante was privileged to take her uniforms and her subvention belt with her into her future. Most important of all, the cape and cowl of that mysterious and versatile material, tekla, were permanently bestowed upon each Vigilante by the Kanshoubu, especially precious gifts to her and her designated heirs forevermore.

At noon, Zude and her Co-Magisters gave stirring speeches. They formally discharged with honor all of Little Blue's Vigilantes, including those high-ranking officers who stood with them on the round platform at the center of the spectator fields. They politely requested the participation of ex-Vigilante Vice-Magisters as well as certain ex-Vigilante bands and honor brigades at the upcoming ceremonies for the disbanding of the Amahrery and the Femmedarmery. At the end of the formalities, the Vigilante anthem, Patrullar, Navegar, Volar, filled the air.

It was 4 in the afternoon when ex-Vigilantes and their guests retreated to designated areas of the spectator fields for food, celebrations, visits, rest, exercise or meditation. At dusk they reassembled before two flags: One was that of the Vigilancia, which was put to bed nightly; the other, that of the Kanshoubu, which was never formally lowered, night or day. As the crowd stood silently by, the flag of the Vigilancia was lowered for the last time. For the first time since the Kanshoubu was founded, a bugler played taps.

Three weeks later in Hong Kong, the two-day rites were repeated, with appropriate variations, for the dismissal of the Asia-China-Insula Tri-Satrapy's 230,000 Amahs. Only one irregularity marred those proceedings. A hydraulic apparatus critical to the raising of the review stand was held up on a bridge from the mainland by the eruption of a religious demonstration. A firmamentarian sect, convinced that without the Kanshou the legions of Satan would storm Heaven's gate, blocked traffic for half an hour while its members exhorted God to give them some sign that Armageddon was not at hand. Amahs relocated the demonstrators but could not make up for the delay in the starting of the first day's activities. Interestingly, the demonstrators were later reported to be covered with small but still very itchy mosquito bites—an answer from God to their request, many concluded.

Three weeks later in Tripoli, in the cheering presence of some half-million civilians of the Africa-Europe-Mideast Tri-Satrapy, 190,000 Femmedarmes were mustered out of the Kanshoubu. Many of the exercises took place against a background of date, olive and orange groves, or under frequent pockets of greenery provided by the desert reclamation project. Again, the planning was smooth, the presentations impressive, and the speeches brief.

After the discharge of the Femmedarmes, and the final singing of the Femmedarme anthem, each of the Magisters formally held up an earthen jar filled with sand and painted the color of the Femmedarmery, the Vigilancia or the Amahrery. One by one, each turned her vessel upside down and stood silent while the sand drained completely from it.

Yotoma held up her green jar. "Form, empty of members," she intoned, "Femmedarmery, you are no more." She raised a regulation Kanshou baton and smashed the jar to bits.

"Amahrery, you are no more." Lin-ci smashed the red jar.

"Vigilancia, you are no more," said Zude, and smashed the blue jar.

Yotoma held up a fourth jar of red, blue and green. "Form, empty of members," she said again, "Kanshoubu, you are no more." Simultaneously, Lin-ci and Zude struck and shattered the jar.

"Steward Lin-ci Win," said Yotoma, flipping the edges of Lin-ci's Magister cloak to off-duty position, "you are Magister no more."

"Steward Zella Terremoto Adverb," said Lin-ci, turning Zude's cloak in the same manner, "you are Magister no more."

"Steward Flossie Yotoma Lutu," said Zude, folding back Flossie's cloak, "you are Magister no more."

The Kanshou anthem filled the air.

That evening, after the flag of the Femmedarmery was lowered, the flag of the Kanshoubu followed it down. The bugler played taps for the last time.

Present at each of the three disbanding ceremonies was an odd couple: Two women, whose flying spoon landed at dawn on the first day and departed after dusk on the second. One of the women was tall and middle-aged, with shoulder-length brown hair and a unicorn earring; she was dressed in soft pants and a lightweight shirt. The other was equally as tall, of undetermined age, possessed of only two upper and cusped teeth, her long silver hair in ringlets bobbing boisterously beneath the wide-brimmed sun hat that was tied in a large bow under her chin; she was clad in white organdy, an ante-bellum gown with hoops and a bodice that revealed scrawny shoulders but no cleavage whatsoever.

The younger woman clearly appreciated every aspect of the ceremonies. The older one seemed to listen more carefully, smile more readily, sing more lustily, cry harder and dance with more abandon than any other attendee.

They had come because they liked to think that, after all, they might have played some small part in the drama unfolding before them.

III. Shifting Citizens

Of all the changes, even the violent ones, that began at once to take place on Little Blue after the Heart's decision, the one most keenly and universally felt was the sense of speed with which life seemed suddenly to be happening. Daily chores and interactions became almost breathless, and even traditionally molasses-bound bureaucracies began to move with purpose and dispatch.

Little Blue's governmental and social agencies endured their expected struggles, but on the whole they found themselves taking unusual risks and challenging orthodoxy at every turn. For example, all nine Sifters at the Kitchen Table and all fifteen Websters in the Central Web immediately ratified the Heart's Desire; moreover, in the spirit of the Kanshoubu's example, each of those bodies entertained a proposal to abolish itself, thus setting in motion the processes that would leave Little Blue's global infrastructures not only without law enforcement or interpretation of the law, but without law itself. The Global Energy Commission formed the Task Force on Personal Desire and Thought Focus. In some demesnes, optimism about the future restoration of both children and animals swelled to new heights: Home transmogrifiers were called upon to produce toys and children's clothing again, and amidst a flurry of controversy and speculation some food processing plants began creating a limited line of vegetarian meals for cats, bird and small fish.

The global interconnections of commerce, transportation and communication sustained Little Blue as an integrated world, but in truth, daily life became increasingly local and autonomous. Small villages of fewer than 500 inhabitants became the norm; dwellers in large cities tended to coalesce into distinct neighborhoods of about that same size.

As the occurrence of extraordinary events increased worldwide, miraculous became a useless word. Any randomly chosen day was rich with new experiences. For example, on July 18, 2088, Manuela Osias discovered that she could carry out her plant-wide duty as materials regulator for a zinc alloy company in Manila by commanding her computer with neither voice nor touch but entirely with her mind.

On that same day, near Idfu on the Nile, the colossal stones of a newly discovered pyramid were faultlessly dismantled and reassembled on safer ground by a sister-brother team of telekinetic engineers. Four women flew alone for the first time without the companionship of a spooning partner. A man and a woman flew in spoon together from Sicily to the Balkans, and two men accomplished that same feat from Timor to Australia's Melville Island. Inch-wide striations of pure gold appeared in the granite of a Quaker Meeting House in Manchester, England. When an angry Lua Phra Meo of Thon Buri picked up a fist-sized rock to throw at Pa Nong Samut, Samut disappeared.

And, still on that same day, a companion section to Egypt's Rosetta Stone was washed up on an Amazon levee; along with its original hieroglyphics and its demotic and Greek characters, this basalt stone included a new undecipherable language that remotely resembled electronic computer code. Its final line included a single pictograph that could only be described as an opened cage.

12

2088 C.E.

> Praise me with rainbows, sing to me in savors,
> touch and move me with your Presence,
> and I will know your mind
> by all its scented whispers.
> *Song of the Lumari*

Steward Zella Terremoto Adverb and her Swallower companion had been living for a week in a barren rockface cave. Here in her Andean sanctuary high above the jungles of Peru, Zude could see, hundreds of kilometers to the east, what she believed to be the joining of the mighty rivers Marañón and Ucayali.

The bailiwicks were closed, the habitantes free, the Kanshoubu dismantled. In the months since the Heart's decision, Zude had lived almost constantly in a state of exhilaration. She awoke every morning to a world vastly changed from the day before. She entered her dreams each night, as did most citizens, with prayers for the return of the animals and the birth, again, of children. Waking or dreaming, Zude breathed in and out her profound knowledge that all was indeed well.

Asleep on the wide ledge at the door of her cave, Zude was traveling inner roads with her Swallower. She was warm within her body-bubble and further protected from the cold by her tekla Magister cloak. Three Indios, two women and a man, sat beside her pallet. They wore ruanas, hard-worn straw hats, gloves and heavy foot-wrappings. Their singing was reminiscent of the *Song of the Lumari.*

255

The taller woman removed one glove and laid her bare hand on Zude's head. A corridor opened, and Zude was filled with a flow of information and wisdom, not one bit of which she could remember upon awakening. Instead, she awoke alone, enveloped by a myriad of intriguing images and haunted by the feeling that she had traveled for years in the space of one short dawn. Puzzled and beguiled, she nevertheless gave thanks to the dream for its mystery and its still pervading sense of well-being.

She leaned against the face of her mountain and watched the sun, that star of life, as it mounted the low horizon.

Minutes later she rose and stretched. As her fingers encircled her comunit for her daily check-in with the Stewardry, she was startled by an object on the floor of her cave, just by its door. Lying there, still curved with the form of the hand it had covered, was a gray glove. Zude knelt to pick it up, rubbing it gently against itself. Tekla. No doubt about it. The precious stuff of her cape and her cowl. Tekla.

She scanned the mountain's rockface, then searched the canopy of the jungle below her. She flashed her lumestick within the cave itself. She came back to her ledge and searched the sky. With a slow smile, she folded the worn glove into a small flatness and tucked it into her belt.

Later that day, she shouldered her pack and left her bleak aerie, picking her way cautiously down the rough rocks of the mountain. When, much later, she reached flatter terrain, she stretched her legs into long strides, heading for one of the upland basins and the timberline below it. Just before noon, she perched on a ruin at the edge of a grassy plateau and watched the back-sensed presence of a busy Inca village six centuries gone. Hundreds of gold- and silver-bedecked craftspeople executed their everyday tasks around these walls, over this gray dirt.

When she hoisted her pack again, preparing to set out, Zude suddenly froze. A presence encompassed her that was without any reference in her experience. She sank to the ground, fighting off a mild dizziness. She felt herself being slowly embraced by swirls of warm, appreciative, chocolate air. Its strongest emanation came from behind her.

Balancing on one knee, she made herself turn in a smooth motion until she faced the serene torrents of attention. "Mother's Magic!" she whispered.

The vicuña stood there in broad daylight, less than the length of two bodies from her, the light chestnut of its flat dorsal wool barely a contrast to the reddish-yellow shag of its chest and underparts. Its total height, long graceful neck and all, was close to Zude's, and its weight a little less than Zude's own. It was looking at her.

Zude dared not move. Frantically, she searched for behavior appropriate to the meeting of a being the likes of which had not been seen on the planet for nearly three-quarters of a century. She swallowed. And smiled. Very tentatively, she tried out her new art of mindreaching. "You're beautiful," she sent.

The animal's head shot upward, its body becoming rigid.

"Wait!" sent Zude, "don't go away! Please, please don't go away!"

The vicuña started, as if to run.

Hastily, Zude stilled her anxiety and made herself feel only calm. And admiration.

The vicuña eased.

Mindreaching was apparently an intrusion. Zude concentrated on simply appreciating the furred being before her. She paid close attention to its big unblinking eyes, praising them; she took in the detail of the thin pointed ears, cherishing them; she adored the dark brown nose. She did not let words in, but filled herself with warmth and gratitude.

The vicuña turned toward her.

Zude's heart beat faster. She focused on staying completely still, feeling nothing but her admiration, her affection. It's a mirage! she thought, and in that instant, the animal froze.

Zude tensed.

The vicuña stepped back.

Zude reimmersed herself in wonder and fondness.

The vicuña eased again and swung its head in agreeable arcs. Carefully, it took several long steps toward Zude, its big eyes looking down at her.

Zude looked only at the shaggy fur, imagining its texture, almost reaching out her hands to touch it. The brown head was near, close above her and bending lower. Zude closed her eyes.

Hot, cordial breath grazed her ear. A nose, cold and damp, nuzzled her chin. Hesitantly, Zude nuzzled back, her lips on that strange cheek suddenly lost in the gentlest home they had ever sought. She shifted her weight to both knees and steadied her hands. Carefully and incredulously she placed them on the length of the neck, and felt there…yes! the unmistakable pulse of solid, warm, vibrant life!

Zude pressed her lips together, feeling a low moan climb to her throat. When she gave her cry its freedom, she sobbed aloud, releasing into the thick fur a burst of emptiness, hunger and disbelief.

"You're here!" she announced in a hoarse whisper.

When the vicuña did not move, Zude flung her arms over the sturdy back, around the big chest, pummeling, hugging, kneading, scratching. The animal endured it all with calm patience. It collapsed its callused knees into a camel-like resting posture so that Zude could press every possible part of her body against its every possible part.

Moments later, Zude lay watching the vicuña. Its long eye-lashes rarely blinked, but its jaws worked in a rhythmical chewing of a clump of grass; occasionally its short tail jerked back and forth. Zude could smell the animal's fetid breath, and with her every stroke of its broad shoulder she raised from its fur the taste of dust. She blessed it all.

"How do I reach it, Swallower? Thoughts seem to drive it away!"

"Enworded thoughts, yes," replied her guide. "Relax."

Lazily, Zude began good-natured attempts at a non-verbal connection. Feeling her way into the vicuña's body, she tried seeing through the vicuña's eyes, experiencing the world from its point of view. The animal did not respond. Changing tactics, Zude drew a picture in her mind of ways the two of them might interact, charging it with intense desire and the conviction that the vicuña would surely understand her. Nothing. Then she tried opening her own mind to the animal, inviting it to come into her head, to exchange pictures with her, even to trade minds with her. To no avail. The vicuña responded only to Zude's physical attentions and, it seemed, to her feelings of pleasure or praise.

Zude sighed. She had just resigned herself to a simple gratitude for the pleasure of the vicuña's company when she noticed the bright pink midday sky above them. She blinked. And the sky was its normal pale blue again. No, wait! Pink. Zude raised herself on one elbow. Crazy. It seemed pink, yes, but...ah, there! Blue. She started to lie down again but felt her vision faltering in a peculiar way. Everything was in motion: The low wall of the ruin moved back and forth, the scrub brush beyond the wall moved side to side, the far horizon beyond the plateau moved up and down. Zude shook her head. Things stabilized. And then began moving again.

Zude sat up straight, willing the scene back to normal. Instantly she was blasted with a cold wind. She stiffened and looked up to confirm that the sun still shone brightly. It did, but in a pink sky, and over a plateau that swam in a jumble of movements. Fear touched her bones. And now the pebbles under her swayed in a tantalizing syncopation against her buttocks. The fear became pleasure.

A thousand pungent smells assailed her nostrils, sparking a sharp desire. An array of colors rose from the rocky dust, colors with such rich deep textures that she hungered to touch them. In her head were humming sounds, both distant and close. They pounded a commotion of disparate rhythms in her head and, to her consternation, they enticed into bizarre actions some parts of her body that were ordinarily quite sedate.

It was the vicuña! For sure, this tumult was springing from the animal beside her!

Zude struggled not to cry aloud. She closed her hands over her ears, clenching her eyes into sightlessness, trying to slow the rush of feelings, the attacking images. One thing at a time! She concentrated visually first, focusing on the orderly building of a scene. She closed out the tumult, then selected and placed together two parts of it, attempting to arrange the disorder into a stable, comfortable picture. Crawling tree under a pink sky. Okay. Now drape the caterpillar shawl over the square cloud by the river of watermelon heart. Good.

It was working! Doggedly she continued, choosing each single element from the chaos and adding it to her judiciously arranged milieu. At her side, the vicuña lay in camel posture, eyes resting on a distant clump of grass.

Without warning the chaos broke out again. It cluttered Zude's sequences and razed to their quaking foundations all her careful architectures of reason. Desperate, she summoned the Swallower. "Help!"

"Align your energy!"

Yes! thought Zude, of course! She closed her eyes and slowly inhaled, mentally watching the rising of her abdominal muscles, then their falling with her exhalation. Several breaths later she was shaking gently with relief as her mind calmed and began its clearing. The craziness subsided. She faced her internal depths where the spaciousness waited, and found at last her still-point of balance. She sighed, and began her rubrics of gratitude.

This earth, this air…my nose, my mouth, my singing health, my strength, my loves, my sparkling days…Her hand rested again on the vicuña. This solid life…these ribs, this beating heart…this being! The incantation hastened, broadening to include each part of the vicuña, the dirt, the grass, the plateau, the Incas, the pre-historic animals, the mountains, the seas, the world.

Zude's face glowed, her cheeks were wet, and now and then an easy laugh punctuated her deepening breaths. With each acknowledgement of a precious gift, her flesh grew more buoyant. Beside her, and with the same resonances, the vicuña's body quivered and matched each new level of Zude's vibration. Both of them were light as air.

"Here's the place," Swallower whispered, "here's where it can happen!"

"Yes!" said Zude.

"Open!" said Swallower. Zude unveiled her senses. The turmoil rushed in, overwhelming her again.

"Allow it!" said Swallower. Zude opened once more. Sensations and feelings smothered her.

"Invite it all!" said Swallower. "With full appreciation!" Zude shook off the last of her resistance. "I honor it all!" she articulated aloud. "I welcome it all!"

Immediately the pandemonium ceased.

Out of the haziness that replaced it, Zude observed the coming into being of what she could only call the vicuña's vibrational language. It sprang from the animal's energetic vitality that was matching Zude's own, but it bore a cargo far more vast. It was in fact the vibration of the Vicuña Matrix itself, the dwelling place of the experiences and knowings of all vicuñas who had ever lived.

The language, as it were, shaped itself into a boundless array of sense imagery and emotional dynamism, including the rosy sky and arctic air, the dancing drums, the passionate pebbles. Zude existed within the images and emotions. They did not come one by one; nor did any one of them compel or motivate another. They were not a sequence, or a summation, or separate parts of any whole. They arose together, simultaneously and synchronistically, as the melon comes into being in its altogetherness, its totality yearning toward substantiality.

The more Zude opened to it all, the more abundantly it arose. The sharper her focus on any one part of it, the more intricate the internal order it revealed. She watched sense impressions and effects solidify into existence, then fade back into billowing waves. All the while, like a master of the bagpipes supports both drone and breath beneath a melody, Zude sustained the world around her with the constant alignment of her energy. The vicuña vibrations entwined with her own.

She could not have imagined how it would proceed, that exchange of meanings, patterns and volitions. Yet it was clear that transformations of intent were stirring, and that the vicuña's panoply of sensations and feelings was shimmering with a message for Zude.

There was no explosion into symbols, no hint of the precision or subtlety of telepathically delivered words. The message now awaiting Zude dwelt in the vicuña's full perception of itself, including its desire to communicate. Zude invited that message.

Had she been able to garb it in words, the words would have been: "I am Tutea, She Who Is a Vicuña!"

As if immediately fluent in a new language, Zude sent the meaning of, "I am Zella Terremoto Adverb, She Who Is a Human!"

In the shade of stunted bushes, on a plateau in the eastern Andes, a vicuña and a woman sat silent in the just-past-noon sun. Inside their motionless bodies, whole worlds of images, formations, effects and even complex ideas were being exchanged.

When Zude asked if other animals were returning, she was treated to the experience of thousands of members of thousands of species, all of them creating their bodies anew as they joyfully arose from a cosmic stream of energy to reinhabit the earth. When she asked why the animals had left, Tutea's meaning clusters, if enworded, would have said, "We left, among other reasons, so that you could understand. You are understanding."

"No!" Zude sent. "You left because we acted against your will! Killing, trapping, abusing!"

"To eat, to drink, to breathe…to be enfleshed is to act against another's will."

Zude almost shouted, "But you suffered! We did unspeakable things to you!"

"We felt pain, yes. Suffering? No. Suffering is your human invention."

"What?"

Tutea's intentions washed over her in waves. "We left," the vicuña told her, "because you acted against the will of others without knowing what you were doing."

Zude sat stock-still, repeating, "Without…knowing…"

"You know now," said the vicuña. "And many more will know each day."

Zude felt the deaths surrounding her—bears eating fish, hawks snapping the necks of hares, snakes striking mice. Tutea's meanings mingled with the images. "We are always present to each other as we take each other's life. Killer and killed. We Ratify Each Devour. And now, so will you."

"It is a New Covenant," Tutea continued. A new understanding between humans and animals, she told Zude. The eating of meat would be quite circumscribed, she explained to Zude, and any forced curtailment of an animal's freedom virtually impossible. There followed examples of insects, hogs and crustaceans who remained happily enfleshed until a human intended them harm or imprisonment; then they simply vanished.

Zude's head swirled. She hardly breathed. "They'll disappear?" she croaked.

Did Tutea laugh? Or was it simply a gentle humor stroking the underbelly of each intention? "Yes. And so will you, if you wish," she said.

"Of course," said Zude, nodding helplessly.

Thus it went, there on the plateau: The vicuña brushing the human ear with her lips, almost as if whispering, and Zude stroking the long neck, frustrated, exhausted, incredulous, ecstatic. At last, woman drew herself tight against vicuña, and the two beings slept. They clung together under a warm sun, in the company of the ghosts of an empire long since gone to dust.

More than an hour later, the sun was losing heat to a cover of thin clouds. Zude awoke scratching her neck. Puzzled, she reached to scratch again, and saw a tiny culprit for just an instant before it leapt off her sleeve and into the paradise of the vicuña's shaggy coat. "Tutea! What was that?" she whispered aloud, her fingers searching the animal's flank.

"Flea." Tutea snatched some nearby grass with her tongue and lips. "They're back, too." She chewed.

Zude nodded wisely, as if she really understood what it meant, having the fleas back.

The vicuña shifted slightly. "We have to go."

Zude's alarm was instantaneous. "No!" she cried, shutting her eyes tight and clasping the big body closer to her own.

"I have to lead you to a friend." Tutea nuzzled Zude's hair. "Someone who needs you to take her home."

"Hush!" commanded Zude aloud, gripping tighter and burying her face in dusty wool. "We're staying right here, Tutea. Our bones forever entwined, come hail or sleet or snow!"

"Zudie, you have to let her go, now."

"Forever! Right here! Wait, what?" Zude froze.

"Zudie." Again. The voice was not in her mind. Or from Tutea. The voice had form, and melody, and texture! And it came from behind her, over by her backpack. I'm still dreaming, Zude assured herself, holding Tutea tight again.

"Listen."

Zude made her taut body relax. She held the big animal more lightly. Another breath, and more ease. She listened. A child's voice sang:

"*¿Dónde estás pelícano?*
¿Dónde estás cordero?

> *¿Dónde estás elefante?*
> *¿Dónde estás salmón?"*

Zella Terremoto Adverb, lately the Commander-in-Chief of 180,000 courageous Vigilantes, began to tremble. There, in bright sunlight and next to a warmth so deep she could not name it, Steward Adverb shook uncontrollably. "T-Tutea!" she whispered, desperately, her eyes still closed, her face buried in sweet, strange wool. "Wh…what's…"

"She's here."

Slowly Zude's arms released Tutea. She rolled over onto her back. She opened one eye and turned her head toward the voice. Her other eye snapped open.

Regina sat astride Zude's backpack, bouncing up and down with her singing, her black hair swaying as her head tossed left and right. She saw Zude staring. "Zudie!" she shrieked, and flung herself across the grass to land on top of her madrina.

Zude could hardly bring herself to place her arms around the child. When at last she did so, the substantiality of that body overwhelmed her. She released a long cry and held the bundle of gladness tight in her arms. She's here! Zude told herself, solid and here! They rolled together, the two of them, hugging and kissing.

Zude was talking aloud, her words an incantation. "I cannot bear this joy. I shall become a puddle! I shall discorporate, be no more! I cannot bear this joy. I shall…"

"¿Dónde estás, Tutea Vicuña?" sang out Regina, scrambling atop the vicuña.

Tutea rolled Regina to the ground and then kicked two hooves in the air, the sounds from her throat clearly saying, "¡Estoy aquí!"

Three bodies tumbled, holding and singing and crying and laughing. Until each was assured that the others were really there, indisputably, authentically, enfleshedly there.

Once Zude said in her mind to Regina, "How can you be here? I saw your body slide into the ocean!"

A rain of sheer delight showered over her. "They taught us," Regina sent to Zude. "They taught us to make our bodies over again. From the blueprint."

Zude frowned.

"Like tekla, Zudie! Like tekla. And like flying!"

"Who?" said Zude aloud. "Who taught you, Reggie?"

Child and vicuña looked into each other's eyes, then burst into throat noises that Zude could only call laughter. Zude forsook her questions. She rolled with the two of them, happily, in the dust. "Estamos aquí," they all whispered in unison. Then they held one another for a long time.

When Zude felt Regina squirming, she sighed. The day's magic was coming to an end.

"It will never end," she heard deep in her heart.

"Let's go home, Zudie," Regina said, kneeling between her and the vicuña.

"Yes," said Zude, "let's go home."

When Tutea offered to carry the child, Zude protested. In her newly acquired language, she sent, "You are not a beast of burden, Tutea. You are not here for our use!"

Tutea closed her eyes and waited the length of a full breath. Looking at Zude again, she sent, "I am here for the adventures of the body: the excitement, the learning, the love. I choose to offer my back to Regina. It is part of my adventure."

Zude blinked and nodded. As Regina climbed onto Tutea's shoulders, the animal lifted her head. Zude basked in the grace of a vicuña smile.

Regina sang lustily all the way down the incline to the edge of the lush selva.

They stood in the night-time forest. "I'll leave you now, my friends," said the vicuña as Regina reached up to hug the long neck.

"You'll be all right when we go?" Zude asked. "I mean, will you, ah, be safe from, you know, from other animals?"

"Never safe. I'm too tasty, and they know it."

Zude was suddenly anxious. "But if your predators are back, if they…"

"I run." The shaggy shoulders did not quite shrug. "And if I'm caught, I drop my body and let the big cat feed."

Zude sought the soft eyes again.

"One last thing, Tutea, She Who Is a Vicuña. How may humans gift you, the animals, now that we are bodies together again on Little Blue?"

Tutea's meaning clusters were glazed with humor. "You've answered your own question, Zella Terremoto Adverb. And in front of many people."

Zude was puzzled.

"'The most precious gift of all,' you said to the world when you cut the ribbon, 'is freedom.' For those of us like me, who are bodying, freedom is our fundamental desire, even though at times we may set it aside in order to build a companionship. Freedom is more important than comfort, more important than respect or love, more important than safety, even more important than food or drink. Freedom."

The vicuña lingered only a moment in her goodbyes. Then in an instant she was gone, bounding upward toward the plateau.

To Zude's delight, Regina ate a hearty camp meal. When they cuddled together by a balata tree, they listened to the sounds of a living forest that human ears had not heard for seven decades. It was a night of wonder, and of gratitude.

Just after the next dawn, they made their way to the banks of the Great Marañón, where a Stewardry cushcar awaited them.

13

Excerpt from

The Memoirs of Magister Lin-ci Win————————

[2089 C.E.]

> If you cannot fly into the arms of God, run.
> If you cannot run into the arms of God, walk.
> If you cannot walk into the arms of God, sit and attend.
> Her arms will find you.
> *Vade Mecum for the Journey*

Within a year of the Kanshoubu's dissolution, Lin-ci Win resigned her post as Steward of the Asia-China-Insula Tri-Satrapy and became Citizen Win. She made a gracious and loving fare-well speech over global flatcast, announced the release of her Memoirs and disappeared with several members of her household before dawn of the following day. The most popular part of her Memoirs, in both its written form and its subsequent fullsense dramatizations, was the following account of her decision to sup-port the Kanshoubu's abolition.

In retrospect, it is clear that the coordinated eruption of the three bailiwicks, each in a separate tri-satrapy, was a watershed event marking Little Blue's radical global change. The uprisings did not, of course, cause the changes, but—in the manner of the West's best tragic tradition—they occasioned our discovery of the vast changes that were afoot, even the dying of the children.

My own destiny began its most torturous unfolding some months later, when Vice-Magister Khtum Veng Sanh, so long my friend and comrade, left her post. Without her at my side the world was both short of comfort and less stable. With the subsequent defection of two regiments of Asian Amahs, my days deteriorated into dramas of increasingly bad fortune; my nights found me tossing and turning in my bed—behavior that could better be called bouncing and flinging, for it involved straps and pulleys and lifts that I could manipulate with my arms so that the position of the lower half of my body could be altered.

All I could see around me was the demise of the Amahrery, and the global rise of a reinvigorated violence; I watched our decades of progress in understanding human motivation retreat into oblivion. The dying of the children seemed only the proper consequence of a world too evil to sustain life, a world in which an age-old bitter cycle of violence reasserted itself with redoubled force: Parents cursing and beating upon their children, who then cursed and beat upon their children – on and on, the legacy passing down to eternity.

What could save us now, I asked, from that dread cycle? In vain I thought and wrote and analyzed. With every failure of the faculty of intelligence, I drew further from the outside world and closer to the secrets of my heart.

It was there that I found him. He lurked in the shadows of cognition, and he fouled the purest corners of my soul with his venom: Yeh Su T'ung, who a quarter of a century before had put the paralyzing bullet at the base of my spine. There he was, the culprit, the villain on whose shoulders the blame belonged! By rehearsing his single act of terror, I could charge him with all the evils that now assaulted the Amahrery, the Kanshoubu and the tottering globe.

That fool had robbed me of my mobility, my desire, my physical ease. He had tinkered with Fate, bringing to her knees one who was touched by Heaven for her role as peacemaker. He had destroyed the fulfillment of a destiny I had acknowledged from my childhood: the leadership of a world of justice dispensed by the only rightful peacemakers, the women. Had I my full physical faculties, I could stem the tide of this present disorder...if only he had never fired his weapon!

Crazed reasoning. Yet the only thinking that afforded me an ounce of satisfaction. So crazed that, one dark night in the silence of my rooms, I carved Su T'ung's full-sized figure from balsawood, dressing it in greasy rags like those he had worn that night. I painted in his black eyes, his leer, his insolence, and I ruthlessly imprisoned him with the technologies of the Craft. I laughed as he writhed in my punishment of his act, ridiculing myself for the decades I had spent laying roses of forgiveness across his path.

Su T'ung suffered that night for more than his crippling of my body. My revenge, I discovered, had been eons in the making; the cycle of violence overflowed the present to reach back in time. In my mind I saw the parade of history, the catalogue of atrocities and massacres, the worldwide epics of slaughter. They did not come as events happening to others, not as pictures on a distant screen, but as my own lives, in bodies I had occupied over millennia, over kalpas and yugas: Yhe countless generations of emerging into flesh and departing, again and again, avenging in one lifetime the torment of the lifetime gone before, only to suffer retribution for that vengeance in the life to come. In the ongoing replay of vengeance I had only two alternatives, one role or the other, either the ravaging warrior or the plundered, the slayer or the slain, the rapist or the defiled. If today I were victor in Burma, I would tomorrow be victim in Rome.

273

And I discovered a motive much deeper than revenge, for I touched in these visions—at least those in which I was perpetrator rather than victim—the elation that accompanied cruelty and killing. The anticipation of rapture seductively drew me toward every destructive act. I played the rapacious, pillaging tribesman to perfection, surrounding him in ever more subtly acceptable accommodations, garbing him in the armor of protector and defender, transforming him into the hero or savior who wore the trappings of righteousness. But whether villain or champion, footsoldier or emperor, I harbored in every case the thirst for blood. I loved its salt and its succor.

Revenge, I decided, was only a flimsy excuse for the exhilaration of my rage and uncompromising desire. What truly drove me was the love of violence; for that prize I ruthlessly protected the cycle of vengeance. In my present existence, ironically enough, I could hope to experience my shrouded exhilaration only by being an Amah, by being a part of the control of violence.

Then Adverb and Lutu proposed to me the abolition of the Kanshoubu.

I refused their proposal, and I descended into an indescribable despair. In those weeks before the meeting of the Heart, Adjana, my long-love, held me when I could allow it, sang to me when I could hear her, and fed me when I would eat, but we no longer laughed or played or loved together. I withdrew from friends, from the chosen familyship of our household. Now as never before, Adjana and my aides—Dani, May, Hu Wei Chu—were my caretakers, those who stood by with open hands to soothe me in my deliriums, to clear away the wreckage of my howling rages. In all the world, only these four women might be able to describe my frail mental state or the wild visions of bloodlust that nightly overtook me.

I slept fitfully if at all and rose to every day exhausted, able to function only by becoming an automaton and by delegating increasing responsibilities to my Vice-Magisters. In particular, I refused audience to anyone wishing to discuss the abolition of the Kanshoubu or my silence on that matter. The affairs of the tri-satrapy lurched forward.

Then, in yet another dream, Confucius himself came to me: The only male in all of recorded time whose thinking I had ever respected, whose doctrine I valued enough to take as my creed, probably the single most influential person of Chinese birth in all of human history.

He sat in formal pose, an old man plucking a sanxian, there in a softly lit corner of my room. He was garbed as it is said he always was, in his girdle and high court dress, his big sleeves dangling. As he played, he sang of the spear, the bow, the hunt, and of the wild boar finally taken by brave men and dogs.

He ended the song with a flourish and looked at me with earnest eyes. "You must not let them do it, my daughter," he said. "You must not let them destroy the Kanshou."

"The Kanshou are lovers of violence, Master," I replied. "We pretend to protect the innocent and punish the violator, but we are the true sadists, exhilarated by the drama of conquest, and addicted without hope of release to the intoxication that chaperones our cruelty."

"Your sadism is a lie," he said. "Your exhilaration is false. The True Way is hidden beneath both." He struck an intricate chord on the sanxian.

"With respect, Master!" I spat. "It is not my cruelty which is false! What is false is your hope of governing by the sheer force of moral example! The Kanshoubu has been committed from its inception to being that example, but it has failed because it, too, is corrupt! It, too, loves violence!"

"You are impatient, my daughter," Confucius smiled. "I have said that if rulers were virtuous for one hundred years, then crime would be negligible. The Kanshoubu has lived barely half that long! It has not been given its chance. Let it live another fifty years, my daughter, and you will see. The Kanshoubu is wind; the people are grass."

Before I could speak, he continued. "You believe that you love violence. But what you truly love is Order. Great Ones must teach lesser ones the way. You are a Great One, my daughter. This is your exhilaration."

No! His words intensified my grim and relentless despair.

"Then, Master," I said, "my Greatness rests upon the small-ness of others. My Order depends upon their waywardness." What seemed a final darkness closed around me. "And you, my Great Teacher, have required the violence of millions upon which to rest the millennia of your fame. Like the Cross-Broken One of the West, your salvation depends on others' sin. Behind your exhortations of Beneficent Order, you are as great a lover of vio-lence as I!"

He sat a moment, his hands hidden in his sleeves. Then with-out another word to me, he took up his instrument and resumed his formal pose. He sang of the spear, the bow, the hunt, and of the wild boar finally taken by brave men and dogs.

I watched the vision fade, heard the sanxian sounds recede into silence.

If in the weeks after my encounter with Adverb and Lutu I had doubted my sanity and my worth to humankind, in the days after my meeting with the Master I was a madwoman drowning in self-loathing. In consigning my Great Teacher to the flames of eternal vengeance, I had consumed the last remnants of my own soul. I grew terrified, not just of the daemons who lurked behind my eyes, but of the outer world as well, where I saw malice in every glance. I heaved my body behind barriers. I hid in corners and flinched at sharp sounds. My every breath became a retreat from life.

Two days before the Heart was to meet, I slipped into an oblivion that even with use of the Full Disciplines I still cannot recall. I am told that I refused food, that my eyes stared steadily without sleep or blinking, that only Adjana could force my lips apart for the taking of liquids. The best healers in Guangdong Province, and some from far beyond it, were unable to bring me to any brink of communication.

In desperation my loved ones transported me to The Mother's Healing Springs on New Zealand's North Island, there to immerse my rigid body in waters that had often been a balm to me. They tell me that, when they placed me in the pool, I broke my trance for the first time, wailing for the Mother of Heaven to give me a vision; I ate ravenously, then closed my eyes, and slept without waking for three more days.

Toward the end of that long sleep, I was visited in my dreams by two smiling Kanshou whom I knew well: Femmedarme Magister Flossie Yotoma Lutu and Vigilante Vice-Magister Winifred W. Glee. They moved like clouds around my aching heart. Why these two, I do not know, or why they should bring with them, of all things, affectionate wild turkeys, flights of butterflies, dancing swordfish and slick black cats. I only know that, with the vision of those animals, I lifted my eyes for the first time in weeks and asked for life again.

My loved ones rejoiced. They fed me, cleaned me and immersed me again in the sulfur springs, for though I could not speak, it was clear that some awful danger had passed and that I actively craved those easing waters.

There I was joined by Jezebel Stronglaces, an adept of profound talents and intelligences. We Sat Hearkening to the

Fundaments of the Craft, and within those hallowed pools this patient Witch heard what I had heard, saw what I had seen. I felt fully known. She suggested to me that the age-old paradigm can be broken, that there is a dwelling place where I am neither victim nor perpetrator, that the twins of Violence and Order are our own best illusions, and that violence itself is in the eyes of its beholders.

Jezebel Stronglaces did not know the extent or the importance of her gifts to me. She left me floating under a starlit sky, watching my useless legs as they stirred with the occasional pressures of the pungent waters.

The snort that startled me came from my own throat. It was rough and guttural, like a coarse snore, but it carried with it the sure knowledge of where the Quick One masqueraded. I laid my snout into the deepest thickness of the brush and drew it aside with my tusk. There she was, no longer darting but frozen against the bronze grass, lost in it except for that fat stomach bellowing out and in.

We Ratified the Devour.

"You beauty," I sent to her, "you are my life!" I snatched her, teeth sinking into her back and her fleshy underbelly.

She blinked out quickly, but not before I held the Here of those who had felt the flick of her tongue, the life of Those-Who-Had-Become-Her-Life—the beetles, field moths, caterpillars, flies, mosquitoes, mites, ants, larvae, arachnids—including one especially delicious brown water spider—as well as Those-Who-Had-Become-the-Life of Those-Who-Had-Become-the-Life of that luscious lizard.

"You are so-o-o scrumptious!" I told her as I folded the lizard body into my throat. I was still relishing the taste of her when I caught the scent of the hunting party. I made for my den only to find myself cut off by the yelps of a pack of dogs. They were on me in an instant, and I upon them. I gored one badly and frightened two more, but still others attacked me from behind. The sound of the fray brought the men with their arrows and spears. One shaft wedged between my shoulders and struck me to the heart.

I caught the eye of my slayer, the Householder himself, and in that moment we Ratified the Devour. But he did not hold the Here of Those-Who-Had-Become-My-Life, and I was forced to pass from my body without his full acknowledgment of what was taking place between us. Puzzled and uncompleted, I tarried above my lifeless form as it was borne to a cookhouse, there to be gutted, dressed, spitted, roasted and splayed upon a flat dish, a sweet boiled apple forced between its distended jaws.

On impulse I entered the soft flesh that had so lately belonged to me, and rode inside it to a cheering banquet hall on the shoulders of two young men. I steamed with the cooked roots and greens that garnished my platter. I would be scrumptious, I knew.

The hall fell silent. The Householder rose to his feet and spoke for all those gathered there. He addressed me and, to my great relief, began to hold the Here of Those-Who-Had-Become-My-Life: all the acorns and fruits and truffles, all the grains and roots and voles and crawling creatures, including of course the luscious lizard. I became the bridge over which the thankfulness flowed, from the hearts of hungry men and women to the endless layers of all who had invested themselves in the flesh and flower of my dark body.

"You have not died," the Householder said to me and to the foods surrounding me, "for you will live in each body here, in each spirit here, whom you will nourish. Everything that lives does so at the sacrifice of other beings. If ever we forget your sacrifice, and that of those who nourished you, then we forget who we are as true men, and we become capable of all manner of cruelty. Thus, for our part, we live each day in simple gratitude for the life you give us here tonight."

There was a trembling in the breaths that filled the eating hall as the people held the Here of Those-Who-Had-Become-My-Life.

The Here-ing was complete. As I lifted from the body and turned toward Home, the voice of a bard followed me. He sang of the spear, the bow, the hunt, and of the wild boar reverently taken by brave men and dogs.

I drifted in the shallow sulfur pool, my eyes adding salt to the waters that lapped at my chin. I still felt my four hooves, my curved tusks and my black bristles…the apple in my mouth. I quivered in the acclaim of all those upon whom I had fed; I was celebrated by the people who were feeding on me. I barely could distinguish any one of us from the other. The Devourer and the Devoured.

All was acknowledged. All was well.

I began lifting myself apart from the flesh and turning toward Home. I had not felt such peace since I was three, not since Little Tz'u and Big Tz'u held me between them in the broad bed.

I remember Home, I thought. Home was the daffodils and azaleas and orchids that crowded our little house in the city. Home was a pale blue, eggshell-thin bowl filled with peaches or with wine-softened quince, it was rain on black tiled roofs, and bamboo fans in the heat of summer. Home was Big Tz'u's arms swinging me high and Little Tz'u singing in the twilight before my bedtime. Home was everything I knew.

But on that New Zealand mountainside, what I thought I knew was suddenly expanding in bursts of vibrating energies: in patterns, axes, languages, and architectures, all of them exploding simultaneously before my eyes, like cherry blossoms at the sudden birth of spring. Home was becoming vast.

Home was a Stream of vibrant joy that flowed through me, through every living thing—and every thing that was, was living! Home was the banks of that Stream of joy, where I stood with healthy legs and reached out to hold a blue-white marble that hung in space against a velvet black eternity. My arms enfolded it all, its oceans, its icecaps and its clouds, its mountains and its cities, its rivers and towns and plains and forests—and all its inhabitants. I held it in my arms, my planet home, my Little Blue. And it in turn held me.

Home was both peace and wild excitement, a birthing each moment of new life, of a hundred billion new ideas and things. It was All Infinity, varied and still All One.

I stood in that flow and understood that we live forever.

There was a lurch. I wasn't Home anymore. Nor was I in the healing pools. I was in another body, dressed in greasy rags and holding a .30 caliber Garand I'd lifted from a Wuhan museum. Across my back was a clip belt, and in my craw all the pent-up rage of an upbringing filled with poverty and abuse. The Girls in Red were scaling the north wall of the Wuchang cotton mill, and I had the topmost one in my sights. I checked my magazine and took up my easy bead again. Give it to her in the head? No, T'ung, give it to her in the back. That'll drop her and stop her, maybe for good. I lowered my aim and started breathing back the trigger.

"You will not harm me, Su T'ung."

It was my own voice, the voice of the young Adjutant Major Lin-ci Win, the voice of the Amah scaling the wall. But it was in his head…in my head…in the head I was wearing, the one looking down the sights of the Garand. I let up on the trigger.

"You will not harm me," the voice said again, "because now you are a conscious man, aware of who you are, of what you do."

Su T'ung and Adjutant Win stood in the Stream, both of us At Home there, both of us washed over by peace, joy and well-being.

And there was only one of us.

"I'm in your sights," the voice reminded me. "You have a choice now, Yeh Su T'ung, a real choice."

"I see what I'm doing."

"Yes."

"I can still fire."

"You can. And if you do, that same world in which you and I have lived since that night will continue to be."

I did not fire the rifle. I had fired it once in another where, but I did not fire it here.

Then I was drowning in bad-tasting water, flailing at the rocks, struggling to right myself and keep my head in the air.

"Adjana!" I was shouting.

She came immediately, up from the lower camp to the side of the pool. I clutched her arms, almost dragging her into the water with me. "Get Chu, put the low rocket on standby," I gasped.

"The rocket?"

I clung to her strong body above me, my face close to hers. "We're going to the Marquesas, Adjana! We're going to the meeting of the Heart! Hurry!" I laughed. "Adjana, I have decided!"

Before she could obey me, we were assaulted by loud shouts and the sounds of a struggle from the direction of the camp. I heard the voices of my Jing-Chas above the scuffle, then a man's long howl.

"Magister!" It was Dani, ascending the path. "Magister, we have subdued an intruder! Please stay close to Adjana while we dispose of him!"

"No!" I called to her. "No, bring him here! Adjana, my sark! Quickly!"

"Magister!" Dani was protesting.

"I said bring him here! Bring him now!" I took my sark from Adjana, pulling it over my head and torso even as I remained seated in the pool. The light material floated like a tent about me. "Help me," I pleaded. Adjana tamed the long shift, covering me with it and tying it about my waist.

Dani and May were dragging a man up the hill. When they had assured themselves that I was ready for this strange audience, they pushed him to his knees directly across the pool from me and stood close behind him.

His robe was saffron, and his tonsure familiar. I had heard that he had entered a monastery upon his release from the baili-wick. He knelt now with his head bowed.

"Why have you come?"

Very slowly he raised his head, revealing eyes so full of love that I quickly looked away, lest they consume me with their fire.

"I have come to beg your forgiveness."

"You are already forgiven."

"And to see you whole."

I could no longer avoid the embrace of those eyes, and in the moment of meeting them with my own, I felt a tingling in my lower body that I had never hoped to feel again. I was suddenly aware of my feet! I knew without looking that they rested on the rock shelf that inclined slightly downward to constitute the bottom of the pool. Still holding his eyes with my own, I leaned forward and cried out in astonishment. My legs, my own legs, were pushing me upward!

Yeh Su T'ung's face was radiant. I saw myself through his eyes: a thinly clad woman with water sliding down her body, a woman slowly straightening to an upright position, a woman standing on her own in a shallow pool.

From behind me, Adjana moved to steady me. I did not need her, for I was filled in every part of my body with strength and life!

Still through Su T'ung's eyes, I saw myself moving by my own power. Then I felt myself walking…at last. Practicing the lifting and placing of my joyful feet as I covered again and again the length of the northeastward speeding rocket, back and forth, back and forth, without rest! Then walking at last, in full Magister regalia, into the meeting of the Heart. Walking at last. Striding! Striding swift, striding long. And with Adjana soaring again and forever over the Gorges of the Yangtze, trailing clouds of glory as we flew!

It can be truly said that out of the Heart of Darkness I came running.

14

> So still does spirit long for matter
> as matter longs for spirit.
> *Wisdom of the Ancients*

Still on low fusion power, Jezebel banked the little solocush into a wide circle and looked down on the long, luminous path of the Canal. Limón Bay was just beginning to glisten in the early sun. Before her and to the east, low mountains began their reach for Colombia; far to her right, Chiriquí—or another mountain almost as high—capped Panama's more rugged western range. Below her, a small flock of jaçanās rose from one of the inland lakes and circled toward the south. She began her final descent.

Jezebel loved the anarchy of craftlanding pads. The Air Traffic Conditions Service, available only in the greater congestion of metropolitan areas, served a good purpose in describing prevailing circumstances to hovercraft, but after dispensing such information, ATC usually left flyers alone, trusting them to plan and negotiate their own take-offs or landings.

All four of her air jets puffed in perfect alignment as they lowered her to her parking berth on the chartreuse ring. She cut her power and checked the console for all-systems par. Voicing-in the necessary information about the hovercraft's most recent journey, she set the Maintenance Check Needed flasher, snagged her trip-pack, and kissed the solocush a thank-you-and-goodbye. She squeezed out of the little vehicle into a day already hot and humid.

She stood a moment, transfixed by the dense life that pulsed over the cush-rocket terminal's lush grounds, just beyond her. Carefully tended gardens mingled their tender fragrances with the metallic smells of cushcar operation and light fusion afterburn; deep shade trees were filled with the sounds of birds and small mammals; fountains and waterfalls were ringed with reeds and tall grasses; a wild diversity of insects and amphibians animated the occasional ponds.

Through the crowd, Jez watched the passengers disembarking from the latest rocket. She caught sight of an old Magister cloak and the handsome figure who wore it.

Even before her smile had opened to its fullest measure, Zude was enveloping her. "Bella-Belle, Jezebel!"

"Steward Adverb!" Jez breathed into the graying hair. "It's been too long, Zudie."

"Years without the sweet touch of the fair Jezebel!" Zude held Jez at arm's length. Her eyes were shining.

Jez's hands explored the muscles in Zude's arms and her back. "You feel great," she sent mentally, planting a brisk kiss on Zude's lips.

"Again!" urged Zella Terremoto Adverb. "Again!"

"Zude the Insatiable!" Jez laughed. They held each other in a swaying embrace while busy travelers stepped around them, carefully avoiding the bubble of their mindtalk.

Moments later Zude mumbled aloud, "Holocommunication is an admirable application of science, but there's just nothing like real flesh."

Jez gave her a parting squeeze. "We have to get moving," she said, steering Zude out of the arrival area. "I have plans for you."

"Oh, I hope so," Zude sighed.

Jez set their packs on mindtote just to her right in midair where she could shepherd them effortlessly, then slipped her left arm under Zude's right one. Easily, and with an old comfort, they entwined their fingers and held their forearms in a horizontal lock that kept their bodies close to each other as they walked.

"Bosca's staying in her sanctum," Jez said. "Bosca, that is, and a family of howler monkeys. She won't come out until day after tomorrow and won't vacate her body until next week. You'll have plenty of time to be with her."

"Why so soon, Jez? Her last message assured me she didn't want to go for another six months."

Jez veered their course toward the terminal's baños and restrooms. "She says she's feeling too big for her skin," Jez explained, "like one day soon she's going to explode. She says she has to do it now, get on to her next level. She wants us to take her body to the mountains of Sierra Madre del Sur for the wolves."

Zude smiled. "Of course." She sighed. "It'll be a great celebration. Folks will come from all over Aztlán to Sit Last Circles with Bosca."

"Will Yotoma come?"

Zude shook her head. "We won't be able to lure Flossie away from that godforsaken aerie in Sierra Leone. Not even for Bosca."

"She's still communing with the great red condor and family?"

Zude laughed. "Yes. She's cold, she's high, and she's getting younger by the nanosecond."

They dodged a shyflyer who materialized in front of them with a baby in a hip sling. He shrugged a quick apology and made off toward the main terminal.

"Reggie. How's she doing?" asked Zude.

"Fine, as always." Jez was angling them toward the restrooms. "Living in the Yucatan with Bosca has been important for both of them." She guided them and their trip-packs through the baño's door sphincter.

Over the top of a multicolored comfort stall Zude commented. "I haven't seen her for months. She's probably shot up like a beanstalk."

"When you see her at Bosca's Last Circles you'll be looking up!" Jez turned a refresher funnel on and basked in its cool air.

Zude had to raise her voice to ask, "So how about Dicken? Will she get there?"

"No chance. She's pledged to a three-month deepsea expedition near the Tonga Trench. She sent a new ballad for Bosca that the elders will sing." Jez scratched her head vigorously with both hands and finger-combed her hair back into place. "Dicken's performing for the whales now. Drumming and singing. They charm her, then she charms them, then they charm her, and so on. I'm not sure we'll ever get her back."

Both women emerged from the baño in fresh clothes, and cooler by many degrees. Jez straightened Zude's collar, then led the way back to the terminal proper.

"So, best beloved," Zude grinned, "your plans for me! What are they? We rocket up to Cancún right away? We do Colón's games and races? Sail the mighty Caribbean?"

"There's a learning neighborhood over in Cativá that I want you to see. One of the teachers is especially noteworthy." Jez spoke easily as they walked. "They don't expect us at Bosca's until tomorrow night." She shot a glance at Zude. "And I figured Bosca wouldn't mind if we had a little vacation before we go to be with her."

She halted them by a flatscreen monitor and faced Zude. "So, Zudie, will you spend the day with me, here in Panama?"

"Jezebel, I'd spend the day with you under the Arctic icecap if you asked me."

"Good!" She swept Zude and the trip-packs toward the terminal's underwater restaurant. "Food first, then Cativá, then some culture. And in the meantime there's so much to tell you!"

"Food!" Zude replied. "Now!"

They spent the morning in the festive ambience of Cativá, sampling lectures and demonstrations in the town's learning snugs, and strolling through the bustle of vending stalls and street performers. They were laughingly attempting to grasp the basic steps of the tarantella when they were drawn to a sudden commotion that arose just beyond them.

A small child was bawling her heartbreak to the heavens. Her cries were enhanced by the squawks and whistles of a hundred or so disturbed grackles in the surrounding trees. A thin boy was trying in vain to comfort the child.

"Lina-Lena," he cajoled, "you were a little too rough."

"She's gone!" wailed the child. "She just went away!"

"Maybe you were hurting her," the boy suggested.

"She wouldn't let me ride her!"

"Dogs don't like to be ridden, Lina, so she went shy."

Lina frowned. "Will she come back?"

"Maybe. Maybe not."

"Look, Lina," interrupted a nearby woman. She held a grackle on her finger. "Here's a bird."

A few people sat by, watching. Jez and Zude rested under a tree within hearing distance.

The child, the boy and the woman sat with their eyes closed while the grackle explored the woman's hair with its beak.

"I'm in it, Señora Casco," the boy whispered earnestly. "I'm in the spacious awareness."

"Not if you're talking, you're not," laughed the woman. "Hush."

Another moment of silence, then Lina wiggled and whined. "I won't do it, señora! I don't like to!" She squirmed in the boy's arms. He released her.

"It's all right, Lina," said Señora Casco, "we can do this another time." She smoothed the girl's hair back. "You go along, now." She gave her a pat on the behind. "Raúl and I will be with the birds."

Suddenly, Lina's hand shot out. It grabbed the grackle. The grackle screeched.

"Let it go, Lina!" exploded the boy. "Let it go!" He tried to pry open the child's hands. The grackle struggled and squawked. Lina squeezed the bird tighter, pulling away from Raul. She and the grackle were shrieking together.

Then the bird disappeared. And the grackles in the trees hushed their cries, moving from branch to branch in silence.

Lina stared at her empty hands. Her face contorted into an agony of disappointment and betrayal. She tuned up from a barely audible whimper into an escalating scream. She screamed again and again, gasping with each intake of breath.

With only a glance between them, Señora Casco and Raúl closed their eyes again and sat calmly. Some others nearby did the same. Lina continued to scream.

"Find the presencing place, Raúl," the señora directed, softly. "Make it empty, no thoughts."

Raúl nodded.

Lina howled.

Then another grackle, or perhaps the same one, landed on Señora Casco's head. The child hushed, galvanized by the bird.

"You can presence with us if you want to, Lina," said the woman without opening her eyes. "Just make yourself very calm and watch how you breathe."

The little girl collapsed to the ground, staring at the grackle. She closed her eyes.

"When a thought or a feeling or a sensation comes, say hello to it, and then watch your breath again."

They sat for long minutes—the child, the boy, and the woman with a bird in her hair—interrupted now and then by words from the señora.

"To play with birds, or with dogs or other animals, human beings have to be present with them. They must go to the quiet place inside and invite the animal to join them there."

A few moments later she said, "This is the place where we let the animals teach us. The animals always know what they are doing, but we have a different kind of mind, and it often makes us forget what we are doing. And who we are."

A little later she said, "When the inside of your head is very big and empty, that's when you're in the Matrix, and that's when you can invite the animal into your quiet place."

While Zude watched the enduring silence, Jez closed her eyes, seeking her own place of welcome for the grackles. Suddenly, Zude gripped her wrist. Jez's eyes flew open. Zude was staring at the little group and grinning.

With effort, Jez focused her eyes. Only one thing had changed in the picture that had been before her: The grackle had abandoned Señora Casco's head and now stood immobile on the head of the relaxed and smiling little girl. Her eyes still closed, Lina raised her hand and extended a forefinger. Immediately the bird leapt to the perch and settled there, its head close to the child's happy face.

The tableau remained for minutes more, the only sounds an occasional whistle or squawk from the trees. Finally, people opened their eyes and stretched. Life resumed its regular pace.

"And that," Zude observed, as she and Jez headed toward the lake where Maestra Kathleen would be holding classes, "is why we don't need Kanshou anymore."

"That's a little overstated, Steward," Jez suggested. "Plenty of people still can't do what the grackle did."

"Ah, but we're learning, Bella-Belle."

"And you aren't bored, Zudie? You don't miss all the blood and thunder?"

Zude was thoughtful. "I was afraid I would," she replied, "but no. No, I don't miss it." Speaking in mindreach, she sent haltingly, "I've missed you, Jezebel."

"I've missed you too, Zudie," Jez sent back.

"We're both so busy, I know," the words tumbled out of Steward Adverb's mouth, "I mean, I'm supposed to be running a tri-satrapy, and you, you're still pushing frontiers, not even sleeping much. It's like we have a thousand more commitments than we ever did before, and we're doing more and more things and getting higher and faster and...but maybe we could..."

"Zudie."

Zude stopped. She blinked, deliberately slowed her breath.

"Zudie," Jez said aloud, her eyes crinkling, "there's no end to the things we can do, or be, or have. We can do together whatever we both want to do together."

Zude blinked again. "Well," she croaked. "Well." She cleared her throat and steered them into motion again. There was an added lilt to her steps.

The day scorched well into afternoon before they found Maestra Kathleen and her students. Atop a slope of lake grass,

Zude stood watching sixteen children in a stand of trees below, intently busy at a group task.

Maestra Kathleen sat on one of several high-backed benches, leaning forward, observing the group. She wore a plain ankle-length dress of smooth cotton that protected her ample body from the sun. Her long brown hair was held back with a scarf. Suddenly, her voice rose above the low murmur of the children's activity.

"Aurelia! Lift up Luka so she can see better! Good. Thank you!"

Steward Adverb had a frown on her face. "Jez," she said, peering down the incline, "Jez, that woman looks a little like…and her voice, her stance, she's…"

Jez stood beside her, an innocent smile on her face. "She's what?"

At that moment the teacher shielded her eyes from the sun and gestured to the figures on the hill. "Welcome!" she called to the visitors. One or two of the children followed her gaze.

Zude did not take her eyes off the woman below her. "Jez, is that…Edge!" she shouted, "Captain Edge, is that you?" She burst down the hill at a run.

"Magister!" the woman exclaimed in astonishment. She rose and moved toward Zude. The two women met in a large, loud, back-slapping embrace, laughing and talking. Lest they lapse into a marathon of old-times-at-the-Shrievalty-Building, Jez drew the three of them toward the benches. "What are the children so engrossed in?" she asked the maestra.

"They're learning how to construct a holocosm." Kathleen smiled. "That technology is actually way beyond anything they could do from scratch, but we have a young cosmotech to show how it's done. He brought his holo and splining generators with him and carried everything he needed here in his pockets!"

Jez and Zude looked over at the group of children, who were focused with rapt attention on a dark young man.

"May we watch?" asked Zude.

"Of course," answered Kathleen.

But Jez was already on her feet, pulled by a tremor of familiarity, a tug of memory, toward the lesson-place. The instructor's back was toward her. "Now," he was saying, "once you have the silver orb at low-spin, you start on the white one. It represents the Stream, so the Matrix orb has to revolve in that direction, and intersect with it…like…so."

The young man's deep voice, where had she heard it before?

"Once you have these two set," he appeared to be weaving a third globe now, "you produce the golden orb, the Journey, and…set it spinning…that way…into the first orb, the Matrix."

The children held their collective breath as he ever so delicately maneuvered the three glowing spheres into their interlocking rotation. He turned his head slightly, and Jez caught her own breath. Another circle of children, another time…She was back in a schoolroom in Arabia. Shaheed!

"Now all we have to do is en-cube it with the crystal-lumer, like this…" He straightened and set aloft the completed holocosm.

"Ahhh!" the children breathed out.

The wondrous artwork shimmered, its vivid colors dancing as the spheres turned each into the other, suspended and revolving, stillness and motion all together.

"Wonderful, Shaheed!" exclaimed Maestra Kathleen, moving around the clutch of children and gazing at the holocosm floating just above their heads. "Matrix," she said, speaking to the group and reaching toward each globe as she spoke, "our source and home, delivering us into the Stream, our realm of active force and creativity, which births us into the Journey, our physical life, and then back again to Home!"

Zude, who had come up next to Jez, was awed. "What a dazzlingly simple demonstration of it all," she observed.

Shaheed looked then from his creation to the two guests. His reply stopped at his lips when he saw Jezebel. His dark eyes widened, then his face burst into a radiant smile. Jez grinned back. He gestured with mock-futility at the small wall of children between them. She gestured an I'll-wait-for-you-here reply, and he turned back to wrap up his demonstration. He presented Maestra Kathleen with the holocosm, which she accepted with a little gasp of appreciation, then they both answered a cascade of eager questions from the youngsters.

One child in particular wanted to know about the jet-black pyramid in the center of the holocosm, the place where all three orbs intersected. "There's no light at all there!" she said.

Kathleen laughed. "Good for you, Yolie! That part is hard to explain. It's called the Realm of All Possibility, where everything that we can't yet imagine, is imagined."

"Then it's all empty?" Yolie persisted.

"Yes," answered Shaheed, "all empty. And…all full!"

Yolie laughed and rolled her eyes.

Jez and Zude stood to one side, enjoying the cosmological pedagogy. When it began to subside, Kathleen said in her carrying voice, "Let's finish up today by showing our guests what we've been practicing all week!"

"Yes!" "Let's!" "Good!" came the piping voices.

"They're learning how to shyfly in a group," the maestra told Jez and Zude. "All right," she called. "Here!"

Immediately the scattered students poured over her, forming at her feet a mound of human flesh. The maestra hugged or stroked each one as they clung to her. Satisfied that all her brood was accounted for, she kept her voice in command timbre.

"What is the most important thing in the world?" she sang out.

The excited unison shouting was accompanied by many tiny waving hands: "Nothing is more important than that I feel Good!"

"And how do you feel when you feel Good?"

A litany of answers from different students: "I feel whole!" "I feel glad!" "I feel love!" "I feel free!"

"And do you feel Good?"

"Yes!" Clapping and cheers.

"And what does it mean when you don't feel Good?"

"It means I'm not in vibration!" one child said.

"I'm not in synch!" said another.

"And how do you get back into vibration?"

"I imagine happy things!" came the chorus. "I imagine!" they shouted again.

"Let me see how you feel Good!" sang out the maestra, and sixteen pairs of eyes squinted in concentration.

Strong, bright striations of light sprang from the group and glistened in the air. The guests nodded awe and approval.

The maestra spoke again. "Now, this will be our goodbye exercise. We four bigs won't be going with you, so Sol Serrano will be your center." She pointed to an older boy.

There were shouts and whispers of goodbye to the teacher and the visitors as the little group drew eagerly together.

"All of you be sure you are touching Sol somewhere on his body, or touching someone who is touching him. And hold each other, touch as many other people as you can."

She drew back from the group, standing at its edge. In a chaos of grunts and squeals and giggles, the mass of children shifted and squeezed more tightly together.

"Sol, you are also nonce monitor, so you get to make the count when you arrive. You'll signal if anyone's missing, right?"

The boy nodded and scrunched into his classmates, eager and waiting.

Kathleen turned to Jez. "Doña Jezebel, would you do us the honor of articulating our shyflight incantation? I've been sending them off in a simple group transport, shy-and-reflesh."

"Delighted," said Jez. She hunkered down, close to the children and touching several of them. She raised her voice. "Can you all see the bicycles on the broad path by the lone rubber tree?" she asked, pointing about 80 meters beyond a nearby grassy knoll. The children shifted so everyone could clearly see the destination, and then all heads nodded in fervent affirmation.

"In front of the bicycles, that's where you want to be, where you'll reflesh. Look at the place, see yourselves there, in exactly your present position. All of you got it?" Again, excited endorsements. Jez's glance at Kathleen asked if the specified distance was an appropriate maneuver for her crew. Kathleen pointed upward with her thumb.

"Do you feel Good?" asked Jezebel.

It was a chorus of yeses, followed by individual assurances: "I feel wonderful!" "I'm flying already, maestra!" "I'm going, I'm going! Hold me down!" The vibrations rose, shimmering in the air, tugging at the group; everyone hugged harder in an intensifying anticipation, trying to stay grounded a few more moments.

Jez's voice took on a louder, firmer quality. "Good. Study your destination carefully and set the image of it in your mind. Now close your eyes! Hold that image steady." She paused. "Now raise those vibrations higher! Even higher!" Delight rode every face. The group was quivering. "Keep the image! Don't let it waver! You're about to go now! Up the vibes! Keep the image! Here is your incantation!" Then Jezebel Stronglaces sang, strong and clear:

> *"Sister-Brother, in an instant,*
> *in the twinkling of an eye,*
> *we shall course the Stream together,*
> *for we are go-ing shy!*
> *So touch my spirit lightly*
> *and hold the image true.*
> *(We'll put on immortality for just a moment, too!)*
> *I love my separate body,*
> *its sweet delights I know,*
> *but I place it in your keeping now,*
> *and off…with you… I go!"*

The children were gone! Zude, Jez, Kathleen and Shaheed sat alone. In the next moment, the entire cluster of children reappeared down the path by the big rubber tree.

They cheered loudly as they got to their feet and waved. "We did it!" "Goodbye!" "Hasta luego, maestra!" Sol Serrano did a hasty count and sent Kathleen an okay sign. One of the older girls rose in an awkward but finally successful solo skyflight. Then all of them were off, several on bicycles, but most walking or skipping. Two older children carried a smaller child in hand-saddle.

"Wondrous!" Zude exclaimed.

"Well-done, Doña Jezebel!" exclaimed Kathleen.

"Well-done, maestra," Jez replied, "well-done!"

She turned to the tall young man. "Shaheed," she said. "How wonderful to see you. And as a teacher, too!"

He smiled. "My life changed after that day, Jezebel Stronglaces."

"So did mine, Shaheed."

Jezebel held out her arms and Shaheed walked into them.

It was after midnight. Jez and Zude rested on a grassy promontory near Colón's cush-rocket terminal, watching the lights of the city. Jez leaned against a giant mahogany tree, Zude's head in her lap.

"It's been a magical day, Jezebel," Zude said, after long silence. "Actually," she added, "it's been a magical Journey."

"It's always a magical Journey," Jez agreed.

Into the silence Zude said lightly, "We don't have to go at dawn, you know. We could wait until noon and take a Belize rocket."

Jez looked at the dark face below her.

"And in the meantime," Zude continued, "we…"

Jez's voice covered hers.

"I know a hideaway in an old army town. Peace Point, just across the bay, there. Small rooms, bed-and-breakfast." She ran her fingers through Zude's thick hair. Her fingers touched the unicorn earring in Zude's left ear. Matter-of-factly, she pulled the hair away from Zude's right ear, took the matching unicorn from her own ear, and hung it on Zude's.

Zude lay motionless.

"So," said Jez, "the pair's no longer split." She smiled. Zude searched Jez's face, then pressed Jez's hand to her lips.

It was moments later when Jez spoke again. "We could shyfly to Peace Point in an instant."

"Or we could spoon."

"Spoon! Zudie."

"It's been a while, I know, but the stars are bright…"

She sat up and faced Jezebel.

Jez raised her hand to Zude's cheek. She laughed. "You think we still could? Zudie, it's been so long."

"We can do together whatever we both want to do together," Zude reminded her. "Come on." She rose quickly and pulled an unresisting Jezebel to her feet.

They swung their trip-packs into place and stood face to face. Jez leaned forward and kissed Zude, just long enough.

"My pleasure, Cadet Lieutenant Adverb. I'll navigate."

She turned and placed herself squarely in front of Zude, facing north.

Zude drew the long body tight against her own. Then both women bent their knees and closed their eyes, breathing themselves into intimate alignment.

"By all the dreams we've walked together," whispered Zude.

"By all the love with which we've filled the vessels of our lives," whispered Jezebel.

They intoned a harmony, tumbled inward, touched familiar reaches of a vista that opened to the stars. They lifted Earth-free feet and leapt above the twinkling lights of Colón to sail rejoicing toward the Caribbean, then west again to Peace Point.

Common Era Date

2003   World Health Organization announces that alternative and complementary health practices lend hope for long life to persons of HIV-positive status. Deaths from Virus I (HIV) balloon in Indonesia, Bengal Bay, and Hong Kong as a result of contaminated blood supplies from the 1990s.

2004   Pan-European medical establishment announces first truly effective vaccine (Vaccine I) against Virus I, to be available immediately.

2005   *Flossie Yotoma Lutu* is born in the Sudan, fifty miles from the White Nile River.

2006   Precipitous emergence of mutant virus (Virus II) from the Virus I vaccine.

2007   Beginning of decade of escalating natural cataclysms, such as spikes in global warming, earthquakes, hurricanes, tornadoes, floods, droughts, famine, malaria, rivers poisoned by acid rain. China, India, and southeast Asia are especially stricken.

2008   Effective vaccine (Vaccine II) against Virus II is announced.

2010   Emergence from Vaccine II of a new strain of drug resistant virus (Virus III).

2012   Vaccine III against Virus III is announced.

2014   Emergence of new viral mutation (Virus IV) from Vaccine III.

2015   Global riots against medical establishment take hundreds of lives.

2018   Global crusade to inoculate every citizen against Virus IV with Vaccine IV, "the vaccine to end all vaccines," which has been tested extensively on cloned animals.

2019   Widespread drought resulting from ecocide and global warming sends masses of starving people northward from Central and South America into southwestern United States. The defensive response of the U.S. military includes releasing upon the invading people swarms of Culex tarsalis mosquitoes carrying an influenza virus against which its own troops are inoculated. Tens of thousands die.

2020   The international outcry against the U.S. use of biological weaponry deals the deathblow to the global power of the United States as it had existed and assures the inclusion within North American borders of the newly formed Reclaimed Territory of Aztlán, extending from Los Angeles to the Mississippi River.

2021   "Empty Monday," April 12, the day of the Animal Exodus from Little Blue. The death or disappearance of all multi-cellular animals except Homo sapiens. All subsequent attempts fail to clone stored animal DNA.

2022 Beginning of a decade of upward-spiralling global unrest, exhibited in street wars, food riots, homeless rebellions, increased martial law, worldwide disruptions of power, communication, and transportation services.

2023 International Disarmament Accords end the possibility of biological, chemical, or nuclear war worldwide.

2024 Announcement that Vaccine IV has irrevocably suppressed the Y chromosome in men and reduced fertility in women by 80%. Estimates concur that by mid-century, global population will be just over one billion and that the ratio of women to men will be 12 to 1.

2026 *Lin-ci Win* is born in Hong Kong.

2027 Worldwide secession from their parent nations of religious fundamentalist sects whose precepts include enslavement of women and individualized strains of racist theology. Their staunch defense of their sovereign communities initiates the bloodiest decade of Little Blue's 21st century.

2029 Formation of International Congress, representing nearly 75% of the nations of the world.
Founding of the Amahrery's Kanshou Academy in Hong Kong, ushering in the era of women's peacekeeping principles and practices.

2033   Founding of the Femmedarmery's Kanshou Academy in Tripoli.

2034   Founding of the Vigilancia's Kanshou Academy in Los Angeles.

2035   Worldwide legal reforms begin the conversion of prison facilities into containment areas called *bailiwicks*, whose inmates become *habitantes*. Local police forces formally adopt Kanshou peacekeeping principles, practices, and ranks.

2036   Inchoate governance model based on values and practices familiar to women begins to emerge for Middle East geo-political territory, spearheaded by *Presiding Sifter of the Syrian Kitchen Table, Flossie Yotoma Lutu* and called a "satrapy."

2038   Transmogrifier technology is tentatively approved for worldwide distribution by International Congress. The profusion of world credit systems is standardized to accommodate the rapidly changing economy. (See TERMINOLOGY.)

2039   Beginning of worldwide efforts to integrate and codify among nations economic and governmental relationships based upon values and practices familiar to women. Hearings, forums, and convocations in every major city explore the requirements of world government, delineating legislative, judicial, and implemental functions.

2041   *Jezebel Stronglaces* is born in Lakemir, near Lake Michigan, North America.

2042   *Zella Terremoto Adverb (Zude)* is born in Barranquilla, Colombia, South America.

2043   The Kitchen Table, international judicial body, is formed, initially with five sitting Sifters. Half-trap, quarter-trap, and demesne tribunals are established upon the Kitchen Table Model.
        (See GLOBAL GOVERNANCE.)

2044   "Earthclasp," April 12, the day that citizens all over the world celebrate Earthkeep priorities, including the hoped-for return of the animals.

2046   Centralizing of global peacekeeping policy by the formal merging of Amahrery, Femmedarmery, and Vigilancia into the Kanshoubu. First convening of the Heart of All Kanshou, composed of Amahs, Femmedarmes, Vigilantes of all ranks and charged with determining policies of the Kanshoubu. (See GLOBAL GOVERNANCE—PEACEKEEPING.)

2049   Central Web, with 15 sitting Websters, is officially established to replace International Congress as world legislative body. Half-trap, quarter-trap, and demesne webs begin forming on the Central Web model. (See GLOBAL GOVERNANCE.)

2050   International census for the first time categorizes "satrapies" and "tri-satrapies" as geo-political entities. The global population is reported to be 1,242,000,000, of which female citizens are 92.3%, male citizens 7.7%. "Little Blue" is officially acknowledged as the most common popular reference to the planet Earth.

2053   The Year-Long Plenum in Tokyo formulates precepts of new global governance. The Plenary Constitution, a planet-wide governing document, takes shape. "Global" begins to replace "international" in the daily parlance of citizens. Newly formed bureaus and boards take up the regulation of economic affairs and the implementation of legislative decisions.

2057   Nueva Tierra Norte Satrapy, after long negotiation with its southeastern precincts, finally confirms both the spirit and letter of the Plenary Constitution, thus completing the ratification of that global document.

2062   *Amah Captain Lin-ci Win* is wounded and paralyzed at a cotton mill looting skirmish in Wuchang (Hupeh Province).

2066   *Flossie Yotoma Lutu* becomes Magister of the Africa-Europe-Mideast Tri-Satrapy.

2067   *Zella Terremoto Adverb (Zude)* enters the Amah Academy in Hong Kong.

2078   *Lin-ci Win* becomes Magister of the Asia-China-Insula Tri-Satrapy.

2080   *Zella Terremoto Adverb (Zude)* becomes Vice-Magister of Nueva Tierra Norte Satrapy.

2084   *Jezebel Stronglaces* becomes the unofficial leader of a global movement to eradicate violence.

2085   *Zella Terremoto Adverb (Zude)* becomes Magister of Nueva Tierra Tri-Satrapy.

2086   Global Consorority of Neurosurgeons reveals proposal to use bailiwick habitantes in "the search for a physiological violence center in the brain" (Habitante Testing) and the possible institution of Anti-Violence Protocols, surgeries to eliminate any such physiological center.

bailiwicks Containment areas for offenders against society, similar in function to 20th century prisons.

"ballbakers" Contraband crystals, tuned electronically or by a witch, which are being illegally distributed and sometimes used to castrate violent men, particularly rapists.

breathshine Creation by breathfriction and focused intent of an independent and "totable" source of light, as in the creation or rejuvenation of a glolobe.

breeks A Kanshou's loose-fitting black pants of light cotton.

cape, cloak A Kanshou's black cape of tekla, hanging to mid-thigh and kept folded in her subvention belt, except when used for warmth, balance, or protection. Magisters wear the near ankle-length cloak instead of the cape.

Central Web Little Blue's global legislative body of fifteen Websters, the highest level of the planet's Legislative branch of government. (See GLOBAL GOVERNANCE.)

chela A beginning Kanshou cadet.

com-, commu- Referring to "communication," as in comcube, comunit, comline, or commuflow.

comfortsuit A Kanshou's skintight bodystocking of rhyndon.

compu- Referring to "computer," as in compucode, compufile, compukiosk, compupost, compusite.

cowl A Kanshou's tubular neckpiece of tekla that can be spread and extended upward to cover her head for protection from weather.

credit system Little Blue's primary method of value exchange, used in all metropolitan districts and in most rural areas, except where citizens have opted to be a barter or gift society. Generally replaces currency used in former eras.

cushcar A hovercraft used primarily for personal transport, such as the "solocush" (borne on only four air jets) or the "standard 24" which can seat four passengers and is sustained by 24 jets. In contrast to the cushcar, a "cargocush" is the transportation of choice for freight and is borne on 48 jets. Cushcars have replaced vehicles powered by a four-stage gasoline combustion engine in popularity.

Daily Voice The ongoing global opinion poll, offering citizens of Little Blue the opportunity to voice their opinions regarding proposals being heard by the Central Web and lower webs or cases being heard by the Kitchen Table and lower tables. One vote allowed per citizen per day.

dartsleeve A close range personal weapon through which a Kanshou may blow darts laden with "sodoze." The sodoze is a neurological inhibitor that temporarily disables the person targeted within seconds.

demesne (duh-<u>mane</u>) The governmental sub-division of a quarter-trap, whose size and shape are determined by discussion (and if necessary, by referendum) among the citizens who are involved.

dreamwork The mutual exploration undertaken by two women who are physically touching while sleeping, and in which they inhabit the same dreams, as in dreamwalking, dreamweaving, dreamwatching.

Earthclasp April 12, 2044, the day that citizens first celebrated the highest of Earthkeep priorities: the rehabilitation, preservation, veneration, and appropriate "use" of the Earth for citizens and for the hoped-for Return of the Animals. Pundits and cultural analysts have since marked the day of this celebration as the turning point in the global economy from scarcity to "No Hunger, No Poverty." The day is also commonly regarded as the time at which women were acknowledged to be the uncontested leaders of socio-political affairs on Little Blue.

Earthkeep The prevailing mass consciousness on Little Blue, derived in response to the disastrous events of the first half of the 21st century. The values attendant upon the Earthkeep consciousness are: a reverence for the planet and its biosphere as a living organism, an awareness of the interconnectedness of all beings, and a celebration of diversity and self-determination within Nature and among the human family.

Empty Monday The day of the Animal Exodus, the 48-hour period inclusive of April 12, 2021, when every non-human animal on Little Blue mysteriously died or disappeared.

Exodus The Animal Exodus from Little Blue in which all multi-cellular animals, including insects, gave up their lives. No bacterial, fungiform, or plant life was affected. Phytoplankton survived.

flat Used to distinguish "regular" objects or processes from holographic reproduction, as in flatfilm, flatcopy, flatcast, flatfone, flatmap.

flex-car The Kanshoubu's multi-purpose and variously-powered vehicle capable of movement on land, in air, and on or through water, usually combining only two of these capacities in the ability to operate both vertically and laterally.

forcefield wraps Spheres of energy established by set nodes and used by Kanshou in the detention or transfer of violent offenders. Different areas of the harmer's body can be quickly immobilized or released.

free enterprise The encouragement of private industry or commerce under open competitive conditions, a part of Little Blue's mixed economy but strictly within the boundaries of Earthkeep priorities. A Board of Use must deliberately grant to a commercial or industrial enterprise its use of any land, water, and/or airspace, however large or small, that is under the Board's jurisdiction. Boards of Use may revoke any grant at any time for violation of the conditions of use.

gert To fly together as Kanshou, designated as, for instance, Rhoda-Gert-Longleaf. Or a "spoon" of two Kanshou women who are able to fly together because they are or have been lovers. Applied specifically to the Flying Daggers of the Amahrery, the Femmedarmery, and the Vigilancia.

gift society A community committed to the development of an economy based upon the gifts that its residents offer and receive. Central to such a society's philosophy is the individual's subsistence solely upon the largesse of her/his neighbors.

glolobe A source of light generated by breathshine and sustained by a pattern of ambient influx. Glolobes may be suspended in the air or carried to other locations by mindtote.

habitante A person remanded to a bailiwick because of his/her violent behavior.

hempbrew A tea-like hot drink made from processed hempstalks.

holo Designating some feature of holotechnology (e.g., holotech, holosize, holoscene, holoroom, holofest).

hovercraft Any air conveyance, usually a cushcar or cargocush, used for public transportation or personal short-distance travel. It is powered by fusion thrust or hydrogen-enhanced photovoltaic units but kept aloft by air suspension in the form of multiple jets of air in constant pressure against the ground (or water).

hurtfield Invisible electrical "fences" which surround most bailiwicks to prevent the escape of habitantes.

Kanshoubu (kahn-show-boo) The global peacekeeping body, composed of Amahs, Femmedarmes, and Vigilantes. A part of the Implemental branch of Little Blue's government.

Kanshou (<u>kahn</u>-show) Peacekeeping officer or officers, either an Amah, a Femmedarme, or a Vigilante, depending upon the tri-satrapy in which she serves. A guardian or watcher.

Kitchen Table Little Blue's global tribunal of nine Sifters (justices). The highest level of the planet's Judicial branch of government.

learntogether A companion in study or experience, often the term applied to a life partner.

lonth The lower body's balance-and-sustain point, between the second and third chakras, which with practice can be used to maintain any psychic or physical state. A kind of "automatic pilot" for spoons or gerts during long flights.

lovetogether Any two people who share intimate erotic or spiritual experiences of lovemaking.

lume Any source of light used to dispel darkness or to accent texts or drawings. An electronic pointer, as in a lumerod, lumestick, screen-lume, or lumepoints.

magnopad Electronic writing tablet for memoranda or brief expendable messages. The pad's magnetic field can be programmed to save data or messages for short time periods.

Mother Right Feminist ideology built upon the primacy of the female, essential female values and sensibilities, the necessity of women's self-determination apart from men or patriarchal structures or processes, and the inalienable principle of a woman's authority over her own children and those of her species, exclusive of any male influence.

paque By a holo-imagery system, the simulation of walls, rooms, and 3-D projections of distant views in areas otherwise transparent or without walls. Whole environments can be paqued, depaqued, and repaqued quickly.

plastiped A soft, durable, and flexible polymeric compound that "breathes." Used universally as the substitute for leather, particularly in the manufacture of footwear as in a Kanshou's mid-calf boots.

Plenary Constitution Little Blue's globally negotiated constitution, ratified in 2057, delineating the responsibilities of Little Blue's Legislative, Judicial, and Implemental branches of government and the interrelationships of the planet's geo-political territories (e.g., satrapies, tri-satrapies). Further, the document sets out the values attendant upon the Earthkeep Consciousness and names those values as the spirit from which all legal statutes will thenceforth derive. Certain caveats attach to the Plenary Constitution, pertaining to specific indigenous cultures and sovereign communities.

Pr-24 The Kanshou nightstick, modelled on the traditional Monadnock Pr-24 Police Baton. Its hard plastic is featherweight and its flexible design offers two working ends. It is, however, used primarily for restraint rather than for striking.

protofobe An opponent of Little Blue's emerging proposals for Anti-

Violence Protocols and Habitante Testing.

protofile A supporter of the Protocols and Testing.

Rainbow Sunday April 14, 2041, the day of the appearance of a double rainbow in the western sky, first sighted at Amsterdam, then globally for twenty-four hours thereafter, a phenomenon interpreted as a promise of the Animals' Return because of its near coinciding with the twenty-year anniversary of their Exodus, but also understood as a symbol of peace and diversity. \

Rememorante Afortunada/o One of the fortunate persons who can remember the non-human animals; an especially respected elder.

rhyndon The material of the Kanshou's comfortsuit, automatically controlling the temperature range selected by its wearer.

rolling beltways Part of the public transportation system in many large cities, powered by hydrogen-enhanced photovoltaics and consisting of both fast and slow lanes for pedestrian travel. Ordinarily coordinated with "swings," individual hanging cables that swing from rooftop to rooftop. Swings are accessed by elevators or moving stairways.

Rwanda Accords Internationally endorsed compact (2028 C.E.) delineating a prisoner's rights and the limits of a detaining institution's use of force.

satrapy (say-trap-ee) Any one of nine geo-political territories, roughly the equivalents of the traditionally named "continents:" Africa, Europe, the Mideast, Asia, China, the Pacific Islands, South America, Central America, North America. A "tri-satrapy" is made up of three satrapies.

Shrieve Any Kanshou.

Sifter One of the nine "justices" to sit at the Kitchen Table global judicial body. Members of lower tables are also called "sifters."

sleepwork The field of psychic training that enhances one's capacities in the state of sleep. On Little Blue, sleepwork is the particular passion of women who wish to acquire the language or dialect of another culture, and they pursue the most immediate, thorough, and enduring acquisition of such material by sleeping with a native speaker of that language or dialect. Where both sleepers are equally trained and skilled, the language or dialect transfer can take place in a single night.

softself The spiritual echo of the physical body which may at the will of a trained practitioner of psychic skills leave the "hardself" and move independently in physical space. It may occupy the body of another (willing) person and thus experience what that body experiences. Not to be confused with a person's "soul."

spoon To fly together. Or a pair of women capable of flying together because of their present or past relationship as lovers, so named for the position their two bodies often occupy in sleep. A spoon is capable of carrying in flight almost double its own weight.

subvention belt A black belt of plastiped that is worn at the Kanshou's waist. It provides compartments or slings for weaponry, the folded tekla cape, magnopad, force-field nodes, stunner, and comunit.

tabard A Kanshou's sleeveless shirt or tunic of heavy cotton that is lightly fitted to the torso. Its mandarin collar bears rank and/or division pips. Its color is that of the Amah (cardinal red), the Femmedarme (shamrock green), or the Vigilante (cobalt blue).

tanglestick Restraint device used by Kanshou that is made of netted strands of a loose nylon. The strands can be cast upon groups of violent offenders, temporarily immobilizing them by impairing muscle function.

tekla A mysterious material that is light, flexible, and apparently indestructible, whose chemical composition has not yet been determined. It was discovered simultaneously in southwestern Nueva Tierra Norte (old United States), central Australia, and the southern edges of the Sahara Desert in the third decade of the 21st century by three unrelated women, each on her personal Visionquest, and turned over to the newly developing Kanshoubu. The Kanshoubu has had exclusive ownership of all tekla resources on the planet ever since that time, constantly recycling it for use in Kanshou lariats, capes, cloaks, and cowls. Tekla "breaks" apart with ease and can be reconstituted as a seamless mass or sheet; it can be flattened into fabric or molded into a rope. Fire- and water-proof, it can nevertheless be dyed different colors. Also known as "zennatekla."

tote, mindtote To carry or sustain an object in midair without physical support. Preliminary exercise for training in telekinesis or the mental initiation of an object's propulsion in space from one place to another (as if it were being thrown).

transmog Referring to "transmogrifier," that replicative technology which allows the manufacture of any small artifact from natural products or from the material of other artifacts by reconfiguring existing elements into new molecular compounds. Transmogrifier technology thus makes possible the filling of basic physical needs (such as food, clothing, tools) and the ownership of small items of personal property that have historically been available only within a system of currency or barter or which have been acquired as the plunder of war or theft. Over the past two decades, all nine satrapy governments have provided their citizens with the intaglios or templates necessary for any individual's manufacture of "a thing or a substance," and the transmogrifiers themselves are universally available except in techless enclaves that have themselves rejected the use of such technology. With the exception of controlled substances or weapons whose intaglios are proscribed, any person can "own" anything she wants, and "personal property" has thus acquired a new meaning. Anything beyond or different from the capacity of the transmog to produce must be paid for with the appropriate credits.

Transmogrifiers are the critical element in Little Blue's recycling program. Though sewage is treated by separate processes, over 90% of the world's remaining wastes are transmogrified. Transmogrifier technology has altered the entire planet's economy.

vaporose A soporific mist developed for crowd control which when inhaled, induces sleep or deep relaxation.

Webster A member of the Central Web, the global legislative body. Members of lower webs are also called "websters."

work credits Value vouchers earned by one's labor or skill and deposited by employers to the accounts of workers. Transmogrifiers guarantee the free distribution of any of life's basic needs to Little Blue's citizens, but if an individual wishes to own or use something beyond or different from the capacities of the transmog, then she must sell her labor or her skills in order to buy those materials or items.

ziprocket A long distance air vehicle, powered by fusion thrusters and typically used as public transportation between Little Blue's large cities. "Lowrockets," more lightly powered, can make shorter jumps between rocketports, but do not boast the ziprocket's speed.

GEO-POLITICAL TERRITORIES OF LITTLE BLUE

Little Blue is divided into three geo-political areas called tri-satrapies, and each of these is further composed of three satrapies (<u>say</u>-trap-eez). The civic affairs of each satrapy (<u>say</u>-trap-ee) are under the directorship of a Kanshou (<u>kahn</u>-show) Vice-Magister. The civic affairs of the tri-satrapy as a whole are under the directorship of the Kanshou Magister of the tri-satrapy.

The *Asia-China-Insula Tri-Satrapy*, made up of the areas traditionally called Asia, China, and the Pacific Islands (including Australia) is currently administered by Kanshou *Magister Lin-ci Win.*

The *Africa-Europe-Mideast Tri-Satrapy*, made up of the areas traditionally called Africa, Europe, and the Middle East, is currently administered by Kanshou *Magister Flossie Yotoma Lutu.*

The *Nueva Tierra Tri-Satrapy*, made up of the areas traditionally called South America (including Antarctica), Central America, and North America, and now called Nueva Tierra Sur, Nueva Tierra Central, and Nueva Tierra Norte, is currently administered by Kanshou *Magister Zella Terremoto Adverb (Zude).*

Each satrapy is further divided geographically and demographically into local areas, usually called half-traps, quarter-traps, and demesnes (duh-<u>manes</u>). Except for the global laws articulated by the Plenary Constitution and the Central Web, a local area typically lives by its own laws, traditions, and values, though it has a financial obligation to the satrapy-as-a-whole and is responsible for providing candidates to the Central Web Pool of Qualified Websters and Sifters (justices) to the Kitchen Table Pool of Qualified Sifters.

BRANCHES OF GOVERNMENT
Legislative
The Central Web
Little Blue's global legislative body, composed of 15 Central Websters, five from each tri-satrapy, chosen by lot from the Pool of Qualified Websters whose members have been elected by each satrapy. This body formulates global law in accordance with Little Blue's Plenary Constitution.

The Lower Webs
Legislative bodies in satrapies, half-traps, quarter-traps, and demesnes which support the structure, processes, and responsibilities of the Central Web.

The Boards of Use
On the satrapy level and below, Boards of Use are elected to govern the use of land, water, and airspace within their area of jurisdiction.

Judicial
The Kitchen Table
Little Blue's global judicial body, composed of nine Sifters (or justices), one from each satrapy, chosen by lot from the Pool of Qualified Sifters. This pool is composed of citizens trained and/or experienced in arbitration, mediation, and the study of constitutional law. Its

duties are to interpret the meaning and the spirit of Little Blue's Plenary Constitution and to determine the justice of claims that come to its hearing on appeal from lower tables where interpretation of the Plenary Constitution is involved.

The Lower Tables

Judiciary bodies in satrapies, half-traps, quarter-traps, and demesnes which support the structure and processes of the Kitchen Table. Their responsibilities include the settlement of disputes that are appealed from Boards of Arbitration and Mediation, particularly those which may potentially be appealed to the Kitchen Table.

The Boards of Arbitration and Mediation

Bodies on satrapy, half-trap, quarter-trap, and demesne levels, composed of citizens trained and/or experienced in conflict resolution and mediation. The majority of disputes between or among citizens are settled by such boards.

Implemental

Civic Bureaus

Little Blue's global, tri-satrapy, satrapy, and lower level governmental organizations handle the needs of citizens in accordance with the priorities set forth in the Plenary Constitution. The planet's mixed economy requires cooperation between government agencies and the free enterprise system. The Civic Bureaus thus complement and support the free enterprise elements of the economy in their mutual effort to meet the needs and desires of individuals and groups of citizens. Their responsibilities are largely regulatory in nature and include Bureaus of:

Size Control (of Population and Enterprise)
Air-Land-Water Use
Health/Sanitation
Recycling/Transmogrifying
Employment
Art-Culture-Language
Science-Technology
Industry
Transportation
Communication
Education
Citizen Opinion
Public Media
Value Exchange
Weather

The Kanshoubu (kahn-show-<u>boo</u>)

The Kanshoubu implements the legal statutes and decisions made by the Legislative and Judicial branches of the government. In the absence of national military forces, peacekeeping and public safety services have developed into a quasi-military global responsibility that is the purview of the Kanshoubu.

Earthkeep *PEACEKEEPING*

ORGANIZATION OF THE KANSHOUBU

<u>Geographical Orders</u>, each under a Magister chosen by her tri-satrapy's Kanshou (<u>kahn</u>-show) and ratified by The Heart of All Kanshou.

The Amahrery, training Amahs and serving the Asia-China-Insula Tri-Satrapy, bearing the color of cardinal red.

The Femmedarmery, training Femmedarmes and serving the Africa-Europe-Mideast Tri-Satrapy, bearing the color of shamrock green.

The Vigilancia, training Vigilantes and serving Nueva Tierra Sur-Central-Norte Tri-Satrapy, bearing the color of cobalt blue.

<u>Branches (within all orders)</u>

The Ground Shrievalty, composed of Kanshou officers known as Foot-Shrieves or Flex-Car Shrieves and holding one of the following ranks:

Brigadier   (A Femmedarme Hedwoman) Marshal
Matrix Major
Adjutant Major
Captain   (A Femmedarme Aga)
First Lieutenant   (A Femmedarme Sub-Aga)
Second Lieutenant   (An Amah Jing-Cha)

The Sea Shrievalty, composed of Kanshou officers known as Sea-Shrieves, sailing the high seas, coastal waters, large inland lakes or waterways and holding one of the following ranks:

Sea Admiral
Sea Captain
Sea Commander
Sea Lieutenant Commander
Mariner First Class
Mariner Second Class
Sea Ensign

The Sky Shrievalty, composed of Kanshou officers known as Sky-Shrieves, piloting rockets or cushcars and holding one of the following ranks:

Sky Admiral
Sky Captain
Sky Commander
Sky Lieutenant Commander
Flyer First Class
Flyer Second Class
Sky Ensign

Note: Although usually associated with the Sky Shrievalty, Flying Daggers (Kanshou who fly in gerts) serve in all three branches of the Kanshoubu.

Kanshou Cadet Academies

The Amah Academy, Hong Kong, graduating Amahs into the Amahrery

The Femmedarme Academy, Tripoli, graduating Femmedarmes into the Femmedarmery

The Vigilante Academy, Los Angeles, graduating Vigilantes into the Vigilancia

Each Academy trains cadets in every branch of service (Ground, Sea, and Sky), and the core curriculum of each

Academy is standardized to include intense physical fitness and combat training; the study of science, technology, law, government, commerce, ethics, computation, and communication; the study of the humanities (literature, history, language, philosophy, the arts).

The Bailiwicks

Offenders against society are remanded to containment areas called *bailiwicks*. As *habitantes* (those contained in bailiwicks), they lose their status as citizens. The maximum sentence they can receive is thirty years, and the credits they earn working in the bailiwicks are sent to designated family members or friends or are held for them until they are released. When they are released, habitantes resume their status as citizens. Bailiwicks vary widely in their rehabilitation programs, their job training or educational opportunites for habitantes, the privileges accorded to habitante trusties, and the work that is available to habitantes during their confinement.

Of Little Blue's 1,240,000,000 people, about 1,000,000 (or .08 % of the population) are habitantes living in bailiwicks. Worldwide, there are 780 bailiwicks, each holding from 500 to 4,000 habitantes. In addition, approximately 120,000 citizens choose to live near or (in the rarer cases of habitantes who are trusties) with habitantes in bailiwicks.

The management and regulation of the bailiwicks are the express responsibility of the Kanshoubu. Of the 600,000 Kanshou on Little Blue, some 375,000 are detailed to bailiwick duty.

GOVERNANCE OF THE KANSHOUBU

The Heart of All Kanshou

Eighteen retired Kanshou of all ranks and branches, two elected by the Kanshou of each of the nine satrapies, whose responsibilities are:

to determine the policies of the Kanshoubu,

to choose, review, and retain or dismiss its three Magisters;

to approve or deny the Magisters' appointments of Vice-Magisters,

to serve as the highest appellate body in disputes within the ranks of the Amahrery, the Femmedarmery, or the Vigilancia.

The Amah's Ear, The Femmedarme's Ear, The Vigilante's Ear

Courts martial, or boards of arbitration elected by Kanshou from within each satrapy, operative as-needed on varying levels or at various locations, whose responsibility is to hear and resolve internal disputes or grievances.

The Congress of Active Kanshou

Ninety active Service Shrieves representing Little Blue's 600,000 Kanshou, thirty of them elected by Amahs, thirty by Femmedarmes, and thirty by Vigilantes (ten from each satrapy) whose responsibility is to advise The Heart of All Kanshou on matters of concern to all active Kanshou. Though technically this body has no legislative power within the Kanshoubu, its influence is great and its opinion is actively sought by The Heart on every matter of consequence.

THE KANSHOU CODE

The Kanshou are pledged to implementing the statutes enacted by Little Blue's legislative bodies. Kanshou of whatever rank or branch of service are ultimately commanded by the Magister of the tri-satrapy in which they serve, and they honor the culture-specific traditions of that geographical area.

The Kanshou keep the peace and secure the physical safety of Little Blue's citizens, most frequently by restraining individual violent offenders. First and foremost, they are warriors, champions who choose, if necessary, to forfeit their own lives for those who depend upon them for their safety. Further, Kanshou administer the bailiwicks and protect the habitantes. They take into custody those who trespass against "commonweal statutes," laws that have been enacted to prevent harm to others or to the Earth, such as the global moratoria on cloning and genetic engineering or the statutes that outlaw the distribution of controlled substances or weaponry. Kanshou constitute frontline emergency forces in the case of flood, fire, hurricane, earthquake or other natural disasters.

The Labrys Manual, sacred to every peacekeeper, reflects the values and practices of each Kanshou and Kanshou cadet, including her priorities:

"As Kanshou, I am Earthkeeper before all things, for the Earth and Her biosphere are essential to the existence of all life. I protect and honor Her above all that is simply important or desirable. She is my highest priority.

"As Kanshou, I am guardian of each individual person's physical safety, for an individual's safety or assurance of continued existence is the most important element in one's life and, ultimately, in the life of our species. I protect the safety of our planet's people above anything that is simply desirable. This is my second-highest priority.

"As Kanshou, I am protector and preserver of diversity, for diversity is the most *desirable* quality of human existence. I hold in my heart the vision of the return of one of the Earth's most extraordinary ranges of diverse beings, Her non-human Animals. Until their return, my desire for diversity includes the Natural World and is centered especially in the variety of human phenomena—our genders, our cultures, our myriad physical forms/colors/textures, our abilities, our ideas, our beliefs, our emotional expressions, our communications, our creations, and our delights. The protection and preservation of these things is my third-highest priority."

Sally Miller Gearhart grew up in Virginia and found her first love at a women's college. After inhabiting a dark closet for twenty years, she burst onto the political scene of the San Francisco Bay Area in 1970. San Francisco State University hired her as an open lesbian and tenured her in 1977. She taught there for two decades, helping to found its radical Women Studies Program and publishing three books. Scores of her articles and stories have been anthologized in feminist publications.

Sally is well known for her leadership, along with Supervisor Harvey Milk, in defeating the 1978 "Briggs Initiative" in California which was designed to bar homosexuality and homosexuals from schools. This decisive victory helped turn the tide for lesbian and gay civil rights across the country. In 1984 Sally appeared in "The Times of Harvey Milk", the Academy-Award winning documentary that chronicled that political era.

Sally has also been an activist for animal rights and Earth First! and now lives on a mountain of contradictions with many cats and a blue-tick coon hound in a Mendocino County, California, women's community.

Other Titles Available from Spinsters Ink Books

The Activist's Daughter, Ellyn Bache	$10.95
Amazon Story Bones, Ellen Frye	$10.95
Angel, Anita Mason	$14.00
As You Desire, Madeline Moore	$ 9.95
Booked for Murder, V. L. McDermid	$12.00
Cancer in Two Voices, 2nd Ed., Butler & Rosenblum	$12.95
Clean Break, V. L. McDermid	$12.95
Closed in Silence, Joan M. Drury	$10.95
Common Murder, V. L. McDermid	$10.95
Conferences Are Murder, V. L. McDermid	$12.00
Considering Parenthood, Cheri Pies	$12.95
Crack Down, V. L. McDermid	$12.95
Dead Beat, V. L. McDermid	$12.95
Deadline for Murder, V. L. McDermid	$10.95
Deadly Embrace, Trudy Labovitz	$12.00
Desert Years, Cynthia Rich	$ 7.95
Dreaming Under a Ton of Lizards, Marian Michener	$12.00
Fat Girl Dances with Rocks, Susan Stinson	$10.95
Finding Grace, Mary Saracino	$12.00
A Gift of the Emperor, Therese Park	$10.95
Give Me Your Good Ear, 2nd Ed., Maureen Brady	$ 9.95
Goodness, Martha Roth	$10.95
The Hangdog Hustle, Elizabeth Pincus	$ 9.95
I Followed Close Behind Her, Darleen O'Dell	$14.00
The Kanshou, Sally Miller Gearhart	$14.00
Kick Back, V. L. McDermid	$12.95
The Lesbian Erotic Dance, JoAnn Loulan	$12.95
Lesbian Passion, JoAnn Loulan	$12.95
Lesbian Sex, JoAnn Loulan	$12.95
Lesbians at Midlife, edited by Sang, Warshow & Smith	$12.95
The Lessons, Melanie McAllester	$ 9.95
Living at Night, Mariana Romo-Carmona	$10.95
Look Me in the Eye, Macdonald & Rich	$14.00

Spinsters Ink Books is one of the oldest feminist publishing houses in the world. It was founded in upstate New York in 1978, and today is an imprint of Hovis Publishing Company, Inc. in Denver, Colorado.

The noun "spinster" means a woman who spins. The definition of the verb "spin" is to whirl and twirl, to revert, to spin on one's heels, to turn everything upside down. Spinsters Ink books do just that—take women's "yarns" (stories, tales) and enable readers to see the world through the other end of the telescope. Spinsters Ink authors move readers off their comfort zones just a bit, pushing the camel through the eye of the needle. These are thinking books for thinking readers.

Spinsters Ink fiction and non-fiction titles deal with significant issues in women's lives from a feminist perspective. They not only name these crucial issues but—more importantly—encourage change and growth. We are committed to publishing works by women writing from the periphery: fat women, Jewish women, lesbians, old women, immigrant women, poor women, rural women, women examining classism, women of color, women with disabilities, women involved in social justice issues, women who are writing books that help make the best in our lives more possible.

To Order Books

Spinsters Ink titles are available at your local booksellers or through Spinsters Ink Books. Call 1-800-301-6860 to place an order. A free catalog is available upon request or visit www.spinsters-ink.com. You may order directly online, or mail your order to: Spinsters Ink Books, P.O. Box 22005, Denver CO 80222. Please include $3.00 shipping and handling for the first title ordered, 50¢ for every title thereafter. All major credit cards accepted.